DEATHLESS REPUBLIC
(#1 OF TEETH & BLOOD TRILOGY)

AINIKA KAMBO

AINIKA KAMBO

Copyright © [27 JULY, 2023] by [AINIKA KAMBO]

All rights reserved.

No portion of this book may be reproduced in any form without written permission from the publisher or author, except as permitted by U.S. copyright law.

TO DAD, AWA & MIKE THANK YOU FOR ALL THE HELP AND SUPPORT. I LOVE YOU ALL.

CHAPTER 1

REAPERGROUNDS

Kamili

I lay in the quagmire, bow in hand, waiting for my prey to come into view. With bated breath, I count the seconds as they draws near. Madi lays beside me, holding his breath to avoid inhaling the scent of the locust beans that smothered my body. We had been tracking our quarry for an hour now, from the forest all the way to the swamp where they come to feed. I stared at the doe, innocently grazing on a soft patch of grass, occasionally nudging the buck by her side. Beside them was a sizable calf, its maroon-brown glossy coat a stark contrast to the seven matching snowy teardrops on its forehead. Such beauty and grace in a world that deserved none. I regard the snowy white coat of its mother; it would fetch a handsome price, less than its actual worth, but enough to cover necessities.

I notch an arrow and let it fly with a distraught sigh, echoed later by the heart-rending bleat of the calf as both its parents were brought down by our arrows. Another beauty wiped off from the world by my hand. And I would do it all over again if need be because that's who I need to become; a killer. I avoid Madi's penetrating gaze as he made his way to his kill, he inspects it before putting it out of its misery. I pull the arrow free and gave the doe peace with a flick of my dagger at its supine, elegant throat.

"We should head back before night falls," I say to Madi.

"You know Kam, you don't have to do this," he finally says, breaking the silence.

"Don't I," I reply without looking up from my work.

"I mean, you could do something else with your life. You could leave the hunting to me."

"And do what? Sit around twiddle my thumbs and wait for death to come knocking at my door?" I retort, finally glancing up at him.

"No, of course not," he quickly replies. "But you could do something more... meaningful. Something that doesn't involve killing." he says a cryptic look in his eyes.

I pause in my work and look at him, studying his face for a moment. "And what would that be?" I ask, genuinely curious. He's acting strange.

"I don't know," he admits with a sigh. "But I'm sure there's something out there for you. Something that doesn't involve this kind of life."

He nods and drags his kill to the waiting cart tied to his horse. I mount mine, and with a flick of my reins, I start forward carefully behind Madi. His form's impressive sitting atop the horse. I snort, gaining a cursory glance from him.

"What's up?" I quip.

"Nothing,"

I urge Namia forward with a little pressure of my knees. Madi and I ride in silence, the only sound coming from the wheels of the cart creaking and groaning under the weight of our kills. I can feel his gaze on me, but I refuse to meet it. I know what he's thinking, what he wants to say. He thinks I'm too young to be killing, that I should be out there, living my life. But he doesn't understand that this is our life, that every day is a fight for survival.

I ogle the suns through the goggles that lends a layer of protection from the two supernova suns glaring down on us, the ones that were lowering too fast for my liking. Sunlight's our ally now, a foe to the darkness that comes, death riding on its wings. Spreading tendrils out, bringing with it, a war we have to fight every single night. It makes us dread it like nothing. Every child knows the risk of living in our world, and to cherish every sunlight, no matter how fleeting.

A hair-raising screech had me spur my horse faster. An early riser probably caught the scent of our kills. Damn it! I thought the locust beans paste was going to mask my scent , one of Calla's endless experiments but it just isn't helping. My body itches in this damn scorching heat, and I can feel the paste flaking off me with the amount of sweat leaking out of my pores. It made Madi complain the whole way to the hunting grounds about how much we both stink like we just came from the sewers of hell.

My skin prickles even more, I scratch at my arm and catch Madi's smirk, and direct a look that says he's enjoying my scratch-fest. I will kill Calla when I reach home. If I make it home. I wrinkle my nose and stare at the suns again. Anxiety swamps me, and I wonder if we'll make it. This is bad, we're running out of time. I share a worried look with Madi and spur Namia to run even faster. Leoe matches her pace for pace despite carrying the bulk of Madi and the cart. I lithely turn in my seat, grab my bow, and cover us, praying to everything that I hold dear that it will be enough if we're attacked. Our hunting fortress looms closer, and I spur Namia on in a faster gallop, clamping my knees tight on the sides of her belly.

This is the game we play with death every time. We play it knowing the price that will be asked of us, a tithe we all dread and welcome, a thing that keeps us fed and alive. With the knowledge that it will cost us a date with death, but I knew what I was signing up for when I agreed to come on this hunting journey so far from town. Mama's against it, but I can't stand the thought of another season without having proper food on the table. God knows Calla needs a little bit more on her bones. And I need a little bit of adrenaline running in me, instead of just picking a reaper or two behind the safety of high walls wasn't much experience for a huntress.

And the weekly quotas the granary gives out aren't enough. When I hunt, I can keep the other half of my catch. The rations could barely keep us afloat for a whole season. Another screech has me gripping my glass amulet in the shape of a falcon in flight, praying that we'll be on time. I pat Namia, reassuring he , she knows what to do. I've trained her for this countless times.

To them, a girl needn't fight; she just needs to pretty herself up, choose a mate, and pop out a couple of rug-rats. Leave the fighting to the men. Only a select few of us want to be huntresses. To me, they are the wise ones, a world like this needs more fighters than it has. What happens when there aren't enough fighters to save us? What happens when the suns don't shine anymore? What happens when they grow into something more than what we're used to? And as the eldest, I have to be the man. Just like Papa made me vow that fateful night that bred the family's heartache. I swallow down my grief and force my body to focus on surviving this sunset.

A screech pulls me out of my thoughts. I let go of my reins, pulled out my compound-bow and arrows. They swarm towards us. I break out in a cold sweat when I caught sight of the suns dipping below the horizon completely, heralding the almighty darkness. We had less than a ten-minute' window of light before everything would be claimed by complete, unforgivable, utter darkness.

They come in hordes, harbingers of our death. Their skin a cold, ashy-gray tone. Their eyes were a sickly, pale, yellowy-gray color, showing that they were from the ranks of Reapers. They had ghastly, hooded, deep-set eyes, domed foreheads adorned by a network of blue veins, and wicked, sharp teeth. A horn rings, lacing the air with its deep and frightening cadence, it lodges a sliver of ice in my heart.

The closing horn made my throat close, restricting my airflow. Bile rose in my throat, and I choked when I thought of not seeing my family, of turning into those things, of hunting them to join our ranks. It's so primal I couldn't breathe. Goosebumps pucker to life on my skin, and I shiver ,becoming more pronounced. I turned around, bow and three arrows in hand, and let loose my deadly rain of projectiles. They hit the Reapers in the front row, but more soon took their place. Our fate did not look too auspicious right now.

It's unthinkable, a torment from the darkest pits of hell.

With a slight twitch of my reins, I let Namia run for both of our lives. Her eyes were wild, with pupils barely discernible. They fell, but it wasn't enough, and more soon took their place; there's always more. Madi's the first to go through the gates, a Reaper jumps me as the gates click shut behind us. I elbow it in the throat just as it tried to swipe at me with the small, clear-orangish blade in its hand. I got a hiss in return. Undeterred, it clings onto me like a spider, while Namia went crazy under me. Sensing the danger, she bucks both of us off her. I fell, rolling with the small, wiry bundle of death. The Reaper a child of six seasons and robust. I wrestle with it. Madi steps forward, but Jagne claps a hand on his shoulder. It took four of them to adequately restrain him.

I'm glad that they stopped him before he could. I would never forgive myself if he got hurt on my behalf. That thought spurs me into action. I had to finish the fight fast. Cursing, I draw the blade I had stowed in my boot for such situations and slash at the Reaper's throat. It grips its throat and lets out an animalistic growl that should never have come out of a human's lips, but it was no longer human. Snarling back, I met it halfway, gripping it by the hair and slip my blade into the hollow space of its neck, severing its spinal cord in a second. I gently lowered its slight body to the ground, closed my eyes, and whisper the farewell prayer for the departed, "Te'dal 'ak' jam'aa, hale' bi."

Sleep in peace, little one.

Pinching sand between my fingertips, I sprinkle it on its forehead. The spider-child combusts, leaving only fine gray dust on the ground. A tear crept out of my left eye and trails down my cheek to splash on the spider-child. It was the little ones' death that is the most tragic, yet they were the most dangerous. Chances of surviving a spider-child's attack are minimal compared to a Reaper's. Dozens of spider-children could end a village. There's something about them that's almost unholy, a hunter's true nightmare. No hunter, even the ones worth their salt, want to ever encounter any of these infernal creatures. I took Madi's proffered hand, letting him yank me up. 'Are you okay?' his eyes probed.

I nod and let him check me for cuts. He curtly dips his head to Jagne to say that I was clear. The bastard smirks, and I sent him a nasty glare. Jagne had hated me the first time he had set eyes on me. Well, it was mutual. I never liked him then and hated him even more now. He was too perfect for my liking, slimier than a batch of newly hatched maggots and nastier than a nest of starving Reapers. It's still unbelievable how he could be blood to Madi, just a few years older than him, tall, wiry, with corded muscles. He's got a face that most girls would swoon over and glacial-gray eyes that could stop a deadly Reaper in its tracks, an air around him that tends to make a lot of people stay out of his way. Ruthless, arrogant, controlling jerk who cares not if he hurts anyone, even those closest to him.

I don't even know why he had to lead this expedition. Couldn't the council have chosen a better hunter? A more responsible hunter, one who feels emotions. Because he sure doesn't. There's Adilo, who is far more experienced than Jagne, hard as nails but sweet as coconut candy. He's got a level head on his shoulders and can feel your plight, someone who will not watch on while you die, a real front-runner. Yells have me snap my eyes to the front gates, and I run for the watchtower.

Another hunting party of five rode for the gates, with a sea of Reapers chasing after them. They're sealed off on all sides. Desperation and fear coat their shouts as they fought for survival to see another sunrise. I recognize Muna, Saliu, Corr, Moro, and Brime riding for the gates. What in the name of all Kendulusu made them so late? The hunting fortress isn't too far away from the hunting grounds. I stare at Jagne's grim, tense mien and know that there's no way in the underworld he was going to let them in.

I once had the misfortune of watching him lock three hunters out for the Reapers to get. It was my first night as a huntress after being awakened. No one did anything as the hunters fought to survive the enormous wave of Reapers and spider-children. They fought well, but their sheer numbers overwhelmed them. I sensed their desperation and had clashed eyes with one of the hunters and saw the accusation and acceptance that we did nothing to help. But he was a decent hunter, a good man, with a family waiting for him back in Kendulusu. He didn't deserve to die.

That night, I vowed to never let that happen again. Even now, when I close my eyes, I see the same look in his eyes. Some lines should never be crossed. In the end, the inevitable happened; they got them. Only one made it into their ranks, the others died because they weren't worthy of becoming Reapers. I don't know how they could do such things and sleep at night, watching people die in front of them. This time, it will be different, because I won't just be a bystander. This time, I will not let them die while I watch. This time, I will give them a fighting chance. I'll grant them life.

"Open the gate; it's Muna's team!" I sprint for the watchtower.

"That gate stays shut!" Jagne growls out, a hand on his blade.

The silence is heavy with the stench of fear, as people sacrifice others to save their own necks. No one wants to cross Jagne, he had put the person in the infirmary for weeks Even Madi avoids my gaze, not willing to help. No one wants to take the risks of being on the receiving end of Jagne's displeasure.

"You can't just let them die Jagne, this is cold-blooded murder. The least you could do is give them a fighting chance!" I plead.

"Everyone is trained for that horn, disobeying it means death. That is our edict, the very thing that keeps you and me alive. Don't try me, little girl," Jagne hisses, invading my personal space, he bumps my shoulder, nearly toppling me off the watchtower. "But you're welcome to save them, Kamiliana," Jagne mutters under his breath,.

His words only meant for my ears. Ever hunter has fear in their eyes, fear of retribution, fear of the steel hand of judgment that could hit them once they reach Kendulusu. I meet Jagne's eyes, which shine with raw, pure arrogance and hatred, daring me to accept his challenge, to defy him, to break a rule older than even him. Even the most daring of hunters wouldn't do it. The horn regulates us, our way of life, the closing horn is not something to be played with. It's a matter of life and death. It's archaic. What makes us exist still? I seethe, knowing that Jagne knew how much I hate being challenged. I grit my teeth and ignore Madi's look that tells me not to step into Jagne's trap. But I'm not the kind of person who backs away from challenges or fights.

Sacrifice, honor, and obey.

The lives of a few, so others could live, a blood tithe, a way of the obsidian hunters.

I eye the Reaper-stones that hang from the watchtowers, Kryptonite to them. The fortress is built on a bedrock of Reaper-stones; they won't be getting in. Within the four walls, we're safe. I bite my lip and stare at the five hunters fending for their lives while we watch. Would I do that? Is it what I stand for? Papa taught me better. Screw Jagne. I will do what is right by them, no matter what comes my way. I can't let them die like that. Casting Jagne a repugnant look, I take Madi's quiver full of arrows off the floor and jump off the watchtower, ignoring Madi's cry of my name.

I land in a crouch on the balls of my feet, looking back to see Jagne holding back a struggling Madi determined to follow me. I grin and run for the five hunters coming my way, dusting Reapers that head for me with the blade on the tip of my compound-bow. I take Muna's extended arm; she grips mine and swings me up on her horse. With a high-pitch horse-like neigh, she spurs her frightened horse in a gallop through the crowd of Reapers. I slash at them, covering Muna as we make for the southern gate.

"Are you crazy!" Muna yells out.

"Is trying to save your lives crazy? Faster!" I scream as we approach the southern gate, the weakest defense of the fortress.

Muna's eyes widen in understanding. I clasp onto her forearm as we change seats. She urges her horse faster, and soon the ground is just a blur under its hooves. I pull out my lucky daggers from my boots and braced myself for what's coming. Eyes closed, I took a deep breath. Here comes the tricky part. On tiptoes, I stand on the horse's neck. A stinging blow to my rear had me opening my eyes in shock. I cartwheel in the air, limbs tuck close to my body, daggers out, and a swift approach of the gates. Broken bones will be the least of my worries if this doesn't work.

They can hold off the Reapers for some time before I could climb over and open the gate from within. I barrel on the gate with a bone-jarring, teeth-gritting intensity that had me gasping for breath, my daggers held true. I start the slow laborious ascend. A battle rages behind me, I jump down, falling in a breathless heap on the ground. On quivering legs, I rush to the opening wheel that operates the gate. Jagne's outraged bellow emerges from far behind me, his footsteps fast approaching me. I turn the wheel, and the gate swings open. Muna surges in with a group of Reapers behind them, followed by the others.

I twist the wheel back, and the gates slide close, cutting off some of the Reapers. I kick out at a Reaper that came at me, a craving to conscript me in their ranks. Sheathing my daggers, I pull out my long blade, when it flew at me, I swung my blade in an arc and decapitate the Reaper with a flick of my hand it dusts at my feet; I sprint into the fray of bodies, dancing to a lethal tune in my head, macabre dance of death. A blinding flash-wave claims my vision, agony lances through me and explodes in my head. I went down, still clutching my blade. Madi shouts my name, it seems far away, like my head's plunge in a barrel full of rice water.

I could feel blood seep out of my pores, nose, ears, and eyes. A flash of blue claims my vision, it paralyzes me, my limbs refuse to obey my brain. Inside, I yell for my body to move, but not a muscle obeys. I could smell the stench of burning flesh. In my periphery vision, I see Corr fighting off a group of Reapers that were heading for me. He throws out a dagger, it sails the air and cut off a clawed hand that's about to claw my face off; the dagger san ground, blood drips from my nose and whooshes down ...it, sliding in slow motion.

The hand fell down the ground and gripped my wrist, before dusting off into gray powder the last ray of sunlight bathing it in glorious, lethal light. A gigantic Reaper makes its way to where I crouch paralyzed, steps slow, confident and steady, blade out teeth bared, much more fearsome than all other Reapers, . What the hell is a Zukai doing here? Where was its ride, the gigantic hyena could put my family's abnormal-sized, wolf-dog back in Kendulusu in absolute shame.

I open my mouth to shout a warning, but no sound comes out, more blood seeps into the ground, I lock eyes with the creature that saunters towards my protector. All I could do was stare as it sink the blade his into his calf, unprotected by leg bracers that the other hunters wore. He went down; I screw my eyes shut, as his pained scream rang out with frightening cadence, Muna's sorrowful one soon follows, I open them and watch as she leaps in the air, her limbs fueled by adrenaline and desperation. She dispatches the Reapers in front of her, making quick work of them to reach him.

In her eyes, I glimpse an ocean of pain and suffering the likes I have never seen. The Zukai reaches Corr before Muna did, it sink its clawed hand into his chest.

"Aydareh' makamah Baba."

Bless this worthy one, Baba.

My brow furrows. How did I know what it means? None from Kendulusu knows how to speak Reaper-tongue. Who is the Baba he talks about? Corr screams out, but it turns into a wet gurgle. Static crackles and snaps, the Reaper release a haunting roar, and the others follow suit. Reveling, that a worthy one has joined their ranks. Daggers flew past me, cutting off a strand of my hair. They fell in slow motion. It clips each one impeccably. Corr slumps on the ground, trying to stem the flow of blood from his neck.

Muna brush past me, I pant as every cell in my body's electrified, my skin buzzes to life. Something awoke in me, all-powerful and hungry. In that moment, the world explodes in blue light, and I was on the Reapers in a split second, blades out I met them halfway. I behead one and whip my body around, meeting another that has its eyes fixated on me. I dodge, and cut another Reaper in half, it fell to the ground and crawls towards my legs; I step aside as a Reaper a little faster than the others rush for me, nearly stepping on the crawling Reaper.

I crush its head under my boots and lunge for the Reaper, scissoring my blades at its neck, it crumbles into the dust, when a massive beam of sunlight wreathes him. I finish off the last Reaper and turn to the group huddled around the boy on the ground. I don't know him that much, but I know that him to an easy-going guy, fun to be with, a good fighter. Muna clutches him like a lifeline, not caring that he might turn soon. I didn't need to see her breaking heart, cracking piece by piece. All I had to do was look in her eyes - the torment in them is enough for me to swallow guiltily and look away. I know it was my fault. I should've had the Reaper's blade and claws sunk into me, not the love of her life.

She cradles his head in her lap, while he rasps his last breath, his eyes starts to turn opaque and showing the first hint that he 's becoming one of the doomed. His forehead knots, and the first stage of turning takes over his body. Tendrils of opaque threads made their way to his pupils, swirling into masses, until they covered his pupils. His body seize once, twice, and his fingers twitched uncontrollably. Muna reluctantly let go of him, not ready to witness what would happen next.

A roar echoes all around, and the air vibrates as a Buki land before us. It's bares its canines , the spikes on its back stand on end, a sharp, forked-tail glistens in the meager light. It opens its jaws and gently clamps the Zukai's body between it's lethal jaws. It's forked-tail flared out to keep us at bay, and with a huge leap, it jumps over the gate. Its fur brushes against the Reaper stones, and it eliciting a painful yelp, then clambers off into the distance.

I spin on my heel and walk right into a fist. I stumble back, my eyes smarting, and starlight burst in my vision. "I never knew you were so attention-starved that all you had to do to get a girl's attention was bring her some flowers," I sneer at Jagne. "But I guess the only way you get to make me see stars is by hitting me," I simper, batting my lashes at him and twirl a lock of my hair with my finger.

Jagne glowers, his eyes full of malice, anger barely held in check. A muscle ticks in his jaw, and a vein pulses madly on his temples. I stared at him in defiance, licking the blood on my split bottom lip.

"How dare you! You could've had us all killed! Just be ready for the council when we go back!" He snarls glacial-gray eyes darkening in anger.

I shiver, but stand my ground. I will not show any fear as a huntress of the Kendulusa tribe. If I had the chance, I would do it all over again. Not a thing would I change.

"With pleasure, at least I'm not a monster ready to let his people die, let the council judge me; in all our eyes, you're judged even if none tells you otherwise."

He moves fast, a muscle quiver was all that I see, I stumble back from the blow, lava-hot pain bubbles on my jaw. I deflect a second hit, dodging to the left, I attack furiously, switching into a defensive mode, and follow it with an uppercut that had his eyes widen in surprise, then morphs into slits as he lays a barrage of punches that went on ceaselessly. A wicked punch had me wobble a few feet back and land onto my ass. My red hair come off its ponytail, shrouding my face from view, a scarlet puff of cloud, a sharp contrast to my ebony skin and bright blue eyes that spit fire at him. Another factor that draws the line between me and the tribe, it makes me stand out.

Some superstitious people even call me the devil's spawn, some devil's whore, I'm bad luck to them, bad juju they really need not tell me in person, the whispers were enough to follow me around. But I bore my cross well, drudging day after day, not showing that it hurts me. He strides forward, gray eyes an enraged hue darker than usual. In that moment, he should be the one called the Devil's spawn, lifting hands to strike me again, but a hand catch hold of his. He seems startled that any dared stop him from carrying out his punishment. For a moment, you could feel the air literally freeze, turning glacier-cold as he whips his body around to see who it was that dared touch him. Much more stop him from punishing me, interrupting his little court.

"Enough, leave the punishment to the council," his second-in-command Adilo bit out strongly, his voice leaving no room for argument, face vacant. One look at Madi's furious eyes had him nodding grudgingly.

"Fine, monitor her. One wrong step, and I won't think twice about teaching her where she belongs."

"Obviously not at your feet, bastard!" I glare at him as I take Adilo's hand, he hauls me to my feet.

Another hunter took care of Corr, while Muna sobbed uncontrollably in Saliu's arms. Every tear, every sob, makes my heart clench and crumble piece by piece, that sound will haunt me till the day I die. I wished I had died today instead of him.

* * **

I take a sip of the moon-brewed cashew-based drink, Keju, I relish the trail of icy fire that it left in my gut. It would help me stay awake and warm amidst the chaos that surrounded us. Madi had followed me to the tower, but he remains silent, giving me the space I needed. I sniffle and take another sip of booze. Sometimes, it felt like he knew me better than I knew myself.

Madi would have been what they call model-material centuries back, tall with muscles that molded against his body armor. The agility of a sprinter made him graceful like water flowing over rocks. He had a sculpted face, with a proud, strong nose that looked like it had been broken one too many times from our rigorous, merciless training as hunters and countless fights.

Dark, flashing, warm eyes, full lips, a stubborn chin with a cleft. The obsidian glass piercing in his left ear didn't detract from his looks; in fact, it made him more appealing to the opposite sex. The poor boy didn't even notice, and he was happy to bumble along in life. I recall the day he got his piercing to convince me to get my ears pierced for the first time. It was when we were just rug-rats, and he got mercilessly teased for being a girl, but he overcame it in that gentle, quiet way of his. People like him didn't deserve to live in this hell we called our world. But who did? Even the worst of us didn't deserve it.

I gaze at the beads that adorned his neck, wrists, and ankles. The same ones adorned mine, only mine were more elaborate. They even formed part of my body armor that covered my vitals made up of precious, hardened Arkor beads found in the Arkor mountain somewhere far from here. In the colonies all the way to the Hinters. More valuable than even food supplies. Beautiful, silver, and red markings in swirls of ancient calligraphy of a long-lost tongue, the very cradle of our language, symbols given life in glass-like beads symbols that are part of our everyday life.

The art of making them long lost through time, so is the power to harvest the gifts they have within them. Etched on my forehead were the images: one of a sun, a shield, bordered by twin lightning bolts, marking me as one of the Kendulusu tribe. To people, we are a savage tribe, I wouldn't blame them because we do everything with an astounding passion.

Love, hate, and fight.

I glance at the Reapers standing yards away from the gate, some trying to find a fault and bring down the weakest defense of our fortress, I shudder at the thought of facing the council. Goosebumps fan all over my ebony skin, but I wouldn't have it any other way. If my penance meant that others could live, I would gladly make the sacrifice again in a heartbeat.

The world before me is a landscape of ruin and rot. A world that was unpredictable and unforgiving, where one never knew when or how it could end. Enslaved by Reapers centuries ago and were still struggling to defy them. Our efforts seemed paltry compared to the Reapers' relentless attacks, which increased their ranks with every passing day. Staring up at the sky, lost in thought. I thought about the world we lived in, the beauty and the horror, the love and the hate. I thought about Mama's cryptic message, about being the answer, and wondered what it meant.

As one of the remaining human settlements in the world, we were all that was left of what was once a thriving civilization. It's a fading memory, being wiped off from history with each passing second. Our only hope was that we could somehow stop the Reapers from wiping us out completely. Hope was the only thing that kept us going—the hope of a better future, the promise of better lives, and the dream that one day we wouldn't have to worry about the Reapers. It is a dying hope, but we clung to it with all our might.

The nuclear EMP and sun flare that hit simultaneously had killed almost half of the continent's population, and I often thought of them as the lucky ones. For the survivors, the game had changed; it is now a game of survival at any cost. Anarchy had run rampant.

As I nestle into Madi's arms, I hugged him tightly, thankful for his presence. I miss my family, and couldn't wait to see them again. Closing my eyes, I succumbed to sleep and the fatigue that weighed on me, ignoring the frantic sound of the Reapers calling out for retribution. I wait for the sunrise, our ally in the dreams of a better future. Even though I knew we were already damned, I still believed that we had a chance at survival, one shot at it, and we wouldn't go extinct like our people feared. I can't help but think about what Madi said. Is there really something out there for me? Something that doesn't involve killing? I don't know. All I know is that this is my life, my reality. And I'll do whatever it takes to survive.

CHAPTER 2

ZUBELA

Kamili

I lithely slid off Namia and take in the picturesque view that is Zubela. Nestled between two hills, shaped like horns, fenced with military-grade steel barb wires, manned by men with guns. On top of each hill, were towers mounted with automatic firearms. Despite being so heavily guarded, the occasional Reaper slip in now and then. We were scanned and let in. I smirk smugly at a glowering Jagne; he had no intention of letting me out of the wagon, but Madi must have had a word with him. He had yielded unenthusiastically and let me out to trade, which I know irks him to no end.

Laid out on stalls were everything from tools, weapons, clothes, medicine to bits and pieces. I eyed the Mborrmborr and Kinkilibaa tea leaves that Mama told me to look out for, I'll get them later, I follow Madi, and we inch deeper into the heart of the town. We step into the stall with half our catch. My eyes went to a beautiful, flowing, sun-kissed Mbuba dress that would fit mama well. Decorated with pretty cowry shells that complements the multiple patterns and hues.

"Three bronze coins for the pretty, little lady." The merchant said a predatory glint in his eyes. I want to run him with my dagger for scouring my body with his eyes, poke his eyes out slowly and give it to Bukis to feed on. His oily gaze makes me want to go scrub my skin with the coconut-scented soap that mama makes at home.

"We are here to trade!" Madi halts him in his tracks.

He smiles wide, showing broken teeth that were yellowed and blackened, probably from poor dental hygiene and bad habits. He scans my body boldly this time, jiggling his body a bit." Well, I know that we could agree to a favorable price for a young thing like her."

Madi shoves me behind him in an instant, I huff and give him a glare that said I can take care of myself. I'm no damsel in distress and certainly don't need a knight in shining armor. All he has to do is lay one finger on me, that was all I need to find an excuse to beat him to a pathetic bloody pulp, that won't be of any use to anyone for quite a long, long time. He gives me a tight smile," I don't want Jagne to crucify us both and have the Diola tribe throw us out, think about the proscription that would be placed upon both of our heads just because I help a comrade fight for her reputation if we are lucky, and if the worse comes, the council would have both our heads for the banning of the whole tribe."

That sobers me fast, I already had smut to my name, an ax that Jagne will surely grind on my head when we reach home, I needn't cause more trouble for us. "Fine, but you should just let me punch him, at least a little bit."

"We are here to trade this, not her, sir."

"Hmm pity, with that skin, hair, and eyes. She could make an absolute fortune all over the continent." He rubs his hands together, muttering," An absolute fortune, even with her scrawny build, nothing a little bit of prime meat wouldn't fix."

I ball my hands into fists and bit the inside of my cheek to keep from flying into one of my notorious rages that only brings nothing but trouble for us both, instead, I said, " And you would do with going on a diet, what with that fat belly, it's a wonder you're still alive, but maybe you're just to be fatten up and given to some Reaper Lord like a sacrificial pig."

How dare he call me scrawny? But Madi's right, I don't want Jagne or the guards crucifying us.

"My! My and with such a mouth on her, she will absolutely do."

With a death-glare. I slink out, wishing that I could gouge his eyes out with a dagger. Outside, I watch hawkers hawk their goods, girls in clothes that left little to the imagination stood on the sidewalk. I can't judge them; with a twist of fate, I would have been any of them. And it takes a lot of guts to survive in this world. I close my eyes and lean on the lean-to-shelter, waiting for Madi to make an appearance. A girl catches my gaze from where she stands in the farthest corner of the street. She looks to be around my age, her skin a bronze-brown color that gleams even in the meager light, her hair's shaved off, tattoos lay all over her exposed arms, a short skin-tight, rainbow colored dress and matching perilous, high heels.

When her gaze collides with mine, her mouth quirks in a half-smile. She nods at me, then disappears around the corner. Curious, I paused a beat, then two, and followed her. Soon the sounds of Madi bargaining with the merchant over an item he wants to buy fades away. I find myself in a deserted alley, a flash of bronze-brown skin and tattoos lured me into another alley, I sprint towards it without hesitancy and come to a complete halt and stared at the girl.

What really had me widening my eyes were the three other people with her. If I wasn't good with hiding my emotions, I know that I would've been cowering in fright at the mere sight of them. I don't know how I could feel them, but the waves of danger and otherness waft off them, swamping my senses can't be ignored. My hand crawls automatically to my dagger at my waist. I don't know how I could feel whatever they had switch on; it doesn't feel human, even though they look human.

"It's okay; we mean you no harm!" The girl steps forward, palm towards me, in a gesture of peace. I stop but didn't pull my hand away from my dagger, stance defensive, waiting for any sign of attack from them. But none came. Slowly the waves diminished, and the girl nods at her companions.

"What do you want?"

"We want to talk, I thought that you would not come. We've been watching you for a quite a long time now, I can't tell you much about us or what we do, but what I can tell you is that we want you to join us."

"No, tell from you equals to a no from me." I quip.

"All I can tell you is that you would belong with us, telling you anything more would put your life in jeopardy, Kamili."

My eyes broaden at the mention of my name. They are no ordinary gang or whatever they are, if they had taken the time to scoop me out, that makes them dangerous people, all the more reason to avoid them.

"I'm not going to ask how you know my name, my answer still stands."

She bobs her head, her face giving nothing away, but her eyes told me that she didn't like my answer seems like she doesn't get rejected very often. Well, there is a first for everything, my gaze went to her three other companions, one thing I noticed is that nothing about them is mundane, even in a crowd of a million people they would stand out, that I know of. The three guys were all tall, impressive bodies that rippled with muscles and a formidable, mesmerizing air of danger that would make any sane person to turn tail and run when confronted. The girl looks like a frail doll next to them like she wasn't a threat. In my bones I could that she's velvet clothed in steel, a killing machine on two legs, pure and simple. It's all a mask, and like any mask, it can be peeled off.

I meet steel-grey eyes set in a strong, almost handsome face and held his gaze not willing to look away, it soon became a battle of wills. He breaks eye contact and looks at the girl; they exchanged words, without speaking, then with no warning, he peels away from his companions and come towards me, not even bothering to turn off his danger waves or whatever the hell it was. What the hell happened to we mean you no harm join us speech? I wonder, backing away, I don't know if I should be worried, at a disadvantage, and clearly, out of my elements, I am fresh out of ideas. Those little gems seem to have deserted me. Sucking it up like a big girl, I ease into a defensive stance, on the balls of my feet, muscles loose and wait. Counting my breath, slowing it down. I dodge a mean swipe from him and counter his next clout. He grips my arm with his other hand and fling my body towards the wall. From my vantage point, it all seemed effortless.

Bastard.

Pain streaks my back on impact, I roll out of his way when his elbow comes crashing on where I lay seconds ago. I stand unsteadily, swaying a little, a new hole on the wall. I swear a slight smile grace his lips. The bastard was playing with me as a cat play with a mouse, time to play dirty. I let him get closer, dodge a blow, and introduce his jewels to my knee.

He lets out this yelp that sounds like a hyena in pain and crumples to his knees, eyes narrowed in pain and rage. Good, I thought, and tackle him to the ground, scissoring my legs around his throat, I bang his head on the ground for good measure. He came alive underneath me, looking startled at my actions, I was past caring. The street narrows and went out of focus; he grasps me by the hair and tries to rip me off him, but I held on. I poke my elbow in his throat, choking him, he gasps. In an instant, he has thrown me off him with a surprising force that was faster than the blink of an eye. My body slams hard on the ground; the might of it jars my body, rattling my teeth, my jaw ached. I gasp, back-arching, body spasming in pain.

"Kamili" Madi runs to where I was trying to get my bearings, I stared at the empty street not believing what just happened. Who were those people? Why would they who want me to join them? I thought Madi hauls me to my feet. Maybe this is all part of a game to them.

"Why did you wander off?"

"I just wanted to do a little exploring." I shrug my shoulder like it's naught, hiding from him the fact that I am a little bit rattled, ego battered by what had happened moments ago. My ass kicked, I grimaced in pain and glimpsed bronze-brown skin, when I glance back a second time, I was met with an empty alley. Madi stiffens, and tracks my gaze."

We should get out of here!"

I couldn't agree more on that, quickly, I tail him out of there, pausing in mid-stride, I could swear that I heard someone say" Till we meet again" but only the wind whipped on my face trying to pull at wayward strands of my hair from its ponytail. Maybe the beating and all the pent-up stress was finally getting to me, but I had a feeling that this isn't the last that I see of them. An intuition that I knew never lied to me, next time. I will surely be ready for the doll and her crew. Next time super guy would have his ass handed back to him on a silver platter.

CHAPTER 3

PLEDGING EVE

Kamili

Kendulusu comes into view, I gawk, eyes drinking in the scenery, not believing them. The huge stone fences, four watchtowers strategically placed at each corner of the town root me in the moment. The sea lay down the right bend, the forest on the left. But it is a decent defense system against the Reapers because the water keeps them away, leaving us with the defense of the gates. A smile came to my lips when I thought of seeing Mama and Calla again. The welcome song rings out, drums pound in the air, beating in time with my heart. I urge Namia faster, ignoring Jagne's piercing gaze, and push forward to the front. I spot Mama at the front of the group, welcoming us. Dismounting off Namia, I led her towards the gate.

A brown-haired girl with extraordinary, silver-grey eyes came bounding towards us. A huge giant wolf-like dog that dwarfs everyone in tow. Cleo bound towards us, heading straight for me, nearly knocks me off my feet. I laugh, hugging the silky mane of fur around her neck, rubbing her favorite itchy spot. She yips in pleasure; I slip her a treat of antelope meat from the pouch that I had reserved for her. Jumping off Cleo, I plop Calla on her and let Mama put the feather-cowry embellished headdress on my head, tying the strings at the back of my head, her tattoo of a bracelet in white ink stark against her skin catches my eye.

Mama leads Namia towards the center of the town, people give us a wide berth. I breathe in the sweet, fresh scent of my homeland and smile. This moment is perfect, and I don't want anything ruining that perfection. I close my eyes to the anguished cries of a woman. I snap them open and glance back, a light, brown-skinned woman sobs in the arms of a man. I wince when she meets my eyes: In them shone a beacon of raw, pure accusation. I know what she thought; that we didn't do enough, if we had, her son would have been alive by now. If only she knew what I did? That it's all my fault, Muna sits on her horse, head hung low, silent tears course down her face.

"You tried everything Kamili, it wasn't your fault, You can't save everyone" Mama whispers, and tucks a lock of my hair behind my earlobe. The drums change the beat, strumming a message that we all knew and cherish. The start of new beginnings', a deep thrum that fills my veins and lifts my spirits. Mama gives me a grin that lighted her comely face.

" It's pledging eve."

"Indeed."

"Here, I almost forgot." I hand her the Mborrmborr and Kinkilibaa tea leaves.

"Thank you Petal, I've almost forgotten the smell and taste of them."

I had forgotten about this day; we celebrate Pledging eve every year, I ogle the girls in traditional garbs, beads on their waist, wrists, some braided in their hair and around their ankles, those who could afford it even flaunt Arkor-beads. Eying the many pledging staffs in the town square near the huge bonfire would be with excitement, trying to see if their scarves would be tied.

Tomorrow they will hold the games, and pledgers would be bonded; the final pledge bond would commence next full moon. It is as if no one died, but this is our way, there's no room for grief, just trying to live every moment. Every moment you breathe is a blessing, every blessing a miracle. Because in this hell, nothing is set in stone, only in fire and blood. And happiness is as fleeting as the wind, change could occur any moment, you just have to be ready for it. Our house comes into view, a small house that was painted an earthen brown sporting a thatch roof identical to all homes in the town, caved in the center to let in rainwater during the rainy season, that would fill the house water reservoir. I dismount off Cleo and hurry to help mama with the supplies, while Calla went to the backyard with Cleo.

"Anything you want to tell me, petal?" a shimmer in Mama's that I know too well in her eyes glimmers; she's too intuitive.

"No mama, nothing." I lied and force my gaze to meet hers.

I had to do that, Mama would ask every time I come from a run, it was her way of prying, trying to know what happened. I have found a loophole; show nothing away when Mama asks. Moments later, she nods, relieved, satisfied with my answer, it's the same question she asked every time I come from a hunting trip. It was her way of asking if anything unusual happened during the journey. She always has this haunting look in her eyes whenever she asks me, makes me wonder what she's afraid of?

I want to tell her that I have broken a rule that I had risked everyone's life on a whim and would be awaiting trial from the council. But I don't want to break Mama's heart. She has never been the same after Papa disappeared. Calla and I were the only ones tethering her to this world, she would have wasted away like so many others who've lost their mates and would succumb to their grief choosing an early grave rather than face a lonely, meaningless life without their loves.

"Kamili, you protect them no matter what!" He had said the night we were attacked. I can still see his extraordinary, gray somber eyes, so like Calla's. He knew that we'd never see him again. That night Calla was born, I could never forget it because it was the night that an exodus of Reapers, the likes of which we had never seen before, flocked to our town trying to get in, killing everything and anyone that stood in their way, we lost papa forever. He never came back. That night, I had my first kill, and some part of me was lost since then.

Nothing was ever the same. Bits and pieces were missing from that night, and every time I tried to remember, a sudden headache just reared up. It was like a part of me didn't want to remember that traumatic night. I didn't blame that part for not wanting to remember. No one should remember such things, and once summoned up, you would never be the same

"So tell me, Petal, anyone pledging for you yet?"

"No, Mama!"

"A little birdie told me that you had chosen your pledging colors like the other girls! You mean to compete? Do you not?"

"Is that birdie Calla? Madi dared me to choose one!" I fight a grin, itching to hunt for my little mischievous sister. Most guys see me as their equal, and I tend to squash any romantic behavior coming my way even before it could bud into something else, something complicated. Since my first day of joining the hunting guild, I had shown them that I'm uninterested in any romantic ties when the closest they've ever had was my fist in their faces.

The most intimate relationship I had that didn't entail fists was Madi. And he's my friend, I don't think of Madi in any other way than a friend. The only one I had to look out for is my chosen mate. It's our sacred duty to make sure the tribe thrives and doesn't die out. There is no way out of it unless you pack your bags and don't look back. That is not an option for me. There was no way in hell that I'm leaving my family behind.

"What about your chosen?"

"That's something I don't want to talk about, I'm just praying that he does not make it this year."

He was the only person who Madi didn't like, and he liked everyone. He could even stand his brother, Jagne. And that's a lot to take in my eyes. One more year, and I won't have to worry about taking a mate; because none would even look at me in any other way apart from the way I allow them to, with fear or hatred. I'm praying that I don't have to see his face.

"What about Madi?"

Surprised, I turn to Mama; she waits for my answer. "Eew, Mama, Madi's just a friend, I see him as nothing but my friend."

Mama chortles, shaking her head. I didn't miss the glint in her beautiful blue orbs that say she knew something I don't. Is he? Madi never tries anything with me, even when he has hordes of girls mooning over him. Besides, he's my friend, that's enough for me. I don't think that I want to change our relationship status; I don't require romantic attachments in this world. I know that mama would want to see me settle with a guy, but I just don't think that I need anyone right now. Well, not in this world, and I have to take care of Mama and Calla. They have to come first, just like papa said, just like I promised.

CHAPTER 4

CHOSEN

Kamili

The girl who stared back in the mirror isn't me. Mama has outdone herself. Beautiful cowries and beads were braided in my hair. A choker of cowries interlinked with aquamarine blue crystal-like Arkor-beads grips my throat, the same hung from my earlobes, dark blue, charcoal, ochre powder lined my eyelids and lips, the Kendulusun tribal mark of shimmery, white Arkor-ochre decorates my forehead and cheekbones.

I wore a traditional wrapper that reached my knees and a short bustier clings to my bust, beads worship my waist. It's meant to tantalize and lure unfortunate souls to their demise. My red hair is braided with a myriad of Arkor-beads, more than I thought Mama possessed. Several diamonds winks in different places in my hair. Scattering a smashing array of colors whenever I move my head.

"You look beautiful, petal."

I feel beautiful. Mama's eyes shine with pride, and I grin. She steps back and surveys her handiwork, then hug me. I step outside and joined Cleo waiting for me outside. "How do I look, Cleo?"

The giant dog huffs at me in annoyance and did a dog version of rolling her eyes. She points at the saddle of arkor diamonds and precious stones on her that Mama and Calla had coerced her into having on.

"I know right, but we girls have to pretty ourselves just to humor the masses." I giggle and give her another treat of antelope meat, then hop on her back, Cleo sprints towards the town square. I run my hand on her fur, enjoying the feel of fuzz on my skin, I wonder who Madi would be pledging for, the pledging has been going for days, even before we came from our hunting trip. I haven't so much as seen him look at another girl. Maybe he also harbors a secret infatuation for Buma, his chosen mate; I bet most of the pledging staff would be in her color.

I glower at the blue fabric that matches the color of my eyes fluttering forlornly in the wind and sigh. I wonder who Mama had convinced to put up a pledging staff for me; she is just wasting her time because no one would pledge for me. Well, except for my chosen-mate, fat chance of that happening, I snort. My hand brush my waist, where my blades should be, a habit of mine. I had left them behind when Mama commands that I do. And I had tried persuading her, but she won. I had to grudgingly do as she wish. A smile tugs on my lips as I envision Madi's face when he sees me all decked out in female finery. Good, I thought, knowing that Mama's makeover of me wasn't futile because some part of me liked what I saw and how I felt right now.

Cleo gives me an irritated huff, "What?"

She growls; I lift my head up and see that we have reach the town square. "Sorry Cleo, I'm a little engrossed."

She grumbles more, and bounds off towards Calla playing with other kids. Parents took their kids, leaving Calla alone to play with Cleo, casting looks of fear and repugnance her way. Hissing and cussing, I ignored them. Some of the townspeople haven't yet come to terms with Cleo being here.

She has been with us for as long as I can remember; she is family, her abnormal size and height was the real problem. Complaints have been made to the council about the safety of their kids, I don't know why they can't believe that she is tame unless you mean her harm, or us. I don't know what mama did to make the council to not take action towards Cleo. And that was how Cleo was there to stay for good. I made my way to where the obsidian hunters sat drinking Keju, the liquor that most hunters are so fond of drowning themselves in to escape everything that they have seen and done. I took the wooden cup Adilo offered and brought it to my lips, perusing for Madi's form, but found him nowhere.

Bai sits on the left playing the kora, he did a double-take, fingers stilling. He recovers quickly, and continued on playing, his gaze still plastered on me. I don't know if I should be offended or pleased that I'm garnering such attention.

"Someone looks ravishing tonight, you will give the girls green gills Kamili. Buma will have stiff competition tonight" He exchanged a look with Muna, and she chuckles.

"You are too kind, Adilo." I salute him with my cup. Then take another greedy gulp of the Keju, stared at Muna, who belts out a song, her words slurring.

"Though I love her, she knows not what she means to me,
An enchantress of unknown origins,

A siren who would lure me down the depths of the Mediterranean,

To my watery grave, I will gladly follow.

She, who I would die for, the one I will lay all the riches of the world.

At her feet lay the nirvana of all,

A treasure I will covet to the end, my siren, the one with the skin of a Nubian Empress,

The lips of the softest flower, and eyes of the brightest sapphire,

My heart is yours for everlasting eons." Muna finished the love song, hiccuping in her cup, at first glance she looked fine, but I knew that she wasn't, she was drowning her sorrow, trying to show the world that she was alright and she was doing an excellent job. A sad smile sat on her lips; her eyes had these faraway look in them that yanks at my heart. I sighed, eyes on where people gather waiting for the drums to start. Adilo chuckles, taking a sip from his cup. He shook his head and stoked the fire, sprinkling Keju on it. The fire blazed to life, burning brighter.

The drums start beating, darker than usual, bringing forth a sensual heat. I downed my drink in one go and nearly choked when the liquor hit my throat with a vengeance. Warmth coursed in my veins chased my worries. I tap a beaded sandaled foot in time with the beat, a couple dance closely together, staring into each other's eyes too focused in their own world to notice anyone.

"You should dance Kamili, don't you want to join them?"

I bit my lip and shook my head.

"Aww you are shy, Madi's been waiting for ages for you to show up he should be here any minute "

My lips twitches, and I down my cup, handing it to him. "Crazy I am, but shy I'm not Sir," I answer.

Adilo chuckles to himself, I know that he just wants me to prove him wrong and dance, he knows that I don't back down from a challenge no matter what. Adilo bequeath me a salute, eyes twinkling with a knowledge he won't impart, with a one glance, I hurry towards the bonfire and the circle of girls dancing to the beat of the drums. I hope that I haven't forgotten the pledging dance Mama taught me.

A series of hand gestures, gyrating your hips and shaking your backside. Putting a hand on your partner's waist, going round in a circle. With seductive moves, eyes, and shoulder gestures. Meant to seduce, to lure a partner. Buma gives me a startled look, eyes widening in recognition and disbelief when she sees I was the one at her back with my hand on her waist, I put the finger on my lips and wink; she laughs and shake her head. She looks like a goddess sent down from the heavens, with her smooth, baby bronze-brown skin, light-gold tinted eyes and flawless face, perfect curves that I yearn to have, she was every guy's dream of the ideal mate.

Dressed in a beautiful, small orange wrapper and a matching orange top that showed off her beautiful midriff to perfection, painted with shimmery orange Arkor-ochre powder in ancient, sacred runes of mating as everyone's, her beautiful blue-black locks decorated with an abundance of Arkor-beads and diamonds, enough to feed a settlement. Not a surprise, since her family's been in power for almost ten decades before losing it to Madi's family. They still have some control over Kendulusu, a reason why Buma gets what she wants; always.

I gaze out in the crowd of people meeting the warm eyes of a guy I have seen before, stirring a bygone memory, and a couple of light, gray-honey gold eyes stared back at me with warmth, and something more, something I couldn't identify. His light, gray-gold tinted eyes rove my figure in quiet male appreciation. I gawk back, spellbound, even though my body went through all the moves I was in my own world, he was just too handsome, taller than any guy I've seen, even taller than Madi, with impressive features and body that I know is holding women prisoner, the same smooth, baby bronze-brown skin of Buma's, the same regal air that commands attention in any room he stands in.

"I see that you have met my brother again, I thought you would recognize your chosen mate." Buma's voice penetrates my foggy, bespelled brain, and I blink, coming back to my senses.

"Err brother? Meet again, chosen..." I stared back, the uncanny resemblance is there.

Bekine!

I gulp. By the wings, I can't do this, I will not do this. When the mating decree was declared, I was but six. Bekine traveled out of here to rent out his services as a Deag' a, an elite blade-slinging mercenary, with not even a backward glance.

"Don't worry, Kam, he's got that effect on people. I'm glad that he's around this time, maybe he might pledge for someone." She winks knowingly.

I just blink dumbly at her, I meet Madi's angry, stormy eyes and stumble. A furious storm brews within them. He looks like he wants to murder someone. I track his gaze to where Bekine stands. And meet a smoldering gaze that holds enough fire to devour me, is that even a good thing? I grin and wave at Madi, and let go of all inhibitions. Madi stands in front of the crowd watching me, a strange look I can't decipher in his eyes in his eyes. My skin prickles with unease, the gazes of the two plastered on me. He grins and waves back, Buma gives him a seductive glance. He gives her a curt nod; in his hand I spy a lot of scarves.

He's got pledges from almost all the girls dancing here, except me. An orange one stood out from them. Well, he should choose Buma, and everybody in town knew that they would make a lovely couple. It was the expectation. Then why does his face look like he had sucked on the bitter crab-wood fruit? The dance comes to an end, and I hurry towards him, swaying a little. My body paying the price for indulging a little too much of keju, bring me hordes of Reapers I can handle, but a tiny cup of liquor I can't, oh the woes of being me.

"Hey."

"Hey, beautiful."

Beautiful? Was he feeling okay? Did he have too much Keju to drink? Was he coming down with something? The Madi I knew never calls me beautiful.

"I believe that we haven't been introduced yet gorgeous again?" a honeyed, silky voice that burrows in my skin rang behind me, Madi scowls, I whirled around and saw Buma with her brother in tow heading for us, Madi's grip on my wrist tightened, I made a face at him. But he didn't notice. Too preoccupied with directing corrosive, deadly stares at my chosen mate.

"I thought that it is time to meet again," Buma interjects, her demanding, seductive gaze on Madi.

"Hi."

His hand envelops my left one since Madi didn't want to relinquish my right one. The drums start again, this time more seductive, a ripple of excitement went through the crowd, here comes the climax of the night. I watch the crowd part, and I stared at the staff with the blue fluttering scarf in the middle of the crowd; I turn my gaze on Bekine, who grasps hold of my hand.

"I know that it's been some time since you heard from me, or seen a hide of mine but I pledge for you Kamili, I want to be yours, and you mine. Blood, bone, and flesh until the suns don't shine again until we cease to exist. My heart belongs to you and only you." He slips a bracelet in the form of a falcon in flight, where its outstretched wing tips conjoin outstretched, an impossibly huge, blue Arkor-diamond wink down at me on my wrist. I open my mouth and close it, repeated the process all over again. He puts a finger on my lips. My blood flames, creating goosebumps all over my arms.

" You don't have to say yes yet, but can I please have this dance with you?"

I ogle the beautiful, exquisite, lush, expensive piece of jewelry on my wrist. As tradition demands, males have to give token pledges to their chosen or pledging mates. Dazedly, I nod at him, Madi hesitantly let go of my wrist. I let Bekine guide me towards the bonfire, we join the bodies of dancing pledgers when I glance back, Madi and Buma were nowhere in sight, knowing him he has taken her someplace where they could be alone. It's common for first-time mates to want to be alone, it's a start for paving the future. Would I want a future with him? I stared at Bekine and don't know what to think. When I look at him, all reason flee out the window. He gave me a charming smile; I gave one back. My brain went all cottony, I felt like my senses have been turned off.

I gaze at the pledging staffs, staffs with orange scarves scattered all over the pledging field, Buma sure has a lot of admirers. Another blue scarf flutters forlornly in the wind. Who pledged for me?

And why would he? A second pledge? Who is it? My gaze went to my handsome chosen dancing with me, and I thought of why he would do such a thing? Pledge for me? The voice of reason asks. I need to find out who the second pledge belongs to.

"I want to show you something."

"Anything good?" I ask my voice a little flirty and breathy.

"Close your eyes."

I gaze at his face, my hesitance in my eyes, he gives me a crooked smile. " Trust me, I won't bite." He drawls out and pulls out a black scarf from his pockets, and blindfold me before I can even utter a word of protest. "Trust me, "he whispers again, his breath tickling my earlobe. I shiver.

He led me away from the festivities and farther into town. My hand in his guiding one, it only took some minutes, but to me, it felt like an eternity before he took my blindfold off, and I stared at the Aerie in all its glory. Trees come into view, tall, wide, and majestic, heading towards forever. With thick, ropy-like vines hugging them, some hung down the branches kissing the ground. All around the trees were ladders of ropy-like vines cascading to the ground. I can never tire of seeing that. The feeling of watching the aerie is something I can never describe.

Bright lights pulse and flicker up in the air." What is that?"

"It's a surprise." Bekine jumps up a vine, scramble up a branch, and soon was out of sight." Why don't you come up and find what it is?" his voice boomerangs down.

I grin and jump a vine, landing on a hollow branch, a blue flower lay at my feet, smiling I pin it on my hair then climb higher. Collecting the tokens of flowers he left behind. I couldn't wipe the giddy smile on my face, even if I had wanted to. Each time I find one, I pin on my hair. I pick the last one and tuck it behind my ear lobe, Bekine jumps down, a blue flower in hand.

"This reminds me of your eyes every time I see one, for you, beautiful." He hands me the flower, his finger touching mine, a jolt of electricity zings up and down my body. I repressed a gasp.

"Thank you," I whisper, enchanted as I gawked at everything in awe. Hurricane lamps hung from vines, illuminating everything in gold and shadows, flimsy white curtains enclose us inside, it felt intimate, a warm lover's nest. The moon shone down, bathing us in its silvery light. My gaze fall on the wooden telescope that hangs from a vine, I move towards it.

I close my eyes and take a deep breath, When I open them, the star-speckled heavens greet me, so many stars it takes my breath away "Beautiful." I mutter to myself, I wonder if papa is one of them. That he has ascended to the heavens to become one of the stars. Death is just a phase we have to pass through to become immortal and live on in the heavens as one of the stars.

"Yes, beautiful, but a greater beauty stands before me, something that nothing can hold a candle to. And my heart is but a slave to her desires."

I smile shyly at my chosen and held my breath as he stands behind me, his body blankets mine. Breathe stirring the fine hairs at my nape, arms wound around me, supporting them. I shiver. For a second, it felt perfect like I have just found something missing, a vital part of me.

"Cold?" he pulls me closer to his body.

"Come, let's eat before it gets cold. I hope you are hungry because I'm famished. "The look Bekine gives me could set the Aerie on fire. He takes hold of my hand and lead me deeper into the treehouse, I sit on the soft carpet laid on the smooth surface of the branch, Something I haven't noticed while I was star struck by Bekine and the heavens, I stared at the sumptuous feast laid out on the carpet. It's a rainbow of delicacies, some I'm well acquainted with, and some I have never seen, taste or heard of before.

"I thought I would give you a taste of some of the dishes from my travels."

He washes my hands in the clay bowl, his fingers caress mine. I watch him take an empty wooden plate and a wooden spoon. He put spoonful after spoonful of the Findi; the steamed tiny grain that almost the whole town eats, on the plate, then came the chicken peanut soup with chunks of chicken floating in it, it tastes delightful, I haven't eaten it in so long, I wonder how he got ahold of groundnuts, even the well-offs would have to pay through their noses to get it. I widen my eyes at him when he scoops some with the spoon and held it towards me. Slowly I open my mouth, and he put the spoon in. The spicy, hot taste had my taste buds in a frenzy. He hands me a plate, I stared at the honeyed-bread in wonder, then back at him.

"My treat."

I take a bite out of the honeyed-bread and close my eyes. And moans, I have gone to heaven and back, right now I don't care if a Reaper comes running , because I have reached the highest pinnacle.

" How is it?"

"It's divine," I whisper, taking another bite of the treat, savoring the taste of the honey, flour was not easy to come by, and honeyed bread is something only people like me dream of, Only the rich could afford such luxury. Even they find it hard to get. How in the name of the ancestors did he get his hands on honeyed bread? I take another greedy bite.

I stuff the rest in my mouth as soon as I had enough room for more. Buma comes hurtling upwards, tear streak track marks on her face, her lower lip quivers. Bekine takes one look at her and ushers her into the next treehouse. I wait for him, something's going on, on a hunch, I sneak after them.

"He does not want me, is she falling for your ploy?"

"She's eating out of my palm, soon, I will have her where I want her. She's an attention-starved, a poor devil spawn. Who knew that all it took for the hell-spawn to feel loved is a little bit of attention?" Bekine's cruel words plunge a knife so deep in my heart that I took a step back, and let out a small sob into my palm, a hand on my chest, I know that I don't love nor harbor any feelings for him , but I can't believe that all that wooing was for his sister.

"You think that I want her as a mate? My heart belongs to no one; I live only to make you happy. And it will make you happy to be with Madi. And it will help us get power in our grasps again"

"Turn on the charms; he wouldn't resist you, Buma. Has he pledged for anyone?"

"No! I don't think he did. But I can feel that he loves another, he will not talk about her to me. When the heart's given, it can't be revoked brother."

"Well, let him refuse you in front of the council when you bring your case tomorrow."

I knew the voice of reason that's questioning all he did was something that's not to be ignored. He had been making a fool of me all along, even though tradition dictates that I don't object on pledging eve until the next day unless I have more than one. Madi will have no choice but to accept unless he pledges for the mysterious girl Buma's talking about. Fighting back the tears, I was the fool of fools, how could I have been so naïve to think that someone would just like me for my ' sunny personality'? I nearly snort, well even if I had, none would ever want me. No one would look past my blue eyes and red hair; in their eyes, a devil's a devil.

I pull all the flowers out of my hair, lay the bracelet on the weathered, smooth floor of the branch floor, and flee. Jumping from branch to branch tears flow down my face, I hit the ground silently. I find Madi in our favorite spot overlooking the forest, scarves in hand, he held a blue one to his nose, a faraway, longing look in his eyes. I stared at my right wrist, where I have tied one and found none. He must have taken it when he had the vise-like grip on my wrist. I turned my gaze on Madi.

"That's a lot of scarves."

"I nearly thought that you won't show up?" Madi said, voice hollow.

"I will never miss this for anything," I replied, equally hollow.

Madi snarls, taking in my disheveled state, the scratches on my arms and legs." What happened to you, Kam? Did he do that to you? I swear on all of Kendulusu, if he harms a strand of red on your head, I will kill him." He growls, chest heaving. He shoots to his feet, ready to confront Bekine. I block his path, hands on his chest.

"He did no such thing; I'm fine, Madi. Bekine is a scum-sucking, Reaper-eating asshole. Are you going to tell me who you pledged for?"

"No, I have someone already."

"Really, is it Buma? Don't tell me yes, because I know you went off with her, but she came back in tears, so she's already ruled out. You just crush her and her family's hope of getting back in power. Are you even sure that it's a good move?"

"I don't love her, never have and never will, but she wouldn't take no for an answer. She mistook my friendliness for interest. I'm sure if her family wants power, they can wrestle it back in the right way. Let them challenge mine for the right to head the caucus, let them invoke the right of the Erul'e. "

I nod, what he said is right. If Buma's family wants to rule that badly, they can use the Erul'e to challenge. And the two can choose their champions to fight to the death, the winner ushers in a new era of reigning, using the same tenets of the founding settlers. "All right, let's forget about political sabotages, no secrets between us, remember? Tell me who she is."

Beautiful Buma that I know has almost all the boys on their knees pledging for her; she's a goddess with every guy clamoring for her attention and favor. My brow knits, and I stared at him, dumbfounded as if he had sprouted another head. Why won't he be after Buma? She's the perfect match for him, a match made in heaven as the people love to gush about. I stared at Calla and Cleo, circling the perimeter, playing mock sentry patrol. While a guard eyes them warily, eyes set on Cleo.

"Then who is it? You have to introduce us. Come on, spit it out, you know you can't keep secrets from your only friend, huh."

Slowly, reverently, he kissed me, surprise wings into me, and little hesitantly I kissed him back, this is a thing I never dreamed of. It awakens a strange kind of sweet-heat that I don't understand a tad bit, it coursed in my body, filling every pore and setting it on delicious, decadent fire. It's forbidden. I have always wondered who my first kisser will be, just never dreamed that it would be my best friend who would, I pull away and take a step back to create some space between us. Trying to ignore the intense charged air, I swear that I could cut with my dagger if I had it with me right now.

Everything seemed too much to take in at once; I need some space to think of what I just let to happen. I know what this means. This changes everything. And all it takes is one kiss, one taste, leaving my body reeling, screaming for more, it intrigues and terrifies me, a thing that I already abhor because I know that it's already a forbidden fruit for me. It would make me do stupid things, and I don't think that there is room in my life for silliness. There's no room for that, it could get my family killed. I have Mama and Calla to think about, my promise to papa still holds true, I wouldn't stray from my path just because I have someone who makes me go weak at the knees with just a kiss.

"You are my friend Madi."

"I pledge for you Kamili, I want to be yours, and you mine. Blood, bone, and flesh until the suns don't shine again until we cease to exist. My heart belongs to you and only you." He utters the ancient words that have been with us for as long as my tribe can remember, gazing at me like I am the world to him. I know that his words were real, it rang with candor. He slips a pair of silver vambraces peppered with ruby stones on my arms. Just the exact that I had told him that I will sell Calla to get from the townsmith.

I dash tears away and flee like a coward. Leaving a confused Madi shouting my name, my feelings jumbled, warring within me. My world shaken from its very roots. I run until I couldn't feel my legs anymore until my eyes ache. My breath came in short, choppy sobs, I came to a complete halt when I spotted figures. I slid behind a rock. Looking at my surroundings, I noticed that I was in the southern part of the town on the road going to the sea.

Council elder Eldres and three hunters I have never seen before stood talking. I should turn back and not let anyone know that I have seen this. No one was to come this way at night, it's forbidden. Made clear to all that we shouldn't meddle in council matters, but some part of me refuses to budge. A rebellious voice whispers for me to stay put.

He was handed a suitcase, an image of a hand holding a flaming torch stamp on it, I watch the two shake hands. This is illegal. The muffled cries of someone in distress triggered my huntress instincts to protect, had me moving into action even before I could think of what I was doing. It was part of being a protector; we have been trained to protect the weak and in distress no matter what. A sound had me whirl round, just as a fist slams into my face hard. I reel back, vision blurry, Jagne stands before me beaming triumphantly. A kick from him, had me groan in pain, a hand grasps my ribs the other my nose. Trying to stem the flow of blood.

"Nosy, aren't we."

"Don't you have a Reaper to hump Jagne?" I was in no mood for his games, his cruel theatrics. Trying to jab at me every time he got. He snickers, his gaze scoured my body. "Someone's got a potty mouth on her. Well! Well, a little dressy, aren't we princess? Where is prince charming?

"Not your business,"

"Well, as far as I can see is that you are the one who is not minding her little business, don't you have things to do? Like babysitting your fiend of a Mama?"

I strike him, my blow takes him by surprise, breaking his hold. The punch is like a whip crack. He tests his jaw to see if it's broken, then slams his fist in mine. I reel back, he attacks again. I dodge his next punch and smashed some of my punches home. He groans, savage satisfaction courses in my veins, I'm mad at the world, at karma for making me want to feel things for my best friend. Stuff I shouldn't feel; I was seething, livid at Jagne for the asshole he was. For Bekine making a complete idiot out of me.

Heat surges in me, and I shift on the balls of my feet, muscles tensed, waiting for his next move. He smirked and lunged at me. I dodged most of his punches but missed some. It hurt, but I wasn't ready to feel anything. Right now, my body is closed off from any kind of stimulus. I was in a kill mode, I caught his punch with an open palm, I gripped his hand in mine hard, so hard I heard his bones break. His scream fills the air with a frightening cadence, I whip out my leg at his torso, and he doubles over.

I grasp the back of his neck and furiously slam my knee up in his face, he curses and went down. I jump him in an instant, straddling him and shower punches on his face, not caring that he wasn't fighting back, I just rained my ire. Pain blooms in my shoulder and I slump on the ground, clutching my head, Eldres sneers up at me, in his hand was a sword, its heavy hilt coated red with my blood.

" Do you always have to be a nosy wretch? I guess that blood is just blood, like mother like daughter, huh! "he knelt down checking Jagne's pulse, he groans and let Eldres help him up, he stood favoring his broken wrist. My vision was failing every second that passed by; everything seemed sketchy and out of focus, my strength starts to fade, a heavy boot slammed into my mid-section, and I curved my body into a fetal position, trying to shield my body as best as I could. But it was ineffective.

"You bitch! You will pay for that ." He shrieks and lands another batch of painful, savage kicks that made me grunt in pain. Another kick made snaps bone and muscle. I screech in agony, clutching my side.

"That is enough, I don't want her dead." Eldres snapped. Jagne stops in mid-kick and turned to me, eyes stormy and furious, a lethal promise." This is not over." He hisses vehemently, the last thing I saw was his boot slammed in my face.

CHAPTER 5

CULPRIT

Kamili

Opening disobeying lids, I lick my dry lips. The bitter, aftertaste of the Keju was heavy on my tongue, and so was the intense, metallic taste of blood, my blood. My mouth and throat were Sahara dry, I felt like I could drink barrels of water, and yet it will not be enough to quench this powerful thirst that has gripped me. Even swallowing brings pangs of agony to my poor throat. A wet rag rests atop my forehead, trying to combat the fever that has me in its clutches, "Mama," I rasped out.

"Don't move." a commanding voice rasps out.

I stared in confusion at the unfamiliar ceiling, then at the room, I am in. Where is Mama? Calla and Cleo? What am I doing here?

I sit up and wince, putting a hand to my head it came away coated in blood, my blood.

"Careful, you were hit a little too hard."

A little too hard, I felt like my skull has been pulverized. I gaze at the woman stuffing the tools of her trade back in a grey, worn-out bag. The door opens, and Jagne steps in. His face, a mess of cuts, and dried blood, his bandaged hand rest in a sling he looks like he had been thrown into a Reaper's nest, and left there to fight his way out. A purple right eye stands out on his face. He gives me a look that tells me all I had to know; I don't need to look in a mirror to see that I am a similar mess, my body feeling a Babel of pains it hasn't before.

Well, he deserves every punch and kick. Everything comes rushing in, a tsunami that had me gasp a little. I clutch my head and try to breathe under the onslaught of the crashing wave. Mama steps in, her face worried she hugs me, her face darkened when she takes stock of me Jagne takes one look at us, then hurries out of there when Mama pins him with one of her poisonous stares, it was the stare that makes you shrink into minuscule proportions; her shadow looms over you. I don't know how she manages it, but it always makes the recipient uncomfortable . He shivers and backs away fast.. I breathed in her calming scent of coconut and roses trying to make it last, with no knowledge of when I will do again.

"Mama." I croak.

"Are you alright, petal?"

"I feel fine, Mama."

Her gaze shifts to the healer in the chair, I haven't noticed due to Jagne's epic entrance. The healer has dark brown skin, and huge dark eyes framed by thick, lush lashes. Her cornrowed hair reach an inch past her shoulders, a Mbuba-like flowing dress hugs her lithe form, her scarf tied at her waist.

"She will be fine, she is a fast healer, I don't think that it will disturb her in any way."

"Thank you Rougy,"

The woman flashes a grin, I watch them share a look, and then she's out of there before I could decipher what just happened. What was that all about? I wondered, turning my gaze to my mother. I muster a smile and let her stroke my hair. "

The trial?"

"It is today."

"How long was I out?"

"A day."

"Where is Madi?"

"Trying to make them drop your case."

I chuckle, typical of Madi, it doesn't surprise me that he's doing the last thing I want him to do, but I knew that it was wasted, hell will freeze over before Eldres drop his bone, that is my case; his teeth were sunken in way deep. Too deep.

"What are their grounds?"

"First, third, and blood offense."

I wince.

The world fades, turning sepia. The tsunami wave submerges me, and this time I quit breathing, I forgot how to breathe, the act omitted by my lungs. I knew that they would plan something major, I would be lucky if they don't banish me. And there's nothing that could make them believe me for the blood offense, it is my word against that of an essential member of the council. One of the people entrusted with our well-being, who am I? A pesky, insignificant, bug, obsidian fledgling of a huntress. Who has a year of experience under her belt! Not even a seasoned hunter who may have a sliver of a fighting chance at clemency. Even that will be tricky with the blood offense. I open my mouth to tell mama about it, but the door opens and two obsidian guards step inside.

"Sorry, Madam, but the trial has started the council request the presence of the Kukenu'l."

I try to meet his eyes, but he wouldn't look me in the eye, I try the other guard, and it yields the same result. Is it ignominy that makes them unable to look me in the eye? Or is it disowning me? I don't know, but both refuse to meet my eyes. I watch as they stiffly hurry out of there. They have already deserted me.

"The poison is already at work," Mama strokes my head, and enfolds me into her arms, I breath in her comforting scent, and wished that this wasn't happening, that, when I count to ten and open my eyes everything would go away. I will be patrolling with Madi, and Calla, Mama, will be at home, awaiting our return. I will be irritated by Madi's bugging that makes me want to dunk him in the river or look for a cliff to throw him off.

Kukenu'l!

Culprit!

I have already been judged.

Not huntress, even my title has been stripped away from me. They had no right. I had earned it, worked hard for that name, almost lost my life during the rigorous, intensive training at boot camp in the outskirts of the town in Burila. A place I don't want to venture into again. I bow my head; the drums thrum outside; I knew it too well.

The Djembe drums were reserved for judging, they rarely get used, it strikes fear in all of Kendulusu. A deep thrum that grips you and never lets go. Calling out for blood, my blood. It does not matter who I am, justice is justice. Swift and merciless, I don't know what will happen the moment I step out there, but one thing I know is that nothing will ever be the same once I face the council. I understand that the drums should make me feel scared. Any other person would be undone, screaming, crying, begging for mercy. But I wasn't. The only thing that it makes me want to do is to scream, lash out, or kill . Feel blood coat my blade is the thought of not seeing my family.

No!

I can't accept banishment, I will not. I'd rather be killed than face that thought. Deny me of a life without my family, and I can't be that selfish to take them with me. What if something happens to them? I can never forgive myself. The image of Calla, lifeless, and bloodied in mama's dead arms in the desert, makes me fist my hand and punch the wall. My hand never reaches the wall, Mama snatches it in hers. I blink at her in surprise.

"You are of my blood, Kamili, and I know how you feel. Deep on a level, I share your pain, but I promise you this; you will not lose this family, your father's sacrifice will not be in vain. He believes that strength exists, but true strength only exists within the heart." she rests a hand on my thumping heart.

Papa.

What would he think of me right now if he was here? What would he say when he sees that I have failed in the one and only task he has entrusted me? Perhaps I'm glad that he wasn't around, I can't handle the thought of seeing the disappointment flare in his extraordinary eyes, eyes so like Calla's. I did rather drive a stake in my heart first. Tears pricked my eyes, and I shoved it back and met Mama's baby blues, then nod." This is unfair, the people they need to know."

"I know Petal, but you don't understand the machinations of this world. This world is mired in power, blood, and death. Is a chess game that only the strong can understand and play, the rest become pawns for Monarchs to use, I know that you are being used on a grander scale, but there is little that I can do about it, I hate myself for that, how I wish that I could be more than I can be, but in the end everyone got a part to play in all this."

"You are everything to me, mama." My words mangled by a heartbroken sob.

"As you and Calla are to me petal. Now listen, I know Eldres for the bloody, poisonous viper he is, I have always known that he has something up his sleeves since I came back here, and even before when we were kids, he never liked me. This is his checkmate, right now we would have to wait for ours, the tortoise is not considered wise in the jungle for nothing, for wisdom doesn't need to act, it shows its character in due time." She kisses my forehead.

I close my eyes. Just feeling her soft lips on my forehead, something I know might be the last time I will feel them. Have Mama this close to me, to breathe in her scent of coconut and roses, to hold her close. Just this one time. I vow that I will live to see the end, no matter what it takes.

"He will have the crowd and the council eating out of his palm by mid-trial, whatever happens, don't say a thing, don't defend yourself; it will make matters worse for you."

"Okay Mama."

"Good, I am proud of you. Of the woman you've become." Mama nods and hurries out of there leaving me in crushing loneliness and anguish. Still avoiding my gaze like the plague, the guards led me out of there and into the town square. I am shoved in the center of the megaliths, the stone circle reaches my shoulders, beneath my feet the Kendulusun mark stood out on the dais. The drums change beat, signaling the beginning of the trial, then stop when Chief Elder Malikai held up a hand. I watch as Eldres stand up; the crowd quiets down when he raises his hand.

He has on a predatory grin that gives me the chills. I glare daggers at him and track his gaze to my mother, who sends him a blank look giving nothing away.

"We're gathered today in this place, something that we have not done for so long. And I truly regret having to call all of you here. But I had no choice. I know that you are curious why I have brought one of our own huntresses here, it pains me deeply to have to do this. She's a great asset to us, but at times things have to be done to make sure that law and order are uphold . If not, we wouldn't be better than those animals out there." He screams spittle flies from his mouth to land inches' shy of my feet.

Eldres paces to where I stand, chest heaving, overcome by false emotions. He spins around and give the crowd a sad look. Then touch my red hair, staring at my features as if memorizing them in his mind, at that moment to an onlooker, he looks like a father, like he cares deeply what happens to me but has no control over the situation if only they know what a viper he is? I recoil from his touch.

God, he was such a good actor, as if he wasn't the one dealing with outsiders. My eyes meet Bekine's, my glare is something to behold. Beside him stands Buma, who shies away from my corrosive glare. She wilts more as her gaze fell onto a glowering, livid Madi, angry veins stark against his neck and temples. I stare back at Eldres, who's still weaving out his bloody, insidious web of lies, telling the crowd of my bravery, and how good of a huntress I am.

"She has broken the rules, and I charge her of not only one offense but three, one of them a blood offense." The crowd gasps, and my heart sink down to the pits of my stomach. I meet Madi's tortured eyes, Eldres let the group soak that in.

"Though she is one of the best, I'm afraid that I am not the only one who has suffered at her hands." He opens his Mbuba robe, revealing a bloodied bandage on his stomach, that I had no memory of inflicting on his person.

"She also assaulted her superior when he tried to have her arrested and questioned, she would have killed him if I hadn't intervened and thus inflicting this life-threatening wound. She put the lives of her whole hunting guild in danger when she did not obey a direct order. We all know what such actions entail." He looks at all the council members, holding eye contact with each one of them.

Every eye shifts onto Jagne. Our eyes clash for a split second, and he smirks, mouth curling at the sides. It was that quick; it was for me. He's won, he has finally hammered the final nail in my coffin Even though his eyes wish me a thousand different deaths, each one more painful than the other. He, too, sports the same somber look that Eldres had on. They were such claimants.

"She has broken no rule council Elder, and you know that. Kamili has given them life. If not for her, we would have lost five of our hunters. She faced the Reapers when the captain gave orders to let them die. What offense is there to give people life? One of them, the life of your own son." Madi steps forward, the crowd parted, letting him through. I shake my head. He shouldn't do this;

I will not let him do this. He will sink with me if he dared question Eldres, it would be seen as a challenge of sorts. He strides towards me and slips his hand in mine. The crowd whisper, speculative eyes turned on us, Eldres stammer, at a loss for words.

"Don't do this. Go! Don't look back."

"I can never leave my heart behind," he squeezes my hand. Setting off my heartbeat in a furious gallop, with an arresting smile.

"That is true, we can't go around not having any concern for saving lives, an act of true valor and stupidity. We all know that we can't take the risks of people doing whatever pleases them, that is why there are rules in place if not, anarchy will take root and rule our lives, our settlements gone like so many others lost out there! Is that what we want? I might let that pass, but what reason has she to spy on council affairs? How many out there would love to see us brought to our knees? To face destruction? Extinction?"

The crowd went silent again. Everyone knew that it was a blood offense to venture into the forbidden. I had done that, and the tribe don't want to see if I had saved countless of lives; it was not enough to blot out that blasphemous offense, only one thing will do, only blood would suffice, my blood. Get them thinking about losing their homes, eke out a living in the scorching, hot desert.

The thought of joining another settlement is an unthinkable nightmare. Everybody knows what's out there, Kendulusu's one of the safest settlements this side of Africa, he has them where he wants them.

How can I compete with such a thought? He had planted the seeds of fear of the unknown in their heads, the idea morphing into a plant grows at a fast rate, into gigantic proportions. I know one thing; there's no way I am getting out of this unscathed, a price would be ask of me, huge enough to have me on my knees. Eldres gives me a triumphant smile that I want to rip out with my bare hands. That is what he needed. Angry eyes turned on me, I could see their eyes mete out ways of punishing me. My heroics forgotten, the cause of Eldres's, lethal, poisonous tongue.

"Does that not give you questions people? What does she have in mind spying on us? That, maybe she's with the enemy?" he shouts. "That can't go unpunished by law she should be cut at suns-fall and turned to the Reapers with nothing else but only the clothes on her back come nightfall, or killed by the trial of surei."

I shiver and turn helpless blues on Mama. Not that, anything but that. My eyes plead. I had witnessed that when I was ten, the son of a council elder committed a blood offense, raping, and killing female rug rats, discarding their bodies into the river. He thought that he could get away with that he was above the council. He realized his mistake too late when he grew careless and sloppy. His punishment was a trial of Surei, and banished forever from his roots, but that never came because he didn't make it to morning. None has survived dawn, I'm not sure I could.

The crowd cheers, forgetting that I was part of them once, that I'm Kendulusun, but at this moment, that doesn't matter anymore. To them, I was a traitor, that I have some kind of nefarious agenda to bring an end to this settlement. I deserved to be punished. These were people I have grown up with, I knew them, I laughed, and I cried with them. I help protect, provide for them and saved most of their lives. And right now, all that has been forgotten, nothing else matters, only my penance does.

"I claim immunity; my daughter can't be banished or sentence to the trial of Surei blades when she has done nothing wrong. No matter the circumstance, Eldres." Mama steps on the dais proud, back straight, head held high, facing Eldres, whose face went livid, the council nod at Mama. The crowd quiets down, murmurs and whispers rose to a pitch. Eldres turns angry, narrowed to slits eyes on me, seeing that he's cornered. He balls his hands into fists and stuff in the folds of his grand-mbuba robes. Thank God that Mama has some sort of sway over the council. I don't know the immunity she speaks of, but right now, I don't mind if she pulls in some strings to have me free. Banishment and trial of Surei aren't something I want mulling in my mind.

"That is true Channeh, but that immunity can only stretch so far. You left this town twenty years ago in search of glory and fame, to only come back with a child, and another in your belly, a foreign mate and an abomination that should not be let into our town, we let it roam about free to do what it wants out of the goodness of our hearts, risking our children." He had struck a raw nerve in the crowd, and he knew it. It's a downplay that could play well in his favor, using their hatred and fear of Cleo.

"Kill the beast" a woman I recognize as one of the many who likes to make my family's life hell screams from the crowd, pumping a small, bony fist in the air; her eyes, two burning coals of hatred that made me want to throw up on the dais.

"Why should we let such a thing live among us?" a man screams and takes a step towards Cleo, a hand on his sword. His face a mask of menace and fury.

"You don't belong here."

"Kill it."

"Kill the damn thing."

"We don't need abominations living among us. God knows we have enough out there." Another screams eyes full of fire.

Cleo growls low in her throat, stretching to her full height. The crowd shrinks back, cowering.

"Cleo."

Cleo huffs in annoyane and lets out a small whine, her eyes trained on us waiting for anyone to make a move. Eldres' eyes glint with satisfaction. He gives Mama a smug look; I know that this is what he wanted. He was playing with us, using the hatred and fear of the people of Cleo against us. The harm's done; the poison has been released, already in perfect harmony with the plant growing inside them, nourishing it.

"See what you make us live through Channeh, but we will not take any action towards the poor beast. In fact, we have something that we have been looking for the perfect candidate to do."

"What is that?"

"Your daughter will journey on a mission to Yegun city." Eldres got the right to judge this trial because of his involvement; it would have been the council judging if I haven't wounded him as he had so meticulously put it.

"No!" fear flashes on Mama's face.

Yegun city is months' ride away from Kendulusu, near the tip of the Sahara Desert, a journey that is far too dangerous. We rarely take that journey unless we have to because not everyone comes back alive. Even the best, and the most resilient, daunting amongst the obsidian guild, don't like taking that kind of risk. He might as well turn me away with nothing else but the clothes on my back. Since that kind of journey could kill me. Even horses die on the way before they reach the destination. If the Reapers don't get you first, the wildlife or the strays will get you.

"Your choice, but the council can never let such an act go unpunished Channeh, you know that. You should have tethered your girl instead of letting her be too free," he smirks. "And for her next punishment, she will be taken to Bulira, where the trial by Ankel will be carried out, and if she comes out alive, she will undertake the mission to Yegun city."

My world fades, and I forget how to breath. Mama's blue eyes begs me to not say anything, not to react. A stillness claims my senses, I would have passed out if I hadn't willed my body not to. Not Ankels, the only time I have ever seen one was during the day of our awakening. A hardened, seasoned hunter could take it all by himself alone, but not without significant cost, that's why awakenings are done when there was an abundance of Huntlings, we are fighters, renown by all for our fighting skills and that comes at a high price. Even then, some Huntlings lost their lives. How the hell was I supposed to battle the Ankel all by myself? Mama's face echoes what I think, I could see that she too believes that this is complete, utter lunacy.

Everyone knows what destruction Ankels are wont to do when sicced on humans. Bred by the council, none except the council are familliar with the beasts, it's council business, but I sure don't want to go near one. I had the misfortune of seeing it once.

"This is crazy! You can't send her off to her death, Eldres, Malikai think this through. As chief Elder, I know you can see that this is complete and utter murder. You can't allow Kamili to be sent to her death, Yegun city, yes, but not the Ankels." Mama pleads, her anger barely held in check.

"I'm sorry, Channeh, but I can't override council elder Eldres's decision, especially when your child has attacked him as he had said, you have seen the evidence. You know what our laws say about such things. I wish that I could help you, but in this, I can't."

Mama nods stiffly, her eyes pools of dejection.

I gaze at the council, and none of them could meet my eyes. They know that there's more to the story, but without proof to counter Eldre's outrageous, false claims, none can help me. They could do nothing, it's the law that created our very foundation and existence. It's the reason why we still live without anarchy and not fade years ago, like so many lost settlements.

"Papa, you can't let that happen."

"Madi!"

Madi strides towards the council, eyes beseeching. His father sits in his seat, avoiding his furious gaze. I could see the helplessness in them, even though he is the Chief Elder, there's nothing he could do about it. My body went cold, with the thought of leaving Mama and Calla. " Please, Papa, you can't let her go to Burila; she's mine, as I'm hers." Madi went on his knees, head bowed. Gone was the proud young hunter I know. In his stead stands a lost little boy.

Malikai's lips thinned, unshed tears gather in his eyes, I could see the helplessness in them, at that moment he was a father, torn between consoling his son, wiping his tears, knitting back his world that is being threatened, and still try to be the stern, just Chief Elder he is known for been. "I'm sorry son, the decision of the council can't be reversed, it will be against the law to do so, and the price too high. I can't take that risk."

I nod, letting him know that I understand.

"I understand Papa; I hope you understand that I'm going with her." He says, determination shining in his eyes.

"No." Malikai's face blanches. He looks like he was going to faint. A hand on his chest, he gasps. He's undone, unravelling before his son. Grief shone in his eyes, grieving for someone not yet lost, but already lost. "Madi, I can't lose you too!" A disobedient tear splash on to his hand.

"I'm sorry Papa, I will not let my mate die, I know you would not." Madi meets his gaze, teeth gritted, jaws locked.

"Me too, I can't let you go alone, owe you one Kamili, heck I want to do something exciting" Muna jumps on the dais to stand beside me, her sad eyes flare alive for a moment before dimming to the natural distressed look it had adopted lately. She hadn't been the same after Corr's death had turned her into this machine that does what everyone expects, but one look, you see, she's a husk of her former, happy self. Guilt prickles my skin, surfacing for a moment. Saliu, Moro, and Brime came forward and stood beside me.

" We are going too," Saliu strides onto the dais.

"You will not," Eldres takes a step forward.

"No papa, you made your decision. Let me make mine, there is nothing you could say that will make me not go with Kamili."

"If you go, you are dead to me."

"I have been dead to you for a long time Papa, how can I die again when I'm already dead?" Saliu whispers back in a voice, laden with emotion.

"No, I forbid it," his mother steps forward.

"I'm sorry Mama I have already given my word."

"Please Saliu, don't do this,"

"Eldres, how could you?"

"What do you mean, Sambel?"

"It's all your fault if not for you he would never join the guild, and now it is cause of you I will lose him. He was never enough for you, you never saw who he really was, and because of you bastard and all your politics and power play, I will lose him." The slap reverberates in the air, and everyone stares as the cool, collected, small woman lost her cool, facing the inevitable knowledge that she could lose her son. People will gossip about for months. Eldres raises his hand, the small, frail woman stands her ground unafraid, not caring that there is an audience watching, the slap didn't reach her, Saliu catches hold of his hand before he could reach his mother.

"Don't you dare hit her, I wouldn't be held accountable for whatever happens if you try touching a hair on my mother's head." He hisses and tightens his hold on his father's wrist until he grimaced in pain, and nods at his brawny, angry son who was waiting for any reason to vent out his anger.

He lets go of his father's wrist and angrily stride out of there. His mother followed imploring him to reconsider, tears trail down her cheeks,. Eldres turn angry eyes on me, I already know what he was thinking, I was to blame for turning his family against him. And I better be ready for his revenge. I give him curt a nod, and a smirk, I expect nothing else from a poisonous viper such as him. Bring it on, Eldres.

CHAPTER 6

BURILA

Kamili

Bulira.

That one word makes my bones go ice-cold, quiver like nothing, a slush like no other. It takes less than a day to journey to the outskirts of Kendulusa. It's what we call our prison of sorts. I know the evil I have glimpsed in its shadows. It's a hellhole, a place where we keep things that we don't want outsiders knowing. The familiar half-moon shaped mud building comes into view. An arena sprawls before our eyes, the catacombs lay beneath us housing dungeons and monsters. A tomb for unfortunate souls.

I stand on the sprawling sands below, enduring the stares of the people awaiting for my death, doors whoosh opens to reveal Madi and the others. Waiting for the signal to step into the arena. I wore desert-sand colored clothes and goggles like everyone to blend into my surroundings, light, sturdy boots, a scarf in the same color for my vibrant hair and fingerless gloves that cover only the backs of my hand, the same as the others. The Vambraces that Madi gave me adorn my arms, its stones twinkle at me every time I move my hands; a testament of Madi's feelings, Bekine's actions and Eldres hatred. I flip my dagger in the air and catch it with a fingertip.

I am with light weapons, my long blades lay strapped on my back, throwing stars and small, light blades sheathes stood out on my thighs and hips. Madi had favored his bow and arrows, Muna sports a wicked-looking scimitar, Brime and Moro had opted for axes and Saliu clutches a long spear. I give Madi a sardonic smile. His eyes linger on the Vambraces, and he gives me one of his heart-melting smiles that wipes off the smile I had plastered on my face. My breath catches, my heart skips several beats. I break eye contact and stare off in the distance. We wait for horn to signal the start of the trial. Nothing happens, I squint at where Eldres sit wearing the smug look, he always wear when he is up to something. There's a victory in his gaze, a secret that he has and won't tell.

I went down on one knee, pricked my thumb with the tip of my dagger, and pinch the sand between my fingertips. "Let the sand turn red with the blood of my enemies." I whisper eyes closed, then let the clumps of sand-mixed blood cruise down my cheeks.

From deep within the building, a horn resonates three short bursts. The air vibrates, burrowing in our skins and straight into our thumping hearts. The ground trembles, cracks snake on the ground. As something live runs under the surface, eager to come out, ready to feast on bone, blood and flesh. I stare at the mark of Kendulusu etched on the lid. The lids slid back, and the only thing I could do is open my mouth and forget how to close it.

It's the biggest beast I have ever set my eyes on; the Ankel opens dark, malevolent eyes and stares at us, it sniffs the air, sizing us, one after the other until it's cold, unsettling gaze rests on me and it screech. The horrible sound that grates my ears came out its mouth, it shows wicked, sharp teeth that made my heart clatter in my chest, and then it heads for me. I gawk at the Ankel making its way to where I stood rooted to the spot, while people cheered at it to finish me, an arrow whizzes in the air and slams into the ground, inches from the creature's face.

"Hey, tentacle face, get your ass over here."

It spins around and snarls, snapping the arrow that lay a foot away from its tentacle and gobbling it all in one go, then spews pieces of broken wood, feathers, and spittle mixed gore with a roar. It launches itself at where Madi stood moments ago the Ankel crashes to the ground, its stinger arcs towards for Madi, creating a huge sand wave that slams into the others. I unfroze and jump on the ugly creature.

My blade parry its stinger, I dodge an incoming tentacle, another I haven't seen threw me at the wall, Muna lunges at it, scimitar flaring into motion. She avoids a tentacle whip in her direction by a hair's breadth. Saliu's spear sails in the air and pins the lethal appendage to the ground, Moro and Brime slashes at the tentacles that tried to wrap around them. I threw several throwing stars at it.

The Ankel bellows in rage and shakes off my companions as an angry child would with their toys, it lopes in my direction, snapping its pincers in the air. It is not typical Ankel behavior, Ankels know only their hunger, and bringing deaths. Never picky. It doesn't matter who it kills. This Ankel is wild, too wild. But the strange thing is that this Ankel's hell-bent on destroying me and not the other hunters. I stare at Eldres, a triumphant smile told me all I need to know curves his mouth. I pull my other blade free and lunge at the creature, slashing at it, then move out of the way. Beginning a game of tag and evade, I inched my way towards the hole it came from, there is only one way that this could end.

"Cover me," I yell and stuff my blades back in their straps and swap them for two daggers. I dash for the hole, behind me, arrows whizz trying to stop the Ankel, I know that it's fruitless, there's nothing that could stop this creature because it is here for me, it will not stop until one of us dies. I could hear the swish-swish sound it made as its legs pierces the sand it in close pursuit. At the edge of the entrance, I jump in, and the crowd went silent, stunned at what I had just done, I knew it is, but I had no choice, the only way to do it is to trick the Ankel into following me. The Ankel growls as it brushes past me to plunge down it's size quickening its descent. Sucking in a deep breath, I slam the daggers into the wall behind me, but it didn't hold, I continue falling, the daggers continue cutting into the wall trying to find purchase, it looks like I will be falling for ages, just how deep is this hell hole?

The light is blotted out from above, I glance up and stared at the Ankel heading for me, I twist out of its way, my daggers dancing in the wall as I tried to get away. It snarls angrily and, whip all its tentacles in my direction, below me I spy a small alcove in the wall, I look back at the Ankel, its eyes twinkle intelligently, it gives a warning snarl as I twist my body for the alcove. Tentacles wrap around my wrist and I am tugged forward, I slash at it with my other hand, and kick at it, the blade in my boots slashes deep into an appendage, greyish-green blood spurts, with a pained screech it led go and fall below. I pull out a dagger and stab it up above my head and held on, I pull the other free and made my way towards the opening. An enraged bellow below me quickens my climb. Madi grabs my hand, I give him a grateful smile, happy to see him, he enfolds me in a tight hug. He lets go and picks his bow on the ground.

"Phew, tell me that it's dead, "Muna puffs and tie her hair back, eyes alive with excitement. "I don't think that it could make the climb back. It's a long way up."

"We did it, huh, want to hang out with me at my place Muna?" Brime winks.

"How about you jump into that hole? I see an Ankel that needs hanging with."

I felt a tiny pressure on right ankle as something latches on to my right leg and tugged hard I fell down. I am dragged on the sand by the tentacle wrapped around my leg, I cough into the ground, watched in slow motion as the four run for me. There's not enough time for them to get to me, Muna and Madi both lunged for me. Their hands clutched mine, Brime, Saliu, and Moro holding onto their legs, the Ankel tugs harder, my limbs are killing me with the strain of being used for the tug of war. Our bodies moved towards the hole inch by inch; the next tug nearly rip my leg.

" Let go, guys."

"No!"

"Don't be stubborn, I can't let you, don't you get it? It wants me, not you."

I stare at the ground shaking as the Ankel went berserk, nearly ripping my leg off, I hissed in pain.

"She is right, Madi, we will only make this harder for her. We need to let her go, or she will lose the leg or worse." Muna eyed another tentacle wraps around my right leg.

"You stay Muna, I'm going with her, I'm not letting you face that Ankel alone Kam." He whispers his forehead touching mine, I lean into him, touching him as much as I could, taking in his scent. I lower my lips to his and kiss him. His surprise's palpable. The crowd went berserk, calling out for a lovers' death.

I let go of their hands and fall into the hole. Their faces the last sight I saw before the lid slid close with a soft click, plunging me in darkness. Madi's furious punches thuds on it, he screams at the council to let him follow me. I hit the ground with a thump and suck in a lungful of stale, musty air. My head bangs on the ground hard, my vision went spotty, my body's dragged on the ground, I let go without a fight. It is inane to be free of an Ankel when it was this mad and injured. After several minutes it stop, and I peek through my lashes and stare at my surroundings.

Tossed on a mountain of bones littered the ground, mixed with personal effects that belonged to people who died by Ankel. I grimace but kept quiet. It huffs and went off after several heartbeats. I tried to sit up and groan at the twinge of pain in my right leg. I test it to see if anything was broken but found none. I can tolerate the twinge of pain. I stand up and crept out of there. I navigate the network of corridors, guessing a way out. I had found myself in the same room four times. Whoever built this place is evil or crazy.

I step into a different corridor and froze when a growl emanates from my left. I sprint out of there with the Ankel in close mortal pursuit. Endless twists and turns of corridors that faded into nothing else; I have no sense of direction, only getting out of here alive matters now. The suns provide little or no light in patches of sunlight. Its hot breath waft behind me, impelling me faster. I must look for a battleground soon, somewhere that I could've my last stand, with enough space to swing my blades. The corridor end in a deadfall that I realize too late; I vault up, lunging at the thick rope of vine hanging from the ceiling, throwing everything I had in me at trying to get it. My hands close around the vine; a splash resonates below me.

I stare at the Ankel, and could not help but sag in relief. A snap had me glance up and let loose a string of words that could Mama's scarlet hair go gray. The vine's fraying fast under my weight. It would not hold me any longer, I would be lucky if I last a second, a tug on my boot had me sneak peek down. I kick the tip of the stinger, trying to get to me. I've got only seconds to act, jump in or wait for the vine to snap and hurtle me in the dark, murky waters below if it's stinger doesn't impale me first.

I let go of the vine and pulled on my blades, I somersault and plunge towards the Ankel underwater, its maw wide open. At the last second, I twist my body to the left, sucking in a gulp of air. I hit the water with a force that rattles my bones, a tentacle lash at me, and I slash blindly . More tentacles latch onto me and pull me out of the water, hovering a few feet in the air with a tentacle wrapped around my midriff squeezing the daylights out of me. I cough, my vision getting sketchy, but I didn't let go of my blades.

"Hey, ugly, get it over with already."

The Ankel growls, showing me its arsenal of weapons housed in its mouth. And shook me like a rag doll.

"Is that all you can do? I know granny Ankels that can shake harder than you."

It snaps its teeth at my face, spattering spittle on my face, and threw me at the wall. My back hit it, I gasp in pain. My body plunge back into the water. Somehow, by some miracle, I have held on to my blades, and this time when it lashes at me, I was ready for it. It wrenches me out of the water, its grip slacks around my waist like I'm not a threat. Think again, beastie. I slashed at the tentacle holding me; it let go immediately, and I jump at it with all I have got; tired of playing with the ugly, miserable beast, it is time for it to die or me. Either way, one of us has to cease to exist, I know one thing it was not going to be me.

I plunge the blade in its eyes, bringing forth a maddening bellow I dance out of the way, slashing at tentacles that head for me, keeping an eye out for its stinger. Tentacles wound around my body and I'm raise in the air, it screeches, my blade sticks from its eye, then my world fragments into pieces, an agonizing pain blooms in my rib cage, inches from my heart. I gasp and stare at the stinger protruding from my abdomen.

Sticky, murky, blood trickles from my mouth, and my body shudders. I fist my hands and wrestle the urge to give in to vertigo lulls me to close my eyes and let nature take its course. I would've if the faces of Mama and Calla's didn't pop in my mind, the victorious glint in Eldres' eyes, he knew what I didn't, no one could survive out of here fighting this Ankel. Its mouth looms closer, it released me, and I hurtled towards its cavernous mouth. At the last second, I twist my body to the left and land on its slits passing for a nose. I lunge at the blade stuck in its eye and pull it free. The mind-splintering screech it gives off, made my ears bleed when it gave off another I drove the second blade on the side of its head, stopping it in a mid-screech, I pull my other sword from its side where I had stabbed it, and stick that too in its head.

It stills and went limp before its body submerges in the water. I pull my blades free and swim out of there. The water led outwards; I followed it. Holding onto the wall for support, I limp in the darkened, narrow, water-filled corridor, and cough globs of blood into my palm, and continued putting one foot after another. My family's faces were the only reason that kept me going, made me want to see them one last time before I die. Madi's face swam in my vision, and all the moments we shared together grips me with startling ferocity. I sob into my palm; the damage's already done, and I know that. I'm dying. I close my eyes and lean on the wall, I can't accept this damnable fate. I slid down the ground, hugging my knees. My body shakes from tremors wracking it as the poison courses through my veins, I don't know how long I have been sitting there with my eyes closed. A faraway snarl had my eyes snap open. Drawing my sword, I use it as a crutch of sorts to hobble out of there.

Time flew by, every step I muster brings pure agony, my clothes stuck to my body mixed with the blood of the Ankel and dirt. Sunlight spills out from the left corridor, splashing my boots in golden-orange rays. I run towards it. Light streams out of a door, and I shuffle towards it; it was locked. Hands trembling, I pull slim daggers and slippe them into the lock, and turned. A slick click rang out in the silence, I push the door open, and bolt it. In case there is something in there that should not escape, who knows what kind of nasties Eldres has stowed in this natural closet? I study the forest, the gigantic trees before me.

A coughing fit grips me, I cough harder, shoulders shaking and spat more globs of blood on the ground. A faraway shriek ring to my left, I pull out my blades and take off sprinting. Too late trying to use stealth and sneak out of here. I'm bleeding, a sure magnet for lone Reapers, answering shrieks bounced all around, my legs shook, but I kept on running even with the knowledge that I won't make it in the state that I'm in. But I could try, I could try to climb a tree and hope that I don't bleed out before they got bored with waiting for me to climb down or fall off from the tree. The suns were already high in the sky, but not one ray of sunlight pierces down below, a bald Reaper come crashing in the forest, it looks new, spells trouble. A lot faster than the older ones. This one had a look about him that told me all I had to know. What troubled me was the malevolent look in its eyes, it terrified me. Something in me flared alive, a hidden extension in me tells me one thing; run.

With a burst of speed that I didn't know that I had in me, I run out of there; it follows. I take a path that I know to be the fastest out of the forest. I trip and fall on to the ground, my blade flies from my hands, rib cage throbbing, more blood gush out of my wound, splashing on the ground. A tripwire, this's a trap of sorts, someone had done this in case I lived and get out of Burila, wants to make sure that I don't survive. I dodge the huge Reaper's hands, he crashes on the forest floor. I put a hand on my ribcage to stem the flow of blood.

The bald Reaper lunges at me again, and I slash at it with my daggers, cutting at it; it screeches. I gaze at its human-like teeth, except for their deadly, piranha-sharp, lethal tips, crafted to the finest of needle points. Looking at him now. Something's off about it. It's no simple Reaper. I stare at some Reapers that kept their distance; I know that on a cellular level, they could feel it's difference like I could. I smash my fist in its face, and it staggers back. I lunge for my blades, my fingers shy inches from them, then I was dragged back from them. The Reaper snarl, I tried to throw him off me, but it was not budging. It lunges for my throat and miss.

Somewhere, a howl fills the air, the Reaper's head snap up, as confusion rove its features, searching for whence the sound came from. I bury my boot-dagger in its throat and kick it off me. Calla and Cleo hurdle into view. I wheeze on the ground, clutching my wound. The Reaper still advances to where I crawl towards my blades, dragging my body on the ground. In a split second, it lunged at me, and I close my eyes. I could hear Calla screaming my name in the distance, I felt the air whoosh as it nears me, then nothing. I open my eyes and saw just as Cleo rips the reapers head off.

"Kamili." Calla pulls my head in her lap.

"Hey twit, what are you doing here? How did you know I was here?" I gasp.

"I had a hunch, can't explain it, Kamili. You're hurt badly, we need to get out of here before they come." She gestures at the Reapers that still stood motionless yards away from us in their own fog of fear. A thing I'm not accustomed to somehow; they don't want to come near the new Reaper's body. Cleo comes towards us and went down on all fours, Calla hoists me up on her, I didn't know how she could muster the strength, veins stood out, bulging on her forehead, she breathes heavily and wound her thin, wiry arms around me. Blood pours down from my wound, staining her hands.

"It's okay, it's not that bad." I lied, trying to reassure her. But another cough rips from me, shaking my frame.

She shakes her head, her eyes haunted, worry aging her small face giving it a decade's worth of gae. "You are dying Kam, Mama and the others are yet to come, you wouldn't last the day."

"You know me Callarxa, I'm very hard to kill."

Calla snorts.

Cleo runs out of there, and back the way, they came from, soon sunlight splashes on my face, warming my cold body, a smile tugs at my lips when I thought that I had escaped death, but it is inevitable; nonetheless, I am dying. There's nothing I could do about it. I wonder what Madi would be doing right now. I hope that he doesn't follow me in the catacombs, knowing how headstrong he is. He's probably in there searching for me. The gates come into view. Calla shouts at the guards at the entrance to open the gates. They did, reluctantly. What does Calla have on the guards to make them obey her? I know that they would not if it was only me, they'd leave my body for the Reapers to find come dusk. My head lolls to the side, my lashes heavy as I dark spots claims my vision

Calla slaps my cheeks hard, and I open tired eyes to scowl at her. "Don't die on me, Kamili," she orders.

"Yes, boss, anything else?" I almost grin at the thought of her bossing me around. We stop at a lone shanty, and she dismounts and pulls me off Cleo's back.

"Rougy, "Her screams deafen my ears. I never knew my baby sister has such a strong, pair of lungs in her. The dark-eyed, dark, brown-skinned woman with the cornrows came out. She takes one look at us, then rushes to our side, she helps Calla put me inside.

Her room is Spartan, herbs, and flowers cover every surface, some grew from the floor, but most grew from the ceiling. A peppering of red, yellow, violet, fuchsia, a smash of a rainbow taken from the heavens and painted on the ceiling. A beautiful welcome sight, I can't remember a time I have seen a flower. "Pretty flowers," I slur.

Rougy scoffs, "You are bleeding out, and all you can think of are pretty flowers. Where did you find her?" Rougy cut off my clothes with a small, glowing dagger.

"In the forest," Calla replies but didn't tell her about the hunch she had. What was my little sister hiding?

The healer nods and eyes my wound. She traces a finger around the edges of my smoking wound, and I hissed in a breath when it stung like she was ripping my flesh off from my bones.

"That is Ankel poisoning, its stinger is the only thing that does this. It carries compound in its venom that stops wounds from closing. Something is not right about this, I have never seen poisoning like this, "

Eldres, I will kill that scum-sucking man, shudders claim my body before I could voice the profanities that I was thinking about, I am so killing him. If I do die, I wish for his dark heart in my hand. Only then would I be appeased. Calla hurries to do as she bid, I watch as Rougy put a hand on my wound, and I wince. She closes her eyes; a glow emanates from within her close lids. Her hand warms on my wound, scratchy sensations spread out, ballooning out all over my body. Calla gasp, I would too if I could muster the energy, I know what she was doing to me; she was healing me. it is impossible. "How?"

"It's my secret, Calla, as you have yours. So you can't expect me to explain it. Do you?"

Speechless, she gawks at Rougy, then nod, letting the matter drop. But I could see a flicker in her eyes that says that she wants more answers, but she clams her mouth shut and grins impishly.

"You should rest, I don't know if the poison is still inside you, but you are healed for now," Rougy says looking tired, it has to do with the healing that she did. I nod and close my eyes let my fatigue weigh me down an endless, dark tunnel.

CHAPTER 7

LAWLESS BLOOD

Jelika

The murky, dust covered lamp swings from one side to another, shrieking every time it moves, I stay in the shadows with the rest of runners, watching and waiting. Blood rushes in my veins, thumping louder with every passing moment. The lamp overhead shrieks again, and then abruptly stops, a figure in tattered clothes lopes into view, it chitters loudly, eyes searching for motion. The whoosh of my blood increases tempo, a vein in my body threatens to burst, sweat trails down my body. The figure gives a huff and starts towards us.

A hand touches my shoulder nearly making me jump out of my hiding spot. I glance back into Jin's blade-sharp eyes, he scrutinizes my face, and mimes calming down. I nod, and try slowing down my heartbeat. One beat at a time, Tida's face flashes in my mind, a hand on the wound on her neck as the dreaded transformations takes her over to the brink of humanity and monstrosity, her eyes so full of fear, fear that's being slowly wiped off by the menace taking over her mind and body the same in the figure searching in the corridor. Out of the corner of my eyes I see Zenenga pull her blade out its sheath, eyes narrowed on me, ready to silence me before I give us away. Her mocha-skin almost visible in the dark room, curly brown hair with white tips and dark obsidian flashing eyes.

The figure stops shy inches of where we hid, and heads back the way it came from, and soon disappears into the shadows, Jin and Zenenga were the first to start for the two great wide elevator doors that would lead deeper into the sealed zones. I suck in a deep breath and follow after them. I was the last to get in the rickety elevator, Zenenga press the button, and pierces me with a malevolent glare, the elevator plummets heading deeper underground, splashing us in darkness.

We are told that we are the last of humanity that we are unique. That it depends on us to make humanity live on. To repent for the sins of humankind. And through us, we will find salvation before damnation comes our way. Then why do I not believe them? Why do I have these memories of a blue sky? The wind on my face? A burst of bubbly laughter full of warmth and sunshine that I wish I could take and wring every drop of. Phantom arms wrapped around me, making me feel safe, loved. I stare at the strange, ancient symbols that I know nothing of. To me, it's some kind of branding system, another one I need an explanation as to why its inked my skin.

The elevator screams open, and we step into a corridor, blades at the ready we stand back to back and eye the playing shadows, waiting and watching for the chittering, blood, claws and fangs to start. We jog out of there and towards the green house , I meet clear eyes with not a hint of the sickness in them watching me , I take a step forward and it disappears in the shadows. Something about all of this seems wrong, something scratches my mind to remember, but when I try I couldn't. We need this stuff if we want to get pills from our trading this time, if not, I shudder to think of that happened last year when the Reapus ravaged our bunker.

The same will happen if we don't get this. Jin fiddles on the keypad, and the door hisses open, I step in with a relieved sigh and watch the door yawn close. I turn around to look at the shelves that go on forever , roomful after roomful of canned food, wreathed with plants, fruit and vegetables hang on, rotten ones litter the floor, they could've help my bunker instead of going to waste rotting on the floor.

I pull off my huge duffel back and starts stuffing them with cans, it will be hard to run with it if we get attacked, which I see coming but I will take my chances, if the worst comes I will ditch the duffel, even though one can is equal to a hundred units of Re3 pills. A dog-eared book with leathery covers lay few feet away from me, I jog towards it the duffel weighing me down , I snatch it off the floor and stuff it down my shirt. I spin around and meet Jin's sharp eyes; they give nothing away and I offer him an awkward smile.

"Come on let's get out of here this place is giving me the jitters." Balu says hurrying towards the doors .

I turn to Jin who hasn't moved from where he stood, for a moment his eyes went all silvery-grey, when I blink they were the same sharp, dark, foreign tilted eyes. Balu is bent over the keypad punching in the codes.

" Stop," Jin's scream slices through the room. The doors whoosh open, and a claws cut into Balu's throat, he staggers back blood spurting from his throat, a Reaper slams into him, his body slams onto the wall, the Reaper lifts its head from where he is feasting on his flesh and shrieks at us. More answers behind him, trickling into the green house, Jin punches in the code, closing the door into a Reapers hand, the door cuts through bone and flesh.

Zens hands flames, Jin pulls his dual blades free, I pull my blade and machete out, and rush at the Reapers hurling themselves at us. One bounces on its haunches, it clings to the ceiling and drop down towards me, Jin barrels into me, and with a quick flick of his hands had the Reaper's head thump on the floor at our feet. I turn to thank him, my eyes fell on the Reaper creeping on us, I held out a hand and pale-fire leaps out from my hand and slams into the Reaper, incinerating it before it has a chance to lunge at us.

Zen has a smile on her face, she stands amidst Reapers torching them. Smoke wreathes her in a gray cloud, her fiery eyes latch onto mine, and a chill creeps up my spine.

"Are you alright.?" Jin's hand grazes my shoulder, I whirl around to face him breaking eye contact with Zen. Jin backs a step when I take a one towards him, I took one back to keep my distance, biting back the question that burbles up in my throat, for once I want to know why he keep his distance from everyone. Kaima took him in when none of the elders in the conclave would, vetoing for him to live in Toulasi. I held back the sigh, and give him a curt nod, and turn my back to him, my eyes on where Zen crouch pulling at something.

"What in the hell are you doing Zen?" Zunaif inquires, tone mocking. His eyes fixated on her lithe form.

She ignores him, and yanks hard at the floor, the floor creaks shifting beneath our feet, revealing a step-ladder, she throws her heavy duffel down and hops in after it. Jin's brows had hitch to his hairline, I cast him one look and follow after Zen, I clamber down the step-ladder, and rush in after her, her flashlight beams on my face and I utter a curse shielding my eyes.

"I didn't take you for a fool Jelika never thought you had it in you huh."

"Where does this lead to?"

She stops in her tracks, and glance back at me. "What? Too chicken to step foot in there?"

"No I'm not! We're just not suppos..."

"To step foot in here! You want to follow that crappy rule Kaima and the council enforced. Your choice, go back in there and pray that the Reapers go away, you know that they don't give up, they'll get you sooner or later if you stay in there."

"She's right." Jin steps into view barely winded with the climb and the duffel almost bursting at the seams. He brushes past me eliciting a gasp from me, I follow after him, falling in step with Zen. Better in dangerous tunnels than the green house.

What if....

The ground gives way under me, and the world tilts around, my hands claw at empty air, the duffel weighs my body down the tunnel hastening my fall, a scream wells in my throat. But never came.

*** ****

I crack an eyelid open and wrack a cough, my leg has gone to sleep I manage to wriggle my toes, and stared at the tunnel we seem to be in. Zenenga tilts a can to her lips, and shrugs when I direct an accusing glare at her. She's meant to know the tunnels more than anyone as the only tracker in here. And here we are in the middle of nowhere.

"Where the heck are we in?" Zunaif whispers groggily, eying Zenenga angrily.

"Not my fault, this is the only way, shouldn't you be thanking me instead?"

I shakily got up, and retrieve my duffel bag from the ground. I slid the flashlight from its sheath strapped at my thigh, and turn it on the others followed suit. I turn my gaze on Zenenga this time not glaring at her. "Do you know where we are right now?"

She shook her head, unsure for the first time. Zenenga is always sure.

"I have mastered a lot of tunnels, but this one isn't one of them. I knew about it by accident from tracking and tunnelling classes." She runs a frustrated hand through her curly hair.

"Any guesses where we seem to be in?"

She unfurls the skin map she has tied to her duffel, and crouch on the ground. With a glove hand she pointed at a location that sets my heart racing, we all exchange looks, bodies instantly tensing. We seem to be in the lawless tunnels or nearing it. And there's no way around it except go through them, or bypass them. The latter would be a miracle. She whispers silently. But looking at it we have no choice, I'm surprised they haven't found us yet. She rolls the map up and puts it back in its place and turns to us. Well what are you waiting for, we need to get going.

We troop after her silently, blades drawn , eying every shadow on the wall. Ready to slash and maim anything. Nothing but eerie silence kept us company in the tunnels, I stared at the water slowly creeping up our legs, I grip my machete and blade like a lifeline and follow Zen's lead into the known unknown territory that would gobble us up and spit our bones out.

CHAPTER 8

BLOOD & WATER

Water laps at my chin ready to fill my mouth and drown me. My hands scrabble on the wall as I navigate the tight space that Zenenga's leading us in. Jin huffs behind me, I glance back and meet his apprehensive eyes, with a touch of fear in them, he looks like he's living in his own personal hell. I wonder if it has something to do with the past he never speaks of. Even when Kaima tried everything in her books to make him talk.

Animalistic shrieks and tongue clicking fills the space, goosebumps flare to life, air whooshes above me, I glance up, a hand pulls me backwards, and I bump into Jin's torso, his hand grips my midriff, grounding me for a moment and then lets go. A blade slashes where I stood a moment ago, sickly laughter echoes, and then a figure swoops down from above. It gives us a smile, from where he stands he looks like any of us, but you take a step closer and you sees the telltale lack of humanity in his eyes, his skin, and his lethal, jagged smile.

"Lawless-man." Zunaif whispers, his hands shook uncontrollably.

"Yess, little pup, I bet Kaima didn't think her precious ones would never venture here," He gestures at the tight space we're in. With no sight of Zenenga and the others.

" What do you want."

"Guess little girl." He licks his long blade-like nails.

I swallow, and take a step into Jin. I know from combat class that fighting a lawless is like committing suicide. They're hard to injure, and harder to kill. Immune to most of our powers, and yet the only way out of this situation is to fight. I step out of Jin's arms, and into a fighting stance. Pale-fire shoots from my hand and up my arm, Jin closes his eyes, and I watch in awe as mercury-grey metal covers his skin, a helmet shields his head . We both lunge at the lawless man, water sluices everywhere, his grin spreads wider, and I got a good look at his second row of teeth, his mouth splits wider, my sword comes crashing down towards him, pale fire engulfs him. Jin shoots metal darts from his hands.

A shockwave slams into us, we went airborne, I hit the water hard, it fills my mouth, I choke. A hand wraps around my neck and pulls me out of the water, the Lawless man snarls in my face, his other hand has Jin in a chokehold.

"Now, now Precious ones, didn't Kaima teach you anything about us. I'm going to take my time with ..."

"Bogeys.."

Neon bullets shower the air, I grab his wrist with a scorching hand, he shrieks and let go, I hit the water again, bullets continue peppering in the narrow space and into the water. I surface , and catch a glimpse of figures in gas masks shooting at the Lawless men. I watch the retreating back of their leader as he beat a hasty exit, he cast me one last glance, a promise of retribution within their sickly depths. I jump up on a step, and a gun presses at my back, and Freeze mid step. My hands starts smoking, I try to move aim my hands towards the figure at my back.

"Don't even think about it."

I went still, and let the smoke dissipate from my hands. And watch helplessly as they round us up, and herd us towards a narrow passageway tucked into a dark corner. a shriek boomeranged from it, and my skin crawls at the thought of going through that, I gnash my teeth and let them lead us towards uncertainty. I spare a glance at Jin, blood trails from his temple to stain his shirt scarlet .I sigh of course he will deem it fit to resist our captors, Zen was deceptively submissive and quiet I could almost see the cogs and gears working in her brain. Fiery Zen wouldn't be submissive unless she possesses knowledge I don't.

Brown briny water crawls up our calves inching higher the deeper we venture in. I catch a glimpse of a Reaper up on the grates above, they're herding us, I recognized the hunting calls, I exchange a look with Zen, she has picked on it too. If we don't get out of here we will become Reaper chow soon. The passage way spits us into a huge yawning room, flanked by doorways, the water sluices down in huge curtain of briny water into a huge watery abyss. A very close screech has my eyes snapping high above me, a Reaper gives me what guess was a grin that it got me. The first of our masked captors executes a perfect jump back to the waterfall and shoots at a reaper, its death shriek muted by the cheers of the masked captors. They soon follow suit and shoot at the Reapers that have jump down from above to attack us. I scorch a Reaper to ashes when it lunges at me, I throw one at another that's almost one of the our masked captors. He dips his head in thanks and shoots at a huge one.

I hit the water hard, and try to hold in my gasps, but I couldn't. Stale water rushes in my mouth, and I follow the lead of our captors, who's just punched in codes of a tunnel door, it swung open and he quickly swims in, I quickly swim into it, a hand tugs at my ankles and drags me out of the tunnel. I kicked hard but it's vise grip was too strong, I cling to the lip of the door but it's futile with one last yank it has my hands off the door. I throw a silver firebolt at it and it moves fast anticipating my moves, it almost seems like he's playing with me. Are they supposed to do that? I wondered brows hitching in frustration.

It swipes at me with razor-sharp nails, I move out its way too late and shredding pain slices across my abdomen. Guess we've to do this the old fashioned way, I spare a glace at the automated door that flashing a countdown, if I don't act fast I will be left alone out here with no way out of these unfamiliar tunnels teeming with Reapers. I pull the dagger tucked into my boot, and blast at him with pale fire, it moves easily out of my way, and I attacked in one smooth moves, stabs it into its heart. it struggles for a moment , claws wound around my wrist, blood pools before me, and then it went limp. I retrieve the dagger from its disintegrating corpse and tuck it back into my boot, I swim towards the slowly closing door, every inch it moves, makes panic churn in me. Jin stands at the lip of the tunnel, his eyes linger on my moving form egging me on, Zen and Zunaif stands behind him. With one last flap of my limbs I manage to make it through the tunnel, and it clicks close behind me, a Reaper thumps hard on it.

I gulp in a huge lungful of air, and turn grateful eyes on to Jin. His slightly slanted eyes survey me from head to toe, and linger on my wounds, that could be clearly seen through my torn clothing. without a word he tears the hem of shit and wrap it around my wrist.

"Thank you!" I mutter , trailing a finger on the piece of garb.

Jin just nods, and walks out of there.

" My lord, you've got an admirer. I thought you were a goner there, come on let's go before they grow impatient and come looking." Zens says and strides out of there. Zunaif close on her heels.

I haul my body up and follow Zen, every step painful as Reaper poison lances into me, inching deeper. I need to get some of the

Re3 pills soon before it gets out of control. Even though Reaper claws won't turn me, it could incapacitate me if I don't take care of it. A gas-masked guard open the door and I stride into a room filled with blinking, bleeping machines set on a table. A tall dark skinned man in his late prime, with a gas mask clutched in his hand studies our little ragtag group with hard, calculating eyes. Strangely there isn't any question in his eyes, he knew who we are.

" Does Kaima know that her pets have strayed too far?"

" We're lost, if you could kindly show us the way, we will be out of your hair sir."

" I see. You're not supposed to know . Clever bitch." he seethes.

" I will grant you one wish, ask for a what you want. Do you want to know if there's a topside or you want to go back to your home?"

The word seems like a fantasy. Existence of life topside, a vague hope that I've been torturing myself with, I don't know what I'm doing. Dare I hope that I could have something better than this? That we could ever be free. For a moment, I could almost taste the freedom. But it combusts on my tongue before I have the chance to savor it. Take a tiny step forward, it snags the man's attention.

A slow satisfied smile spreads on his face, an approving light glints in his eyes.

"Yes!"

"I want to find out about topside."

" Good choice." he waves at one of the masked guards, and they proceed to tinker with something on the wall. " Anyone have a different objective."

Silence is the answer to his question. I look at my companions, each curious to find out if there's a topside; breaking Kaima's cardinal .

CHAPTER 9

BOGEYMEN

The floor tremors under us when one of the guards punch a code on the wall display, I clutch at the edge of the huge desk to stop myself from falling, walls before us melt away, and blinding light invade my eyes, forcing me to squint. Air whoosh all around me, it feels strange to be in such a huge space, I fight the urge to curl up in a small fetal ball. I gaze at the two suns that hang high up in the sky, like two flaming balls that Zen summons when she's in one of her kill modes. Jin look as shaken as we were, only Zen didn't.

"There's a topside, she kept it away from you. Do you not wonder why?"

"Topside is survivable, and you're not mankind's last hope, you're its destruction. All bigger pawns in a grand game, that only the powerful will survive." he slashes a hand in the air and guns point at us." Much as I hate doing this, you possess knowledge that can bring my end, you have to die."

"I..." I lift my hand up in surrender.

The Bogey-man leader turns his back to us, and his guards cocked their guns back, a millisecond away from releasing the bullets into our flesh.

A sonic boom rends the air, I took cover, shielding my head, and laying on the ground. A fly-ship comes into view, it shoots another shockwave blasting the bogeys off their feet. The Fly-ship comes to a standstill and Kaima steps out, a catty grin on her face as she surveys the Bogey-men at her mercy.

"How does it feel when you think you've won, and you didn't Kyrem?"

"You think this victory Kaima, I've just shown them your lies, I already have victory. Good luck, because you'll need all the luck in the world."

"Hmm, Pity, with all your might, this is where it ends. I'm sorry comrade I think this is our goodbye. Come on kids."

I fall in step with Jin as we follow her into the fly-ship. Her hard gaze fixed on us, warning us what will happen if we try anything. I don't doubt her willingness to end us here . I watch this new world that has opened my eyes, widen the chasm of my my wanderlust, with a pang I realized that there's no going back now. I watch in amazement as the fly-ship shoots a beam of light into the earth below, a sinkhole opens up, and it dives into it. Curtains of dust rain down the sides of the fly-ship as it made its slow laborious descend into the bowels of the earth. It lands on the fly-pad, a guard waves a hand , and the shower of sand slows down to a halt, and the earth knits back.

We step down the fly-ship, Jin looks lost in his head, he didn't react even when I bump into him. A scuffle has me spin around to see Kaima slam Zen on the fly-ship, the metal gives way on impact, I grimace in sympathy. Kaima let's her crumple at her feet, and turns to us with a wicked sneer. "Not a word to the others, or I wouldn't hesitate to make an example of all of you."

We all nod wordlessly, and she breezes past us and disappear into the looming gates ready to put us back into a world I don't want to be part of anymore.

CHAPTER 10

Jelika

50 years After The EMP.

Dear diary,

Last night I saw my best friend's death, she turned into a Reaper. She got stab by a Zukai when they raided us, she had pleaded that she still had time. But we weren't sure. Because we can be wrong when it comes to it. We couldn't take such a risk. She knew that. I couldn't blame her for wanting to hold on to life, even if it meant being a Reaper. But who doesn't want to hold on as long as possible? Because no matter how terrifying it is to live in it, the unknown was even more so? Everybody wants a respite from all these madness, and yet death's the only thing that could bring such a thing, and yet none of us would embrace it.

When I close my eyes, I could still see her amber-colored brown eyes pleading with our Njitt, our leader, I could see his hesitation shining in his eyes as he cocked his gun to kill her. See the helplessness in them, I had wanted to do something; I don't know. It's crazy. I wish the torment, the acceptance of her fate, and the sereneness of her demeanor to end.

They say that you see the world in different shades of death, that life flashes before your very eyes, as you stare death in the eye when he comes for you. How did our world go to hell? How did we lose our way? I'm chronicling this so that anyone reading this might know of how we lost our world and ways. My grandma told me of how the world was alright one moment, and the next, a nuclear electromagnetic force wiped off everything we had. The sun flare was no help as it rendered the world almost unliveable everything bowed to the hands of nature or died, along with the humanity in us. Taking us back to scrabbling for the simplest of basic necessities. And then the Reapers came, filling their ranks.

Our families, our neighbors, came back for us. It made us desperate to survive, no matter what. It turned us all into what we hate most. Monsters! No crime was too high; anything was right if you wanted it. To go by the law of Anarchy, to survive another sunrise, to see enemies everywhere, Reaper or not. Trust was a rare commodity to come by because it exists no more. A fable that dusts like so many things. Being on the run, running to survive, or die trying to survive.

The alarm shrills, and I put the dog eared book back in the hole and jog out of my cell to the training room. Everyone wore the standard uniform; a black T-shirt and gray sweatpants. I didn't look at my sparring partner; it's easier to not look at the person you are beating to a bloody pulp. It never matters. To survive on the ark, you have to be cold-blooded, unfeeling, a monster. Nothing should faze you, nothing's new. We have seen everything and survived. There is no mercy in my world, no love, no kindness. Only the unadulterated purpose of reaching what we are here for.

Salvation.

I slug the girl with a mean uppercut, watched with grim satisfaction as her body was lifted in the air, thumped hard on the wooden floor. She cried out, cupping her chin; it's a human thing; it's against everything to be human because being human ended the world. Never show pain. I stare at the slowly blinking red lights in the cameras, everything is recorded, nothing escapes their notice. I kick her, and she went down. Right now, I hate who I must become, who I am. It's my opponent or me, and I had already decided it was going to be me. Taking hold of her hand, I snapped her fingers backward. She screamed, hard, and breaks free of my grasp. She lands a good, solid kick at my legs. I stumbled back and righted my balance. Then I was on her like an angry storm, not even giving her any time to react to my attack. Gripping her head in my hands, I slammed my knee into her face, the sound of her nose breaking made the monster in me giddy and dance with glee, a faucet of blood streaming out, coating my pants, she let out a pitiful groan falling face down on the sparring mat and blissfully pass out. I sigh, grateful that it was over.

Somehow seeing her on the floor, broken bones, and helpless made me want to help her out or kill her. I snap out of the haze and glance at Kaima stands, the glass partition separating us. She writes on the clipboard she had in hand. And for the first time, an idea fills my mind. Something that could bring the end of me, something that the girl I was before reading that diary, and seeing the bogey-men would never have thought of such a thing. A drop of blood slides out of my nose and falls onto my palm. Ready to take the chances of being caught. Because I'm curious about what it holds within its pages. And now I had this feeling that it would be the death of me because I now knew one thing, I will never stop trying to find a way out of here.

CHAPTER 11

BLADE, TEETH & NIGHT

Abiyanna

Dear diary,

We are headed towards a place said to be secure. Where there's food, shelter, and no Reapers. We are trying it out ourselves; I don't know what we will find there. But we have to cross the vast desert and past places that are risky. I don't know if we will make it. I haven't eaten in days, can't remember when I have last eaten decent food. We have been on the road for weeks now, banded with some survivors heading that way. And I pray to whatever power listening that we make this journey. I know that the desert is a treacherous foe to everyone living and that there is strength in numbers. I don't like the way our guide looks at me; I want to tell Papa about it. But I might only be paranoid. His gaze makes goosebumps break all over my skin. Something about him is not right. I can feel it, the way his oily, leering gaze stares at us girls like we were prized mules to him. I am not too bothered because I can take care of myself. I make sure that I go to sleep every night with my blade in hand. I see the hope dying in Papa's eyes every daylight when we count our fallen, and the determination to not let the Reapers end our lives, where ever this place is, we have to reach it soon.

My sleep was getting lesser as every night Mama in my dreams, I would wake up every night screaming for mercy, In her eyes was the fearless, selfless love as she sacrificed herself so that I could live. Papa had gone out hunting with some men. That night our security is breached when another group of desperate survivors attack us, leaving us vulnerable to the Reapers. It makes me furious at how useless I was back then after Papa taught me how to shoot a weapon and wield one, he even threw in some self-defense moves. She came again, Mama, with arms outstretched, she walks in the stiff gait of the Reapers. Calling for me. There was no love in her eyes, only eternal, savage, insatiable thralldom.

"Child, you can't run away from death," she mocks a stranger speaking through her lips. She give me a smile that had me trembling in fright, then she was on me in a blink. She wrestles me to the ground, her mouth opens to take a bite out of me, small blades in her hands

. My eyes spring open, and I gasp for breath. My chest felt heavy, I cough a few times, then still when I hear footsteps. I shake Chika awake and put a finger to her lips before she made any noise. I gesture that she should wake others and hurry out of there. The air was heavy I could scent something in the air that I can't pinpoint what it was, the blue force field Papa and the other men had put up surrounded our camp to keep the Reapers out, according to Papa it costs an arm and a leg, complex to set up, but a good thing for an effective Reapers defense mechanism, it looked okay to me, my instincts told me that something was amiss, and I have to find out what it was. A hand clamps on my mouth, and pulls me to a body.

I react without wasting a moment and bit into his palm hard, blood floods freely into my mouth; he groans, and I slam my head into his chin. I whirl around, coming face to face with a man. He wore military fatigues, an arsenal of weapons on his belt. A blast rocks a tent to my right, I ran towards it without hesitation. How did they hamper the force field? I stare as another strode through the force field. A silver light pulsed on his chest, bathing his whole body, shifting the force field back. I realized that it was what made it possible for them to walk through it.

Papa.

The world darkens, and everything seemed far away, a whooshing claims my senses, I watch a man ran him over with his blade a savage satisfaction on his face. The other one he's fighting with slashes Papa's throat open, and scarlet-red blood gushes out. I barge into him, my sword's in him before he knew what hit him. I slammed the blade over and over in his throat, not stopping. Blood mixed with my salty tears coated my face, trailed down my chest and dripped on the ground. Screaming the whole time, I was a savage. White-hot pain explodes in my head, and I slump on the ground.

I woke to find myself in a dark room, scanning the room my eyes fell on a small form on the floor. A girl with a petite frame, brown hair, and light-brown almost fair skin sat on the floor. She rocks back and forth, whispering words I can't hear. I stood up from the bed. Bright, impressive, aquamarine-green eyes surveyed me from head to toe. I wore some kind of light blue hospital frock that stops at my knee, a band made of strange metal I had never seen before with a winking green light. Barefoot I padded towards the door of the room.

And tried the lock pad on the door, trying to find a way to open it, but found none, damn it, I have to get out of here. I swipe the wristband on the panel. But nothing happened, I bash my head on the bars of the door, silent tears gliding down my face to drip on the floor. Papa I could still see the shock, surprise, and the pain as the blade sunk into him.

"*Don't bother, no one gets out.*"

"*What do you mean?*"

"*I meant what I said. No one has ever escaped here. You are here to stay for good, so get used to the idea. I'm Izzayatu.*"

"*I'm Abiyanna! What is this place?*"

"*I call it purgatory, the first step to the ark because that is what it is,*" *Izzayatu whispers, green eyes glowing in the dark. She looks like a small, forlorn, lonely doll. I slid down to the floor and hug my knees, trying to take in all of what I knew.*

CHAPTER 12

MBETU

SUKUNDA

I splash water on my face, stared through my goggles at the blue sky with the flaming suns hanging above our heads, cold water sluice down my face, chasing away the intense heat of the desert. I snuck a glance out of the corner of my eye staring at the girls dotted out in the courtyard, raiders with weapons in view stood at attention eying us all like we are pieces of rare delicacies that they want to devour. Goosebumps rose on my arms, footsteps rang behind me, I stiffened my back and stuffed back the urge to turn back and run, get as far away from those footsteps as I can. I know that I could have an ocean between us, and yet it will not be enough for me. I gripped the lip of the fountain and braced myself for what was to come.

Hard hands caress my hair, and I flinch away from the touch, I can't help it. Even though my body tells me to endure the touch, that it won't last. That I am a passing fancy. That Mbulla would see someone and forget about me. But when? A voice asks within me. Fingers tunnel in my hair and grip hard, so hard that tears came to my lashes, I refuse to cry or struggle. It only makes things worse, I had tried all that, but it just doesn't work.

I close my eyes and reach the place that no one can reach, only I can, the place that I wished that I'm still in. How I want to turn the hands of time, to be what everyone expects, accept my fate, as I should have, instead disobey the very thing that I should have obeyed. A place that is not like this hellhole that I have dug myself into. I wanted to know more about the forbidden world, and everything that it holds, it was taboo, and I knew it. But I wanted it, I must know more about it, a desire that would not fade away, I was too selfish to see what it would do to me. Pinpricks of pain attack my scalp, forcing my head up to meet the cold, merciless eyes of my handler's son. He leers at me, a hand clamp at my waist.

" I've been looking for you everywhere, my Mami-water." His eyes roved down my body in a way that made me want to lose the contents of my stomach.

Mbulla grins, flashes his whites, I see the nauseous lust lurking in his eyes as he drags me by my hair. He had taken a sick liking to me the moment he had set his sight on me I let him drag me farther away from the courtyard. A girl with fair, light golden-brown skin hid behind a column. Her loose clothing did not hide the bump that was showing. Her face a mask of fear, for a moment I forgot my situation, she wipes tears from her face, she must be new here, not yet broken, a little girl about ten grips at her skirt, hiding from the world. She looks to be around eleven. They share the same complexion and lush, long hair that fell past their shoulders.

"Mbulla!" a voice boom out, making us stop in our tracks.

We both turn around to look at my handler, Balla stands before us, face furious and nostrils flaring. A mountain of muscles that threatens to pound anyone into dust. The two are polar opposites, where Mbulla enjoys meting out pain, and sadistic, cruel jokes. Balla, his father, is excessively stern, a force that I have never seen hurt anyone except if it is as punishment to make sure that we obey rules, a reason why I never want to cross him.

"What in hell's gate do you think you are doing with that breeder?"

"Father, I was just taking her _."

"Silence, I told you to leave the breeders alone." He slaps him hard, so hard he smacks into a column. Blood trails down the corner of his bottom lip.

"Yes, sir," he whispers and let go of me, loping off, but I felt the weight of his stare, this was not the end of our meeting. Next time his father will not be here, he'll make sure.

"Did he hurt you?"

"No."

He nods curtly, and stride out of there, I sag to the ground in relief, not believing my luck." Here, drink this." A small voice said, I look up and meet the eyes of the light, golden brown-skinned girl. I took the wooden cup and take a greedy gulp from it.

"Thank you."

"I am Amisha, and this is my sister Anushka. It is nice to see a new face, you new here?"

She nods, giving me a small smile that lit her beautiful face." Where are you from?" she whispers shyly.

"Mbe'tu, "

"Mbe' ti."

"Mbe'tu, it is a place far away from here. Where are you from?"

"Somito,"

"What are you doing so far away from home?"

"The same could be asked of you."

I should have never left my tribe, but I had foolishly made my choice in a fit of anger that has buried me in the purgatory of my own deed. Now, because of me, more of my own people will perish. Girls my age gaze at everything with vacant, cold eyes. Eyes that tell you all you need to know, eyes that have seen the fires of hell and beyond. We live, but our souls are not present in our bodies, we are shells of our former selves, vessels where new life would spring forth. A curse I did rather not have. If I had known this is what our world really is, I would stay home and suck everything up as I should have. But no, I lost count on how many times father told me that as the Matriarch of the land, my role is to stay close to home, marry and continue the line.

Mbe'tu. How I missed home, a word that I have forgotten. I have forgotten how it tastes and feels like, the arms that hold you close and vow to never leave you. I missed the festivals, the food, the joy of belonging. Not the poor excuse hunk of bread and water we are given, in Mbe'tu we have delicious, nature defying food that is just too unbelievable. We are the Mbe'tu people, my tribe has been living solitary lives, not interfering in the world and its affairs. We see it as tainted; it was something that worked well for us, for me until I stumbled upon what I later learned is a taint of the world. Father was aghast, but I was not, I was entranced with the thing. So I stole it from where father hid it. I wished that I'd never done so.

"Bad choices," I stand up, and hand her the wooden cup, then with a soft smile that I haven't summoned for some time, tousled Anushka's hair.

"I see that you have gained Mbulla's attention. Not a good thing. Keep your head down, keep a low profile. It will help you survive in here, but I know it won't work, someone as beautiful as you will not go unnoticed in a place like this, believe me, it will not work, I tried, but in the end, it never helped, he still got his way."

"He did that to you?"

"Yes, the miserable bastard did this to me, he threatened to kill Anushka, he would have if I didn't give in to him." she bit her lip and met my eyes, her eyes tearing up. She held the girl closer to her, her posture protective, her eyes going hard for a moment. And I could glimpse the fact that she would give up her life protecting her.

In Mbe'tu, the crime such as the one he committed will not go unpunished. I would rather kill him first. That very thought of him forcing himself on me made me fist my hands. I already hated him. Killing him would be something that Amisha should do.

In Mbe'tu, it would be an honor .

CHAPTER 13

PRIMA

Chima

Junk district.

"Five bronze coins,"

"You know that is one of my biggest scavenges Tin" I glare at the fat man with the double chins giving me an evil grin. He knew that he was ripping me off because he's the only person who I could sell my scavenges. I sigh, not having any choice, and take the coins. He knew that I had no choice but to take it, instead of the unsavory alternative; go savage girl on him, I could get lucky with a few punches to show him how riled up and volatile he has made me feel. But one glance at the towering mountain of muscles on either side of him made me reconsider and go through my option of surviving such an encounter with his infamous bodyguards that he had hired to guard him. Tin was one of the most secure people from here to the Sahara, his infamous trade was known throughout Junk district. And being one of the most hated people in this territory, second only to the Obra family, I don't hate him that much because he contributes a quota to junk district's security, but even that wasn't enough.

"You sure that you don't want to enroll in my recruitment program doll? I have got a special coming up."

"No, thanks, Tin."

With Tin, you would be selling your soul, his program entails his security, dove, and private rat for the Obras, which's being a spy for them in their territory games. They've been playing since their territories were created, as each master falls, another rises up the ranks to take his place. If you let your guard down, you'll have your throat slit before you can blink. I have no intention of being one. A private rat's life span is even lower because the punishment when caught is death. There's no question asked about who sent you because private rats aren't known for their candor. The first thing done when found is a tongue removed. Being a dove is out of the question, letting him pimp me out is the last thing I would consider doing even if the suns do not shine again and he was my last hope. I know that some girls opt for option one because it has a higher chance of surviving, well except if your Patreon is a sadist and likes to dole out the pain. I'm not cut out for a life of servitude because it offers life insurance that's not even fifty percent safe. If the Obras want you dead, you will be before you know it.

"One day, I will get you, Chima." He runs a hand on my wrist towards my forearm to my braids. I scoop up the coins and quickly shoot out of his reach. My skin crawls, and I wish that I would cut off my hand if I had no need of it I would. I shiver and stuff the bronze coins in my pocket scurrying out of there. Those words were a promise to me because I know that Tin never fails when he sets out to get something. There's a reason he's one of the most hated and feared men in my world apart from the six. I knew that he didn't play fair to reach where he's now. Neither did I. I hurried out of there and towards home. Thinking about what I was going to buy with the money I had. I stare at the dilapidated buildings and picture that I was somewhere different. Soon I smile, soon I will be there. I will make you proud Mama.

I have to fulfill the promise I made to Mama about making sure that I am better off. Safe and well-fed, one day, I will be in Hope city. A dangerous journey that I'm willing to take for her sake. Things are getting harder every time, scavenges lesser, and Reapers attacks more frequently. But I'll soon have enough for the journey, I hope. My nape tingles, and I stiffen spinning around, I'm met with only people walking around. I walk faster to my shanty. Nothing follows but trouble when my nape tingles. Perhaps I'll have to talk to Zahra into letting me sleep in her shack tonight. In the junk district, there's no loyalty, only every man for himself. We are like a bunch of hungry Bukis circling a massive chunk of meat call survival. And the Reapers make it worse, occasionally Reapers make their way in. Which begins some kind of sweep-purge. Disobeying the curfew will have you shot on sight, staying in your shanty and pray to God that a Reaper doesn't find you inside before morning, so many lost their lives during purges like that. Pray that you don't see the 'devil-children' as dubbed by Junkers; they were the most troublesome of all Reapers, faster than the Reapers. Soft, cold, and buttery touched my cheek, and I looked up, getting a face full of snowflakes.

No!

I hate this; I run as fast as I could to my shanty, banging the door behind me; I lean on my door and close my eyes. I hope that no one saw that. People don't understand what they fear, and fear brings the worse of monsters in us. Fear kept us living, fear is the reason why we fight every sunset. I peek out of my window and stares at the soft fall of snow from the sky. I thought I spot the shadow of a man in the farthest corner of the street, but he was gone, it left me feeling if it was my mind making it all up.

"Let none know what you can do Chima, there are people who will kill you for what you are. And others would make a weapon out of you. Hide what you are in plain sight." Mama's voice rings out in my head. More snow rains from the heavens, reacting to my mood. I tamp it down a little. And released a sigh, when I look up at the sky and see that the snowfall had lessened.

"I thought that I could find you here."

I twirl around and come face to face with a girl; she looks to be about twelve, with huge doe-like, innocent brown eyes, that makes you want to drown in them. I lift a brow, silently asking what she wants. Right now, I'm in no mood for anything less than business. She gulps a little, and I let my features soften, the anger and fear melting away to show friendly features. That seemed to relax her a little, but it didn't chase the clouds of fear and doubt in her eyes.

She still maintains the wary look that had come into her beautiful eyes. "I need…. We need your help, please follow me." she intones, her eyes darting everywhere as if looking for potential danger that could jump out of places that it might lurk in. "This isn't a trap Chima, please come." She adds, striding out of there, I sigh and follow the girl. Taking a risk that I have never done, something that could prove fatal to me. It will suck if it turns around and bites me back when I least expect it to. The girl led me deeper into lower junk. Something I avoid by all means because this place holds the worst of the dregs of our society. This place is where only the poorest of us live. They had no choice. She led me into a rundown shanty that looks like it could be blown over by the smallest of storms; she disappeared in, and I followed a heartbeat later. A girl around my age sat in a sturdy, rocking chair, I don't even need to ask to know that she spells trouble for me, or anyone mad enough to step into this shanty.

"I thought that you will not come.

"I shouldn't have."

She nods and pins me with solemn, reddish-brown eyes that made me want to take back my words. My eyes fell on the noticeable, telltale bump that is her midriff. A voice in my head was telling me to turn back and go home, that, this isn't my fight, I can't save everyone. Whatever they wanted isn't going to bode well for me, but another argued that what harm is there to listen to what they want since I came all the way here? Might as well hear them out.

"As you can see, my state," She gestures at her baby bump, giving me another sad smile, makes me wonder if that's all she can do. "I need to get out of here ASAP, and I heard that you might be the right one for such a job."

"I was, but not anymore, that was a past trade? And no pay could make me do that again." I wasn't lying; I had stopped making people disappear without a trace a long time ago. It was what I did when I first came to Junk district. A little girl with no way of earning her keep, it was either that or let Tin take me under his nefarious wings. The scavenges weren't enough to take care of me. Thus, I had to be 'Wisp,' the assassin and smuggler wanted by almost all six authorities of the colonies in Kambuya, the one at the top of Tin's list, no doubt, and some other people I have crossed out there. Whether you want to have someone assassinated or you need a smuggler to smuggle you out. I wasn't afraid to keep my hands dirty, and dirty them I did. What would he do if he knew who I was? That I had been under his very nose seemed laughable that a resourceful, powerful man such as he should be bested by a small slip of a girl like me. Karma must be laughing at him right now.

"That's half of the payment, it will be completed when the job's done. I want out of here, "

I eyed her right, inner wrist where lay the tattoo of a drop of water entangled with a drop of blood, a shield lay underneath it on her, a symbol of a skull and crossbones on fire perched on her left bicep. She's a breeder, not an average breeder, but a prima breeder, property of the Obras by the tattoo branded on her skin. But that doesn't explain her reddish-brown eyes, maybe it is the side effects of all drugs being administered to her to make sure that she is in peak health for the baby, Primas have everything they needed, no expense was spared, everything they need was being given to them. When the virus came, it created some kind of infertility disease that made almost all women barren, breeders are treasured, and so you will see why I was adamant about taking on such a risky job. If caught, I'm dead. Doornail dead. Might as well commit ritual suicide and leave a note for Zahra to find. Because there will be no mercy when Obra goes on a witch hunt for my head.

I picked the velvet pouch and stares at the Arkor diamonds nestled within its velvet embrace worth a small fortune, something that could help with my planned expedition. I shook my head, "Sorry, I can't, there aren't enough Arkor-diamonds to make me cross the Obras, I have crossed them enough already." I threw the pouch back at her, and she snatch it in midair with quick, startling reflexes. I strode out of there before I reconsider and help. I try to forget the anguish, I glimpsed in her reddish-brown eyes. I want to kick myself, but what could I do? I have to think about it. What was so hard in her life that she wanted to anger her master? She's got everything that anyone would wish for, the only downside of it is that she has to have his kids. Only the best for the masters, they are to have whatever they want.

Years ago, when they were on a witch hunt for 'Wisp,' I was in my shanty with Zahra, Obra and Fex were the people on my list that I will not cross. Maybe I could give second thoughts about the others, but not him. I have never seen him, but there's a rumor in Junk district that you should pray to never cross the path of Obra's; he's the kind of person that can kill you for just doing the right thing, killing was a hobby for him. You will live so long as it suits his moods, except for the occasional thefts that I do now and then, stealing his weapons. Drawing the red smoke that I always drew before I disappear, the signature mark of wisps. Arms were a must in Junk district. And what better way to have it other than from the best? But I went cold-turkey a couple of years back when the number of people who have an ax to grind on my head grew, bodies piling up. And a week didn't go by when I don't hear that a Wisp wannabe is executed. It always leaves me feeling guilty about the loss of life in my name.

CHAPTER 14

SANCTUARY, NAIL & CLAW

Abiyanna

Dear diary,

Izzayatu is right, this is purgatory, my worst nightmare in the flesh. My life has taken a downhill, no one tries to escape, it was useless. Security here is tight, even a fly can't get out undetected here. Izzayatu has withdrawn more and more into the far edges of her mind, I get to see the other kids my age at mealtimes, when we are not, we would be in our cells. Forced to follow a rigorous schedule that is ticked by the alarm that everyone fears to miss our very life depends on it. Some of us are relieved to have a roof over our heads, food, water, and no worrying about the Reapers. Because they don't seem to be a problem anymore, they are. I wanted my world back; I want Papa back and the thrill of living to see sunrise after sunrise.

I don't know why they killed all the adults and took us. This sure doesn't look like a sanctuary. The last refuge I was in don't have people in cells. And following a schedule that does not tell you anything. In the gym following the instructor that I disliked at first glance, we push our bodies past limits we thought possible, and I fear that they are trying to bring out the fighters in us, Papa says that when everyone brings out the soldiers in them, monsters will emerge. I stare at Izzayatu, where she was whip-cording her body in the air and slammed her leg into the jaw of her sparring partner, a savage look in her eyes, from afar it looked effortless to me.

She has changed these days, retreated into herself day after day. She was turning into a stranger, she said to me when I asked her what happens when they come for you, and she had replied. "Survive to see the end." I'm scared. By the looks of it, my time would come soon. I don't know what happens when they take you. All I know is that they change you.

* **** *

I backed into the wall, holding my breath as the guard hurried past me. I was trying to look for a way out of here. I have got to get out of here, staying back and being helpless does nothing good to help me with this situation. I have been sneaking out of my cell late at night, always trying to avoid the cameras, sticking to their blind spots as best as I could. Tonight I have ventured farther than I had ever done, I rushed out of there when I was sure that the corridor was bright; I tried the door and found it open. I stare at what layout before me, bodies lay on steel tables, cold and lifeless, with some kind of liquid of an indeterminate color oozing out of the drip into their bodies. I walked towards one, it was a girl with her hair in cornrows, her skin had taken on a grayish tint, I lay a finger on her cheek; it was as cold as ice.

She's dead.

"She's not dead! They are all in stasis."

I met brown eyes under the table. On the floor was a guy. He crawled out from under the table and stood beside me. "guess you are running away too."

"Yes, do you know a way out?"

"I might."

Footsteps rang out, and I looked for a way out of there and found none. "Quickly get on a table."

"What?"

"I know that you won't like what happens to you when you are found here, it's either that or you wait for whoever those footsteps belong to or get on one," he said, getting on a table, and tucking the needle into his wrist band. I rushed onto an empty table and tucked the needle into mine, I just hope that I don't get discovered. That would be a tight situation to get out of. Through my lashes I peeked out at the man in the white lab coat, he punched a button of a remote, bands of steel retract out from the sides of the table, strapping me to the table, slowly the floor dipped, and the tables slid down all in neat rows.

I don't have a good feeling about all this, but do I have a choice? Nah, the floor yawn open, and my table tip over. Following the trail of other tables bearing bodies. Stasis, he had said; they don't look like that to me; they looked dead and cold. I narrowed my eyes. No, it can't be. Izzayatu lay lifeless on the table. They got her too. What did they hope to have from doing this? I knew that they were lying to us, a conspiracy of some kind. Either way, I have to get out of here. The guy push back the steel bands and hurried to help me out of mine."

Abiyanna, my name's Abiyanna, but you can call me Abie."

"Tarafa Balafo at your service, but Taraf would do fine," he bowed, a smile plays on his lips. *"Oh, she smiles."*

"How do we get out of here?"

"We have to reach the alpha sector on the other side. I guess this is the transcendence sector."

"Trans what?"

"It's the final stage to change you into something that I hope you won't have to be if I have my way."

My gaze roved Izzayatu's prone body. I yanked the needle out of her inner wrist, Taraf deactivated the steel clamps. I shook her, trying to wake her up. Heart in my mouth, I shook her harder.

"That won't do, "Taraf came forward, I watched him close his eyes and put his palms on Izzayatu's chest, a silver light emerged out of his palms and sink into her chest. I stare in shock, not believing what I was seeing. He opens his eyes and gazed at me with pupils that have gone mercury-silver, and sighs. "I don't think that she will wake up, maybe she is too far gone, we should get out of here before it is too late."

"They did that to you?" He nodded and strode past me, I clamped my mouth shut, gave one look at where Izzayatu lay and hurried after him. I was a few feet away when the gasp had me whirring back to see Izzayatu sat up; I ran to where she sat, Taraf on my heels.

"Abie."

"How're you feeling?"

"A little wobbly, but fine."

"Perfect, she will be fine, it will pass away. We should move on." Taraf strode forward and left me to assist Izzayatu down from the table. She swayed a little, but I steadied her. We follow the guy to where he has disappeared.

"Who's that?"

"His name is Taraf, I met him minutes ago, " I noted the pale hue that clung to her skin was fast fading; I felt a little twinge of apprehension for not trying to help more, but it was risky. We could have been discovered at any moment. We walked into the lift, and Taraf punched in a code, and the doors swung close. The alarm blared to life; I knew it. It was too good to be true. That we are getting out of here with no obstacle laid our way. It was a pipe dream. Heart thumping, I wait with bated breath for the doors of the lift to open into the alpha sector. My blood hummed with adrenaline, I was *tired of letting people control my life; I am tired of everything that life threw at me. I am ready to fight back, and I will. By the grim set of my two companion's mouths, I knew that they were not going down without a fight, and a fight they will get. I was ready to get out of here or die. Freedom is mine. And I'm prepared to fight tooth, nail, and claw.*

CHAPTER 15

ODE

Chima

I run like the hounds of hell were chasing me, branches snatch at my clothes, scratching my skin. My breath erratic as I run, fear lending my feet wings. Tears swarm my eyes as I force my body to move forward. To not turn back and help her. Mama I could see the cold determination in her eyes, as she gave herself up . I nearly spins around and go back. But a voice spurs her on. The howls and vicious screeches carried by the wind chases me, embed in my mind, forcing me to move faster. She sobs but didn't stop. Then I saw them. Bodies swinging from the trees, ropes tied at their throats, it's a monster's work, and I know who that monster is.

I want to wave my hands and make everything right like the stories Mama used to read to her, about magic, how she wished that she has the power to do so. As it should be, this isn't right. Her eyes widens, as the ropes frayed, and the bodies fall to the ground and rise. They circled her, chilling vengeance in their gazes. They want my blood. They close in on me, and I raised hands to defend myself but I couldn't move a muscle, rooted to the spot. They tore into the helpless me; I screams for help and cried, but none came. I gasp awake, body saturated in sweat, hands tingling.

"A nightmare?" a voice whispers within the shadows,

I scoot back, sitting up to stare at the girl in my shanty. Her Reddish-brown gaze found mine, and she puts a hand on her swollen stomach." How did you get in here?" I wheeze, still, in the grips of my nightmare, body quivering, I try to stop the quiver. The first people to witness Wisp's undoing. It makes me want to gnash my teeth in frustration.

"I never knew that the great wisp has nightmares."

"Everyone has one little girl, makes me wonder what yours are?"

"She got me in." The girl tilts her head at the petite girl. Who grins, proud of her feat.

Great, there's no way in deterring the two. I huff and run a hand through my sweat-soaked hair. And by the look in the girl's age-old eyes, I know that I wouldn't like the answer if I probed how she got them here. I clamp my mouth shut and take a gulp of water from my canteen, eying the two. Fine, I will admit that they were relentless in their pursuit for my aid, that they have sneak up on me without detection. "I told you that I'm retired, now if you two would let me have my little beauty sleep. God knows that everyone needs it in this shit hole of a world."

"You are my only hope of getting out of here, I don't want to lose this baby. Please help, he wants to experiment more on the baby when he's born."

I heave a sigh and curse. I just can't let that happen to the unborn baby. Great, I might as well put a noose around my neck and write my will. Hating the words that I was going to utter next, "How long before he realizes you're gone?"

"Another more day before he looks for me,"

"Good," I lay down on my small bed as the two eye me curiously. "Get some beauty sleep ladies, we won't have one for some time.

"Thank you."

"Don't thank me yet, just pray to whatever you believe in that we don't get caught."

*** ***

"I've got a run for us."

I quirked a brow at her, and she gave me a smile. Her beautiful dark hair glinting in the sun, I wonder where Azuiga is. They live in the outskirts of inner junk, not part of the better offs, but not Junkers either. It wasn't common for Junkers to make friends; our society doesn't give us that option. What will she think when she discovers what I'm about to do? "Okay, let's hear it! How much is it worth?"

"Half a million bronze coins."

I gawk at her in disbelief; she has to be kidding. It could be one of her pranks that I fell for one too many times. I turn my back to my shanty and glimpse a flash of reddish-brown eyes, I had them stay inside while I make sure that the carriage I have bought from some of Red's Arkor-diamonds that I peddled for a lot of mints. I hadn't wanted to buy it, the Junker in me had wanted to take her money and get out of there, but I couldn't when I've already given them my word that I would help, I see too much of me in her. So the carriage it is, it's the only way I could make the guards believe that she's Fex's niece passing through from a visit, and was going home to the provenance.

"Where?" I whisper, throat dry.

"Ash mansion."

My mouth went dry; it's a death sentence. Ash mansion is a no-go zone that the Obra family has no tolerance over. Whoever is paying for that must be high up, wealthy and ready to cross swords with the Obras. Only a master or mistress will dare try such a thing Anyone who does, won't live to tell the tale, a testament of the Junk-gallows. Whatever was in that mansion must be valuable to them. Coveted; that death sentence is why it's that high, I shook my head at her. There's no way in hell or heaven that I was going; it could mean everything and nothing for me. With money like that, I could go into Hope city no problem. Hell, I could even live off the money till I die. And so would a noose around my neck, my body hanging lifeless from the Junk gallows.

"What if it goes wrong?"

"It won't trust me, Chime. This is a run of a lifetime, are you going to let it slip through your hands like that?"

When she puts it like that, she knows that she got me, so says the victorious glint in her eyes. Zahra always had a way with words, she had this uncanny way of knowing what you are thinking, and the right words to sway you, it's a dangerous tool that she wields, and she knows it, never hesitates to use it whenever she needs to.

"Okay, but if we get tagged, it's on you."

"We won't. "she gives me one of her trademark, winning smiles that never fails to win people over, and I am no exception. Like the people, I suck at saying no to her always putty in her hands. What Zahra wants, Zahra gets. God, I hope that nothing goes south.

One day I will get you Chima.

Those words raised goosebumps on my skin, I quiver, got a concerned look from Zahra and she gives me the are-you-alright-look we tend to give each other, her gaze on the carriage that I'm prepping but she asked nothing, I shrugged and watched her mount her mountain bike parked a few yards away from my shanty. That's what I love about her, we both have secrets, we want to keep it that way, it's for the best to not get sucked in the other's life.

I released the breath I was holding and gestured for Red and the girl to step out of the shanty. She emerges, a deep, midnight-blue, print dress that drags on the floor, hiding any evidence that she was expecting clung to her frame, hair pulled back from her face, with crisscrossing braids and gold nuggets that formed a network of twists, then trail down her shoulders to stop a few inches' mid-back. She looks influential, beautiful, perfect, untouchable. A poster girl for the rich, I nod at her, pleased that her clothes are baggy enough that her pregnancy wasn't showing. I'm a goner if someone suspects what lay beneath her beautiful, expensive clothes. I turn my stare on the girl standing beside her. She also wears finery that made my fingers itch to tear it off her frame and sell it off to Tin. The mere thought of Tin brings the jitters, I rub a hand on my temple.

"It will be fine, Wisp."

"Don't call me that. Chima, it's Chima."

She gives me a small, knowing smile. "But you're, are you not? Deep down, you know that you love being Wisp, untouchable, invincible. The only person feared and wanted by all. If only you know that you are one of the reason, Obra doesn't sleep well at night, especially with that rumor about you going to assassinate all masters and mistresses of the colonies. It seemed laughable that you shy away from that kind of power, instead of embracing that mantle of authority, which anyone would kill to put on, you hide away from it. Fearing power is inevitable for people like you wherever you go, it will follow. Power is the only thing that everyone wants in this deadly world of ours, and you were born to wield it."

"Call me Chima, "I whisper stiffly, muscles tensed and locked.

"Very well, Chima, call me Odah'e, but Ode's fine."

She hops in the carriage, I take the driver's seat and with a twitch of the reins I had the horses out of there heading towards inner Junk.

CHAPTER 16

MEMORIES OF HUNGER & HOPE

Jelika

Dare I hope that I could have something better than this? That we could ever be free. For a moment, I could almost taste the freedom. But it combusts on my tongue before I could savor it. My core warms, I whip my hands out, raw, pale-white fire blasted out of my fingers, and slammed into the dummy white-ice fire eating at it, burning, leaving nothing behind. I stare at Kaima. I disregard the painful feeling of having a knife stab into my skull, the urge to scream like an enraged animal. My eyes burn, I fought it. I won't let Kaima see my full capabilities, this one will suffice.

She's the only one that I'm afraid of. Nothing escapes those eyes of death, nothing. She wasn't named angel of death for no reason. We usually see her once every month, but this's a surprise visit. Kaima writes something on the small board, I step back and Zen, almost all the people on the ark, feared her; I watched her close her eyes when she opens it. Gasps ring out in the room, but I held it.

Show no fear, it could be used against you, if you want to be feared, you have to be a monster like her, with no fear or weakness. I meet eyes that have gone night-sky with flames licking at her lashes, ready to come out and play. They played in her palms; her skin had taken a death red-pale shade. I shudder, as a memory of pitch darkness blankets me. I feel the hunger, the need for flesh, a voice telling me to hide. The memory is gone before I could grasp what that was all about. The shrill ringing of the bell pulls me out of my trance.

My core warms up, I whip my hands out, raw, white fire blasts out of my fingers, and slam into the dummy in front of me white-ice fire eats at it, burning, leaving nothing behind. I stare Kaima. Her skin had this flawless look that showed like she hasn't been missing the sun, a beautiful, cocoa, golden-brown skin with not a wrinkle in sight, eyes of death stare back in the face of an angel, dark hair in a low bun.

I disregard the painful feeling of having a knife stabbed into my skull, the urge to scream like an enraged animal. My eyes burn, I fought it. I won't let Kaima see my full capabilities, this one will suffice. In my whole life, she's the only one that I'm afraid of. Nothing escapes those eyes of death, nothing. She wasn't named angel of death for no reason. She's here to assess us. We usually see her once every month, but this's a surprise visit. Kaima writes something on the small board,

Show no fear, it could be used against you, if you want to be feared, you have to be a monster like her, with no fear or weakness. I meet eyes that have gone night-sky with flames licking at her lashes, ready to come out and play. They played in her palms; her skin had taken a death red-pale shade. I shudder, as a memory of pitch darkness blankets me. I feel the hunger, the need for flesh, a voice telling me to hide. The memory was gone before I could grasp what that was all about. The shrill ringing of the bell pulls me out of my trance.

CHAPTER 17

BLOOD, RAGDOLL & FLASH

On combat grounds, Zen spars with a boy. She fluidly attacks with quick, accurate moves, a spinning kick from her had the guy slams him on the wall, crumpling into an unconscious heap on the floor.

"Excellent," Zama, our instructor praises.

His gaze latches onto me, "Jelika, Zunaif. You're next." I stared at Zunaif, I guess we're being punished for our little sojourn topside, I crouch in a defensive pose. Standing on the balls of my feet. Zunaif gave me a smile that didn't quite reach his dead eyes," Don't worry, wormy I won't be too hard on you!" he smirks.

I clench my teeth," Bring it on."

He moves before I could blink. A tremor of muscle was all I saw before I went airborne, crashing on the wall. Super strength is one of Zunaif's abilities. I hated being treated like a rag doll. Zen takes a step towards me, but one look from Zama's narrowed, dark hazel eyes stopped her in her tracks. I know the drill. Staying down for ten heartbeats means you are defeated. Three defeats, and you are under review. None knows what happens in evaluation, only that no one comes back, I force my body up at the seventh heartbeat and blearily stared at Zunaif. Blood trails down my face and drips on my gray tee.

"Again," Zama commands.

I bound towards Zunaif, pure fire in my wake. He counters all my moves grinning; he's toying with me; I want to wipe off that stupid grin. Replace it with something more suitable.

"Is that all you've got wormy?" he taunts, throwing a punch at in my solar plexus so hard that I gasp for air, my limbs spasming painfully. With a roundhouse kick, he had my body cartwheel in the air before thumping hard on the floor. Bones and tendons n my leg snap, and I cried out in pain.

"Get up, wormy." Zama screeches.

My heart thumps wildly, the world narrows, and my vision turns gray. A roaring fills my ears, accompanied by the sluggish whooshing of blood. I ball my hands into fists and pull my body up. I knew that I shouldn't be capable of doing even that, battered and bruised as I was, but a creature had taken over my body. Commandeering every limb to cooperate, a hidden puppeteer tinkers with my strings and I had to obey. Singing a blood song in my head, I was ready.

Zunaif lunges at me, an astounding blood lust in his eyes, angry that I still stood. Defying everything, defying my mortal body's limits. I met him halfway. A hit that I barely felt had me stagger back, holding my side. I attack in a flurry of moves, countering his punch midway, I clutch his wrist in a vise grip. I smirk as fire roars out of my palm to burn his hand. The scent of burning flesh fills the room. He screams the sound boomerangs in the room. Grinding my molars, I give him a grim smile showing only teeth. He's never known defeat. Not used to pain, the pain would be more than he can bear. Well, he gives this pain to his opponents every time he spars. He switches to offensive, throwing out his hands. I was slammed on the ceiling. I grip my neck; he's choking with his telekinetic power.

Zama takes a step to intervene, but Kaima stops him with a hand. Her eyes pinned on me. My sight starts to fade as Zunaif chokes the life out of me, Zen steps towards me, but two guards stopped her. She turned on her pyro-self, and more guards poured in. I clutched my throat, sucking in limiting amounts of air that was getting scarcer every second that went by as Zunaif took me towards death's doorstep. With a last desperate burst of energy, I scream out. Releasing a flash of blinding light that blasts at everything. And everyone. The lights went off, and I fell down. My last sight is of people taking cover as the blinding flash lashes out before I passed out.

CHAPTER 18

OBRA

Chima

Sweat streams down my back in waves, I stared at the long queue keeping me from getting out of there. Why in God's name did we choose the day that seemed to be the busiest in Junk district? In front of me stood guards in Obra's insignia of a flaming skull and crossbones stamp on their chests, I watch on as one slugs a man; he fell and got kicked several times, where he lay curled in a tight ball, another kick from the guard made his head snap back, blood flow out of his nose. A wheezing mess, he crawls away, the guard sneers down at him, then run him through with his blade. Two more came and drag his lifeless body out of there. The next person steps forward, hands shaking in fright. I hope he has a genuine reason in getting out of here, it's treason if you unlawfully try to get out of here. If caught, you are thrown in the dungeons.

The line crawls forward, I soon find myself staring at the guard's face. "Papers?" he barks. I would have jumped if I hadn't been expecting the intimidation, I blink coolly and handed over the engraved thick parchment-like paper that Ode had given me, I don't know where she got it, but right now all I care about is that it does the magic trick I needed it to do, he snatched it from my hand, and stared at it, a scowl already forming on his face. An eternity later, he nods and hands back to me, reluctantly, he motions for me to move forward. I waste no time in brushing past him. Bounding for the gates, each second feeling like an eternity as it came closer.

A horn blares behind me, and I crack my whip harder. The horses run faster, heading for the gates, only to have it shut in front of us. I don't have to look behind me to see that a mass of guards was hurrying towards the gates. Obra has already found out that his Prima breeder's missing. I hop down from my seat and hurried towards the guards at the gate." We are in a hurry and will want to reach Tendabar soon, I would hate it if Fex's niece is being delayed."

The guard's eyes widens a fraction, he didn't even think of the lie I had said, only the fear of Fex's name was enough to have him moving. He gulps, throat working and went to open the gates. I turn back to the carriage but stopped when a gunshot pierces the air. The guard's body crumple on the ground, I whirled around and came face to face with a man; he barks out orders at the guards to look for the prima breeder. Ode crawls out from the carriage, her beautiful clothes stripped off. A long, high, swan-necked tunic slash on both sides over dark, rough pants had taken its place, a look of desperation in her eyes. I lunge for the button on the wall, my palm pressed on it, gunshots rang out. I flip my body in the air and dodge bullets. With a wild scream Ode starts the carriage forward, I soar in the air, hovering weightlessly over people's heads, eliciting gasps, bullets whiz straight at me, but fall down before they can even reach me, I land with a soft thud on the hood of the carriage. Guards give chase on horseback, some on motorbikes.

Closing my eyes, I tilt my head back and tap within me, to a hidden part that I have been pushing back all this time. I know that there's no going back once this deed is done, no undoing what I have already written in my blood, my essence. He will find me; it's a matter of time before he does; I hope that I will be far away from this place. A gamble I'm willing to take.

The thought brings forth my a painful twinge in my chest, I will miss Zahra, but this can't be avoided. I might even be too late. Perhaps he has already found me. Thick mist streams out of nowhere, thickening in the very fabric of the air, knitting into it. Horses neighed as the guards pushed further in the cloying mist before them refusing to go any further. Ode increased the pace of the carriage as the bullets whizzed past us blindly. And with it, an awareness flared to life, making my heart gallop, a fistful of fear clutches my heart, and I knew that it won't be long before he comes for me, I just hope I survive his wrath.

CHAPTER 19

RED ZONE

Jelika

I wake to find myself in a different room, lying on a gurney. I wince, putting a hand to my head, it felt like a hole's been drilled into it. What have I done?

"You are awake?"

I stared at Dr. Kaima, her eyes drill into my very soul, she stepped forward, making my heart seize. "You manifested something I have only seen once in my lifetime, and the world ended that day."

"That would make you..." I trail off.

"Over a hundred years, yes, Jelika, all thanks to science. Many would kill to have your powers, I have someone who wants to meet you."

I nod at her, staring at her perfect nails that were tapered to flawless points." Did anyone get harmed by me?"

"Nothing that could not be fixed." She smiles at me. The smile never reached her eyes, and my stomach churned at the damage I have done. The smile should reassure me, but I wasn't.

"You are something special, and the world is counting on you to make things right."

Kaima never smiles, she never does. She gestures at me to follow her, I mechanically did. It is time to get out of here, I can't let them use me. I know what I saw in her eyes, that look told me all I need. She is monitoring me. Getting out would be a thousand times harder than I could ever fathom. She led me out of there, past our quarters, into a section I've never seen before, she opens the brown mahogany door and shoves me inside. My eyes squint in the darkness, trying to adjust to it. Luminescent lights flared to life, threatening to burn my retinas into ash. I whirled around, taking stock of the room I stood in. My brows hitch at the sleek, twisting banister that arc through the air heading towards the impossibly high ceiling.

"So you're the one that created that impressive EMP that pulled me away from my slumber?" a voice that brings goosebumps and chills to my body echoes in the room. I whip my body around, looking for the one the voice belongs to, I found no one.

The voice chuckled, "Curious one, aren't you? Lights flared brighter, and I shield my face with a hand. I whirl around, taking stock of the room I stood in. My brows hitched at the sleek, twisting banister that arcs through the air heading towards the impossibly high ceiling. I wonder where it leads?

"Who are you?"

"Wouldn't you want to know? Very well, I will indulge you a little."

A figure materializes before me at the foot of the sleek staircase. He wore a gray, metallic-colored Kaftan-like bodysuit, slit in front to show off the pants he wore underneath. His face is awe-worthy, eyes of an indistinguishable color, knife-sharp cheekbones, thick arched eyebrows, and beautifully shaped lips. "Come closer, child, I won't bite."

I take a tentative step forward, another one, I kept putting one foot after another until I stood before him. "Good girl, let's see what's so special about you." A cold hand grips my temples, I gasp as ice enters my veins. My muscles lock in place and refuse to move. The world spins on its axis, I find myself standing on a turret, sword in hand, beside me crouched a man. He wore the same scaled-armor, made of stones I 've never seen in my life, covering his vitals. Helmets made of the same kind of stones sat on our heads. Below us stand an army, stretch all over the horizon.

A horn resonates, I watch as the army rain fiery arrows at the castle. We take cover, I follow into a room packed with armed men, an army. "They've come, tonight we fight for not just our world, but for humans, we're the torch that lights their lives. As their protectors, we would bring them to heel." The scene fades away, and I'm suck back in the room, cold hands on my temples. I pull away, gasping for breath.

"Impressive, very impressive. Now shoo."

I made my way out of there as fast as I could, Kaima was at the door. Her gaze says she knew what happened in there, she led out of there and back into our quarters. In the food court, whispers followed me as I made my way towards Zen. I hate it; I hate the fear in their eyes. Even the number of guards had tripled. It chokes the room, making it hard to breathe, wrapping fingers of dread around their throats. Out of the corner of my eyes, I felt Zunaif's gaze on me, looking like he fought an army all by himself. For the first time, raw fear shone in his eyes. Not wrapped in its usual cocky overconfidence that always mocks everyone. I stared at Zen's arms, which bear crisscross cuts from glass shrapnel no doubt. I take a seat and take a huge bite of my food.

"You okay?"

"Yes I am, how are the cuts?"

"I will live."

"We have to get out tonight Kaima is planning something big I don't know what it is, but it has something to do with you, it's not in our favor, she has been going into the red zone a lot since you have been out in three weeks."

The world swivels, and I stared at her. I have been unconscious for three weeks.

"You didn't know that, I guess she wouldn't want you to know."

"She didn't say, I guess she gave you the special talk about being special, huh?"

"Yes she did, how do you know that she would?" I didn't tell her of the creepy man with the ability to make me see things in my head. Didn't tell her what I saw.

"Let's just say that she is a predictable old, hen. Predictive but dangerous, very dangerous" Zen chews her food slowly, eyes narrowed. The metal spoon in her hand turns red, smoking.

Cursing, she put it on the table, and turned to me." She always does that; she makes you feel special because she needs you. You are an army, one of the things she has been looking for. And once she sets her sights on something, she never backs down. Be careful"

"And your brother?"

"I have a plan."

I hope that this goes through, I yearn to have the sun on my face. Whatever crap they have fed us about being the salvation of mankind, and knowing that I have given Dr. Kaima the powerful weapon she needed, it irks me. A rage deep within me surfaces. I want to raze everything to the ground, I won't stop until everything is gone, I hate being a freak that even freaks fear. She thinks that this is a blessing; she was wrong; this isn't one. It's a curse from the deepest pits of the damn. Here I am burdened with the curse of the very same thing that might have a hand in ending everything. And now I know that my suspicions were right.

She had a hand in the ending of the world. I will not let her use me.

CHAPTER 20

TEMPEST

CHIMA

Three nights without sleep, I hope Zaghra isn't hold responsible for my heinous crime. Knowing how vicious and malicious Tin could be, it will not be a surprise. What was Obra thinking experimenting with his Prima breeder? Was power or whatever twisted agenda he has strong enough to make him cross the line of nature? There's no going back once lines are crossed. On the move, never stopping for anything; the horses were slowing down now; I crack my whip harder and they increase their pace. Every minute that ticks by is a minute that Obra will find us. I wouldn't be surprised if I see expensive fly-ships tagging us from above, the man's got deep connections. The gates of Yegun city come into view, tall and imposing turrets and spires welcome me. Guards stand guard on watchtowers, binoculars stuck to their faces. We are heading towards Zubela. All I have to do is reach Ash-lands; if we make it as far as that place, we are free. Obra will not follow, the people don't tolerate the presence of masters there, he will have to have a death wish to pursue us that far. Let's hope that he doesn't.

"Here, let me! You should get some sleep I will take it from here, if we run into any trouble I will wake you up." Ode takes the reins from me, I slid in the carriage.

Sukunda raises her head, her reddish-brown gaze clashing with mine, her face held a longing that made my heart literally stop, then restart. In her hands, she holds a beautiful, crafted snow globe made of some kind of liquidy-reddish metal. A ruby on top winks at me. Tiny balls mimicking snowflakes rain down from the lid, haunting notes poured out of it. My throat tightened, I fought the urge to hug her. She sniffles and wipes a tear that has escape from her eyes and trail down her beautiful, elegant face.

"You know I wish that I didn't run, but I have no choice I had to. Obra is a monster who would stop at nothing to acquire some kind of cure, to him, it is a way to gain the upper hand over everyone, he likes to say that the world does not need saving, that it only needs him. And I will be the one who hands it to him in a golden placenta. And I fear being caught, I'd rather kill myself first before I go back."

"You will not, as long as I breathe." I sit next to her and take her hand in mine, she pulls away only to throw her hands around me, catching me off guard. I hold her while she sobs, her bump pressing into my stomach.

"I'm sorry for the waterworks, I don't tear up that easy, must be hormones." A shy, embarrassed smile graces her lips.

"You know you're not the only one who tears up, I wish someone could listen to me rant and rave. But I'm not that good with emotions."

"I'm told that I'm a good listener." A chuckle tore out of her lips, humor lights up her beautiful face.

"I'm pretty sure that you don't want to hear about my crazy life."

"The opposite, in fact, I want to know more about the life of the great, mysterious Wisp." She whispers, mirth dancing in her eyes, waggling her eyebrows. I huffed at her, turning my head to the side, a small smile on my lips, "Well." Her face full of expectations, I see no way I can get out of this scrape. So much for making her feel better. Perhaps it is time I talk to someone about my dark past, even if it means dodging and dancing around the truth.

"Where are you from?"

"I was too young to remember the place, but I lived with my family until I could not anymore."

Is that the lie you make yourself believe?

I clench my fist in frustration. Sukunda shrinks away from me. I pull my hand that was inches' shy from her throat. "I'm sorry I didn't mean to scare you," I whisper, and she nods, her eyes wary. I want to slap myself for that slip. Why do I have to let the darker part of me slip past my defenses? The start of a sand storm brewed outside. I sigh and calm the tempest within me, I will not let my past influence this, who I am. Who I have become in a decade, if I let it have the smallest of leeways it will, then I will be doomed. I lay on the seat and close my eyes. Joining the little girl running away from herself and her past.

CHAPTER 21

THE CLOSET

Jelika

I land on the balls of my feet; the guard turns around before he could register my presence. I twist his neck, and he crumpled at my feet. I snatch the gun and the prong from his belt and made my way past the sparring pit. The alarm is yet to shrill, a good sign that Dr. Kaima has yet to detect us missing. The first step in being a deserter, kill a guard; start an ark-break. In the control room, the monitor shows every sector on a large screen on the wall, and buttons on a huge control table. I stared at the buttons, not sure which to press. My eyes fall on a gray dial, then went back to the red one.

I pressed it. An alarm blared to life, I watched in the video feeds as cell doors sprang open, kids poured out racing towards the tunnels. Zen has done her part, I head towards the red zone. Guards pour in the corridors, blocking it. I lift my hand up and blast a way through them, and the rest of the Arkers join in the fray. In the red, I stepped in. I dodge a fireball aim sailing my way and spin-kick a guard Zen torches him. We run in deeper, passing corridors I follow her as she led me. We ste into a massive room with a high ceiling that went on forever.

Wires and steel twine around massive iron pillars that filled the room each one reached the ceiling. Glass pods attached to them. A panel's erected in the center of the room.

"What is this?"

"The closet; it holds the pandora's box."

"The what?"

"Shh, listen."

I did, a brush of awareness caresses my senses, a screeching filled my eardrums, it was everywhere. A movement catches my eye in one of the pods, I made out what looked like a claw on the glass, determined to come out. "What's in those pods?"

"The future."

Dr. Kaima stood before us with dozens of guards behind her. She gives us all a chilling, clinical smile that reaches into my very bones. "You never disappoint me, Zen, a mother, always knows what her child would do next. I see that you took my advice and chose the right thing."

I stared at the girl beside me, my body tensing, white-fire trail from my fingertips, threatening to start engulf my whole body. I stared at the two; the resemblance is there. I want to slap myself for not seeing it all along.

"You are not my mother!" Zen bits out, her hands, bursting into flames. Her voice laden with so much poison, it startles me. Hate fills the room, stroking our skins. Dr. Kaima gives her a beautiful smile, not at all rattled by her outburst, her beautiful, vibrant skin glinting under the intense light.

" Come, son, she's here." Her voice gentle and soothing. A mocha skinned guy stepped forward. He wore a gray sleeveless shirt and black sweats. His eyes, the brightest green I have ever seen on anyone." Zen, is that you?"

"Blyte ." she takes a step forward

I watch them hug. Twins; he was the masculine version of her.

"A happy reunion, now daughter hand her over, and you walk away free, remember our deal!"

I glared at Zen, who gritted her teeth, staring at her mother, "I'm so sorry." She reverses the gun to my head and gestures at me to walk to where her mother stood eyes trained on me. It's a tradeoff. The betrayal stings, burrowing deep into my skin. I tasted it on my tongue, and turned glowing, white eyes on Zen. She met my gaze with her blank one.

"Don't look so shocked, Zenenga's a serpent, with not a bone of loyalty in her body, well, loyal to only her him. You fell for her little stunt, and yes, she told me all about how you intend to start an ark-break. I gave her a choice she could help me squash you, gain your trust, and I will free her and her brother. Or she could stay here with all the Arkers."

The taste of betrayal heavy on my tongue, a metallic taste floods my mouth, the pain that my tongue was forced to endure was horrendous. I take slow steps towards the woman, not believing that all these was a setup, I had let my guard down, and let her play me like a fool. Here I am giving the enemy what she needs, the powerful weapon she wants. I was such a fool. How could I have blindly trusted her?

"I trusted you, I had thought that you were different, but I was wrong!" I spat out bitterly, holding my wrist out to the guard to slam the cuffs on them. I stared in surprise, as she turns the gun on her mother and the guard.

"Really, daughter? What are you playing at, hmm?" Kaima lifts a perfectly, plucked brow at her. Her eyes dare Zen to shoot her, in them held something that only the two of them knew of." You're not the first ones to have started an ark-break. Do you believe that you can get out of the ark? That there's a place in the world out there for you? Somewhere you belong? No one escapes the ark like that Jelika, this place is forged into you, the ark is your parent. Fed you, clothed you and gave you a sense of meaning. A purpose as humanity's salvation, and you throw it back at the ark."

"I am not your bloody daughter" She screams, then aims the gun at the panel.

Panic splash over Dr. Kaima's features, "You would not want to do that young lady?" True fear coats her words for the first time. Zen surges towards the panel, bullets peppered at her heels. She takes cover with Blyte behind a pod. Dr. Kaima signals for the guards to stop shooting. I elbowed the guard in the gut, he wheezed, and I scissor my legs around his neck, choking him, we fell off the catwalk and down below. I twisted his neck, and kick his body off the catwalk. I swiped his keypad on my cuff. It slicks open. I start my hike up. I sling my body on the catwalk, with a tap of my finger, I disengaged the metal catwalk stopping three guards, one fell, the other two clutch the edges of the catwalk trying to stay on it.

"Oops."

Dr. Kaima backs away as Zen pressed activate on the large screen that hovers in the air. The steel pillars groan as a whooshing fills the room, steam fills the room, making it hard to see. I back away with the twins sprinting in the opposite direction. I pump my legs faster as a computerized voice begins a countdown to a self destruct trying to contain whatever abomination Zen had just released. I closed the grate door behind me and scrambled out of there. Dazzling light filled my vision. An explosion rocked my world, it lifted me in the air. Heat licks at my back, my body slams the ground. I know no more.

CHAPTER 22

DAY-STORMER

Kamili

We have been on the road for almost a week now; I clench my jaw at the thought of leaving Mama behind, and I can't push the feeling away that something terrible would happen in my absence. At least Mama knows how to take care of herself. But I would never forgive myself if anything happens to them. Transported back in the arena, I could feel the stinger go through my body, rendering my body cold. Rougy healing me. Madi and the others had come several minutes before the sunsets, moments before the closing horn was blown. I could still see the apology in Saliu's eyes as he stared at me from where I lay on the floor. I don't blame him; it wasn't his doing. We had left Kendulusa two days after. Despite

Madi's protest that I am yet to fully heal, I told him I want to get it over with and come back as soon as possible. He had caved in with no choice.

"Are you okay?"

"Yeah, why?"

"Because you have this murderous look on your face that says you want to kill someone."

"That makes the two of us,"

I huff, I want to kill Eldres for doing this and putting all of us in this mess. I want to turn back and gallop back the way we came when I think of the virus that is coursing in my veins; I have told no one about it, not even Mama knows about it, only Rougy and Calla do. The torment of thinking that I'm a ticking, biological, time bomb ready to explode and bring only death and destruction. That I could end up as one of the reapers makes me gnash my teeth in anger and frustration. It unravels me, I clutch Namia's reigns with a gloved hand. At least we were allowed in the town armory, I had my own choice of weapons, and now I have two sawed-off shotguns, K-bar knives, and a machete. Also standard dark leather garbs that the town purchased from Hope city. Rough, woolen, desert-sand colored clothes went on top, fashioned with a hoodie, it's perfect for camouflage and long-distance travel in the desert.

Zubela comes into view, I release a sigh . I had thought that we would spend the night on the run from the Reapers. At least with enough coin, we could have a decent room and a bath. I glare at the suitcase tied at my saddle buttons that bear numbers. I can't wait to reach Yegun city and deliver it into the right hands and hurry back home. I don't know why I can't put the foreboding feeling that something terrible would happen to my family. In the crowded market we, made our way towards the run down bed-and-breakfast, ignoring the attention we were gaining from people, some even pointed at us. It's very unusual to see the Kendulusu tribe twice in a year.

Muna waves back at a kid who waves at her cloaked in shadows. The kid beckons for us, I stopped, and stared at her, she mouthed, "Come."

Muna rush forward towards her before I could stop her. An arrow whizz, past my ear, and embeds in the wall. An explosion rocks the air, sending us all airborne. I tumble on the ground hard, thankful that Namia and the suitcase were far away from me. Dust and bricks rain on us. Figures effortlessly dropped down the wall, I dash towards Namia, beating the man to her, his fist bangs on the right side of my face before I could react, pain bubbles on my face, and I grit my teeth to keep myself from crying out, he attacks a second time. He's quick, I would give it to him. I jump on Namia, leap-dodging his strikes, I land on my hands and kick him a few yars away from me, he got up, and sprints towards me. An arrow strikes him in the chest, and he collapses. I glower at where Muna disappeared; the explosion had blocked the way. More figures streamed out surrounding us.

"Who are they?"

"Mercenaries." Madi snarls.

Zubela is secure, not as safe as Kendulusa, but it's okay. My eyes fell on the suitcase. They were here for this. The crowd parts, and I stare at the hooded figure coming our way; he comes to a stop in front of us, bronze-colored hands push the hood away, and I stared at a face that's too perfect, the only imperfection was the ugly mass of tissue that started on his right cheek and disappears into his eye patch covering his right eye. His other eye is an indeterminate silver-honey shade. I have never set my sights on, bronze skin, a sharp nose, and a beautiful mouth. He was perfect and imperfect, both sides of a coin. A corner of that mouth curls up, his other eye glides over me. Madi moves his horse beside me, fingers twitching on the pummel of his sword.

"Greetings, hunters."

"What do you want?"

"Ah, I like that, a girl who likes getting straight to business." He saunters to us," You see friends, it is simple, give us that suitcase, and you will get out of here, unscathed." he intones slowly.

"Over my dead body." It's not an option that I want to entertain.

"That could be arranged, I would hate to see all that beauty go to waste, be careful what you wish for "he tutts eying my red hair in its braids.

I gritted my teeth, fisting my hands to stop myself from jumping at him and punching the shit out of him, Madi grips my hand, I give him a look that made him let go of me like I had burned him. I would not hand over anything to him; I would rather die first. And I meant every word that I had spoken. Wishes be damned.

"Fine, have it your way." He sighs, a look that I can't decipher crosses his face. He throws back his head and pulls his eye patch down. Static spits and crackles, air went heavy, it feels different, is that even possible? I watch as the sky darkens, clouds blanket the suns. unmistakable shrieking fills the air, seems to come from everywhere in, my blood runs cold at the abominable sound ripping the air, douse me in cold sweat. Somewhere an alarm blares to life, chaos comes alive as people run everywhere to get away from the snapping jaws of death. That's not human. His gaze lands on me, and I pull Namia's reigns back. She takes a step back in fright. The eye covered by the patch is taken straight out of a nightmare; it was death incarnate; it stared at me with such unholy malevolence that I wanted to climb into my own skin. He grins, and I have a hunch that there was no way of leaving this place alive without a miracle.

Body frozen, feeling out of place, I stared at the Reapers heading our way from every direction surrounding us in seconds. These were different. There's some kind of animalistic savagery and hyper-intelligence absent in the normal Reapers. They are puppets, relinquishing free rein of their bodies to him, their master. I held my K-bar knives tight, waiting for the attack I knew was going to come soon. A spear whizzes in the air, and slam into a Reaper lifting the Reaper's body in the air and strike into the wall. A small figure stood on the roof of a building, sword in hand, a cowl hiding her features from view. Another figure hunkers on a roof threw his spear, it hit her mark with startling accuracy.

I narrow my eyes, they seem familiar. The girl went down in a crouch and leap off the roof without pause; I expected her to fall flat on her face, but; she lands perfectly on the balls of her feet, then rushed into the horde of Reapers. The others followed without pause. The guy curses, screaming out orders to his men. I watch him turn back and sprint towards the girl, an unholy fury etched on his features. The Reapers attack without warning, obeying some kind of hidden command. A Reaper dodges my blade with unerring precision that had me slow down, he nearly takes a chunk off my hand with his blade when I pulled it back a second too late. An arrow struck him in the head. Looking back, I nod at Madi. Who winks and blows me a kiss. I grin and whip my body up in the air, I crouch on Namia, and cut down Reapers that were trying to take a ride on her. Muna drops in a crouch on Namia's back, a wicked smile on her face, body dripping with the same bluish-dark liquid I'm covered in. Shock grips me, I'd thought that she was dead. She must have picked that on my face because she gives me a smirk of her own.

"It's not that easy to get rid of me, Kam."

"Glad to know that." I chuckle.

Another shriek had me turn round, Reapers run for the gates, these were the norm. A hand grips my ankle with a vise-like grip, and wrench me from Namia. Clawed hands chokes the life out of me, mouth wide open to take a bite of my flesh, unholy, wicked, sharp teeth. Ready to tear my throat out. Out of the corner of my eye, I make out Muna carve a path towards me and the Reaper hellbent on killing me.

"Get out of here, I've got this," I scream, and muster a smile. I do not want a repeat of another one of us dying because of me.

She looked unsure for a moment, then she sprints out of there; I buck the Reaper off me, easing its hands off my neck for a moment before it's back to clamping on it with a vicious intensity that had me squinting, gasping for air. With one hand holding him off, I pull a dagger free from my boot and stab it in the head. It slumps pining me with it's dead weight , bluish-dark liquid gush from its mouth. I shove it off me. Madi gallops towards me. I grasp hold of his hand and let him swing me on Leoe and gallop for the giant gate teeming with Reapers.

Long blade in hand, I slash at the Reapers fighting their way in, gore splash on my face. Somewhere, Muna utters a battle cry. Hands claw at us, but Leoe continues running, we rode through them at breakneck speed. Breaking free. The skies cleared, and the suns burst out, streaming and spreading out in the blink of an eye. Madi stops the horse and turned it, we watch as the Reapers combust shrieking, a hooded figure jumps off from the roof, free-running with an agility that had my mouth open in amazement. I caught a glimpse of brown eyes, set in a face that I had thought I would never see again. Coincidence? Not. I thought, shaking my head and ignoring Madi's inquisitive eyes.

CHAPTER 23

MAMI-WATA

SUKUNDA

ONE YEAR AGO

Hate

It fills your veins with darkness, choking you from the inside out. I lay in a fetal position on the floor, blood pooled around me, I sobbed into my hand, muffling the sound. I never want to relive what I have gone through in the last few days, I thought that I will never be used like this, my dress in tatters, I had tied it as best as I could, trying to have some semblance of modesty. Even though I knew that it has no use. It would be repeated all over again. It started the night when Balla had gone out with other raiders to raider-land, on a raid they have been planning for a time now. And he had wasted no time in cornering me. No one will help me. He had a guard put some kind of rag immersed into something foul like he was, clamped it over my nose. Next thing I know I had woken in the dungeons tied to stakes driven into the ground, I wish for a thousand deaths for the things he had done to me.

I don't think that I would ever experience that kind of a pain in my whole life. The lock turns, and the door opens. My eyes snap open. Days back, it would have sparked a response from me, and I would start screaming all over again. But it did not. I lay where I was, barely breathing, thigh bone in my hand, a thigh bone, sharpened on the wall, day after day. It is what remains of someone who had died here, a girl like me who had fallen prey to Mbulla's cruel ways. Never to be found by Balla. Well, I'm not staying here to be killed and forgotten. Mbulla steps in humming a tune, he was in a good spirit today I can tell; I wonder why his father has not detected me missing yet, he should be back. It's either that he hadn't discovered me missing, or he does not care. I grip the bone firmly and let him come closer.

"Hey Mami-wata, I got something for you. You will like it; we have gotten on the wrong foot. I want to show you that I am not a monster." His breath wafts on my neck, reeking of liquor.

I went still, barely breathing, he pats my cheek, the other gropes my breasts roughly. He slobbers on my neck. I moved fast, shoving the bone as hard as I could into his collarbone, he shrieks, his gaze says I have lost my mind. I wrench the bone free and kick at him. He barrels blindly into me, trying to disarm me. That sobered him fast, I smile, all teeth while death dances in my eyes.

" You don't want to do this with me, Mami-water, trust me, lay down that bone and I won't have to kill you."

"Try me," I smirk and run towards him.

He lashes out, using only brute strength, I slash with my crude, deadly weapon, and missed. His fist crashes on the side of my head. My ears ring, and I stumble, almost lost my footing. I move out of range and take a deep breath, I can do this. I have to get out of here, Mbe'tu waits for me. I have my speed and the call for his blood to rely on, I need to focus on that.

I fixed him with an icy stare and rushed to meet him. We exchanged blows; I caught him off guard with a vicious uppercut, slamming the sharp end of the bone on his jaw and pull back, blood streams out of his lips, and trails down his chin, I slam the blunt end of the bone into his groin, and he yelps. I almost laugh at the look on his face.

It's priceless, something I'd cut an arm and leg to see. I wish Amisha could see this right now. Grabbing hold of his hair, I tug it back, hard and introduced my knee to his jewels. He push me away, ripping my hold of him. Mbulla bellows and backhands me, not giving me any chance to reciprocate. A punch had me crumple to the floor, the bone clatters from my stiff, numb fingers, I crawl towards it, a heavy boot slams on my fingers, the crunch of my fingers seemed far away. Horrendous pain blooms in them, spreading up my wrist to my arm, I released a long scream that bounced off the walls.

"E for effort, I must applaud you for trying. Do you think that you could best me in a fight?" he lisps and knelt on the floor cradling my head in his hands, my gaze went to the dagger tucked into his boot, I trailed my hand towards it, his lips slide on mine in a punishing kiss. Taking his time to shove his tongue down my throat, I pull the dagger free and slash his ankles, his body crumple to the floor with a hard thump, I slashed his neck, a neat slashed that made me smile. He releases a gurgle, gripping his throat. Blood gushed on me, an elegant faucet that paints me scarlet, a shower I welcome. He collapse to the floor, and I snatch the bone off the floor and stand over him.

"E for effort." I jam the sharp end of the bone into his heart with my last strength. His mouth opened, but no sound came out, blood gushes out of it, I pushed harder, didn't let go until he stopped moving. I strip and took off his clothes, the trouser was a little too big for me, but the belt helped, so was the shirt, I had it tied around my waist, deciding that it was better that way. They will have to do for now until I can get better ones. I checked his gun for ammo and found some, his daggers went to the sheathes on my thigh and belt, two others from his boots that I have raided from him. I tore my tattered dress and wrap it around my mangled hand, holding back sobs. Without a backward glance, I hurry out of there. Soon I was out of the dungeon and into the corridor. I pull the flaming torch from the wall and sprint towards the east wing of the compound. Never again would I be weak. Tonight it ends. I splashed the gasoline on the walls, and onto everything that I can reach. Tonight we would have a beautiful bonfire. Tonight I will go back home, home. Something that was a dream. I almost thought was a pipe dream until now.

"Hey."

I spin on my heels , a guard sprints towards me. Without hesitation, I grab the burning torch from the torch stand mounted on the wall and threw it on the floor, a blazing fire flared to life, a fiery obstacle. The guard comes to a complete halt, cursing. I turn around and tail it out of there, towards the cells that held the breeders. I would abhor myself if I knew that I had the chance to break them out, but I didn't. The thought of leaving Amisha and Anushka behind was already enough to make me run faster towards the wing the girls were being held, I had to get out of there before the guard alert the other guards or start the siren. I released a sigh of relief when I saw that only a lone guard stood outside. I plaster a smile on my face, I hope that he won't make out the blood on my skin, maybe the poor lighting will do the trick. He looks young, around my age, I am already regretting what I am about to do, but there is no innocent in this bloody world now, only shades of gray and muted hues.

"Hey, I am lost, been roaming this place looking for my cell." I muster a genuine smile.

"Okay, Missy, get in then. You don't want to get into trouble."

I nod, letting fear seep in my eyes and give him the lost puppy look I always fix on my father when I wanted my way. He was no exception; the trick worked like magic; he fell for it. I brush past him, putting a hand on my gun in a fast move that he didn't see until I had the weapon pressed on his back." Get in"

He complied, I herd him towards my empty cell, making sure that he had thrown all his weapons on the floor first, I let him walk in the cell, and I closed it behind him. I hurried towards Amisha's cell. She enveloped me in a hug when I opened her cell, Anushka followed closely behind her." I thought that I will never see you."

"Me too." I breathed in her captivating, exotic scent. One that reminds me of Mbe'tu. The siren blared to life, jolting me out of the comfort of Amisha's arms. "We have to hurry, try to open as many cells as you can."

I strode outside and started opening cells with Amisha's help, the girls, in turn, help open more doors. I had around two dozen of the girls stood before me; we crept out of there, heading for the exits. Creating fiery obstacles for the guards, buying us more time to get out of there. Amisha opened the massive gate. The breeze of the desert blew on my face, on it, I could scent wafts of Mbe'tu and freedom. Soon I will see it, I will see Papa, and my people will rejoice. I will see mbe'tu's familiar haven, the rolling landscape, so many colors, a feast for the eyes. The trees that make you feel safe, there you know that you are safe, not looking behind you every single minute. The thudding of boots broke me out of my trance, and I stared at the huge man heading for us. On his face were a million promises of punishments,

Balla's face held so much anger, eyes crazed and unfocused, the face of a father who just found his son murdered. It spurred me into action, "Go!" I scream, closing the grated door, I poured the rest of the gasoline on it, then set it on fire. I hope that it was enough. The group of girls made it towards the forbidden door they had only journeyed in once, but never out. I run after them, pumping my legs faster with some others who were dispatching the guards. Panic stirs the group waiting outside for us, I was nearly at the door when I saw them. Motorbikes were coming towards Jufureh; they were not the cage-trucks that the raiders to snatch people when they go on raids. These were foreign ones; it didn't bring me any relief at seeing them; they fly the flag of a skull with crossbones on fire. I knew that from the stories that they are here for one of us.

One of us would become a whore in one of their harems for their spoiled masters. One thing was sure; not all be able to make it out in time. Might as well buy some time for them. I stared at Amisha's protruding belly and decided. She deserves to raise her child in peace, with no fear of the future. No doubt that her child might end up as she had. I step outside and head for the truck," Come on, guys, in the truck. Any of you know how to drive this monster?" I asked the group of petrified girls. A hand shot up in the air, and a lighter-skin brunette stepped forward." I do, I mean_."

"Good, get in, I want you to drive us out of here, as fast as you can. Don't let them." I pointed at the incoming motorbikes, and the raiders trying to combat the flames out." Get us."

"I think I can manage that." She said, hopping into the driver's seat. I watched girls scramble into the truck, gripping at the bars, I closed the door.

A girl whimpers in fright, gaining my attention. Her hair lay in a curly, tight mess on her scalp. Scars dot her body, one trails from her mouth into her left eye. Another victim of Mbulla's cruelty. Tears course down her face." Shh, it is okay. I won't let them get you, I promise. He won't hurt you anymore, he is dead."

She smiles, fear lessening in her body posture." He is?" she asked in a small voice.

"Yes, he is. I killed him myself."

She gave me a small smile and touch a bead braid in my hair. "Thank you."

I nod and hurry to the front of the truck, I take a seat next to Amisha. The brunette started the truck, and with a deafening roar from the huge, metal beast, we sped out of there, leaving Jufureh smoking. A telltale of our silent victory.

CHAPTER 24

NUMBER SIX

Mayala,

Keep your head down, walk, do your job. Don't make eye contact; that is my mantra. What kept me alive? Not rebellion. Everyone who thought to fight the chains of slavery did not last long in this place. You don't fight the yoke; you endure it, understand it, live it, and be it. Fighting it has no use, it cuts down your lifespan faster than you realize it. Before you know it, you're dead. We are handpicked from the best of bests. Our obedience is beaten into our very being, our blood, our soul. Conditioned to obey without question, you tell us to cut off an arm, and we will do it; we have seen too much, our souls scarred.

I don't know why people want to come here, all the promises of a better life will not make me come here, this city is a smokescreen that shows the world what they want to see if they only know the power play behind everything else, the sacrifices, the blood that was needed to power such a perfect beast. I push the trolley of vials out of there, and towards a door that makes door my heart pound with every step that I take, sweat poured down my back, triples on my face to drip down the trolley. I wished that I don't have to see this. The door slid open, and I stepped in, knuckles shaking a little as I thought of seeing the horrors all over again; God how I wished that he does not make me stand and watch. More work for me. I wait, breath held to see if they will release me. A hand went under my chin and lifts my chin. I stared at dark, fierce eyes, eyes that held not a hint of remorse, I stared at his lab pocket, my lashes shutter my eyes.

"Look at me!" I lift my eyes to his eyes," Now was that so bad, clean that mess, I see that you have delivered the vials."

I nod and turn to do as he bid. A hand clamps hard on my chin, I grit my teeth, as he forces my face up to stare at me." Don't think that you are better than us, Number six? This is for humanity. You should be thanking us that we are here to do this." He smears the blood from his lab coat onto my face.

I stumble when he let go of my chin, my head bangs on the stainless steel table, He chuckles, and both of them hurry out of there leaving me alone with the abomination on the table. Taking the mop and bucket from the corner of the room, I started the rigorous task of cleaning the splatters of dark gray blood off the floor and walls. A sound made me whip my head back, I stared at what stood before me. My eyes zeroed in on the trolley of vials, and I strode towards it. I took four and pocket it. For the first time in my life, I thought of ways of getting out of here. I had heard of lab outposts that got infected and were cleansed before anyone got wind of it. Right now, I have the element of surprise, I have to get out of here; I took hold of the mop and slam it on my knee. It broke in two; I take the longest piece and deactivated the permanent seal I have initiated on the door; it slid open, and I ran out of there. I head towards the opposite of the dark footprints, knowing that it would buy me some time. My arm hurts like a devil, but I ignored it and head for the fly-ships that I knew would be in the hangar.

I lash out. A scream stops me in mid-strike. I stared at Jandel, who cowers back from me in fright. Blood coats her clothes.

"Mayala, you nearly killed me. What is happening?" she hissed when she saw that it was me.

"Follow me, I'm getting out of here."

She did, I head towards the hangar. The fly-ship comes into view. My breath stuck at its beauty. A scream had me move into action, I hopped in and stared at the numerous buttons before me, looking for the button that I always see pilots touch. I don't know what makes me always watch pilots power the fly-ship; maybe it's how a small button can power such a colossal thing baffles me. I glance back only to find Jandel wasn't in the fly-ship. What the hell was she thinking going back? I thought, prepping the fly-ship for takeoff. I wrap a hand wrapped around the throttle. What any of them don't know is that once the powers that be knows of this, they will stop at nothing to get us back. "I'm sorry, Jandel, "I pull the throttle up. The fly-ship took to the air, going higher every second, a scream made me look down to see Jandel and a group of slaves waving down at me, I flew past them. There was no way that I'm wasting my time helping them out. I might be too late already. The image of Jandel, broken and sobbing in my arms, begging me, making me promise that I will help if there was a way of bursting her out. Cursing myself for being stupid, turning into her will make me die earlier than I should, I turned the fly-ships around, and head towards them, the fly-ship touched the ground.

They jumped in. I hit the throttle full-on, and the fly-ship leaps into the air, a streaming ball of fire speeds towards us, I flipped the fly-ship to the side, and it brushed at it before slamming into the processing center, a flash streamed out blinding us, a vortex whipped behind us sucking at everything in the vicinity including our fly-ship. I gritted my teeth and push the throttle, but it would not budge. My eyes fell on a dark brown button, and I hit it, my pendant, an oval-shaped, purple colored stone, I keep it hidden under my blouse at all times. Buzzed to life. Blue light streams out of it, hitting the screen with symbols I have never seen in my life. The fly-ships started its slow descent downwards to the blinding vortex behind us. I closed my eyes, gripping the edge of my seat. I wait for my death. The fly-ship groaned at the last second, then with a burst of speed, heads deeper into Hope city. I hit all the buttons, but it wouldn't stop, it flies faster. "Where is it going?" Jandel asked.

"I don't know, it's not responding. It's heading off course."

We know where it's headed, no one lives in the third world, after the nuclear EMP and sun flare, all the territories in the third world were considered too poisonous for living in. Everyone knew about that. Our fly-ship heading towards it was a fate worse than anything else we could think of. Right now, there was nothing we could do. The Fly-ship hit an invisible wall, metal groans, the screen flashes red, showing a system failure starting an immediate shutdown. A force field, I never knew that the city has a force field. The pendant pulses faster, the stone went flaming hot, I pull it out and gaze as the light envelopes the fly-ship and slowly started pushing it through the force field. The fly-ship tipped over bit by bit until the tail was left, the roar of rotors filled the air, I stared back and saw three military fly-ship behind us, our fly-ship slid free, and continued on its unknown course, the fly-ship shook, bursting into flames and we went down.

CHAPTER 25

THE NULL

Jelika

Heat shrouds my face in a warm cocoon. I didn't want to open my eyes, lids heavy, I squint at the enormous glowing balls in the sky. Zen's face looms over me, Blyte's bright blues latch onto mine. I blink at them, not believing that I am alive.

"I thought that you were dead."

"Wish I was." I grimace in pain.

She chuckles and went back to her seat. We seem to be in a moving vehicle that I don't know where they got it.

"Where are we going?"

"The null."

"Know anyone there?"

"I have a friend."

"Oh."

I wonder how many of us made it out topside. If Dr. Kaima made it out too, knowing how crafty she is, she could be alive waiting for the right time to strike at us. They will have tails on us and would tag everyone back. Now that I know how important and deadly we are, I eyed a silent Jin, he meets my eyes and gives me a nod. Blyte cough, clutching his throat, his eyes rols back in his head. Zen's on him in an instant, trying to make him stop choking himself.

"What's going on?" I scream.

"He needs his shots; hold him still I need to search him."

I wrestled Blyte while Zen patted him down. When she found nothing, she started rummaging through bags in the car.

"It's not here," she shouts and kicks at his bag, tears rolling down her face.

"What's not here?"

"It's his stabilizer; he can't control his power."

My eyes widen as his eyes went obsidian, an endless, dark pit. Black veins spreading up his arms, I sat on his stomach, a hand on his chest, while Jin Grabs hold of his arms. The ground shook, I watch as cracks appear, zigzagging on the ground. The vehicle veers out of control and came to a stop inches' shy from an endless drop, a maw that went on forever.

"Come on, you can do it, breathe in, and out with your mouth," I whisper, terrified as another crack heads straight for us.

Blyte screams, his body shook with tremors that nearly dislodge me off him. But I grip him hard with my legs. "Do something," I whisper to Zen.

"I can't." she said despair in her voice, her face heartbroken." Mother wanted this to happen."

Blyte blasts Jin away and grips my head in his hands. A buzzing fills my senses. The world slows down to a halt, I could feel every beat of hearts: the wind, every grain of sand, and the unholy hunger to destroy everything in sight. Something snapped in my head, and I collapsed on top of Blyte, aware of my surroundings, I cough, this is what he feels every time, it was impossible, terrifying and incredible at the same time. Zen revs the car away from the death drop, the car ate up the distance chased by the ever-widening crack.

"Do something, Blyte, fight it. Damn it," she screams, pumping a fist in the air, she stops the car just in time, a crack appears before us. Leaving us standing in the middle, surrounded by nothing but a death fall on all sides.

Blyte sits up. His gaze went to where I lay prone." Thank God you are awake, you gotta do something."

"Are you hurt?"

"I'm fine, get us out of here and onto the road, we might already be too late."

Blyte's gaze stared at everything dispassionately, in a kind of detached way. He looks invincible for a second. A terrible thing like that needs a heavy hand controlling it. He closed his eyes. The ground starts knitting back, going back to the way it was until an untouched landscape before us as if nothing happened. Zen releases a sigh of relief that was cut short when bullets sing in the air, I glare up at the drone shooting at us.

"Just our luck," Zen blasts it away with a wave of her hand.

I still could not move, Jin hops into the vehicle looking very pissed off. Blyte hops into the seat next to Zen and took the wheel, she hauls her body through the roof of the car, countering the shots shoot by the swarm of endless drones tailing us. She pirouettes on her feet, dodging a bullet, a wicked grin on her face, she sent a massive ball of fire at the drone.

It engulfs it in flames, and went down, crashing into the ground. A boom shreds the air behind us." Piece of cake, that should keep them off for some hours, we should be in the null zone soon, oh there he is." She shields her eyes from the sun. I glance at the direction she was staring into. A figure stood in the distance with a huge car, tapping one impatient foot after another. Blyte parks next to him.

"About damn time you turn up Zen, who are these people? I thought you were coming alone?" The tall, thin guy asked, a scowl on his face.

"Don't fret Sparrow, here is your pay," Zen hands him a couple of syringes filled with indigo-colored, sluggish gel. Sparrow opened his mouth, but closed it, a coveted look transforming his face. He gripped syringes tighter. And waved us in the car, then took the wheel. We shot out of there.

*** ***

Jelika

I think that we should get out of here because I really don't trust this guy.

"I know; can you hear that?" he cocks his head to the side.

I perk, my ears, trying to listen, but couldn't hear a thing. Blyte took hold of my hand, and I flinch, trying to pull my hand away from his. He held on tighter, and I grimace in pain. The world slid away, narrowing until both of us stood in a room, overlooking a mass of writhing darkness that whirred in a never-ending formation. Trying to reach outwards, upwards to where he stood.

"This is how it feels like, I had no idea."

The ground started shaking; the floor gave way under me a dark hand grips my arm. Another grips my boot, Blyte pulls me up. "It is, but it has changed now. With you, I can fight back, Jelika."

We ran out of there, chased by the dark masses. A doorway stood before us, light spills out from it. Beckoning. We pump our legs towards it; I tripped on a stake driven into the floor and toppled.

"Jelika." I could see the anguish on his features, as he looks at the incoming writhing dark mass coming for us, he runs towards me, and pulls me to my feet, we barreled for the door. We won't make it, yards away we watched as the dark mass formed into one form, something that made me stare incredulously at the figure. Dr. Kaima stands before us.

"Hello, Son."

"Mother," he takes a small step forward.

"That's it we are out of here."

I dragged him towards the door, blasting at his mother. Wrapping arms around him, I jump out the door and into the waters below. I gasp, hands clutching at empty air.

"What in the name of all that's bad was that?" Zen's empty gaze cruise on us.

"I'm sorry, Jelika. I should have never taken you in."

"What is going on here?"

"I took her to the Azure."

"What? What were you thinking?"

"I__"

"Come on, we're out of here, we will have her on us soon."

"What's wrong?"

"Kaima created the zone for Blyte to control his power, and with the help of the meds, he could do so. A place locked away in his mind, but it is also a place to track him when she needs to, she couldn't as long as he doesn't venture into it." She in an accusing tone.

I shrug. Not my fault that her brother wants to give me a tour of his head. An explosion rocks the city, a blinding, blue flash flared out, causing the lights to flicker then die plunging me darkness. A connection opens in my mind, and I could feel the ghost pain gripping me. We have to get out of here. The door opens, and Jin steps in looking yummy in pants and nothing else, his incredible torso bare.

"Are you okay?"

I have to do something about this bond thing, I can't have him look at me like I'm his sun and stars. Zen's fine with it, I know that she is hoping that I stay with them until they could figure out. But when? What if it took weeks, months, or worse years? I open my mouth to answer, Blyte puts a hand to his lips, he moves the curtain to the side. I stared at the figure creeping in the shadows, gun in hand. They have found us; I shake Zen awake and stifle a yelp when she turns pyro. Blyte points at the window; she nods and throws our backpacks at us. Fire licks at her eyelids.

"You are surrounded, surrender, and we would not be forced to use lethal force." A voice booms out.

Slowly we step out of the room, guns shove in our faces. They have us boxed in slowly we made it outside. A huge fly-ship waits outside, There's no way that I was going in there. The ground shook, Blyte grasps my hand as it cracks, splitting. I turned to Blyte in panic." I got this." I watch as the ground got farther and farther. The section where we stood was rising in the air, the ground gets farther every second.

" Jump."

"You can't mean that."

"Is big bad Jelika afraid of heights."

"No"

"Then you have no problem with jumping."

Zen scoffs behind us, "Are we doing this, guys?"

We jump off the raised mounds of earth; I close my eyes when the ground came closer and closer; he held me close to him; I breathe in his scent, we land on solid ground, I opened my eyes, we have landed on another raised mound of earth." That was not so bad."

"No, it wasn't "

I glance back and gawk in amazement as a wall of earth rose from the ground, cutting us from their view.

"Earth to guys, are you going or not, remember that they have a fly-ship," Zen says sarcastically.

We follow her nimble footsteps out of there, several minutes later I heard the whirr of blades in the air, my ears pop as a sonic explosion rings to my left, and Blyte manifested a shield of earth, shielding us.

Zen fumbles for on the ground; she dances out of the way of bullets shot at her." Hurry." she screams, then jumps down, swallowed by the manhole, it's desert colored lid matching the ground perfectly, I jump in, and Blyte follow, hefting the cover of the manhole back in place.

CHAPTER 26

WHISPERA

CHIMA

Sheyika!

Thick fog wrapped around her, the girl, her heartbeat beats frantically. The girl gulps, looking around. Cruel laughter follows, clinging to her bare skin, and she shiver in fright as her eyes scan around the forest, trying to see who was calling out to her. A shape step out of the fog, it more looks like it parted to let him through. The girl steps back, trying to stay as far away from the figure as she could.

'Why run when it means nothing Sheyika, in the end, you will be mine.'

Tears came to her eyes, and she whips around, only to come face to face with death. Merciless eyes, sharp fingernails pierced her skin, blood splatters the ground in scarlet drops. She whimpered and tried to get away from the creature. Who held her in a vise grip that was proving impossible to get out of. The man turns around, leaving the little girl to scream for help. No one came. Soon it faded away to leave only the sound of nature.

A hand shook my shoulder. For a moment, I was the girl in my dreams being ravaged by the reaper. My eyes snap open, and I acted before I knew what I had done, Sukunda yelps as I pressed her face to the floor of the coach, a dagger at her throat.

"Let go of her."

A gun pressed at the back of my head. I blink blearily down at the pregnant girl who wears a panicked look, tears gather in her beautiful eyes. I let go of her. The dagger clatters to the floor, and I scrambled away. Ode help her up, she sat on the other end of the carriage, avoiding my eyes, I snatch the dagger from the floor and poke my head out of the carriage door. I need time alone to think of what I had almost done, I will never forgive myself if I kill the very person that I had journeyed out of my home to save. I scrub a hand on my face and angrily wipe a sole, desolate tear. If it was not the unexplainable feeling that I had that I have to make sure that Sukunda is safe from Obra, I would disappeared e and never look back. I gaze at the desert, at my back lay Zubela, we have passed Yegun city days back. And yet a step ahead of Obra, it makes my heart swell with pride whenever I thought of it. Dust rose in the distance, and I push back that burgeoning pride; it's a matter of time before they find us.

"Wisp, they are coming." Ode grip the reins of the carriage. I met Sukunda's red, frightened eyes.

A few more miles, we would've been in Fonia. Nearly had our freedom. I snort, who was I kidding? Even I know that that was not how stories like this end . In this world, stories like this end in misery, suffering, and then inevitably death.

"You coming?"

I threw my head back, arms outstretched, and called for my power. "No!" I jump out of the carriage and land on the sand. A sand storm brews. It's what I could think of now they need time, I will get it for them.

"Thank you." And with that, Ode shot out of there. The hoof beats got more and more distant. And the sound of vehicles became closer. The wind rose to a roaring pitch; I stare at the grains of sand floating in the air, whipping into sand-shaped funnels that reach outwards towards the gray sky. Not my best work, but sand-nadoes are effective ways to beat the enemy. A drop of blood leaked out of my nose and splash onto the ground. Bleaching the ground bone-white, spreading out. My hair went iron-grey, distressed shouts of panic echo as the spreading tsunami of white sand heads towards them. It whips them in the air, only to be sucked in by the sand funnels when they are about to land. I spread hands, maneuvering the bird-shaped sea of sandstorm as it attacked, pecking and throwing people in the air, its wings fueling the intensity of the storm, every beat making it rise higher and higher.

Finally.

I hope you know what you're doing, daughter mine.

I know that this is dangerous; it takes a lot of energy out of a wielder. I grit my teeth and dig deeper than I have ever done in my life. The storm turns fiercer than before; it went to the point where I was afraid that it would lift me off from the desert ground.

Bravo! Bravo, I think you should stop it and come with me.

No!

I crumple to my knees, gasping for breath. I dab the tears from my eyes and sit up, staring at the calming desert storm. I have to get out of here, but where will we go? What's there to do anymore?

Huge motorcycles shot towards me, creating a loose circle around me. Riders wait for me to make a move. I stood up, a guy with deep brown skin, dead eyes regard me with something akin to fear and curiosity. "Whispera!"

"Turn back, and I won't think about ending you all?"

"Where's she headed? Tell me, and I will let you go free. No one has to get hurt here." I glimpse desperation in his eyes, and I would have given in if the image of Sukunda's face didn't flicker in my vision for a moment. I don't know her that well, but that heartbroken look on her face, while she was holding the snow globe, and staring out the window of the carriage, has something to do with this guy. I met his pleading eyes, and he looks away.

"I know, but the thing is, I gave a promise to my mama that I won't kiss and tell." I snap into a defensive stance and wait for him to attack.

"Very well!"

Daggers at ready I slash out at the guards that came towards me, I dodged a wicked blade and whip my body lithely in the air and slam a booted foot on another's temple he went down. I land in a crouch, with a move too fast for the eye to make out, I slit another's throat. I throw my throwing knife at another who lunges at me. He crumples at my feet. I pull my knife free and wait. Hard, dead, angry eyes meet mine, a fury like no other brews in them, one that's being fed by my hand. Well, what does he expect? I can't yield like that, got a reputation to feed. Something sizzled on my shoulder blade, pain lanced my body. I couldn't stop my body from convulsing, I hit the sands. A shadow loomed before me, I stared at the man who had just shot me down, he held a strange, smooth and sleek, snub-nosed gun. He aimed the gun at my heart and squeeze the trigger.

CHAPTER 27

BLOOD TIES

CHIMA

"Wakey! Wakey sleepyhead, "Something was plunge hard in my arm, I woke up with a half scream and half yelp. A man stands before me, a huge gas mask covers half his face. I was cuffed to a chair, surrounded by tubes and wires. A machine beeps to my left in synch with my galloping heartbeat.

"Glad to have you back from the land of the dead to the living wisp." He bit out, smiling evilly.

I could make out an evil smirk behind his gas mask." To be honest, a slight wraith excuse of a girl is the least I was expecting when I came on this mission. Guess we were all wrong then." He chuckles, filling a syringe with a teal-gray liquid that looks like it holds a swirling, writhing mass within its depth.

"Slight wraith, how about you release me right now, and we will see."

"A tempting offer, but I must pass on that. Right now, you tied up is the best thing for all of us, don't you think so wisps? Right now, I want to see what makes you tick." he tuts.

I snort, he strides towards me with the almost full syringe. My body tensed, "What is in that?"

"Aren't you dying to know? How about we make a deal, you tell me where that little prima breeder scurries off to, and I will not only not refrain from injecting this in you, I will make sure that you are freed,"

His smarmy smile that made my skin crawl, I would've believed him if his words hadn't echoed with insincerity that brought goosebumps to my skin.

" Like I said, I don't kiss and tell, I promise my mama that I won't."

"Have it your way, I thought that you knew what's best for you."

"She is my friend."

"Friendship doesn't exist in this world of ours. I can see that you stopped thinking about that, it is what makes even the mighty fall.

However, you and I will be the best of friends, I am Dr. Klem". He croons, and plunges the syringe into my neck.

I let loose a piercing scream meeting the dead eyes of the guy who stood before the observation glass. One side of the room darkened, sucking all the light to one side, I fought for breath, sucking restricting amounts of air in my lungs. When I had my breathing under control, I lift my head to meet the eyes of Dr. Klem.

"Finally, "Something akin to excitement shone in his eyes, meaning that whatever he has just injected me yielded the positive result that he was hoping for. I watch him write something down, then with one last smirk behind his mask, he was out of there. I stared at the large observation glass and saw no one standing there. I closed my eyes, seeking for my core, the only thing that made up my abilities. And found it flaring but brighter than before. I dig in deep and called for it. Nothing happened.

Daughter!

The image of a girl clutched my mind in a vise grip that didn't let go, no matter how I tried to push it out of my head. She is my nightmare, the only one wisp is afraid of.

Why deny your very blood? I would have you out of there with just a word from you. Just one word, and you know it. Why torture yourself to no end? For what? You know that only the strong live to see the next sunrise.

My head's on fire as I tried to push the voice out of my head. With every push, I find it harder to budge the picture. The girl held the man's hand. He lifts her up and throw her in the air. To anyone looking, it would have seemed like she would be hurt. She stops in the air and hover in the air for several seconds, then execute a couple of somersaults she hit his palms perfectly in a crouch.

"Get out of my head." With the last vestige of my power pushed the scene out of my head. I hung my head, breathing erratically, heart rate hiking.

CHAPTER 28

FEVER-HEAD

Chima

Cold hands touch my feverish skin, I sigh in absolute bliss. "Chime."

I squint. A girl in all black, with a white lab coat on top, the same gas mask on Dr. Freaking Klem's face on hers, I couldn't believe what I was seeing.

"Zaghra! What in the abyss are you doing here?" I slur, trying to keep my eyes open.

"What do you think? Do you really believe that I will let you rot in this place?" She yanks the IV needles out of my wrist. And heave me out of the chair. Muscles complaining, I forced my legs to match her steps. She risk everything to get me out of this hellhole.

I meet her dark, flashing eyes, she smiles, it was 'our' smile that says 'you-look-like-shit-but-you'll-be- alright.'

"Stay here." she helps me on the floor of what looked like a storage room of some kind and disappear. With a trembling hand, I pick a splintered chair leg .Being this weak won't be an excuse to not defend me if the need arises. A couple of minutes later, I heard a deafening explosion, and the room shake, raining down fine dust on me. The door opens, and a guard steps in. I shot up in one smooth move, and attack, the guy's green eyes widens and he dodged.

Dark green eyes.

I stopped in mid-attack, "Azuiga."

"Hey, Chime."

Wary eyes set in a face that's all planes and hard angles, a face that even angels will get jealous of. I stuff the chair's leg in my empty back sheath, "where's Zahra?"

"She is out there, I'm here to get you out. But maybe she should have come seeing that you nearly stake me with that chair leg of yours."

"Getting cold feet, Azuiga?" I follow him out of there, he shook his head, I don't need him to turn around to know that a smile graced those beautiful lips of his.

"You don't scare me Chime."

"Good, because that is the last thing I want you to feel."

He stiffens, I chuckle darkly, and increased my pace. My body was feeling more robust now, the effect of whatever the good Dr. Klem has injected me with was fading away fast. I don't know why I like needling Azuiga, what I know is that it gives me intense, perverse pleasure to see him try not to react to me. I can't seem to stop doing it. Maybe it's having this ginormous crush on him for as long as I could remember and trying so hard to hide it. Being unpleasant is the only thing that could help me in this situation, being Wisps means that I got to have sacrifices of my own. Because I know that he could be a bargaining chip that could destroy me, at least with Zahra, we both know where we have to stop. He's the forbidden fruit.

"Hurry guys, even my grandma can run faster than you." She revs her huge monster bike. Azuiga was first to reach her, a gunshot rings behind me, I whip my body in a side-flip, almost falling onto my face, I jump behind Azuiga, and we speed of there bullets chasing us. She drives past inner junk, past all the shanties, until we stand before one shanty.

"Whoops, we made it." She whoops. It will take time before they could even catch us. I climb off the bike and follow her inside. Azuiga follows behind me, a presence that tickles and caress my senses. I stared at the shanty; it comprises a couch, a small wooden drawer, a cracked sink that was coated with dirt, and grime. "Welcome to the hideout."

"Nice, thanks for coming for me, guys."

"You would have done the same for us Chime, we are family, you gotta remember that us Junkers don't like being fucked with. Now, are you going to tell us what you did to piss off Obra?"

"You won't be mad?"

"Nah, maybe grumpy here would be." Zahra gestures at where Azuiga stands brooding.

"I smuggled his Prima breeder out from under his very nose."

"What?" both scream, horrifying looks on their faces.

"You promised not to freak out guys."

"That is extreme even for you, when did you start being a smuggler. You know that the lifespan of a smuggler."

"I had no choice Zahra, she was pregnant, he was already experimenting on the baby."

"The hell?"

"Yeah, now you see why I had no choice, it was pretty tough to do, I never wanted you guys in a mess. And now look, you are in it with me."

"You're right, you can't just ignore such a thing someone has to help. But are you still on for the game?"

"You bet, I can't wait to head for Hope city, you guys should come with me."

"Are you sure?"

"Yeah, we would fit right in, once we get whatever the bounty is from Ash mansion."

"That I can't wait for."

CHAPTER 29

DRAGU

CHIMA

I Peel from the shadows and scale the wall of the house using the sticky pad that Zahra gave me; she was already inside the house masquerading as a cleaner. I lifted the glass window and stepped inside, I sneaked deeper in the house, sticking to the shadows. Being near them makes me jumpy. It always brings painful memories that I had buried deep in the recesses of my mind.

I close my eyes, and I was back into the tunnels with Mama running away from them, fear lending my feet wings. It grips me in its deadly grip, Mama puts me in a corner, and encased it with ice, I watch helplessly as she decoys them to her. That's the last time I saw her again. I gasp, eyes snapping open. Tingles break all over my body, I shudder, striding deeper into the house maybe I'm paranoid.

Whenever you feel the tingles, know that they are near.

I stared at the snarling wolf's head carved the door. It looked almost lifelike, warning me to not step beyond the door, to go back, that this is the point of no return. But I have already given Zahra my word I won't go back on it. With a deep breath I open the door and tread inside, a dagger flew towards my head, and I whipped my body out of the way, it slammed into the wall its handle ringing out; the echo made me wince out. Zahra drops down from the ceiling, grinning. "You should see the look on your face epic, choking fear girl. What took you so long?"

"Was admiring the décor, should do before we got caught, and besides beautiful things are getting lesser every time."

"Morbid, I like that." She whispers, pulls on a lever that was on the wall revealing a trap door.

I shadow her down the rickety, old, wooden stairs and into the bowels of the darkness within. I stared at the objects in the room. Some dated back to the days before the world ended.

"What are we looking for exactly?"

"I have no idea Chime, but will know when we see...."

"Zahra, look out!"

The floor gives way, and I watch in trepidation as she falls, I tail her down. Using the little air in the room to soften her fall and land smoothly. I wait for my eyes to adjust to the darkness, the slow shift of wind to the right had my me tensing. A ping arcs in the air for a second, then stop.

"It's right here!"

I made out Zahra beaming up at me, albeit all the dust on her face and body; she clutches a small, wooden box in her hand. I pull her up, she opens the box and push the lid back, a dark, bronze dagger, with purple liquid-stones, three empty slots for where some stones use to be stands out etched on its whole body lay on a velvet cushion.

"What is this?"

"Do I look like a crazy mad-cap, trying to know everything?"

She snorts. "We risked our lives for a piece of ancient junk,"

A shriek impales the air, answering howls and snarls bounced off the thin walls of the mansion, and we both stiffen, we don't need to be told what those sounds were.

Tingles still break out on my neck. Damn it, I should have heeded them, all the signs have been there, but I had to be a fool and ignore them. I held my blade tight in hand. Should have listened to my instincts, should have tucked tail when it told me to, and run as far away from here as possible. It's what Mama told me to look out for. Zahra closes her eyes, and the air buzzes slightly it felt like it was charged, or something weird that I can't explain.

"God damn it!" she whispers, body quaking. Fear bleeds in her eyes.

My heart nosedive to the bottom of my stomach, I freed the two blades from my soft, leather back-sheaths I wore, hold slippery. I take a defensive stance.

"What is it?"

"We are in the middle of a nest, a hibernating one, I'm so sorry Chime, I have led us into a trap. I should have known."

I stared at her frightened face. A hibernating nest is one of the most dangerous traps out there. The darn things are expensive to maintain. A whooshing emanates in the room, and we both stood our ground. Lights blink to life, I close my eyes at the bright light, and slowly open them, trying to let it get accustomed to the intense lighting. We seem to be in another room, this one differs from the last dusty one we were in, it looks cold and clinical. It gives me chills that spread out in a cold wave all over my body. Green blink at me up in the corner of the room. It's a camera, Zahra was right, it's a trap, and we have played right into their palms. We went back to back as the door to the right slide open noiselessly, and Reapers ran towards us, endless hunger in their eyes, I struck out at the first Reaper, I chop its head clean off; it went down. I whir around slashing my blades round in a deadly circle of blades, kicking out at the Reapers that came too close for comfort. I leap in the air and cut two Reapers with my boot blades.

"We have to get out of here, I don't think I can control all that's too much practice for me." Zahra stabs a Reaper in the eye and kicks it away from her. Some Reapers wander aimlessly around not attacking anyone, this was the first time Zahra had willingly demonstrated what she could do in front of me, I can't wait to show her what I could.

"Any ideas miss sunshine,"

"Yeah."

"And what is that?"

"We have to get out of here, we can't fight them all."

"Glad to know that you figured that out." She pivots and takes off towards a keypad panel on the wall; I kick a Reaper, and watch in satisfaction as it fall paces away from me and started after her; she slams her palm on the panel, a door swings open. We step in; the door slid shut, cutting the Reaper's hand off, sealing us inside. I kick it off me when it tries gripping my ankle; we are in some kind of dark corridor with flickering lights; it lends a striking, dark, creepy feel to everything. I grasp my blades waiting for something to jump me anytime, heart speeding, Zahra grips her machete tight,

I edge my way towards the very place the light is the brightest, tingles were now a buzz on my nape, I could feel their presence closing in on all sides, I break out in a sprint and Zahra follow closely behind. A figure stands in the corridor, motionless; I taste bile when he drops on all fours. Its limbs contort, bones break aligning into position.; I wonder how they could make their limbs do the unnatural, and impossible, I stared at its ashy-gray skin tone, bony features, eyes of death, and claws that could rip and tear. Separating flesh from bone in seconds. I take a step back when it opened its mouth and hiss at us; pure, insidious evil mists the air.

Zahra's eyes widen into huge saucers, and she starts backing away. Another figure joined the creature on the floor in the same fashion. Spider-like, I gasp as his limbs turned to the same unnatural pose that should never be possible. They bent so that it could walk spider-like on the floor. They're here. I know that I have been toying with the idea of making them up, that they were nothing but a figment of my imagination, the trauma of a child who lost her mother in a world such as mine, trying to survive and not end up being the next meal of some lucky Reaper.

"What the heck is that?"

" A dragu, a poor copy of a Reaper!"

"Damn it, this is getting better and better! How do you know so much about them?"

"I do! Because I can do this." frost appears on my hands and spread all over my arm, icicles decorate my fingertips, I conjure a wind that whipped at her face, her hair flew in the unknown wind nearly knocking her off her feet. "They are here because I am Wisps."

"I don't want to know more! God, I thought that the Reapers were the stuff, but this." Zahra shook her head, waves her hand, encompassing everything. Her eyes say that this is too much to take in.

A low keening faraway call came out of its throat.

"What is it doing?"

A louder one rips out of the throat of the Reaper, its eyes staring hungrily at Zahra.

"Establishing contact."

"There are more?"

"Yeah, they run in packs, that's a sniffer."

She shakes her head, eyes huge on her face. She takes a step back, I mirror her. Her eyes widen more. She gulps and stared at me in horror. I wait to see what she will do next.

"I will understand if you leave me, you should go I don't want you to die here, they will not kill me, I don't want you hurt."

"No! I'm staying, I brought you here. We will get out together; besides, you are not the only freak in here. I'm the reason we are here," she whispers, breaking out of her petrified state.

"Thank You, Zahra,"

"Just get us out of here alive" She snorts, a screech that had my ears buzzing.

Zahra cusses extensively, I was sure that I will be deaf after hearing the things sprout from her mouth. Answering screeches bounced all around. The dragu looks at me with a promise and hunger I have seen before, a memory ago. I led Zahra out of there, it stayed put like I knew it would.

I step back, pulling Zahra out of there. A door opens and Azuiga peeks his head in. "In here."

We run in, and he close the door. Reapers were in close pursuit behind us, blade out I slash at a Reaper's neck when it lunges for me, It slam into me, lifting us both in the air. He fell down with a low whine; I crouch perfectly in front of Azuiga and Zahra. "Go!"

"No, we are not going without you."

"Just go, I will be right behind you, I promise. Please take her Azuiga."

"You better Chime, I'm holding you on to it."

I watch them run and lift both my hands in the air, weaving energy into the very fabric of the air, energy only a select few people could see, opaque threads streams out of my fingertips and weave into each other, forming a pattern invisible to mundane eyes. I stand my ground and watch the horde of Reapers head my way, only to smack into the invisible wall of the shield . The sea of

Reapers part and made way for a man in a long leather coat, his skin an indeterminate color I have only ever seen in my nightmares. Or was it a memory? A faraway memory bubbles to life, threatening to surface, my temples throb, and I gnash my teeth. I will not succumb to the temptation. I knew that worn path well enough to know that nothing good comes out of it. A drop of blue-red blood splash on the floor, the Dragus grew frenzied. His bony features melt away, he flashes a grin, showing flat, white teeth, that's supposed to make me feel at ease. It didn't work; I trembled.

Reaper Lord.

"You are getting good at weaving!" he runs a hand on my shield, a loving, coveted touch. Warm eyes that I knew too well appraised me. The very source that threatens my very existence and freedom.

"Sweetie, you know that you can't run from me, but I will have to congratulate you on staying under the radar for a decade, it only shows that you are your mother's daughter. Shadarka misses you, now take the shield down and come with me and I can guarantee you that your friends won't get hurt, the game is over! It is time to come home, where you belong."

Home.

A place that nothing but death and misery awaits my return.

"If you choose the other option, I won't be so pleased! Do you want to play this tiring game? Maybe I will add the girl as an addition to my Dragus, she could accompany you with Shadarka, "What say you?" he eyed the drop of blood on the floor.

"Where is Mama?"

"Take this down and come with me, your mother would love to see you."

Mama is alive, she's not dead. I thought that she died every single day, regretting why I didn't take that shield down and follow her, the guilt, a wound that ate me inside out every day that goes by.

I will come back for you, I promise.

Like a puppet whose strings have been cut, my knees refused to hold me, I crumpled in relief and lifts my head. Satisfaction shone like beacons in his eyes.

Don't ever trust him, no matter what he says.

"Are you lying to me?"

He shrugs," I will not tell you to believe me Sheyika, you should come with me, why run when we are what we are?"

"Monsters!"

He grins and pierces me with eyes that have gone opaque dead, eyes that have been tormenting me for a decade. "Believe it or not,

Sheyika we are all monsters, the power is in all of us, it depends on how you choose to utilize it."

"Chima, my name is Chima, and I'm not a monster like you." I bit out.

I hate that name, it plunges me back to those dark days. Days when I was nothing but a monster. His right hand. The Lord's executioner and I reveled in it.

"Is that what you tell yourself every day, every moment of your life? You of all people know that you don't belong here, but you do with us, you are my blood. And I choose you to stand by my side while I build a kingdom. You threw it back in my face."

I remember a time when a younger me has done horrible, horrendous things to gain his love, approval and acceptance. Giving in to the evil that runs deep in my veins, I was malleable; after a day of doing what he says, he would hold me close and call me his heart's treasure. The one thing in the world that meant everything to him, I knew that I will continue blaming myself for those actions till the day I die, the destructions I had a hand in, even though this voice in my head was telling me not to blame myself for things that I had no control over. That I was a child, and a child's mind, can be easily influenced. I know that it is partly true, but it doesn't make me feel any better. Because I knew what I was doing, I felt powerful; I felt like I was a goddess, that I could do anything and get away with it. Mama didn't know about it until it was too late, and I was nearly too far gone. She had found me one day starting a tornado at a nearby village when she chances on me, I had killed half its population.

She'd looked at me like I was a monster from the darkest pits of hell. I wished that I could erase the look in her eyes when she saw me feeding the body of a boy to my Dragu Shadarka, the one charged with looking after me. That is what I thought until Mama had tried to take me away, then it had attacked her. She had to kill him before she took me away from him. I thought that he had died, guess I was wrong there.

"No, child of mine is a monster Sheyika, power is not meant to subdue the weak; it's a calling to protect people who can't protect themselves." She had whispered to me, a thousand pains in her beautiful, tawny eyes.

I pull myself up and wipe the tears from my face; I knew what he's doing; trying to have sway over me, going with him was not an option. Not when I have promised Mama that I will do her last will. I don't even know if he's telling the truth about mama being alive, even if she was, she wouldn't want me go with him. I remember a time when loving arms wrap me into a loving cocoon of a world that told me that I would never be hurt, that I was precious to them. It was a lie that deceived Mama.

I weave more energy into the shield. "Tulki'amkieya ayinha."

Your blood no more.

Fury etch his features, his face leach of all color, taking on the look I have always dreaded. I turn round and sprint out of there, the shield will hold off for some time, but not for long. I reach out with senses that I have suppressed for so long, no more will I hide. If what he said is true and that Mama is alive, I will try to get her out someday, I will have to survive and reach Hope city. I weave the incendiary threads throughout the place, dodging the Dragus that take a swipe at me. I slid in, and the door seals shut behind me. Zahra stood in the doorway waiting for me, she hugs me; I closed my eyes and let her closeness calm me down a little.

"We have to get out of here."

We rush out. An explosion rocks the ground, another rips the air, and shrieks fill the air. We've no time. Another explosion fills the air with a force that smacks us onto the ground.

"Oh my God, look."

Dragus streamed out in flames. Reaper-lord's nowhere in sight, I sighed and stood up. He will go for now, but I know that he will be back with more Dragus than these now that he has found me. And when that happens, I'm not sure that I might escape a second time.

"Well! Well, look what the cat dragged in!"

Tin stood before us, smug as always, eyes gleaming with the knowledge that I'm too afraid to contemplate on. He held out a hand towards us, and a guard snatches the small box from Zahra." I will give it to you two, you have done something that no one has ever done." His gaze went to a Dragu crawling towards us. He points at the Dragu and the guard shoots it in the head.

"What are those?" a guy with pale brown eyes, deep brown skin, and close-cropped hair steps into view.

"That is some shit I have never seen, but I assume that our guests here know what they are." He smirks, eyes lands on us.

"What do you want, Tin?'

"Doll, do you even need to ask? You, my Chima, will be a lot more useful with your friends here. I'm still amazed that you have done the impossible, I will let Kalam know that you fetched this beautiful box. Everyone who tried never comes out alive."

"Extraordinary."

My eyes fell on the tattoo of a chained skull in flames on the back of his hand. Everyone knows who those kinds of tattoos belong to. He said nothing, just let Tin give out the orders, so he was not Kei Obra, the master of Junk district. Who was he then? I could still remember his angry eyes in the desert with his guards.

"You won't get away with this." Zahra hisses.

"I just did love, I always do. Cuff them. I want them all secured. These two look cute and all chummy, but make no mistake, one will rip your eyes and feed it to you, while the other pulls out your heart."

I hung my head, slackening my body, goosebumps fanned all over my arms, currents fill the air, then I saw it, a blinding shockwave of blue light jets out, knocking everyone to the ground, my body felt electrified for a moment, power surged in me, and I gasped doubling over. On the ground Zahra feels the same effects as I did, she grips the ankles of the two guards that held her a moment ago; they were up in one fluid motion and attack their partners. I spring into action, fast and slug a guard hard, he went down coughing clutching his throat, blood run down from his mouth and nose. I hurry to a weak and pale Zahra, dark rings stood out round her eyes.

The guy moves towards us with startling grace, beautiful to watch; it hints at a discipline I rarely see; he was elite or near it. Those combinations of moves were hard to learn without the proper training and pain . I pulled the knives out of my boots, and meet his blade halfway, he slash and thrust testing the waters; I let him play with me for some time, checking my boundaries. Trying to see what his fighting tells are. I glance back at where Zahra stood, the two guards protecting her, and turns back to my opponent. The wrong move, a fist pummels into my face, I stumble back and right my footing, another punch heads my way, the blow slams into my sternum. I cough hard, and clutch my sternum, Zahra's breath hitches the guards fighting for her paused a second reacting to her distress. Bullets exit their foreheads to clatter at Zahra's feet. Azuiga stared back to where I collapsed on my knees, he slowly made his way where Zahra sits on the ground drained, and barely conscious.

He wounds my hair around his hand, pulled my head back painfully my eyes watered, but I refused to shed any tear or make any sound, I stared into his face; he held a gleaming dagger at my throat. Stopping Azuiga in his tracks," One move she dies."

"Get her out of here Azuiga, don't worry about me."

Azuiga throws his weapon on the ground, and raises hands in the air, his body shielding Zahra's.

"You should let us go? Those things you see out there would come back, and this time it would not be a pretty sight."

"I don't think so."

"Then you are a fool, I just hope that you are ready for the next wave because few would survive the attack. Believe me, they always find a way to get me."

He ignores me and turns to Azuiga," here, cuff her to you, make it slow, no sudden moves." Azuiga picks the cuffs off the ground and cuff his wrist to Zahra's. His gaze boring holes into the guy with the knife at my throat.

"Good, now get up Wisps, nice and slow."

I did as he commands, following his orders to the letter. The knife digs deep, my neck smarted throat. I stared at the vehicle coming our way, the door opens and Tin smiles at us." Get in for one hell of an adventure, kiddos."

Knife at my throat I'm frog-marched into the vehicle while Azuiga helps Zahra in, and slide in after her. Tin drove us off towards the ill-fated fate awaiting us.

CHAPTER 30

ARINNU

Obra

The man moves the chess piece to the left, a finger on his chin. He hurries to the small table that holds a glass case full of an amber liquid that shimmers from time to time; he pours a generous amount in a tall flute-like tumbler and goes to stand at his window, staring out at the view. He takes a sip of his drink and shudders in ecstasy. Savoring the rare taste that he has weaned himself off for so long, but it was for the best, it takes hardened discipline to master ones addiction. Once you get used to Bengala's Lady Abyss, you are his slave forever. A drug only he knows the formula. He has, for many years, tried to weasel the secret out from him, sending one private rat after another, but everyone turned up dead or MIA. A small smile creeps on his lips. The man knows how to take care of himself. How he had bested him was beyond him.

His ever-growing entertaining empire was another thing, something that he knows too well. It beckons like a siren to a sailor in need of deliverance. His fingers held the oval-shaped glass pendant. As memories surfaced, he let himself feel the crushing pain as it always does, it nearly brings him to his knees. For a moment he could hear her cry as the blade came crashing down, she pushes him out of its way, and it struck her. He closed his eyes and run a hand on his face, his mind had wandered to things that he has put a lid on, a wound that he had let scab, was threatening to burst open. He has been having these nightmares that plague him since he had escaped the pens. And would do anything to make sure that it stays that way,

The slaving pens were something that he would never forget until his deathbed, prime meat that came from lands beyond the third world. If only they knew what they'd let into their midst. The Baba is a fool for thinking that he's the only one with an agenda. Even with an army of Reapers at his command. But soon, he will see all on their knees, one by one, even Fex. He sneers and let the image mull over in his head. Obra scowls and slams his flute on the table; he was the one who should have a say in what happens in the territories. But he knew that he will have to take caution, all who have tried to unseat Fex met their fate mysteriously. He had learned that Fex was not someone to take lightly, and so was he. Who would have known that a slave from nowhere, hell-bent on surviving, with no chances of living in a world that had no hope would be a master one day; none. His bloody coup gave him the right to rule the Junk, he rose through the ranks, until he maintained a powerful enough position, to massacre the Olunu family.

It took agonizing patience like no other to rise through the ranks, starting to poison everything. One at a time, people didn't notice until it was too late, If he had to do it all over again, he would. He had figured out a way to make vehicles from scrap, vehicles that work despite the EMP, despite what everyone thought, even Hope city couldn't do it with all their technological advancement. Making him one of the richest masters in the territories, and like the way he tried to know about Bengala's secret formula, he too and the rest of the masters had tried to return the favor, if only they know whence it came from, no one lived to tell the tale to their masters and mistresses. What he knows is Fex's the only one who wasn't interested in their mind games, so long as they don't cause a war in the colonies, she was ready to turn a blind eye to their bloody mind games and skirmishes. Knowing the sacrifices, the inhumane things that each one of them did to rise to the top or have an ace over the others, they knew that only the beasts in them can take them to the apex they needed to reach. Being the Provenant does not guarantee that you won't die.

What was her end game? Everybody wants one thing, and it could be their downfall if you knew what it was? His gaze fell on a Soft, gauze veil, and he lifts the slight wisp of material to his nose. He could still scent the mild perfume of jasmine and jojoba oil she applied on her skin. What was about the girl that makes him lose his cool, calculated, hard-earned iron control? It was complete and utter lunacy to think that she has such power. He couldn't help that she reminds him so much of Arinnu, the name opens long, forgotten past wounds that had healed and scabbed over the years. He will find her, and when he does, she will never leave him, never. No one leaves him unless he is through with them. Whoever has her better be ready for one hell of a storm. For his wrath can't be withstood. He won't let all his hard work go to waste, the child in her is the future he had hoped for all these years, a prospect that not even the Baba can't replicate.

CHAPTER 31

SOMITO

Chima

"Are you sure about this?"

I wasn't, the thought of going through with what I had in mind terrifies the pants off me. But I've to try my best to make sure that I reach Hope city before it's too late. We had run off, traveling all the way to Somito, taking the risk on a hunch of mine that the Junker in me thought that if Kalam was ready to pay that much for that dagger, he might still want it. And besides, I believe that Obra would mind too much, it's just doing business. And afte barely escaping the gallows by the skin of our teeth, I would do anything to piss the master off.

Right.

Junker loyalty is fickle, nebulous.

So here I am with Azuiga and Zahra masquerading as workers deep in his pharm, he was using technology to pharm food. It was truly heaven compared to Junk district, I don't see anyone going hungry here, Kalam supplies almost half of the food supplies to the colonies and beyond, every Master and Mistress has something that makes them filthy wealthy, Obra has his junk which he creates into vehicles since the EMP, we have found ourselves short of cars, and he has found a way to make vehicles work smoothly Pre or post EMP. Kwim has his smugglers, Bengala runs the Abyss business, Amosia mines the Arkor-beads, which are the most expensive things in our world, due to the wide range of its uses. Safi makes the weapons. It was what makes them one of the most influential people in Kambiya, being able to carve out territories.

"Mmm, this is heavenly; I wonder why we don't have this back at home."

"Because they are damn expensive, they are meant for the rich, that is why? Would you stop stuffing yourself silly before we are caught!" Azuiga hisses at Zahra.

She blew him a raspberry and bit into the hand-sized nut in her hand, it is delicious I was hooked the moment I took a bite out of it, at first glance you will think that it is a nut until you take a bite out of it, that is when you knew that it is actually a fruit. It was sweet with a strange tang that attacks your taste buds with some kind of a strange sensation that was indescribable.

We have been holed up here for two days, being part of the workforce harvesting food and putting it in carts. I plucked another fruit and put it into a cart, and cast Zahra a look as she stuffs another fruit into the pocket of the loose white pants she wore. She winks, I shook my head and turned back to what I was doing, she can never leave the Junker in her behind. The door opens, and a man I have never seen before stepped into the room, he looks to be in his early twenties, guards trail in his wake. His skin was of a light brown hue, brown hair and dark eyes that missed nothing set into a face with sharp features that looked a little on the slender side, his clothes were different he wore a kaftan-like long sleeve tunic that was slashed to show the pants he wore underneath, a slit in front reveals a perfectly chiseled chest. His presence sets off my alarm bells, I stared at Zahra, she gives me a small imperceptible nod; she had felt it too.

"Just act cool," She whispers.

I turn back to my work, and ignored the buzzing of my senses, my instincts tell me to run as far from here as possible, they were worse than the tingles, with the tingles I know what to expect, but this, I'm just blind. It makes me feel like an antelope caught in the headlights of a hunting Fly-ship. His footsteps shortens the distance between us, my hand trembles as I put the fruit in my cart, out of the corners of my eyes I see him beckons to the supervisor over, the short, balding man with dark brown skin and skittish brown eyes. He whispered something to him, eyes on Zahra.

"We need to get out of here."

"How do you propose we do that genius?"

"We need a distraction, whatever brought him here isn't in our favor, we use one of them as a distraction and get the hell out of here."

"Okay, seems reasonable, I hope that they like their workers very much, if not we might as well stab ourselves."

Zahra chuckles, I stiffen as the guy comes to a stop behind me. I continue my work and ignored the fact that I had someone behind me, he was expecting me to acknowledge his presence, when I didn't, he touches my shoulder lightly with a finger, I held back the gasp as a heatwave like no other swept over my body. I was ready to combust somehow; behind me, he sucks in a breath. Glad to know that I was not the only one who had felt it. I turned around facing him, hard eyes clash with mine. I held his gaze, not willing to blink or cut off our staring contest. His eyes roved all over my petite frame, taking me in the white cap and pharm garb, if he was back there in the convention we are screwed bad, this isn't a good thing.

"IDs, please?"

Praying that Zahra's mumbo jumbo works, that he does not overlook the small differences that I had with the real owner of the ID that I had tied off somewhere with the other two workers we had deposed and stolen their IDs, I handed the small key card over. He stared at it for longer than I would have liked, when he looked at me, I knew that he knew that it wasn't me on the key card.

Shit.

Time for plan B.

Zahra moves into action, pouncing on the girl beside her, she presses a dagger at her throat. I jump out of reach. Executing flips on the table till I stand beside Zahra. Azuiga join us.

"One wrong move, and I end her." She intones slowly, her eyes deadly emeralds, she meant every word she had uttered. This is a dangerous game we play with death, flaunting our odds, risking everything to be safe, but I knew one thing; nowhere is safe, not anymore, not when I'm being hunted by the Reaper lord.

"Derre..." the girl voice shakes, tears gathered in her beautiful brown eyes.

It makes me feels like we are monsters, but we had no choice this is the only ace we have over their heads, the guy held out a hand trying to calm the situation, panic flares in his eyes for a moment before he schools his features back to a mask of indifference.

" Easy there, Mister, one mistake, and I will slit this pretty throat of hers." Zahra glides the blunt side blade on the girl's throat, her eyes hard.

"What do you want?"

"Get us to Kalam!"

He calls off his guards. Slowly, we made our way out of there outside. Workers stop what they were doing to gawk at our slow pace with the guy leading us towards Kalam. He led us into a mammoth-sized room where a man stood in, everything about it screamed sheer wealth. The man has his back to us, he turns around and pinned us with a stare that gave nothing away. His eyes the same color as the guy except for the vibrant band of light-indigo around his shrunken, opaque pupils . It gave him an eerie look. He's an abyss addict.

" Papa...." the girl whispers a lone tear trailed down her cocoa-brown, beautiful face.

He fists his hand and stuffed it in the pocket of his trousers. In his gaze, I saw our torment, this better go smoothly, or we will have the wrath of Kalam on our heads. I pulled my cap off and freed my hair from its prison.

"Yes!"

"Uh, sorry about the way we approached this entire awkward situation, but it was the only way we could see you." Zahra started, she looks confident and capable. Different.

"Chime."

I peeled off the white long-sleeved shirt and the pants leaving me in the previous garb that I had escaped the gallows and reach in my pocket and pulled out the vial, Kalam's eyes lighted the moment his sights set on the vial." You were the reason why we broke into Obra's mansion to retrieve this in the first place, we are here to get the bounty if the offer's still up." I said, handing over the vial to the guy; I grit my teeth holding back the gasp as my fingers brushes his.

This is bad, I can't wait to get out of here.

He fingers the dagger and turns to us his sharp, eerie calculating gaze on the girl who called him Papa. "Let her go. Holding her can't make me change my actions, if I wanted you dead, I would have killed you the moment you stepped foot in here."

"We have to make sure, we aren't staying long. Just here to collect the bounty."

"Very well," he says, his eyes say that he does not like that we are not doing what he demands of us.

He sets a small pouch on the desk, Azuiga took it from the desk and put a finger in, he pulled out an Arkor diamond, twisting it around testing its authenticity, satisfied he nods at Kalam." It was good doing business with you."

I doubled over in pain as tingles swept all over my body. Zahra lets go of the girl and lunges for me . Everything seemed far away, and surreal as Azuiga lifts me from the floor, Derre clears the desk and Azuiga put me on it. Ice coats my hands, inching upwards, while red ribbons of heat wound up my arm.

"What on earth is happening to her?"

"I don't know," Zahra whispers

Rain pelts outside, clusters of grey clouds covered the sky, he was here I could feel it. Reapers screech, waking from their sleep.

Daughter.

I close my eyes, this can't be happening. Maybe I should have done what he commanded, yielded when he asked . Their sheer numbers make my head want to implode as they chanted two words. For a moment I was transported back to a time when I was taken in by a family, and I had to watch helplessly from a distance as they got massacred, until nothing was left of them, not even their bones, eaten out of existence. That was when I had made the decision to be alone and not endanger people by letting them help me.

Find her! Find her! Find her! Kill! Kill! Kill! Find her! Find her! Find her! An endless mantra that swirled in my head, making my blood pound faster and faster. He knew what the influence of their numbers does to me. I grip the edge of the desk until the desk groaned under me. A sizeable portion of the desk came off my hands, smeared in my blood. It had cut into my palm, I took a deep calming breath and tried pushing back their influence, slowly. Until I can manage to breathe without screaming in agony.

I met Derre's eyes, something in them told me that he had heard them. But how? That shouldn't have been possible. A drop of blood fell from his nose and splash onto snow white carpet. Marring its perfection. Slowly, I pull myself up and rested on my elbows." We have to get out of here, he's here!"

"Who?"

A haunting shriek filled the air, I winced, gripping my temples. Derre exchanged a look with Kalam, Zahra looped my hand around her shoulders, and we started towards the door only to have it closed shut. Derre in our way.

"Shit." Zahra shudders, meeting my terrified eyes.

"What the hell do you think you are doing?"

"No one's leaving here, stay put."

"Do you even know what's out there?"

"Yes, I do, and you have led him straight to me."

"What do you mean?"

"This." He held out a hand, and I watched as particles of water appear out of thin air, forming into a massive drop that hovered

an inch from his palm. I open my mouth, and he held out a hand."
Just stay." A glimmer in his eyes made me shiver. His eyes didn't miss the action.

"We can't, Obra's hunting for our heads, "

He sighs and open the door, and we ran into the rain. An ashy-grey bony Dragu shriek and lunged for me. I slashed at it, it screeched in pain and rage and retreats whining. A gunshot rings out, and it crumples. We sprint for the bikes, intense sick eyes that always never stops to astound me tracks our progress.

More Dragus than I have ever seen in my life, it wouldn't take long before the place's overrunning with the infernal creatures. I can barely feel my surroundings, my vision starts to blur, and I drown in them, I stumble and right myself in time before I fall on my face. I made out Derre fighting Dragus, his moves fluid and choreographed, moves that I have yet to master, he's impressive. I wanted to know how he knew the Reaper lord. I had always thought that Mama and I were the last of our kind, guess I was wrong.

"That's some shit."

I hopped on a motorbike, I have to lead them out of here, it's the least I could do before more die. Heat flares to life in my head. They hurried towards me like moths to a flame.

"Let's play."

I surged out of there, with the Dragus on my tail, Zahra beside me followed by Azuiga, today there will be a blood bath, I knew it. That's if I don't hurry, I turn around my motorbike and rode towards them, the world narrows until they were the targets that I see. I wove the threads into my ride, I park the bike and wait for them to come for me. In waves, they teem towards me like bees to honey.

"I knew that you'll see it my way." He steps forward, the Dragus making way for him.

"Chima, what the hell do you think you're doing?" Zahra screams and, did a U-turn. Azuiga hops out from his ride, and onto hers, both tumble to the ground. Derre made his way towards us, his face a mask of fury.

"Oh, look the prodigal daughter returns, and with good company."

I turned to the man before me, both blades in him. The explosion blasts me sky-high, spreading out in a blinding, a red flash that hurt my eyes. I slam back on the ground, coughing. Shrieks filled the air, Reapers ran everywhere, bodies aflame. Some lay dead on the ground. Torn limbs, gore, and viscera scatter on the ground, a painter's canvas portraying hell on earth. I slowly got up, swaying a little, and fell back down, hands that brought heat wherever they touched caught me before I reached it. My eyes opened, and I stared into his eyes.

"Are you okay?"

"Is he dead?" I reply.

He snorts, I swing my gaze to the blasted site, it looks like some kind of a mini crater that an asteroid created." Nothing could survive such a blast, if you continue being this suicidal you might not last long"

"Are you calling me stupid?"

"Maybe I am; how do you know the Reaper lord?"

"He sired me," Derre tensed for a moment, then continued on as if nothing happened.

A brother, I had a brother.

Mother never told me about him. I gazed at him, seeing the subtle features of father, combined with Mama's.

"How did you?"

"Wrong time, rotten luck."

"You know that's not an answer, dancing around the truth isn't being truthful."

"Chime."

I let Zahra hug me to her. "Okay, that is enough, Zahra, now you are killing me."

"I should do; you have a death wish or something? You nearly killed yourself."

"I know Zah, but someone has to do something, what if one of you died?"

"He could do something," she nodded at Derre "no one will miss him if he dies!"

"I'm standing right here."

"Well, it's true," Zahra says haughtily and pulls me for another bone-crushing hug that left me coughing. Damn it, the girl is strong. I sent an apologetic stilted smile Azuiga's way. He just lifts in return then turns to his bike. Great, he's mad at me,

CHAPTER 32

NIGTMARE

Chima

Running from them, that is all I have been doing my whole life. I wonder how my life would've turned out if I didn't have to run from what I fear most. Being turn into a monster. My very nightmare becoming a reality.

Sunlight bathes my face in glorious heat. We head towards precinct five. I watch Zahra buy tickets for the train heading towards Sutukoba. Mombess trading post tents stretched out as far as the eye could see. People meander about, talking, laughing, battering to have enough to buy a ticket out of Mombess. We have traded our motorbikes for tickets. The train hoots in the distance,

I watch as the people brace themselves for it. We made our way towards the train, people jostled each other to make it inside, it soon turn into a stampede as people try to make it inside before the time's up. I touch the blade hidden in my clothes, my mouth curves into a smile. Kalam never saw me swipe the dagger. A howl rose in the desert air, I stiffen, I would know that howl anywhere Reapers come into view riding Bukis. I turn my gaze on Zahra and agonizing pain brings me to my knees. I gasp at the blade that protrudes out of my stomach. Azuiga pulls the blade from within my clothes. All friendliness leach out from his eyes. A stranger stands in his place. I should've seen this coming. Shouldn't have let my guard down.

"I told you it won't be hard to take it from her, you can always rely on a Junker to get you what you need.

"What's this guys?"

"It's called taking what we came for."

All these times, I thought of them as friends, they had hidden agendas. "Why?"

Zahra knelt before me because Sheyika, unlike you, I do what my father says. I welcome my monstrosity, rather than run away from it. It's pathetic how you chose to live your life. Afraid of doing anything. There was no way of crossing Obra without help. That's where you come in the picture. Being Whispera was just a bonus."

"What're you?"

"Something you'll never know, tell dear old father The Baba sends his regards."

Zahra kicks at the blade, it inches deeper into me. I fall face-first on the ground, Reapers attack, the skeleton train crawled forward, leaving half the people behind. Zahra made her way towards a Buki, Azuiga jump on its back, and helps Zahra up. His eyes never left mine. Just as soon as they've come, they were out of there.

My baby,

Mama,

What is wrong?

I'm dying mama,

Hold on baby, you can't die on me, remember your promise.

I'm sorry, Mama.

For a moment, I could feel her presence, ghost fingers brush my cheek, I close my eyes. Footsteps force my eyes open and trail on dark-grey pants, and up into the thunderous face of Obra. "Where's it?"

"Nobody steals from me vermin," hands searched me, searching for the dagger that I no longer have.

" Negative, Sir."

"You little runt, where's my dagger?" Obra yells his foot, slams onto the blade, more blood gush out." Kill her, and get her friends too."

"I don't have it, she took it, The Baba."

Obra's face contorts, into a malicious mask I barely felt the pain as the gun went off, the bullet strikes my body, the metallic scent of gun powder invades my nostrils. Tears slid from the corners of my eyes, pooling at my feet, where it touched, dark crystals forms. My head felt like it was stuffed with cotton balls, my body thudded to the ground, and I close my eyes, losing myself in the vortex of pain.

CHAPTER 33

CHAINS MADE OF EARTH

Calla

I gawk at the sinking suns and can't chase the foreboding feeling that this might be my last sunset. Why would I think that? I stand beside Cleo growling at the early Reapers that have risen and were looking at me with such unholy menace, I can't help but shudder. I know that water is the only thing holding them back. If not, they would've made their way in. The closing horn lance the air thrice in a row, each one deeper and sadder than the last.

Something's feels of.

My heart lurches in my chest, I stumble and turn to go but stops when I caught a glimpse of a blur. I motion for Cleo to go on all fours; she huffs but still does as I bid, I mount her. Cleo growls low in her throat, eyes narrowed. She slinks back, heading towards the town. Another horn blared to life but was cut short mid-ring. This one deeper than before. My muscles tensed at the sound.

Mama.

I have watched helplessly as Kamili had undertaken a mission, my instincts tell me she might not come back from. I know that I should head towards the Aerie and await evacuation, but I can't, not with being haunted by the thought that Mama might be hurt. I recognize those caged-trucks.

Ravagers.

I never thought that they will come to Kendulusa, gunshots and screams pierce the air. We are fighting back; I spur Cleo on. She bounds through the enormous gates that hung on its hinges. I scan for Mama in the sea of fighting bodies. I spot her fighting back to back with Rougy, who got an army of plants beside her, a blade in hand, eyes of cold-mud that could freeze any who dared stand in her path, a fae in her element. Both in sync with each other, lethal extensions of the same body, the way they fought is beautiful, deadly, and mesmerizing. Mama looks like a goddess of old. Her red hair had escaped its ponytail, it frames her face, but still reveals her eyes that were full of ire. She decapitates one ravager without hesitation. I can't believe that it's Mama fighting, gone was my Mama. In her place, a goddess of death and destruction.

She leaps onto the town dais stopping two ravagers from dragging a screaming, struggling girl I recognized as Buma into a house, a sharp vine materialized out of nowhere and impales the ravager from behind, the vine drains him of blood and chucks his body away, he hits the ground with a dull thump, Buma picks up a blade and disappears into the house. A ravager to the left has a rocket launcher aimed at Mama, my eyes widens as he releases the rocket towards her.

"Mama!"

She whips around, our eyes clash, horror flits within her sapphire depths, widening, she knows it's too late to react, it does not matter how fast she could be, the rocket is almost upon her. Acting on instinct I lift hands in the air, the rocket flames hover in midair, inches from Mama's face. The world slows down. Time meant nothing to me.

I thrived in it.
Mine to bend.
Mine to will.

It must bow to me.

Mama moves out of the way, I let go of my hold on time. It blasts into the house behind her; the ravager turns startled eyes on me. Then he meets Mama's equally unsurprised ones; he gives her a smile that stops my heart. My grasp on time meant nothing as fear petrified my body, locking me in place. I was too powerless to stop it. He reverses the launcher in my direction and fired.

"No!" Mama screams her sadness coated in desperation, grieving for her loss. I watch a tear seep out of her eye and slowly slip down her cheek to drip on the ground.

I wave hands in the air, but nothing happens. Panic beat at the walls of my mind, I close my eyes, waiting for my end. But nothing happened. Instead, a chill encased my body, seeping into my bones, making me feel safe. When I open them, I was shrouded in a light pink force field that had encased my body, shielding me from the flames. Mama stood yards away, her hand held out in front of her in a half-fist, the light pink force field leaches from her fingertips.

" Look out, Mama."

A ravager shoots two bolts of arrows in her left shoulder, he was dead before he knew it, pain clouds her features but she did not cry out , she stagger back into Rougy who catches her as she fell, distracted she didn't see when a blade sink into her side. Wicked looking vines with sharp tips rear out of her back and slam into the raider, lift him up, I watch it sucked him dry of blood, then let go of him. The ravager's lifeless eyes land on me.. The healer tilts her back, and suck in a long pull of air. I watch the wound heal, leaving only blood stains to show she was injured.

Mama whispers into the healer. Rougy shakes her head. I watch as the healer kisses her cheek, and rush out of there, plants come to life clearing the way as she heads towards of the cage-truck. I start towards Mama, but she shook her head, her eyes tell me to get away from here. I know what she wants. What she's going to do, I want to stay and help. She put a hand on her heart and smiles up at me, then holds a fist in the air. Slowly, she got up and lunge towards the trucks of ravagers streaming through the broken gates. She pick up the discarded rocket launcher.

I knew what she was doing. Sacrificing herself for me, I incline my head in reluctant acceptance. She was doing what papa did for us that fateful night I was born. He never came back, I'm not ready to say goodbye yet. Not in this way, now, I knew what has to be done, with a touch on whining Cleo's head I bound out of there. Leaving Mama behind, but I had no choice, I had promised Mama that I would do it if anything happens to her. I knew that this day would come, I just didn't think it was this early, or that I have to be separated from my family. That I have to face a cruel, cold world without them. A deafening explosion rings out. It's an unthinkable torment that always plagues my sleeping and waking hours. Tears slid down my cheeks as Cleo's paws ate up the distance, creating cracks in my heart, cracks that will never heal.

CHAPTER 34

OUMALI

Calla

Tents lay stretched out in every direction, everything seemed like a war zone, bodies litter the ground. I have been sticking to myself for days, avoiding Reapers and humans, the Reapers I knew what they want, but humans I don't. Treachery runs in everyone's veins in the world. I stared at my small backpack in the makeshift saddle I made on Cleo's back. The little bundle inside's really important to Mama. I have to make sure it reaches the right hands. Then I will rescue her, I have to. I hope that Kamili does not come back to the Kendulusa, I climbed down the makeshift saddle ladder and hurried towards a tented stall.

"Hello, I want some beef jerky and two canteens of water," I told the frightened trader, staring at Cleo in fear. I wouldn't blame him, a lone child is nothing to fear, but a solitary child with a gigantic beast of unknown origins is something to fear. And right now Cleo was looking at him like he was her last meal on earth, I gave Cleo a look to stay, she did so grudgingly, huffing at me all the while, I swear that she acts like more human than animal at times.

He puts the items on the counter, and I lay the coins down. The world sharpens into focus, and I gripped the edges of the counter gasping, my knees gave out, vision turning grey, my surroundings stripped away I was in the same place, but it was different. A brown-skinned, dark-haired girl accompanied by two people, a girl and a guy, I watched them trade their bikes for the coin. The girl touches something hidden in her clothes, a devious smile on her lips. Phantom pain pierces my midriff, I double over, tremors shook my body. She gawks at her wound in disbelief, then at the girl who stabs her in the back. Reapers came thundering on Bukis, the guy helps the girl on one, and they rush out of there.

Footsteps made their way to where the girl lay, hands searched her. The man in the dark-colored clothes looms over her, he asked about a dagger she stole from him. Enraged that she doesn't possess it anymore. He kicks at the blade still buried in her, more blood gushed out, he shot her and went after the girl with the Bukis.

I had heard of such things from Mama when she had told me of places that lay beyond Kendulusa. Territories called colonies, controlled by six powerful families that are all answerable to the Provenance at Kambuya. It was the foundation treaty, the provenance was to make sure that the colonies won't be plunged into chaos again, everything would be kept in check. Tears glide down the corners of her eyes and pooled to the ground, where it touches dark, ice crystals forms. She closes her eyes succumbing to her fatal wound.

"Are you okay."

I blink at the trader, lifting my head. He takes a step back, slashing some kind of shape in the air, warding off evil and muttering about demons coming from hell to take all souls on earth, Cleo growls low in her throat. He shrieks and cowers in a corner, I walk out of the stall and mount Cleo, leading her to where I last saw her in the vision, praying that I'm not too late. Cleo grumbles, and I scratch her ears, she lifts her nose in the air sniffing, run faster towards the railway, she stops at something in the ground, the sand saturated in blood. I wonder how she stayed alive, even if there aren't a lot of Reapers around here. Her body was nearly buried in the sand; a few more hours, she would be fully submerged into the ground." Good girl".

It was the girl, Cleo gave a happy yip and licked her cheek. It elicited a small moan from her lips, I took a canteen from my saddle and put it to her lips.

" Drink." I command.

She took a small sip and turn her face away, coughing. I cap the canteen and put it back in the saddle." Cleo down girl," Cleo went on her haunches, dragging her slight but lithe body and onto Cleo's saddle. I slid in beside her, and Cleo bounded out of there. I pulled back her jacket and stared at her stomach wound. It looks pretty bad, I tore a section of my blanket, and wound it around her midriff, she will have to wait till I can find help for her.

Cleo lopes out of Mombess, heading out of the colonies, figuring that I should get out of there before I attract more trouble. Caravans lined everywhere, people chattered endlessly in multiple colored fabrics that were a sight to behold, a vibrant feast for the eyes. I push Cleo forward, screams erupt everywhere as we swerve amongst the people. The wind whips on my face, I held the girl tighter, and let Cleo run free, she will never let me fall, I trust her. I lost sight of the encampment, a mountain comes into view, it's ancient, rough outcropping a testament of humanity's iron will of survival, I stared at the pass, big enough for Cleo to run through freely. An arrow sails in the air, and struck on my left few inches from Cleo's feet.

A warning not to proceed further. I glance up, the sun's making it hard to make out anything. The shooter's a blur in my periphery, it's hard to see anything with the suns in glaring eyes. I clutch on to the collar of the girl, with the other, pull on Cleo's scruff, she rears back, and the arrow missed her by a hair's breadth. Figures materialized out from everywhere, they stood all around surrounding me high up on the mountain, all wore clothes with hoods on that blends into the mountain, glowing beads on their arms, I stop a growling Cleo intimidated by their swelling numbers.

"You are trespassing on our lands, girl, where did you get such a beast?" a figure on an enormous beast that looks a little like Cleo but much bigger and meaner says striding forward. His animal made this low growling sound in its throat, Cleo let loose hers. I put a reassuring hand on her head, and she went silent, giving me a look that shows her displeasure at stopping her natural impulse of showing her beastly side off, a show of dominance.

"There, girl, be good, and I promise to give you something good."

"Apologies." I lay a hand on my chest and extend it in his direction in the Kendulusun way of greeting." I 'm just passing through, I have someone who needs urgent help. This is Cleo, she is mine."

The man nods and hops off his beast, my breath stuck in my throat when he took off his hood, and I stared at the purest, resplendent-granite hair I have ever seen in my life, his ebony, glossy skin glints like a mirror. The aura shrouding him screams otherworldly, glowing eyes of the purest blade of grass, set in an age-defying face with not one line on it, except for the scar that starts from his brow to the corner of his lips, the embodiment of a vengeful god sent to earth. Rows of Arkor-beads lined his throat, arms, and legs, a large band of it encircles his bicep, another graced his deific head in the form of a circlet. A sizeable Arkor-diamond rested on his forehead, sitting between the perfectly arched snowy, perfect wings, eyebrows that Buma would be jealous of.

"Where are you from girl?"

"Kendulusa, a little far from here."

A murmur rose in the air, his gaze went to the girl in my arms, his eyes linger on the grey garbs she wore so different from mine." And her?"

"I don't know, I found her in Mombess, she needs help, so I helped her."

"Is she infected? If she is, we will have to take care of her."

"No! I mean, she is not, she is clean."

"Good, let me have a look at her."

I let him check the girl for any sign of cuts, or residue always left behind by the blade of a Reaper. His eyes snag on the corners of her eyes, he touched the dark crust that stuck to the edges and frowned. He nodded to himself and turned back to his mount.

"Follow me!"

I trail him into the cave, when my eyes adjust to the lighting. Covering every surface were Arkor diamonds, its brilliance stealing my breath away when I stared at their depths, holding the precious beads within them, bubbles float in the liquid. They led me into a bigger cave, a fire blazes in the center where glowy-eyed people huddle in groups. The room quiets down, excitement fills their eyes when they take stock of Cleo, the opposite reaction; I expected Fear was the first thing that people have in their eyes when they see her.

"You can put her here!" the man points at the fur spread on the floor. I put a hand onto Cleo's head, and she went down on all fours, two rangers took the girl from my arms and put her on the animal skin, I climb off from Cleo, and watch as they stripped her top revealing her ghastly wounds. Dark crust covers her bullet wounds, the same that crusted on the corners of her eyes. The two rangers share a look with the granite-haired man.

One of the rangers prod her wound searching for an opening but found none, one brought out a surgical kit and lay it on the floor. A silver marking etched on to her skin, the same on the granite-haired man's bicep caught my attention A ranger made a neat, surgical cut on her stomach wound. Another wipes the blood clean. He slid in the tweezers and pulled out the bullet coated with blood and ice. She gasped in pain, her eyes slid open, the ranger backs away, looking like he was burnt. Her eyes glowed the color of the purest blade of green grass the same as the man beside me. She lay back on the floor, and her eyes closed. A hand clamps on my shoulder, and I was spun around to face the ranger."

You brought a wielder here? I want to know everything you know about her?" The granite-haired man commands, a frightening urgency in his eyes.

"I found her in Mombess, double-crossed for a dagger by friends, shot by a master who claims that she stole the dagger from him, left to die out there. That's all I know about her."

"What is your name, child? What are you doing so far from your home?"

"I am Calla of Kendulusu, my home was attacked by ravagers. They took my mama."

"Is that all?"

"Yes, it is."

"I am Nusir, leader of the Oumali tribe, but to outsiders, we are called rangers. You are welcome to stay as long as you want if you choose to."

"You are most kind, Nusir, but I'm afraid that I must decline such a generous offer. Under different circumstances, I would have jump at the opportunity to do so; perhaps another time, I will take it. But there is something that I must do."

"Wisely chosen words Calla of the Kendulusu tribe, I hope to see the winds blow you our way one day."

"I hope so too."

A tall, beautiful woman made her way towards us, her dark hair in braids that hung past her shoulders adorned with Arkor diamonds, a glorious diadem made up of multiple colored Arkor-beads rests on her forehead. A long flowing Mbuba made up of a myriad of colors, patterns, and symbols stood out, slit on each side showing off her legs, beautiful sandals grace her feet adorn with Arkor on every surface. Her dark, flashing eyes missed nothing as she stared at the girl swath in furs.

"Veins of my heart, you called?" Her eyes linger on the silver mark on the girl's stomach and then fell on me. Her brows furrow, she met Nusir's gaze, he bows his head. Tears gather in her eyes, she puts a hand to her mouth.

"I never thought I would see this day Damseira, the winds have blown her our way."

"Come child, let me show you to your sleeping quarters." She collects herself, and once again, the regal, confident woman that had everyone enthralled by her mere presence. I follow her out of there with Cleo in tow staring at everything with dazed eyes.

"Here, we are!"

The large room is the biggest room I have ever seen; all around were people going about their business. Catwalks crisscrossed the room, leading deeper into the mountain. We were on one that was high up in the air, we walked into a corridor, passing people who gawked at us, she stopped at a door and turned the handle. It opened, revealing a Spartan room with a bed and a small built-in wardrobe that was part of the wall." This is your room, if you need anything, let me know."

"Thank you."

She nods and hurry out of there, I watch till she was out of sight. Then ran inside, Cleo squeezed herself in the room. I closed it behind me, and flop on the bed. I wonder if Mama and Kamili were still alive, things are getting harder and harder every time I thought that I had it figured out, it takes a new twist that leaves me reeling. Only to find out that my cardinal points have shifted. Whoever this girl is, they know something I don't. Maybe it is better if I don't know anything more other than what I know. Some things have a way of luring you in until you can never back out of it. I open my bag and pulled the sand-colored parchment out. The light glimmer from it, bathing me in its brilliance. Sighing, I roll it up and stuff it back in the bag. I can't figure out what the parchment's for, all I know is that none should get their hands on it only Mama.

How I wished that things were different. That I was back in our town, living the lives we were known for. I close my eyes, succumbing to the fatigue that has been plaguing me for some time. Perhaps when I wake up, the world would be better than it is right now. I know that it's surreal thinking on my part, a dream that I have to wake up from, but what could I do?

CHAPTER 35

YEGUN CITY

Kamili

The city comes into view; I stared at the long queue of people waiting to be let in. Taking the risk of dying, playing with the death and life card. Knowing that, if not chosen, they will be forced to stay out with the Reapers. I spur Namia faster, heading towards the gate.

"Delivery from Kendulusa."

"And what is it that you deliver?" the guard sneers, eying me up and down. His gaze stops at my chest more than once.

"None of your business, tell your mayor that we are here."

"I'm afraid, but we can't do that. So I recommend that you turn back and head the way you came here. the weather looks a little bit antsy." I ground my teeth in frustration, balling my fist I wish that I could slam it in his face, son of a cur. I stare up at the sky, which was turning darker every second that went by. My skin crawls, and I shiver, gaining Madi's attention. He lifts a questioning brow, I shook my head at him? I don't know what is going on here. Everything seems displaced and off. Screams fills the air; a guy run towards the gate. A hooded man jump him before he could reach us. Pandemonium broke out as people run for their lives.

"Open the gate." A man screams in fright, banging the gate, he crumples in a heap a bullet hole on his temple. People scatter in the opposite direction. I start forward and slam into a man head-on. His diseased eyes latched on to me, leaning back in my saddle. I slashed at him with my K-bar knives. I shot at one heading for a girl staring at everything in fright. I jumped off Namia and ran for her. Scooping her up in my arms. I lifted her up and ran towards a car. Sharp pain on my neck had me stop in my tracks.

I let go of her, Reaper-hooded eyes stare at me, a snarl rips out her mouth, I shook my head in disbelief as the little girl went on her haunches, ready to spring into action, a small blade lay nestled in her hand. How could that be possible? Reapers in daylight? Not the ones we encountered in Zubela, these ones don't need nightmare guy to turn day into night. I wrestle her off me and shot the Reaper between the eyes. I stem the flow of blood with a handkerchief, it will have to do until I can do something about it. I pull up the collar of my jacket and hurry to help. Rain pelts on my face, my body moves in a dance of death that I knew too well.

Eldres knew about this, and yet he sent us out here. What was the viper playing at? What was his end game? Does he hate me that much? Who were those people he was with that night I walk in on him, the people with the emblem of the hand holding a torch? What does it mean? Suddenly nothing seems simple anymore. This goes beyond hatred, a bloody thread that I knew that I had to follow and that I won't like where it leads and ends. Forget that all this happened, even if it means not everything would be the same? I have a feeling that all these have something to do with someone called The Baba. All I want is my family. The word tastes like Ambrosia on my tongue, and I increased my blade speed, going back to back with Madi. The others were doing the same. Using the turtle formation, working our way towards the center, and take care of the rest from there.

CHAPTER 36

SANDS & REGRETS

SUKUNDA

One year ago.

I don't know if splitting with the rest of the group was a good idea, but I knew that it gave us all a chance at escaping. It was a possibility that looks less likely as we journey farther away from Jufureh. We have been driving the monster truck for hours now; I don't know how long it will take before it runs out of fuel. A hand stops me, pulling me to the side. Motorbikes whizzed past us, I stared at Amisha who put a hand on her lips and pointed ahead of us, then she lay down on her side. I lay on my stomach and watched the men dismount and started combing for us.

"Negative, sir!"

"Fan out, I want all of them caught, not one less." Balla snarls, turning to the brown-skinned guy before him. He stood beside him, not saying a word, just observing. Beside me, Amisha gasps, staring at the water trickling down between her thighs, wetting the ground. I meet her frightened brown eyes. She bit her lip. Taking her hand, I help her up, Anushka takes hold of her other one, and together we start dragging her towards the cave. Heart in my mouth, I expect to be discovered any minute. In the cave, I released a sigh of relief and turned to go." Where are you going?"

"Someone has to get them away from there."

"You won't make it."

"I know, Amisha."

"Thank you!"

The bone weapon in hand I sneaked out of there. Covering our drag tracks that lead to the cave. I jump on one motorbike, footsteps ring echo behind me.

"Hands up, step away from the bike." A male voice intones behind me.

"You will not shoot me." I revved the motorbike towards him, he jumps out of the way, I sped for Jufureh. It wasn't long before I heard the several hums of motorcycles behind me.

The air pings as several gray pellets head for me, ropes shoot out of it, nets came to life. I try jumping out of it but it snap me in the air, the bike explodes, shrapnel flies in the air, one embedded into a motorbike's tire it went out of control, the guard on it went under, pinned underneath the machine. The two men dismounted their rides and hurry, where I lay trapped on the ground. I watched as the sand peels away and people approach weapons in hand. I don't know how they could achieve such a thing.

"Damn it, sandmen."

A sand-covered hand took hold of my net and drags me towards a manhole I didn't see before, I struggled, trying to get out of the net but I could not. The other sandmen attacked the guards behind me. I stared at the brown-skinned guy fighting with daggers. The blades fan out whenever he strikes at sandmen. His companions fought, but they soon fell. He stood, proud and tall. A true warrior that I knew might survive if he kept fighting like that.

The sandman drag me towards a manhole. He threw me down first, and this time I screamed my way down. My body thumped hard when it finally came in contact with the floor that I thought would never come. I wished I hadn't. Pain jolted into my very bones, tears came unbidden to my eyes, and I bit into my lower lip to muffle the sound. I groan. The sand-man, covered hand pressed the gray pellets, and the ropes shrink into it, I study the sand-covered man before me; he wore pants smeared with a coat of sand, his face a collection of scars, hair matted with sand, only the whites of his eyes and teeth flash. He grips my hair in a herculean grip and pull me up on my tiptoes. I sob, a cold blade went to my throat, and he barks harshly in a strange tongue.

I went limp and let him pull me in deeper, his eyes taunting me to just cry out or make any kind of move. Give him a reason to end me where I stand. A body thuds behind us, the sandman stops body stiffening, he shoves me back into a wall and hurried to the twitching body of a sandman. A figure lands in a perfect feline crouch, daggers out, his cloak flares out dramatically, I would have been impressed if I don't have something equally horrible waiting for me out there. Maybe I should just take the corridor and see what the sandmen would have for me. I meet eyes that hints at danger, and blood lust, I glance away. When I glance back, he and the sandman were engaged in lethal, mortal combat.

I step back, and his eyes snapped back to mine. In them was a warning to not take another step. I gritted my teeth and took another, whirring I ran, the sandmen fell down with a pained yell, and footsteps gave chase to me. I pumped my legs hard, pushing my limbs faster, I have to get out of here. Hands gripped my waist, and I kicked out hard. And was rewarded with a grunt. A smile came to my lips, and I was freed. I whip the blade out of my boot, and slash at him with blurring moves, I knew that it was an offensive move that gave not enough room to defend himself. But desperate times call for drastic measures, I'm not going back to Jufureh or anywhere else, that I am sure of. His hand shot out, gripping the blade, blood ran down the sides of the blade and drips to the floor. He throws the dagger away and lifts me up by my throat.

"Don't tell me that you'd rather die than be saved." He chokes me with his large hands, shaking my body like a rag doll. I gasped for breath when he let go of my throat; I stagger away from him and bump into a body. A rough sand-covered hand grabs me, I widen my eyes when I saw sand-covered figures streaming out of the corridors; they filled the room, weapons in hand.

I gulp.

Maybe I should have gone willingly. I watch helplessly as the guy relinquish his weapons; they weren't satisfied until he had piled everything on the ground, his accusing eyes set on me. I gave him mine back. If he hadn't come to help the raiders, we would not be in this messy situation. I stared at the arsenal of weapons on the floor and thought of why he would need so many weapons were beyond me. The huge sandman before him motions for his clothes to come off. He did so slowly, wearing a feral look I have never seen on anyone's face. He made sure to look in everyone's faces. A promise that he will make them pay. All of them.

I shiver.

They left only him with pants, half-naked. The sandman turn to me. His eyes linger on my intricate, multi-colored tribal tattoo of stars marked on my left cheek, and my braids. He said something to the men, eyes scouring my body in my tattered clothing. His men chuckle, I don't need someone to translate what I saw in their eyes; I gulp, almost hyperventilating.

My eyes seeks the guy's, he looks furious, a glare is all I got from him. Right, I forgot that he's blaming me for this incident. We were herded deeper into their sanctum; I stared at the walls of the tunnels, paintings graced the walls, showing different scenes. It has something to do with their everyday life. One scene claimed my attention, I stared at a sandman beheading the body of a man's, another shows bodies being chopped into pieces with an unerring intensity that made my heart shrank to the pits of my stomach. I pushed the bile back and lowered my gaze.

CHAPTER 37
ROTTEN PROMISES

SUKUNDA

ONE YEAR AGO

I sit in a cage, limbs shackle to the cage wall and stared blearily at the room. Shrieks brought goosebumps on my body; it's what woke me up. I would never get used to the screams, the death, and carnage that we were forced to watch, dreading that each hour that passes means ours is getting nearer. This makes me wish for Jufureh, at least in Jufureh, I don't get to be eaten like some animal. With the sandmen, we are food.

Cannibals!

I never thought that I would encounter such a thing in this fucked up world. No wonder father wanted our people to stay in our lands, and not stray out to these lawless lands, where everyone wants a piece of you. Here, we are their source of sustenance. Something that I vow I won't be. I had seen them dragging the corpse of the dead guards in the tunnels; they are not letting anything go to waste. My savior had twisted his face in a mask of fury when he had seen them cut up the bodies. Right now, those unholy eyes were directed at me in an intense glare that had me wilting under his unforgiving stare.

"Aren't you even trying to get us out of here?" I snapped.

"What's the hurry sweetheart, I thought you like it here?"

I smiled sweetly and rifled in my hair and pulled out a long, thin hairpin that made him hitch a brow at me. I fit it in the lock of one arm shackle and twist it gently. It opens and I turn to the other one, then made quick work of my legs. I stood up and stretched. Sighing in pleasure.

"Well, it was nice knowing you and all, I hope that you got a nice time with these savages, in fact, I hope that you turn out to be their dinner tonight, seeing as they are kind of running low and all." I hurried towards the cage door, my hairpin in hand.

One...Two.

"Wait!"

"Yes?" I turned around with a smug , an eyebrow arched.

"You won't make it out here alive without my help."

"Seriously, are you doubting my survival skills? I really don't need you, what's the use of getting you out of here when you are just going to take me back to become a whore for your spoiled master."

He winces, "What if I tell you I will let you go."

"You'll do that, hmm?" I crouch before him, drawing his eyes to my face.

"Yeah, I promise."

"Okay, deal."

'You believe me?"

"Hell no, I don't, but I can't let you die down here. This is a fate I wish for no one." I work on his shackles.

"Nice knowing that you care about me."

I snort at that, the lock of the cage clicks open, he steps out. Together we crept towards the exit. We were just inches shy from the end of a corridor when mister high and mighty slams me on the wall, lips descend on mine, I gasp in surprise, his tongue swept expertly in my mouth. I nearly passed out from sheer bliss. He pulls away when the footsteps faded away.

"Tasty."

"Jerk, " I send a flare to hide how rattled the kiss made me.

We hurry towards a group sand men drinking from a wooden gourd that lay on the floor a few feet away from them, a couple of sand women with them. A muscled hands stopped me, and I huffed at him in annoyance. His gaze linger on my lips, and I got the urge to bite his nose, just for the heck of it.

"Those are the guards; it should be pretty easy considering that they are already wasted."

"Cocky, are we now since you are out of the cage and not tied up and ready to be sand people chow, huh Mister fantastic?"

"Hamoul, the name's Hamoul, quit the name-calling."

"Not happening, Mr. fantastic."

He creeps towards the group, keeping to the shadows. He pounced on the first sandman, snapped his neck before he could make a sound, Hamoul pulls the knife from the dead sand man's belt and slits the nearest sandman's throat; he fell to the floor clutching his throat. The last of the sand man-made a drunken dash for it, Hamoul clips him deadly precision he went down without a sound.

With a finger to his lips, Hamoul turns to the three women, and they whimper, backing away. He held out his hand to the women and one of the three hands over the keys. I step out of my hiding place and join Hamoul at the door. He waved me through and he closes the door behind him. I quickened my pace, knowing that it won't be long before they detect us to be missing, that should buy us some time.

CHAPTER 38

I AM MASAN

Channeh

The slap has my ears ringing, and I grin at the ravager interrogating me. They think that they could break me, mold me into something for their own gain. What they wanted could change our world on a massive scale, and I wasn't ready to give it to them.

"Let's start again, honey."

"Where is it?"

"Somewhere you will never find it." The prod zaps my body. I would've doubled over in pain if I wasn't chained to the ceiling. One… two…. three… I see Calla smiling up at me, her eyes full of trust and childlike innocence. I kicked myself for not showing

Calla who she was. To show her what she's capable of, to hide her powers. I hope that she had made it. What about Kamili? I hate myself more for not telling her the truth, I just hope that she would not hate me when she finds out all that I have kept away from her, to see that I was protecting her. I stare at the tattoo of bracelet on my wrist and will it to disappear.

"Almost a century, I have looked for you Chey, you are a hard one to catch. I see that life's treating you really well."

"Well, I aim to please, Cheikh."

He chuckles, face thoughtful. I stared at the face that has been haunting me for years, every day that goes by was my victory because I knew that he had lost me.

I study Cheikh, and wonder where was the guy who wanted to change the world? I won't expose Kamili and Calla to a world such as this. When I lost Suleil, nothing mattered, only they did. Escaping with the essence was the most significant blow to them, the very one Cheikh wants to get his hands on. I would've given it to him if I hadn't known who he was walking with. And what he was? Cheikh crowds my personal space, a sharp finger trails down my cheek.

"I admire your loyalty Chey. Frankly, I don't know why you insist on fighting a lost cause. This war was lost centuries before you were born. The Baba has done the impossible; they walk in daylight now, and soon amongst men, he would amass them to the third world. And I don't see any Kunta stopping him, can you?"

"Just kill me and spare me the lecture."

"No, Chey, you know me better than that. Besides someone as great as you deserve a chance at freedom, don't you think? I won't let the last one of the ancients perish like that. As much as I enjoy talking to you, darling, I am a busy man, and I hate doing this to you." Cheikh went corporeal and passed through the wall.

A flash of skin catches my eye as the creature scampers away into the shadows again. The bastard has left me here to die, I grip my chain, gritted my teeth and pulled hard at the chains. The chain groans in protest, and I swing my body out of the way of the incoming silver-colored humanoid creature. It was once human, but now it looked like something taken out of a scientist's nightmare. What the hell was Cheikh creating down here? Well, what more could you expect from a twisted, half-Galaki' scientist? I whip my body to the side, I free-run on the wall and yank at the chain with all my might, it chain gives way, and I crash on the floor;

the creature was on me in an instant. It shrieks and we grapple on the floor, its nails scratches my face, I grip its throat and slowly lift it off the floor. Sharp, knife-hot pain burns my shoulder. Digging deep within me to the place that I haven't tapped in so long.

It doesn't surprise me, he has always been too power-hungry, ready to do anything if it promises the heady taste of power. I don't plan on dying here, I wouldn't let Cheikh win, I wonder how he had joined the ravagers, climb up their ranks to be their leader. I tap into it and blast the silver-colored damnation away from me, it slams on the wall and fell, it didn't get up again.

A savage thrum sings in my veins, I pull the needle out from my arm, and walk deeper into the bowels of the sanctum, ignoring the plethora of screams emanating out from within. There are more waiting for me. Twin laser whips materializes in my hands, casting shadows on the wall. A panther-like creature covered in feathers snarls at me from the left, I crack my whip. And it rears on its back paws, I spring into motion and meet it halfway in the air. My whip slice through its stomach, its two halves fell on the floor, bullets pepper my way, and I tuck and roll on the floor and take cover in a corridor.

"No one gets out of here alive" a hoarse voice rasps out from deep within the shadows, I made out a figure sitting on the floor, his back to the wall. I meet sunken, feverish, bright eyes set in a gaunt face, it was a man, his body that looks like he just crawled out of a grave.

"Not me, I will get out."

"Ooh an optimistic," he claps, a smile cracking on his gaunt face." Well, I have not seen one for some time, see sweet cheeks, you aren't the only person who thought that they could get out of here."

He scoffs, laughter rattling from deep within his chest, the awful sound grates on my nerves. He puts a bony finger to his lips as if in deep thought, stared at it, then he broke out in gales of laughter that had my lips turned up at his antics." Lady, when I said that no one gets out, I meant it because none does, this place is death. I have tried everything possible in the last two years, and yet I am still stuck here."

"Maybe you didn't try everything." I bit out, striding past him, I am getting out of here, and there is nothing in seven hells or heaven that could keep me here, away from my children.

"Where are you going?"

"Just follow me, partner you might just be in luck today."

"Nutty."

It was my turn to scoff," So says the one stuck in here, I think that term suits you more than I. who has spent two whole years in this place. I hear that solitude tends to make people go a little stale upstairs, then bulb's out."

"I am Masan."

"Channeh,"

"Channeh, from where?"

"Not your concern, mister."

"Very well, lady this way!"

I stop in my tracks and stared at Masan; he points at a door. I don't know if I should follow him, but what are the odds that he might just be a trap of some kind for me? I stared at the figure, weighing him and my chances of getting out of a scrape.

"I know that you don't know me, but maybe you should just take a leap of faith and trust me to get out of here. I have found a way out of here, but I don't dare to try it yet, waiting for the perfect opportunity, so I guess you might be my perfect opportunity for getting out of here." he gestures and hurried inside.

"Nicely phrased," Swallowing my uncertainty, I lope towards the door; it revealed stone stairs that go down, holding a blade in hand I inched deeper inside, following Masan's uneven gait, he favors his left leg more. His clothes in tatters have seen better days. I just hope that this doesn't come to bite me right in the ass. A snarl rips in the air, and my muscles tensed, and I hasten my pace.

" They are here, come on, make it fast, inside." Masan squeaks in fright.

"Who?"

"No time to explain."

I step in the room, and he bolts it close, I take a mental inventory of the room, I turn to Masan, and a fist slammed into my face hard, blood spurts out of my nose and I stumble back. He licks the blood that coats his hand and close his eyes in morbid delight. His body shudders, and he moans going on all fours, I take a step back when he opens his eyes and released a shriek that made my blood run cold.

What the heck?

"Shit."

The creature before me didn't resemble Masan, in his place crouches a creature that looks at the three drops of blood with a hair-raising intensity . I wonder what the hell was Cheikh experimenting on in here? I knew him to be dangerous and would do anything to have power, and the world in his palm. What I didn't realize that he was ready to take steps, that both of us knew that there is no backing out. Once done, it's done. You just have to live with it. No room for regret, I thought that I knew him, but I was wrong. This shows it all, I knew that he was using the book he stole to carry all this out, all Cheikh wanted were the resources, and he had gotten it. All he had needed was me. Where was the guy who tried to save the world with me? The one who wanted to right all wrongs done to us? To the world?

"Leap of faith, humans are so gullible." The thing that was Masan moments ago hisses , the gaunt look wasn't totally gone he looks a little less thin than before, blue veins stood out on his arms and forehead, his eyes have gone night sky. It hiss and rears back, wiry muscles tensed and bunched, ready to spring into action. I waited for it on the balls of my feet, another hissed had me whirring round just as another creature slinked out a dark crevice, this one definitely female, her hair hung in clumps around her shoulders, it looked dead and limp, showing her dead, dry scalp. More stepped out, circling me, closing from all sides. Laser whips in hand, I waited for them; I know that the chances of getting out of here alive are slim, but I would take my chances, no matter how narrow they are, I'm not letting these bloodthirsty creatures bring my untimely demise. They would attack any second, I could see it in their crazed, murderous eyes. Tensed, poised bodies, ready to attack any moment.

"Halt children."

CHAPTER 39

DARKLINGS

Channeh

They back away, a whining sound welling from deep within their throats. The man strode forward. Eyes hidden behind shades, slowly they made their way to where he stood, Masan hugs his leg, running his cheek on his pant leg while the guy pats his head, his eyes vast pools of adoration. My eyes scour the room, looking for an escape route, each one I find is being blocked by the creatures. I stared at the endless doors that extended upwards towards a vast ceiling that was way far. I stared at the winding stair that went round and round, all the way to the ceiling. All packed with the abominations before me, more creatures poured out of the surrounding doors to surround us.

"I believe that I have never had the pleasure of meeting one of you! I have heard so much about you, oh yes, the one who started everything." he took off his glasses and polish them with a pristine, white handkerchief, his gray, pale eyes fixed on me. It was meant to make me feel at ease, I was anything but. Anticipation buzz on my skin. All I want to do is just turn on all of them and kill them, I felt threatened. But I held on to the sliver of control I still grasp and try not to give in to the destructive thoughts swirling in my head.

"What do you want?"

"What everyone wants? What you are not ready to part with, the only thing that could help us in our crusade."

"Crusade? I was not aware that Cheikh is leading a crusade now."

"Yes! They were part of the crusade, but something went wrong on the way, and they turned into these creatures all because we thought that we had the right thing, definitely not." He gestured at the creatures that were jostling amongst themselves to be near him.

"Is master angry, master should not be angry!" one of them whined out.

"No, my beautiful, Master isn't angry; you have done a great job, master will reward you greatly."

"Would master give the pretty lady to us." The creature grins up at him, revealing jagged, serrated, black, glass-like teeth. The guy smiles down at her fondly, stroking her head, God, I'm ready to retch. He didn't miss the disgust clearly written on my face, this is the most disgusting thing I have ever seen in my whole life.

"If she doesn't cooperate, yes, master will give the lady to you to play as you like."

The creature claps her bony hands in glee; I took a step forward to just end her or show her that the only one who would do the playing would be me, and no one else. I calmed down and turned my gaze to the man who was studying me with great interest.

"So, whatever I have will fix this?"

"No, it's a little complicated, the Darklings are far too gone to change back, we will have to have another new crop."

"I see; by another new crop, you mean to make more of those. I don't have it."

"Think about it, Channeh, with the essence in our hands, we could fix all this, we don't have to be enemies, you know. We are allies with a common enemy, and the enemy of my enemy is my friend, you know that they will never stop hunting you or your family, and from what I know it has just started soon it will scratch the surface if we join forces we could defeat them, and create something better than this."

"True, but you or I don't have the right to play God. The world does not need more monsters, it needs a savior to save it before it goes to hell, and right now we are teetering towards a hellish abyss. "

"I knew that you would be difficult, I hated that I have to be the one who does this to you. Cheikh had told me that you were iron-willed, I had thought that I could change your mind with a more diplomatic approach. We will find it with or without your help, I hope that you are fast and good as the stories say you're."

His gaze fell on the creatures who have fixed their eyes on me with an unerring, hungry intensity that had goosebumps spread all over my exposed skin." Because you will need all the speed in the world."

I give him a curt nod, letting him know that I will accept this gladly, but I will not forget this, because once I have my family, I will hunt him down, kill him and deconsecrate his pathetic body. I watch him back from the room. I faced the darklings, and watched as their faces morphed into that of monster's, snarls emanated out of their throats, as if acting on a single command they attack fast, I whip out my laser whips catching one in the shoulder; it yelps and fell to the floor, shook its head like a dog and struck again. I vault in the air kicking out at one, claws raked my bare shoulder, and I slashed my whip out, cutting off its arm before it could retract it back. They were an endless wave of claws and teeth; I jump on the wall, flipped, and land on one's back, slashing its throat before it could react. Masan barged into me, we went flying in the air and smashed into the wall, I rolled out of the way of his claws as they descend towards me. I kicked out and stood up, pain jolts my shoulder, I cried out, brushing the darkling off me, bury a blade between its eyes. I whipped the whips out in a loose circle, holding them off at bay; the air whooshed out into a crescendo. I cracked out my whip and let go; it sailed in the air and stops at the lid.

"Ready to die?" I pulled the small grenade, Masan hissed out, closing in with the rest I pulled the pin free and threw it at his feet, one of them lifted it sniffing, Masan's eyes widened, and he opened his mouth to warn the creature, but it was too late, muscles bunching, he springs for the door. The blast rang out, the force field shrouded my body, I slowly stood up, legs shaking. I hurried out of there, shrieks following me, but fortunately, they stayed to the shadows.

CHAPTER 40

DAY WALKER

Kamili

Coated in the blood of the newest trend of Reapers. I don't know if I should call them Reapers. These new ones are stronger, faster, and smarter than the Reapers. They have undergone some kind of evolution. They're not like the ones we encountered in Zubela; the suns do nothing to them. They are day walkers, our worse fear immortalized in the flesh, the suns are no longer our weapons. No longer our ally and protector. I led Namia through the gates of the city. A guard escorts us into the base I stared at the people training, he leads us past a mess-style hall, and into another huge room where a man sat behind an enormous mahogany desk. He smiles when he saw us. The smile never reaches his eyes.

"At last, I thought that you will not make it, I'm sorry for what you have to face outside. Glad to know that you survived it."

He didn't sound sorry, his eyes said otherwise again, that's a trap for us, I give him a curt nod, suitcase in hand." We are just here for delivery, "

"True, but I insist that you stay and rest for a day, at least."

"Thanks, but no mayor, we have to get back," Muna says, her hand twitching on the blade at her thigh.

"I'm sorry, but I must insist."

He rose up in one smooth motion, gun aimed at my head; I eyed his ring with the flaming torch etched on it and kept him in my sights as he walked around the table to where I stood. I didn't have to look behind me to see that he got men with guns trained on the rest of my group. I feel like a fool for not noticing them, so engrossed in delivering and going back home to my family. I should've been able to see that coming, and not too fixated my my desire.

"What the hell is going on?"

"What do you think?" Eldres steps into the room, the same broad, smug smile I always want to wipe off plastered on his face.

I still do.

"What are you doing here, Papa?"

"Take everyone except him, as much as I am mad at you. I will not condemn you to such a damnable fate Saliu, you are my blood."

Two guards drag Saliu towards the doorway. He slugged one in the gut and slashed at the other's throat. He turned to his father, whose face contorts in rage, he points his gun at Saliu and squeezed the trigger, shooting his son in the stomach. Saliu screams and went down, clutching his bullet wound.

"Now, where were we?" He blows the tip of his gun then aims it at me.

I moved fast and lunge at Eldres. I barely felt the bullet when it clips me in the shoulder, I shot at the chandelier on the ceiling and took cover when it came crashing down. It takes a guard under; I down another guard, going back to back with Muna we drifted towards the exit. A dart soars in the air and sunk into my neck, I yanked it out. I stared at the slender needle at the tip of the dart and the mass of filaments writhing from it, eager to embrace my veins, more came for us, Brime went under an assault of darts, he never stood up. My heartbeat slows, and I narrow my eyes at where the darts sail towards me.

Knowing that they don't plan on killing us chilled me to my bones, what fate would they've stored for us? Moro crumples next. I stride in the center of the corridor we have retreated into; I bring another guard down with my shotguns. Sprinting on the banister, I twist a guard's neck. Another dart is shot into my neck, I cursed out, and pull it free. Muna crumples on the floor, and my heart sinks. Sweat trails down my forehead, I whip out of the way of the incoming harpoon; it sailed in the air and embedded in the wall. The guard before me smirked, pulled it free, and slung the harpoon at me again, I dodged it diving out of its way.

It cut into my cheek, blood splashes on my clothes. Madi belts a warning, but it was too late, I turned around trying to move out of its way when it boomerangs back towards me. I shoot at a sniper nestled on the left side. My body slams in the wall with a sickening crash, the wall shattered and rained down on me; I groan in pain, sitting up. My eyes widen on the incoming weapon cruising my way, I roll out of its way, blood coats my clothes, sticky and warm. In a crouch, I put weight on the tips of my fingers and toes and spring out in the air, shotgun in hand, I shot at the chain, and kick the harpoon. It slam into him, his body went air borne before tumbling in a heap. Liquid fire filled my veins, and I went down crying out. A hand grips my hair and tilts my head back. I meet the dark eyes of a guy in jeans, a metallic yellow T-shirt, a beautiful leather jacket, and combat boots. A tattoo of a dragon sat atop his sharp cheekbones, his dark eyes devour me.

Another bronze-skinned guy, with close-cropped hair, stood far behind, his hands outstretched, cold-heat emanates in waves from his fingertips. The liquid-fire reaches my head, and my world explodes into tiny fragments, sliding my hands into my boots I slashed at the guy's wrist, and roll out of reach. He curses, and attacks with a spinning kick, a knife-punch went to my gut. I groan, stumbling back a little. Scales simmer on his skin, claws sprout. His features takes on a reptilian look, golden eyes glared at me with a predatory fury. Let him do his worse. I'm not yielding; I smile, K-bar knives in hand, feeling a little woozy but not letting my body succumb to the whole baggage of aches. I have only one go at this, I have to make it count. We rush at each other; I pounce first with a roundhouse kick, his claws counter my blades with surprising ease. He flings my body at the wall; I rebounded and decked him, my legs scissor around his throat cutting off his air flow. I cling to him, and flip us in the air and lodge my blades deep into his neck.

He rakes claws on my biceps, snagging my arm and throws me out the window. Glass rains down as my body made the slow descent down to the ground. Whatever they put in the darts kicked in at last and the world blurs as I hit the ground, my body broken and battered an explosion went off in the distance.

CHAPTER 41

MALAKI'

Kamili

I lay on an alabaster-white table, my hands cuffed to the sides. Five more tables lined beside me. Bright light floods the room, I squint as my eyes try to adjust to the powerful lighting. A drip holding a clear gray liquid slid down drips in my veins, with every drop in the the tube, I fight the urge to scream bloody murder; it feels like my veins were set on liquid-fire. The bite wound on my neck throbs viciously, I gritted my teeth and forced the pain away. Footsteps approach, and I closed my eyes, peeking through lashes, I stared at the man with the mayor in tow. He switches on a screen on the wall, a woman's face fills the screen. She has the most beautiful cocoa brown skin I have ever seen, her features were above average, she would have been a dream if I haven't looked into her soulless eyes and a nightmare peeks back .There's no humanity. Endless, fathomless death stared back at me.

A hand holding a flaming torch was on the left of her white lab coat.

"Yes, Ifem, what do you have for me?"

"Two of them are first gens, progenies of Malaki', I'm not sure about her yet, will do only if we run some tests on her"

Her gaze flick over us, where it lingers goosebumps spread to life " Ifem,"

The man lifts his head to look at her" Don't let her turn, I want security increased, nothing comes in or goes out without my knowledge. I'm on my way," she says. The screen went blank.

I have to get out of here. I pulled at the cuffs, raising myself on my elbows." Don't bother, these are reinforced steel made especially for Malaki' and Genimions."

"Genimions?'

"Lab-bred enhanced humans, you, my dear are a progeny of a Malaki, a pure-bred that no lab can create, trust me we've tried.."

"You got the wrong people, none of us are what you say."

I try not to squirm under his gaze ,he pushes his glasses up his nose and turn back to write on his board.

"The test's never wrong, sweetheart, how long have you had this red hair?"

"None of your concern."

"Let us go." Brime whispers hoarsely.

"Can't do, let me see this one. Hmm, definitely a progeny." He trails a gloved hand on Muna's cheek.

My gaze went to the suitcase on the table, he tracks my gaze and grins.

"Aaah the delivery, a good move on Eldres part. We need test subjects, and you all fit the bill. Having progenies only sweeten the deal."

"You won't get away with this,"

"Already did kid, you are ours lock, stock and barrel. Nothing could change that, it is a dog eat tail world, but only bigger dogs would survive because they would eat the weak dogs. So don't make this harder for you and me, submit to what we have in store for you." He whispers as he punches in numbers on the small panel . The suitcase clicks open, and I stared at the vial that contains strange looking symbols swirling in its depth . And wonder why did we have to risk our necks for a vial no bigger than my thumb, he caressed the vial lovingly.

"You bag of Reaper shit." Muna glowers from where she lay, for a moment the room felt charged with static, the table shakes, objects clatter and fall down on the floor. Then it stopped abruptly as it started.

"Wonderful," Ifem whispered, his face reminiscent of a kid given a treat. He strides off writing on his clipboard, and I shifts my gaze to Muna, who avoids my gaze. I felt like she had dug us in a deeper hole than she had meant to, whatever that static was.

His footsteps fade away, and I turned to Muna." We need to get out of here."

Muna mutters a curse, and I give her a weak smile

"What are you?" Saliu asked hotly.

"None of your concern?" Muna hissed back with a deathly glare.

"It is when you are the reason why we will die soon; do we have anything to fear from you?"

"I'm not the one who orchestrated this, maybe you should ask your damn father why the hell he would make us come all the way here to be guinea pigs?"

"That is enough guys, we can't have us bickering amongst ourselves and not think of a way out of this mess, it does not matter whose fault it is. Remember that all of you followed me here because you wanted to. You could have chosen differently, but yet you sacrificed everything to come all the way here for that I can't thank you enough, I'm asking you to see the bigger picture and let us survive to see the end together, just follow me one last time."

"Kamili is right, this is the very thing expected of us, I really don't care what Muna is. For all I care she could sprout a tail or something more bizarre than I have ever seen, she is still the girl I know and right now being negative does nothing good for me." Madi says softly.

"Thanks, guys, thanks for accepting me!" Muna whispered, a lone tear trails out the corner of her eye.

I give Madi a grateful smile, and he sends me one of his own heart-melting smiles.

"I'm so sorry Muna," Saliu whispers eyes downcast.

"I am too." She whispers back.

I sighed in relief, having averted something that could be a problem stopping us from not being able to get out of here. Fighting amongst ourselves should be the last thing we should do right now. That's the very thing anticipate; we shouldn't give them any reason to use us like this.

CHAPTER 42

THE SERPENT HAS EATEN IT'S TAIL

Jelika

The human skulls mounted on wooden poles should be warning enough, I thought. Blyte grips my hand tighter as we walk closer into the vast barren territory. Skeletons of humans and horses were littered everywhere, I clutch my blade tighter. We have been on the run nonstop for days. Fatigue fans my body, my body demands that I quit, but I moved on. Every single one of us weary, but we kept moving. I think that it's in our genetic makeup to endure almost everything. We are practically indestructible, our endurance could outlast ordinary people's, a testament of the skeletons we found littering the desert.

I stared at the hills looming above, unease creeping up on me. The trail leads through between the two hills, vines crept on the ground, nature reclaiming back what it lost. It looks different from the desert, a different world. A growl rips in the air, and we stop trying to detect where it came from. We take cover behind a rock, our only best option for protection in this place. Another growl rippled in the air, echoing all around. A gigantic beast strode a bloody limb between its jaws. Blood drips down from its maw to the ground, leaving a bloody trail that heads towards our hideout. It stood on its haunches sniffing the air, grunting, then it went on. Another growl raises the hairs at my nape. I dodged its swipe. The beast in front of us stopped and looked at us, it threw what it had between its jaws then leaps for us.

The other one behind us growled out then the two slam into each other fighting over us. The beasts clawed at each other, claws rip into skins. Biting each other, it's a game of dominance, of survival. It's going to be the winner who takes it all.

"Psst.

"Over here."

We hurry towards the woman beckoning to us; I scrutinize her and just stared. She had beautiful red hair, enchanting, bright blue eyes the most vivid I have ever laid eyes on. Coupled with the smoothest ebony skin. Her body's lean and womanly, lightly muscled, and curvy. An air of lethal, sensual danger hovers around her, I met Zen's eyes, in them I could see that she thinks, what I believe, she was not normal, an average person would not survive without their body paying the price, she's unscathed.

"Who the hell unlocked the pandora box?"

"What do you mean?"

"Those creatures were never here; they must have come from a lab." She pins us with burning bright, blue eyes, those eyes told me that it knew who we are, that they had seen a thousand horrors that transcends ours, and that we would never understand her demons. A screech fills the air. When I looked back one of the beasts lay on the ground dead, the other turns around and growls, ready for his buffet. The woman nocks an arrow and let it fly at the creature; it hit its side with startling accuracy. It blurs hurdling for us; a gunshot blast in the air, hitting the beast it was just inches from the woman I turn around to confront his shooter. Five people stand behind us dressed all in dark shimmery clothes, wearing helmets, dark visors hide their faces.

Even without the crest of Olympus, I knew who they were, Kaima must be really desperate to get us back if it meant sending enough manpower to take out a couple of settlements. But still, their mere sight made my heart rattle in my chest. They have found us; the creature heads for them. They stood their ground waiting. Waiting for what? My answer came when the beast stopped in its track and bellows, clawing at its belly. An explosion rocks fans out and heads towards where we stood. But it didn't reach us, a pink force field enveloped us in a warm cloud, bring it to a halt. She's one of us. The woman meets my eyes, a grim set to her mouth.

"Run when I tell you to, don't look back head for the resistance, tell them that the serpent has eaten its tail."

"We can help."

"No, not with these, you won't last a minute with them, now go before I change my mind damn it."

We nod. My eyes went to the group before us, they look menacing. Maybe we should help her out. She can't possibly take them all by herself. She closes her eyes; the air ripples, two laser whips materialized in her hands with streaks of red and silver running in them. She opened her eyes. They fizzles with power. Every hint of her humanity gone, in it, was the savage urges of a predator. Her jaw set, she leaps effortlessly towards them. I turn with the others and run out of there. Behind us, a battle rages as the blue-eyed goddess fought off the five, I know that she might not win, every second she fights is a second we are out of Kaima's grasp.

CHAPTER 43

OF ARENAS, SMOKE & GLORIES

Jelika

I don't know if leaving the woman behind to face the five was the best decision. I stared at the cave we are in; it seemed like the only way to make it out of there filled with creatures that I think I had released unknowingly. The bones littering the ground should have given us pause to think twice about going into unknown territory. But going back isn't an option that we are ready to entertain. Feet pad lightly behind us, I stared at the spear stuck in the wall, with the skeletal hand hanging on its tip from a rope of hair and human teeth. Zen pulls the spear free, flames dance in her eyes. A chuckle echoed in the dark, more footsteps reverberate in the cave.

Zen's inhale of pain is followed by the swish of steel, pain flares in my thigh, my knees gave way, nets swathe our bodies imprisoning us in their embrace. Torches blink to life, and I stared at the people before us. The ones in front held spears, swords hanging from their waists, we hang in cages suspended in the air created out of rope-like vines thicker than my forearm. A man in a long coat strode forward, staring at us with his dark eyes that held no hint of humanity. His hair tumbles down his back in long, snaky dreadlocks.

"Hmm, this one will fetch a good price." He said, trailing a long fingernail on Blyte's forearm. His gaze land on Zen.

A grin blooms on his face when his eyes fell on Zen. He gestured for one of his men to open her cage. He did so, pulling on one of the three levers on the left side of the cave. Zen came tumbling down, spitting expletives the whole way down. The man licked his lips, gaze alight . She punches him when he touch her curls, he bares her shoulder to expose the flaming torch that we all had etched on our skins. He clutches his nose and stumbled back He grins and then punch her back." A lively one, eh, every catch has one. This one has a spirit, and I like it very much." He cups himself, and his men chuckle. He lifts Zen off her feet and nod at his men, the darts withdraw and fell off her body.

I wait for Zen to torch him, but nothing happened; I tried to call forth my power, but no pale-fire answers. I meet Blyte's eyes, the same in mine mirrors his; I know how helpless he felt because I felt it too. She spits on his face. He wipes off her spittle with a snigger, she kneed him in the groin. He drops, like a thrown stone. Letting go of her, she slowly got up, wavering on her feet.

"Wished you hadn't done that."

"Well, I did."

"That you did." He moves towards her, and she dodges his attacks scoring a few of her own, a kick to her midriff had her crashing onto the cave wall hard, a spider web of cracks appear on it, she slid to the ground into a boneless heap.

"I'm no match for you kid, now all you three are going to make us all rich men." A wicked chuckle escaped his lips. He pulls out a dagger and tease her throat with it, then licks its tip drawing his own blood. "A good day's catch, boys."

Sickened, I watch as they knock Zen out and dragged her out of there. "You don't know what you are doing."

"Oh but I do, get ready we are going on an adventure, something that you will like very much, I promise."

A man pulls the two other levers, and we fell to the floor, held us down before we could move, weapons aimed at us. Hands tied us, I was slung on someone's shoulder like a sack of cassavas. I didn't bother fighting, knowing how futile it is to do so. I stared at the world upside down, Blyte was another story. He struggled until they knocked him out cold.

The men hurry towards horses saddled outside, a cart tied to two horses sits in their midst, they deposit the twins in; I was unceremoniously thrown in, my head bangs on the edge of the cart, I bit my lip, and ignore the pain. With a twitch of the reins, the horses head towards the hills, I wonder what's out there. I stared at everything with new eyes. Not used to seeing things like this, I never thought that topside would be like this, heck I made a mistake of not thinking about the dangers here if people lived here, and now we are to see firsthand what happens when you get caught.

I just hope that the other Arkers were faring better than we are right now. These men knew about us, they knew about Olympus, about our abilities. And they have found a loophole to render our powers useless; I don't know for how long, but I just hope that it does not take long because I'm itching to obliterate them all to bloody pieces. What does the blue-eyed lady mean when she said to go to the resistance and tell them about a serpent eating its tail? It sounded cryptic, and it made neither heads nor tails to me. Does it mean that people are fighting Olympus? Just how powerful is Olympus topside? We have to find some answers fast before things get more complicated than they are. The dome's the first thing that came into view, the cheering was unmistakable, something challenging to miss, I don't want to know what was happening behind those massive walls, guards stood on watchtowers scanning the landscape.

"Welcome to precinct Five, baby cheeks, take a good long look because once you are in, there is no coming out."

"You will pay for this." I meant every word I utter.

He titters and turns his gaze back on the road. The gates yawn open, a man in a black tank top and camouflage pants stomps towards us. "What have we here, Teki?"

"Hey, Keva, my man, something I know you will love."

The man lifts a brow at him, Teki jumps down and roughly drags me from the cart, I glared daggers at him, then turn my gaze on the man. Teki bares my shoulder, showing the man my mark of Olympus in white ink.

"Does that mean something Teki, the last time you brought merchandise claiming that they have some kind of ability, and I had it sic against my dreads, they didn't last a second, Bengala was livid and nearly had my head, you know how sensitive he is on being perfect. I still want your balls for my units, I won't waste my money on you."

"These are the real deal."

"Hmm, how do I believe you?"

"You don't, I will stay here as oath until you see what they can do. The crowd will love these ones. I know that once you see these three in all their glory, you will want more."

"Okay, we have a deal. Get them inside, I will have them as fodder, if they don't survive I will have your balls for wasting my time."

"That is my man, I knew that we will see eye to eye."

Keva shakes his head and hurry inside. Sutokoba is huge, way bigger than I had first thought it would be, I stared at my two unconscious companions and hope that they wake up soon, because I don't know what Keva meant by the fodder part. Blyte and Zen were dragged, I glare at the guy dragging their bodies on the rough ground. He gives me a toothy smile. We wander into a dark corridor, cells lined on each side. A girl snarl and lunges at the bars, spittle drips down her face, the beads in her hair clacking together with every shake of her head, a song of her ill intentions, a guard stuns her with a his prod, she shudders and collapses on the floor.

"Want some baby cheeks?" Teki whisper in my ear. I turn my gaze away from the writhing mess and glare at the man.

" It's not too late to free us, because I promise you that you'll be dead if I get my hands on you."

"Oh, I'm shaking in my boots, I have heard that a lot little girl, and here I am because few survive this place, and even when they do, what makes you think that they are the same? Once you are in, there's no room for revenge. Just survival. Out here, survival is king, bow to it, and you'll live."

"I will have mine."

"I'll be waiting for you baby cheeks, "he blows me a kiss.

I huff and got in the small, cramped lift. At my feet lay the unconscious twins. Damn it, I need them awake, this is going to make this harder than it should be. I toed Zen in the stomach, but she didn't move. Bright lights focused on us and I squint .

"What do we have here people, you all know that only Sutukuba has the answers that you seek, is it gore you seek? The impossible? We have everything and more." a voice rumbles from speakers.

I squint at the crowded stands, all staring down at me.

"I hope you know your game, and now ladies and gents, get ready for the one and only Prince of the dreads, an undefeated champion, groined from the darkest of hells. The likes of which you have only seen in here." I stared at the people peppered out on the sands beside me, a girl stared at me with frightened, huge eyes. A man clutches a woman's hand. His face says that he would rather die than he let something happen to her. It's sweet and foreign to me. Love, it shone in their eyes. It shouldn't be ended here. A growl rips in the air, the crowd went wild at that. The massive gates swing open, and a creature I have never seen or knew existed loped out.

Roped, carved muscles rippled on its form, the colossal creature, It's face hideous and nightmarish, slits for nostrils and a wicked, sharp-looking tail, a bald head, a forked tongue licks the air, and it growls, muscles bunch, juddering, gearing to spring into action, and end us all. It springs at us, egged on by the crowd. A girl screams and run in the opposite side of the arena. I wish that I had Zunai f arrogant jerk or no. "Hey, foul face, you want some of me?"

It swings its gaze to me, stalking to where I stand.

"Well, come and get me."

It bounds forward with a deafening roar. I pirouette out of its way when it swiped at me with claws so long you could have a collection of blades from them.

A glimmer caught my attention. A blade lay on the sand. Red, hot fire jolt my back. I helplessly sailed in the air and thud on the ground. The dread snarled in victory; it stared back at the people cowering in the arena, then turned back to where I was crawling on the arena ground towards the blade. I could never make it to the sword, not with the damn creature hurtling for me, expecting its dinner. I dig deep, calling forth my power, my soles went hot, my body blasts forward, the dread crashes, trampling where I lay moments ago. White-flames streams out of my already ruined boots, blade in hand I attack, it swats me, and I plummet to the ground. The crowd went wild, calling out for blood. Whose? I have no idea.

On the ground, the twins stirred. The dread turns around momentarily forgetting me, Zen's eyes widens taking everything in trying to get her bearings .I'm too far away to get to them before it does. With a burst of silver-fire, I sped towards it, Zen's eyes could only gaze at the advancing creature. A figure drops down from the stands and onto the arena. Cracks spread outwards where he lands. He barrels into the dread. I skid to a halt and watch as the guy takes on the dread, the crowd got wilder than ever as they screamed out suggestions betting on who would emerge the winner.

The guy rips the dread's hand, it let loose a screech that shook the arena, its second limb got ripped off next. I flip in the air, land on its back, and thrust my blade in its back; it tried to shake me loose. I grip the handle of the blade harder and pushed down with all my might; the blade sinks in, bluish-gray liquid seeps out.

"How the hell did you get caught?" Zunaif scowls face painted bluish-gray.

I nearly let go of the hilt of the blade, "You escaped."

"All thanks to you, it's because of you I am enjoying a whole, brave, new world of possibilities, this is better than the boring combat class we have."

He rips off the dread's long, whiplash tongue and threw it at the crowd. They fought over the souvenir. In a quick move, he slashes at the dread's neck; I jump out of the way, hands caught me, Blyte;

he grin and land us on a giant mound of sand, our faces inches' apart, his breath fans on my face, tickling my senses. I wrap a hand round his neck and kissed him.

"What was that for?"

"Let's just say that it's for saving me from having a lot of broken bones." I chuckle.

"Get a room guys, I am ready to throw up. What do you say we have a repeat?" Zunaif wiggles his eyebrows at Zen.

Zen makes her way to him; he takes a step forward, face hopeful. She put a hand round his neck and pull him closer and decked. "How about this."

I snigger, Zunaif collapsed, his face a mask of pain. Blyte lowers us on another mound of earth, still cradling me in his arms. "You know that you can lower me."

"I enjoy having you in my arms."

"And that Ladies and Gentlemen is the fight of the century, I don't know if I will see such a thing again in this cursed lifetime."

Multiple-colored smoke fills the arena, misting it in a thick cloud. I put a hand on my nose and try holding my breath. Smoke filters into my nose forced its way into my lungs, my eyes water. I cough, my knees give out under me.

Beside me, Blyte places a hand on the ground. Calling on his power, but only a handful of sand creeps up his hand. He looked at me, eyes helpless and panicked.

Somewhere in the arena, Zen coughs and screams bloody murder. Zunaif tries fighting, but soon his struggles ceased, and his body hit the ground with a thud. My sight fizzles and form, changing every second that went by, Blyte's hand envelopes mine, and I gave him a soft smile. Figures with gas masks step out of the smoke, the one in front nods his head, and they lifted my and Blyte's bodies into the fly-ships.

CHAPTER 44

SPIRIT & SINS

SUKUNDA

ONE YEAR AGO

The lying, son of a witch, lied. He lied, so Balla did catch up to my presence. My cheeks are still smarting from his slaps. I ogle the charred, skeleton building and meet Balla's vicious glare that already tells me how he feels about my presence. I overheard Hamoul tell Balla that we will be staying the night until dawn, then make our way into the colonies. A place I had only heard of from Mbulla when he was in one of his rare charitable moods. He made it sound like a place the old Sukunda would have loved to see, but not this one, here I'm making my way to a man I'll call master, a man who I will be forced to bear children for. A lone tear rolls down my cheeks soaking my shirt, I wish I had left him in the cell to die, maybe I would have survived when I had figured how to get out of that nefarious, godforsaken place.

"I heard that you got lucky and you got picked to go to the colonies, not just a breeder but a prima breeder." A girl snarls from the other cell, her bony hands grips the cell bars of the door, her eyes alive with flames of hatred.

"Wish it's you?"

"Why not? It's better than this hell hole you've damned us all into, at least there you will have good food, nice clothes, you won't have to worry about anything, you don't even need to do anything, well except spread your legs if you are pretty enough to catch your master's eye."

"I'd rather die,"

"If I 'm you, I'm going to keep my head down no matter what. I hear that the master you are headed to does not tolerate defiance."

"I'm no one's broodmare, "

"You wouldn't say that when you have everything you ever need and more. It's a better life than the one you are damning us to live."

I glance away from her gaze, she turns her back, dismissing me, I wipe away a tear. I don't need her to tell me that I was the reason for putting them all in this mess. A hand touches mine, I raise my head, a girl I recognize from the courtyard, she gives me a smile, her lips quivering, her hair held back by a strip of leather, huge haunting grey eyes set in a small face stared back at me.

" It's not your fault, you saved us all. Gave us back what we lost all this time; the spirit to fight back, because of you, we will never stop trying to be free, thank you."

"I didn't save you, she's right, I damned you all, should have left all of you back there, and now you're all paying for the sins of my crimes."

She snorts, "Is that what you think, don't listen to that heifer back there. Alaika likes to put the blame on people when things don't work out, I hope that I will be part of the ones sent out to the Hinters, maybe life won't be that hard, who knows what could happen there? Maybe working the mines would be easier than spreading my legs for the coming weeks." she chuckles dryly and coughs in her hands. She winced out painfully, a hand on her ribs.

"I wish you luck then; I hope you find what your heart desires most."

"Larkis, but Ark's just fine." Putting a hand out,. A mischievous smile graced her lips, and she winks.

"Sukunda," I let her wipe the tears off my face, she drops something in my hand, I didn't have the time to see what it is before the door open and I stared at Hamoul who refuses to meet my eyes, a guard opens my cell door, I step and follow them out of there, deeper into the quarters of raiders. We stop at a door, he opens it and shoves me inside. I stumble in the room and turn to him ice in my gaze.

"You're safer here," he mutters and sits down on a chair, completely ignoring me.

I snort, and plop on the floor, knees up, I hug them. Safer for whom? Safer for the merchandise to not get damaged by accident in case Balla came for a chance revenge-visit when he decides that the pouch full of coins is nothing compared to his son's life and the damage I did to Jufureh. Right now, I hate the guy like nothing I have hated before, but I can't attempt to do anything until we are far away from here, then I will have to do something about my freedom. I wished I had seen father's point a long time ago, at least I wouldn't be in this twisted mess. All I've seen father is a draconian enforcer of some sort, banning this, banning that. We were forgotten in a world where being known and unknown might be an advantage and a weakness. My land was forgotten just like the third world, a place deemed unfit to survive in by everyone.

I stared at the yellow-green leaves clutched within my hand, wrapped in a thin, dry banana leaf. An herb I haven't seen in so long, Bankanas leaves, how did she get her hands on it? I grin, shaking my head. I wish I could see her right now and thank her properly. Used as birth control by women who knew about it, kept a secret by women. I sneak a glance at the silent guy sitting in the corner eyes closed, breath evened out, play-sleeping. I bit the end of the bankanas leaf and chew, then shove the rest in my bodice when I was sure he wasn't looking.

I stood up and hurry to the water bottle on the floor, inches from it a hand snatched my wrist, I met his eyes with my own icy ones. "What're you doing?"

"I need to drink unless your objective is for me to die of thirst, Mr. Fantastic," I say with bite in my tone, sharp as a blade. He lets go of my wrist, and hands me the water bottle, I chug it down in seconds and throw him the water bottle. He catches it and set it down. First thing first, I have to know where we are headed. But how the hell am I going to make him talk? I lay on the bed and tried to get some sleep, maybe tomorrow I will find a way to do so.

CHAPTER 45

MECHANDISE

SUKUNDA

ONE YEAR AGO

My back aches like a devil's pounding on it, we have been riding since the unforgiving crack of dawn, and still, there's no sign of slowing for the guy. It's like he's not human. Unlike him, I was suffering, how could someone just ride like that and not think that I have got no lady business to take care of? And the view here's just dull, miles and miles of sand are guaranteed to make me want to take a bullet in the head. I wish I had a gun here, maybe I could make him see some sense then. Riding back-breaking long hours shouldn't be part of my hidden survival resume.

The suns hang low in the sky, his body gets more tense the more the twin orange glowing balls dip lower in the horizon. I stared the skeleton of humans embellishing the desert ground, and I gulp, maybe I could see the reason for the mad dash we were doing since dawn. I stared at the three motorbikes and the truck holding a group of girls from Jufureh tailing us. Balla gives me the stink eye when he catches me watching, thank God that I was riding behind Hamoul and not with the other girls.

"Where are we heading to?" I asked speaking for the first time since we embarked on this journey.

Silence met my question, and I bit my lip, I had given up the thought that he would talk to me, but then he answered, "We are going to the provenance, making camp here would be suicidal."

I couldn't stop the full-blown smile on my face, even though he couldn't see me. "And do you think we would make it, ahem with the suns sinking that fast."

"Then pray to whatever you believe in that we do because we are dead if we don't."

I eye the wasteland, the thought of Reapers attacking us if we don't, I just hope that we make it out of here. In Mbe'tu we don't have much Reaper activity to take care of, I'm not sure why that is, we are thankful to live a peaceful, harmonious life unnoticed by the outside world.

A snap boomerangs in the air, I watch in horror as the motorbike in front of us suddenly cartwheel in the air, it's rider's headless body somersaults, spraying an arc of arterial blood and thumps in the truck behind us. A blood-curdling scream that feathers goosebumps to life on my arms emerged out of it, Hamoul stopp the motorbike in a sudden, sharp move that had me nearly topple to the ground, but he pulls me back. Men on horseback ride into view at breakneck speed.

"What the hell?"

"An ambush." Balla snarls his face a mask of fury." Fucking Strays"

Just our rotten luck

"They are a menace that I thought that I had wiped out a long time ago, but I see that I was wrong." Balla chances a look at the fast sinking suns, and I shuddered this is going to be a long, terrible night.

"Can you ride?" Hamoul hands the bike to me.

I snort and hop in his seat. It's like asking a fly if it could fly, I sped towards the strays, Hamoul pulled out two guns from his long coat and started shooting, behind us a guard went down another hidden trap. A horse fell on the ground with a hard thud, pinning its rider beneath its substantial bulk. I dodge bullets fired a sand flies everywhere, eyes narrowed on the stray leader giving out orders, I speed towards him, the motorbike ate the distance between us. Hamoul jumps off the motorcycle. Without a backward glance, I revved out of there, not even looking back. I dodged horses and bullets, deaf to Hamoul's shout. I smile and rode on, let him take care of the stray problem. For now, I have got things to do, and places to hide.

If he thinks that I was going to be a sheep, who won't do anything as he led me to my inevitable slaughter, he should think again. A colossal castle comes into view, and I stared at the sinking suns and shudder. I could make a risky choice and seek shelter here, or I could keep on riding and brave the Reapers that would be coming for the night. A shriek had my hand tremor; with a curse, I turn back towards the gates. Inches from the entrance, an arrow pierces the ground.

" State your business." A voice shouted.

"Open the freaking gates, we are seeking sanctuary." A voice growls in annoyance.

I whirl around and stared at Hamoul. He smirks and aims a gun at my head. "You know I should kill you for that stunt you pulled."

"At least I'm not a dishonorable rat who goes against his words."

"You're naïve if you think that I was going to keep those words, You're already Obra's, there's nothing you can do about it."

"And I give a rat ass about that, just know this, I will never stop trying to escape, I don't care that I'm already damned Obra's" I say vehemently, standing toe to toe with him our noses nearly touching. His eyes softened for a bit, and stared down at my lips, he leans in, and I unconsciously copied the move, breathing in his hauntingly, tempting scent of man, smoke, desert, wilderness, and spice.

"Well this is new, boy you finally have someone who got under that cold skin of yours, come in and finish whatever you two were about to do."

Both of us swing our gazes to the gate, I stared at the opened gate, then at the man with salt and pepper hair and beard carrying an array of weapons. Hamoul grips my wrist and drags me past the man, I bit my lips to stop myself from crying out in pain with the punishing grip.

"Where are the others?"

"Fighting, "

"You left them behind to fight, how could you? The suns are already down."

"If you hadn't tried running away, they would have been here by now; thanks to you, they might die. And I won't let the merchandise escape." He shrugs

"I'm not a damn merchandise, I'm a human being, and it wasn't my fault that I had tried to run away, it was yours. You gave me your word, and it meant nothing to you." I snarl and wrestle my wrist out of his grip. He lifts me and slung me on his shoulder like I weighed nothing.

"Put me down, damn it, Hamoul put me down," I scream, thumping his back; the man chuckles to himself, shaking his head. I glared at him, and he lifts his hands up in surrender.

He opens a door, and throw me down in it none too gently on the bed, and closed the door behind him, the lock clicks into position, and I scream and run into the door hard, screaming bloody murder. The mud-sucking ass hole, I can't believe that he is the only one keeping me away from my homeland.

Gadzooks, I hate him.

A smile came to my lips unbidden when I remembered how his eyes softened, for that moment I could almost see in him a guy I would like if I was back home, well almost. An inner voice scoffs at that. I have got better things to do than mooning over a guy who hates my guts, how many girls has he dragged to be a breeder for freaking Obra? Everybody knows that you get a decent life, but not for long; you either bore out your master or die in childbirth. A thing we don't have in my homeland, we respect and honor life no matter whom it belongs to, human and animal. When it comes to life, there are boundaries one should never cross, never.

And this's one of them.

CHAPTER 46

TICKET

Sukunda

One Year Ago,

I take the gift-wrapped leather and smile my thanks, the smile fades the moment I turn my back to him, at least today I wasn't subjected to the evil hands of doctor psycho. The thought of the man had a trail of hate trickle down my throat, nausea wells in me. I hate everything about this place and everything it stands for I haven't seen Hamoul in ages, sometimes I take a walk outside with the hope that I would catch a glimpse of him, but I never did. I stared at my sizeable baby bump, I just want him to know. I loosened the beautiful bows of the leather, and stared at a beautiful gown, dripping with diamonds and Arkor diamond set off a kaleidoscope of vivacious colors that blinded me for several seconds.

" Do you like it?"

"I love it, it's so beautiful, thank you, Master."

"Anything for you pet," Obra whispers in my ear, a hand caresses my shoulder, the other glued to my bump.

I forced myself not to pull away, there are only three people I hated so much in my life: psycho doctor, Hamoul, and his father. I'm tired of being used for their own games, the experiments were horrifying enough to make me go mad, I don't know what they want to achieve by experimenting on my unborn baby, whatever it was couldn't be good. Every time I was taken down to see Psycho doctor, a part of me dies.

"I have things to take care of pet, you should sit down and rest." He kisses my head.

I obey silently and watch him hurry out of there a happy smile on my face. It disappears the moment he went out, my gaze went to the dress, and I start plucking the diamonds, and the Arkor-diamonds off it. I don't know when it is, but what I know is this. This is my ticket out of this hell hole. A knock on my door has me hide the dress under the covers, several heartbeats later a girl came in carrying a vial with a purple liquid trapped within it. I took it, she waited for me to drink it, doctor psycho's loyal servant, I uncorked the vial and put it on my lips. I meet her lifeless eyes and take a breath. Here goes nothing.

"Hi, I know that you can understand me, and I know that you're playing along. Trying to act like the veggie that doctor, evil psycho wants you to be, I know that you are more than that." I sucked in another breath, "Please, you have to help me out of here, I can't stay here anymore, I don't want anything to happen to my baby. Please help me." I whisper, staring into her lifeless eyes. Which gave nothing away. She blinks, the look she wears fades for a moment before coming back on, I wipe a tear from my face, and proceed to drink the vial. There's no way I was getting out of here without her help. Hamoul, the rat, would not do it resigned to my fate, I tip the vial towards my lips.

A hand snatches the vial from my hand, "You're hopeless, I thought that you will never ask." A hoarse voice says. I met the intelligent brown eyes of the girl. Not the lifeless ones I get so used to watching me every chance it gets. The girl smiled warmly at me, "Odah'e at your service."

"Sukunda," I say, not quite believing my eyes.

"So, can you get me out of here."

"Yeah, I can, a risky, foolish thing to do, but I can bust you out of here."

"Thank you_."

"Don't thank me yet; the hard part is yet to come. If we are to get out of here, we will need the keys to the tunnels, that only two people have."

"Tunnels?"

"Yes, unfortunately, Obras' is off-limits, taking his key would be suicidal. That leaves us with only one person."

"The evil, psycho doctor."

She chortles, clutching her stomach. She gave me a bemused smile." Come on, do you think that I'm blind? Others would be, the smoldering glances he throws your way is hot enough to put the Sahara on fire, it might go unnoticed, but nothing went by me unnoticed. I didn't become the evil, psycho doctor's rat for nothing. That fool thought that he had broken me if only he knows how wrong he was. Who else would be the most powerful after Obra?"

"Hamoul."

"Good, he is the one you should get the key from. Considering he likes you that much to put that baby in you, I reckon that it will not be a problem."

"How did you _."

"Know about you two, I have my sources pet."

I bristle, she takes a look at my face and lifts a hand ." I'm sorry, it's just a joke."

I nod, "Whew since all that is waived off, he should be coming home tonight, get it because tomorrow we get out of here. Obra won't be around, he would be coming soon, maybe by daybreak."

She turns back and hurry towards the door, at the door she pause and turn around. Face passive, the lifeless mode back on, she winks before rushing out of there

Hamoul was coming today, I pull a small brownish paper, and started writing on it. With a shaking hand I write a message. I ring a bell, and a girl came running to my room." Please get this to Hamoul without reading it."

"Yes, my Prima." She bows and runs out of there. Now the waiting begins, I stared at my reflection in the mirror, fidgeting with my hair, I hope that he makes it. I would prefer he makes and gets caught rather than him not making it at all, I could imagine the shock he gets when he sees me. It's been months since I had set eyes on him, months for my bump to grow.

CHAPTER 47

HORNET

Kamili

Time exists no more, only pain, and the need to survive. Chained to the ceiling. Fire and agony ate at my veins, I screamed. The woman wrote something on the clipboard she holds; I glare at Eldres from the glass partition. They had separated us when the woman came. Security has tightened considerably well; the experiments have my teeth clenching in anger and pain. I felt alien, looking at my bloodied wrist. They have been digging into me, raping my gene in every possible way. Mangled it beyond repair.

"She is negative, take her for harvesting."

"Maybe we should wait Ma'am, something is stopping the test."

"Take her for harvesting Ifem, don't make me repeat myself again." My life meant nothing to them. They will harvest every valuable part of me until nothing remains.

Wiped slate clean. Taken from my family, who won't know what happened to me. I glower, wishing that I could wrap my hands around her slender, elegant swan-like neck and choke the life out of her, slowly. I know that I will enjoy every minute of strangling her, even if a part of me protests at taking a life, but I slam that door close. The minute I get the chance , I won't waste it, she is going down. She walks out; the doors slid close, and smoke billows into the room through the hidden vent. I close my eyes, sucked in clean air, and held it. Eyes watering, my heart rattles in my chest, my vision blurs going groggy, my body relaxes embracing the haze it is forced into. Hands check my pulse, opened the manacles on my wrists and ankles. Put on a gurney and wheeled out, air smashed into my lungs. I was up from the gurney before my white coat clad wheeler could react I twist his neck and he crumples in a heap at my feet.

There would be no mercy, I was given none. I pulled on his coat and put his body on the gurney. A coughing fit gripped me, and I double over. Warm liquid drips on my palm.

Blood.

No!

I retch, my body shudders. Sweat speckles my forehead, I force my body upright and wheel the gurney towards the elevator. I expect an alarm to blare to life, but it never does. The doors whooshes open; I push the gurney into the corridor. Veins stood on my skin, I ran a hand on my face, feeling the raised veins. Something live moved under my skin. Whatever they had put into me was doing this to my body. The lamp in the corridor flickered when I touched the wall bracing my body. More blink in rapid succession, I limped to where I guessed that they held the others. Something animalistic surged into me, I flop face first in the corridor. Tears swamped my vision, I grip my head that was ready to implode any moment.

The alarm blares to life.

Voltage crackles on my skin, licking the ground where I kneel. A storm eddies within me, and a blast of current slams at the first wave of guards. I rain my wrath, I start my dance of death. I had no mercy and no intent of leaving any survivor. None will stand in my way while I breathe. They started this, I will see it ended. The door opens at my command, and I step in Saliu lays in a heap on the floor, his pulse steady, Muna's head cradles in his lap. Her hazel eyes were open, a ring of silver circles her pupil.

"Kamili."

"I'm fine, where's Madi and the others?"

" In harvesting."

I sprint towards harvesting heart lodged in my mouth, the two followed, I wish that I could slow down time somehow, God let me not be late, Muna keeps pace beside me with Saliu leading the way, his wounds already healed from all the tinkering we have been subjected to, the veins spread farther up my arms to my shoulder, to my face, a pulse ticks on my forehead, as if on a countdown. Saliu opens the lid of a manhole, and climb down, knee-deep in brackish, gray water."

"This is the shortest way."

"What is this place."

"Hell."

Wading deeper in the water. I follow Saliu as he led us towards a hatch; he pulls the grate and maneuver his muscular build inside. In the vents, we crawl in the small, cramped space, one at a time. I land behind the guard he's dead even before he registers my presence. I throw the gun at Saliu and swipe the key card on the door. A scream spirals in the air stops my heart for a second before I was out of there. I blast the man in the lab coat. His body flies at the wall, smoking, he thumps on the floor dead. I switch off the strange contraption strapped to Madi and Moro.

"You came."

"I will always do what are friends for?"

He snorts, and I help him up. There's something different about him, I could not pinpoint it, something was going on with him. An explosion rocks the ground, vibrations in full swing. The ground gave way behind us, chasing us.

"They want to kill us."

"Not if we kill them first."

The world whirls around, walls appear out of thin air. I slammed my hands on the glass partition that separated me from the others. Madi punches at the glass that separates us. He lifts a chair and slam it repeatedly on the glass; it is shatterproof. The glass goes dark, Madi disappears; air shimmer around me, raising the hairs on my nape, I take stock of the room I stand in. I am in an office, a cluttered desk sat on the left, a glass screen mounted on the wall. There is a stillness to the room that chills my blood. A timer blinks on a huge obsidian glass. It came to life, the woman with eyes of death and doom regards me.

"Hello, progeny, I see that you are doing well."

"What do you want?"

"It's simple; come with us, and your friends will live. If you don't, I will have to take certain steps, I don't want to. Not many will survive this, even you will find it difficult. And besides, we have someone you'd be glad to see."

An image of a red-haired woman floats in the air, she lays on a gurney, her wrists cuffs to the sides. Her eyes gray and unfocused. Not the bright blue I'm used to seeing. She looks small and frail. So different from the effervescent woman I was used to seeing. My heart lurches.

"Mama," I wheezed out.

I hadn't realized that I had spoken out loud, agressive current crackles on my skin, ready to surge. How did they get their hands on her? What happened to the rest of the people in Kendulusa? What had become of Calla? So many questions I want answers to buzz in my head, and no way of finding it. There's no pain more significant than the unknowing, I swallowed my questions, and looked at the image of the woman.

"Don't hurt her,"

She knew that I will do anything for the woman lying on that gurney, and I hate that she knows my achilles heel.

"Like I told you, it's simple, surrender to us, and everything will be okay. We won't hurt her," she gives me a bone-chilling look "much." Insincerity shone in her eyes, she had no intention of letting us all leave this place; we are guinea pigs. And the same goes for Mama, too.

"Why do you want me so badly?"

"You are the key to what we want progeny. With you, so many things will be possible."

It seemed like a reverent prayer to me; she had no right playing God with our lives. No right to hold Mama prisoner, to turn my world upside down, to worsen our world. I fry the screen and wipe tears.

"So be it, progeny, you have made your choice. I guess I should have known better, like mother like daughter. Remember that you're the one who chooses this, I hope that it will be worth it" Her voice echoes from hidden speakers, for a moment she seems sad, I step out of the room. Green light fills the endless corridor I was in, my body tenses in anticipation. I wait for what will happen next.

"The hornet is activated," an electronic voice announces.

"Bring it on, bitch."

I crouch and wait. Neon green light streams out and blasts forward, lighting up the endless corridor.

"The rules are easy in the hornet, play, or die."

I tune her out and went still, I gaze at the floor properly, my brows furrows. The pattern looks familiar. The box-shaped tiles went on forever, each a different color, a puzzle of colors that could either be my salvation or bring my untimely demise.

In the hornet, nothing exists only pure, animalistic survival.

Nothing is below or beyond you for survival.

The eye is the essence.

Only the price of lives would be paid for your soul.

The rule of the peacock must be obeyed to ensure total survivability.

Mama's voice filters in my head, it's the poem she read to me every night to bed when it was bedtime. She had made sure that I memorize it.it. How did she know about it? Was mama an experiment? Memories long buried surfaced, coming to life, I could see mama fighting people in the forest, she looks invincible and deadly, an all-powerful force, she dispatches them without breaking a sweat and kneels down ." Hello Kaima, is that all you can do? Say hi to Baba."

The Baba, Mama, knows about him. Nothing adds up. Another memory surfaces to life; this time, I was playing with the other kids. My younger self touched the boy, blue light fizzles out of my hand and hit the boy; he fell, body seizing. That night Mama takes me to a familiar shanty, a woman had her back to me, she brandishes a syringe, and I cringe hyperventilating.

Mama strokes my hair and tells me that everything will be okay, she spins around, and I stared in to Rougy's, I sucked in a breath as she shoves the needle in my arm and pushes the plunger.

"This is the most potent dose I can give her Chey, it might make it latent for some time, "

"How long?"

"I'm not sure it could take years. But you will know when it resurfaces, it will give her a chance at a normal childhood, but some memories would be lost along."

"Thank you, Rougy."

"Don't mention it, "

"How is Muna?"

"She is doing fine, Musa and Aleku are taking care of her, they give her the doses. She asks about me from time to time, it won't be long before she forgets me completely, but it is for the best I can't take the risk of them taking her." She wipes a tear that slips from her eye and splashes on her open palm.

"It's a brave decision Rougy, I'm selfish for not trying to do so. But I can't bear having my children away from me. You are stronger than me than all of us. Just remember that I'm here for you, we won't let Olympus win. Some day we might be able to go back

Rougy nods and sadly watch us leave.

I gasp, crashing to the floor, blood trickles from my nose. Everything I thought I knew wasn't what it seems. I stared at my grimy hands, coat in blood, wheezing, slowly I stand up and take a step forward on the green tile, the corridor comes to life. It vanishes, I stand in a labyrinthine made of reflective, huge glass pillars that forms corridors as far as my eye could make out in the bright light. My reflection stares back at me, a stranger with vivid blue eyes that has a distorted, glowing pupil in the center. I sprint forward, dodging the traps, each corridor a challenge; varying from the last, but each as deadly as the previous, revolving and self-assembling, becoming narrower every second that ticks by.

I take the last dagger tuck in my boot and vault in the air as the floor collapses beneath me; the dagger slams home on the floor and held true. I watch the floor plunge into forever and haul my body over the edge and stand up. An uppercut cut into me, I gasp in pain and flip back. Dragon guy whips around, the same sadistic glint in his eyes. I caught hold of his next punch with an open palm. Claws raked my palm, blood spurts out, spilling down my wrist.

His roundhouse kick throws me back in the corridor, and towards the vast, dark, endless maw, my fingers dig onto the edge. I fling a leg over and haul my body over and faced him again. His features had morphed to its reptilian look. He barrels at me. Our bodies collide with an impact that shakes my teeth. His claws rake at my arm ripping into muscle and sinew, I hit the floor on my toes with astounding cat-like grace, and he crumples to his knees the dagger protrudes from his chest, charred and scorched.

I dash out of there. It was becoming harder and harder to navigate through the corridors; I crash into someone, and we both tumble to the floor. I gawk at Madi, surprised, and relieved to see him.

"I thought that I wouldn't see you?" relief shone in his eyes, and he pulls me into a tight hug. "Any idea of how to get out of this place?"

"Yeah, we aim for the eye."

"The eye?"

A snarl echoes in the tight space and I stared at Madi. We have to get out of here if we want to live." Follow me." It is the only thing that could stop this death trap.

"How do we stop it."

"It is simple we play the game, we switch off the interface, and it is game over for the hornet." I spring into action, snarls echoing closer. I don't need to look back to see that beasts were heading for us, avoiding certain tiles that could kill them. They were was trained for it, until a few moments ago, I thought it was just a poem, that Mama was just overreacting, as mothers tend to. Claws skitter on the tile; I sneak a glance behind me. A group of big scaly cats with glimmering, silvery eyes and the longest claws I have ever seen bound for us, I increased my pace, we should be near the eye soon.

I dodge a dart; it strikes the wall with a thwack, we come to a complete halt and stared at the tableau before us. A creature with carved marble-like features that looks surreal the trunk is made up off a human's body, its arms looked human but the rest morphs into branches and vines. Eyes stared at us like we are just insects under a microscope, blinking its weird ever-changing eyes.

"What the hell?" Madi whispers and takes a tentative step back.

"I think we just found the eye."

"No way!"

A gigantic vine crashing towards us, we spring apart, and it slams on where we stood a moment ago, another incoming killer branch heads for us, and I moved out of the way. I stamp on the vine that tries to wrap around my ankle, it recoils. I jump out of the way of another incoming deadly vine, Madi dances away from a vine that's tries to wrap itself around him.

How the hell do you kill a human-tree? Or whatever the hell that thing is. I clamber up on a vine; it revolved around trying to dislodge me, a vine wounds around my leg and tug. I grip a branch harder. I hack at it with my dagger, blood streams out of the vine, showering me, I fling the dagger at another vine creeps towards where Madi hangs off a branch; it pins it to the floor.

"Any ideas."

"I'm fresh out of them."

The whirling increased, and I could barely open my eyes. The vines twist over each other. Soon we will be trapped within its lethal, viny embrace. Madi lets go of the branch. He pulls the dagger that pins the vine to the floor and surged towards the tree.

"Madi no!" The vines released me and rear up, I land on my feet and sprint towards him. Everything moves in slow motion, I watch helplessly as he plunged the dagger deep into the heart of the human-tree, it screeches, dark blood mix with pus gushed out of its mouth, vines burst out of Madi's body, it lifts him cleanly off the floor. Then silently let go of him. His body thuds to the floor, and I ran towards him. Pulling him up on my lap, blood trickles from his lips and he tries to speak.

"Shh, don't talk, why did you do that?"

"Because I love you, my heart. Tell father that I love him, tell him it is my decision. I guess that I will see on the other side, just look up, and I will always be there." He points to the ceiling, his body wracked by tremors and went still.

Muna, Brime, and Saliu run into the room, covered in blood. They come to a halt inches from me, I turn to them, Madi's necklace in hand." He is dead, where is Moro?"

"Dead."

One word turns my life into ashes.

"Let's get out of this hell hole."

I strode towards the doors that opens to a transport pod, I stare back at Madi. I expect him to wake up at any moment and tell me that all this is a joke, a bad joke. A dream, anything, it does not matter what it will be. I don't want him dead, his body cold and bloody. The doors whoosh closed behind me, making him disappear from view, Muna puts a comforting hand on my shoulder, tears course freely down her face. They will pay for this, for making me the monster I am right now. For taking Mama, Moro, Madi away from me, for killing the only chance I had at love.

CHAPTER 48

SNOWGLOBE

SUKUNDA,

ONE YEAR AGO,

My footsteps ring in the empty corridor as I wore the floor out with my restless pacing, my ears ready to pick out any sound. I stood in the shadows waiting for Hamoul to make an entrance, my palms sweat I search for his familiar form. Wiping my tears, I stared out of the corridor's eyes vacant.

"Sukunda."

I glance back, Hamoul standsd behind me, dressed all in black garb; a tunic and pants and a tattered coat on top, weapons strapped on him, an iron key hung from his belt. In his hand he held a beautifully crafted snow globe made of some kind of reddish metal, a ruby winks at me on top, I spin around and take a step towards him, stepping into the light. His eyes widen when they land on my bump, sliding over my frame.

"I'm sorry for being late, this's for you."

I accept the snow globe and give him a brilliant smile." Thank you." I hug him, and close my eyes, breathing in his alluring scent, swallowing the pain parting with him. I grip the syringe tightly.

"You wanted to see me?"

"Yes, I want us, Hamoul, what we could have back." I run a hand down his back, and he stiffens.

"I'm sorry, Sukunda, you know that nothing can ever happen between us. You got to think about your condition."

"You bastard! How could you say such a thing? How can you ignore this? I know that you feel it as I do. "I put a hand on his chest, loving the way his heart changed tempo. "You should have set me free, but instead, you had to hand me out to your father, and his evil, doctor psycho. While you were out there, they experimented on our baby, your baby. This's not your father's; this is your baby Hamoul." I whisper bite in my words, tears sliding down my face, he blanches and step back and bump into the wall.

"Suk_."

I attack, plunging the syringe into his arm, I empty the liquid into him. He chokes and grab his neck, I step back and watch as he crumples. I sit on the floor and pull him onto my lap and stroke his hair." It's okay, you will be fine. I just gave you a little something to help you sleep, you'll wake up in a few hours. I love you, I have always loved you deep down. I'm so sorry."

Ode steps out from the shadows and into view, a satchel on her shoulder, I don't know how long she has been standing there watching us, "I'm sorry Sukunda, but we have to go now."

I gently lay Hamoul's head on the floor, Ode bends down and pulls the iron key off from his belt. Numb, I follow her out of there. I want to turn back and check if he was alright.

" Don't even think about it." Ode's voice bounces all around in the dark corridor.

"How did you know I was thinking about that?"

"Let's just say that I'm a little over the norm and leave it at that, huh. Right now, we should be more concerned about how in hell's balls, we are going to get out without setting off the alarm."

I force my feet to follow her quick footsteps, she's quick on her feet. We round up a corner, and she pressed her hand on the wall, her hands seeks a latch on the wall. I hear a quick click, a second later, and the wall swings to the side, revealing another corridor, it looks dark and menacing, smelling of age and dust. I step in with her, it bangs close, sealing us inside. I started to hyperventilate, as darkness descends in around me, Ode's hand burst on fire, the flame chased away the dark several inches away from us. I gaped.

"How did you do that?". light bounces off the skeleton frame of a rat on the floor.

"Come on hurry, we don't have much time."

Ode jogs past me. I gather up my skirt, and run after her, she tries to keep up a reasonable pace with my snail's pace one, but I still find it hard to keep up. She ducks through an archway, I shadow her. We come to a stop in a room. I stared at it, dust covers every surface of the room, skeletons lay scattered on the floor. A ladder leans on the side of a manhole that leads out of the tunnels.

"I will go first and make sure that everything is safe, you come down the ladder and join me when I say so." Ode ties the strings of the satchel around her waist.

She pulls a dagger from an indiscreet sheathe on her back, she pulls at the hilt, it lengthened to the size of a short sword, she put fingers on each side of the blade and pull. The blade broadened, she clamps it between her jaws and give me a wink, then vaults up in the air. I clam a fist in my mouth to smother the scream that wells in my throat. Her feet slam on the first rung at the top of the ladder like a cat's, all feline reflex, poise proud and graceful. The light bounces off of her reflective pupils. I squeeze my eyes shut and take a step back. That's not human. Humans don't have reflective eyes, why was she helping me? Do I even have to trust her? What was I doing? Her head emerges a second later, I back away from her. Her eyes clash with mine, she did not miss my action.

" All clear."

"What are you? How old are you?"

She sighs and ease her down cross-legged on the floor. Her posture non-threatening, now I can see her eyes properly. They were the usual brown until you gazed long enough to discern their exact color, a moving, murky, grayish-brown mass, that glint whenever she moves.

" Not entirely human as you suspect, I 'm a century old."

My eyes bug at that, a century. Right now, her eyes beg me to trust her.

" I mean you no harm, Sukunda, believe me if I wanted you dead, you would not be right here." it's okay if you want us to go back. But you will never be free."

"Does Dr. Klem know what you are?"

"What do you think?"

"Let's get move, you brought me this far, let's see where this tunnel leads to."

"A good choice." She grins, then slowly climbs down the ladder, putting a leg over I followed her up the belly of the manhole.

CHAPTER 49

Rangerlands

Calla

I regard the girl in bed, she's yet to wake up. She has been in and out of consciousness. The weather always fluctuates when she goes under, I wonder why they tried killing her. Was she some kind of anomaly like Mama? The more the weather goes haywire, the more I thought that my suspicions were right.

She stirs, opening hazel-brown eyes, I hurry to the bed she lounges in." How are you feeling?"

"Who are you?" she eyes Cleo warily.

"I'm Calla, and this is Cleo; she won't bite you."

She sits up, wincing, I take the jug of water from the stool and hurry to her." Here drink."

"I'm Chima, where am I?"

"In ranger lands, with the Oumali tribe, I found you in Mombess nearly dead. It's a miracle you manage to pull through."

"Yeah, I remember, thanks." She hands the jug back and she slips on her boots.

I put it back and turned to her,

" You should rest"

"It's not safe; how did you even get in this outpost?"

"It is safe for now."

"Who? No, you don't understand it's not safe for me, nowhere is. I have to get as far away from here as possible. People die when I'm around."

"You are in no condition to travel, and the weather's not stable. The Reapers are out there. I'm coming with you." I believe what she had said about people dying around her, but I'm ready to take my chances. So far, nothing happened to me.

"No, you stay here, you have done enough for me already."

"No, I'm headed that way."

The door opens, and the Nicu steps in, stamping the snow from his boots. His eyes went to where Chima sit, looking frail, a haunted look in her eyes.

"I see that she is awake, Nusir would be pleased, where are you going?"

"I have to go."

"There is a freak weather out there, and Reapers are doing a number on us, we have lost two of our rangers."

A bell tolls in the distance and Chima runs for the door, Nicu follows cursing. Icy cold air whips my cheeks when I step out, guards run to their posts, panicked voices try to know what's going on. Then I saw them, hordes of them heading for the mountain.

Cleo growls low, her fur stands on end. Their bony faces, nightmarish eyes, grey-pale skin, their unnatural gait made my heart gallop. They walk on all fours, limbs contorted at strange angles. They're not the Reapers I'm used to seeing, these ones look like evolution took a step back.

"Dragu, they're here." Chima grabs her throat.

Nusir jogs towards us," You should stay indoors, Calla."

"No I can't, I can't let your people die for me."

"We lost her once, we are not ready to lose her again."

Before I could figure out what he meant, arrows rain onto the Reapers pinning some to the ground, but still, they were unyielding. Their feverish eyes fixated on one target; Chima. The girl can barely stand still, her legs shook, she's kitten-weak.

"And so we meet again, old man! Pity, it's under these circumstances. I will make sure to send your regards to Lela. Now hand her over, or you will have the pleasure of seeing me end the Oumali this very night, come Chima you know that you can't run away from your destiny, spare me the effort of not killing everyone here. They've got bigger a bigger boat to flout than ours."

"The only one to be annihilated is you Serak, this night is for you and your cursed ilk."

"You never learn old man, we are the future, and you are nothing but a glitch from the past. Didn't your own daughter leave you?"

A snarl that should not come out of a human ripped out of Nusir's mouth, a silvery flash rips out from of his eyes and slams into some of the creatures, obliterating them into piles of ashes.

"Now you're just showing off old man," Serak smirks and pins Chima with an opaque, dead gaze. He takes a step forward and stops in his tracks, his gaze lands on me and widens, Chima backs into me, panic etch on her features, she mumbles something, but I didn't hear it.

"Well! Well, look what we got here? Nusir, you're full of surprises. Where did you find this one?"

A thumping envelopes my senses. I put a hand on Cleo to steady myself. The world turns red at the edges, a hunger like no other claims me. a rage like no other slams into me. A metallic tang fills my mouth, a growl forces from itself past my lips. I went on all fours, retching, seizures wrack my body.

"Are you okay?"

I lift my head and stared at Chima she backs away in fright, backing into Nusir whose face blanches when his gaze lands on me. My fingers elongate into claws; my skin takes on an ashy-grey hue that matches Cleo's fur. She lays beside me, licking my face, comforting, purring sounds hums from her throat. She leaps after Chima and Nusir, dodging arrows, and beams thrown at her. She knocks out Nusir with one mighty blow and come back with Chima clamped carefully in her jaws.

Kindred.

I lift my head.

Kindred.

I meet the Sarek's gaze, a smile sits on his lips. I shook my head in confusion, he was talking to me just like Mama did.

I am not your kindred.

Really, The voice chuckles in my head, I fist my hands at that.

What do you want?

Her, what else, hand her over, and I promise I won't harm anyone. And make sure that the Baba won't know of your existence.

The Baba?

"Yes, the Baba, and believe me you don't want that, maybe you want your family thrown in as well."

I can't let that happen, my family always comes first, what if Kamili gets hurt from my actions? If he knew about my family, he could hurt them.

"I'm so sorry," I whisper meeting Chima's frightened, sad eyes, still imprisoned by Cleo's jaws, her head hangs low in defeat, slowly I pull the motionless girl from Cleo's jaws, resigned to her fate, a storm brews, snow plummets heavier to the ground. Cleo dashes towards the army waiting outside. She jumps the high fence. We land in front of the creatures.

The sea of creatures' part to make way for us, I made my way to Sarek. Thunder booms in the distance, lightning split and clobber the ground. A hurricane in full swing heads for us. I hope that I can get away with this. My blood thrums in my veins, a blood wave that I rode. Cleo swerves to the right, trampling the creatures in her way. They gave chase.

"Faster, Cleo."

"You are not turning me over to him?"

"I'm not Chima, I'm not a monster despite the look."

I glance back and saw that the creatures have fallen back.

"They will come back, "

"What are they?"

"Dragu."

"So am I one?"

"No, you are something different, something like my father, you are a Reaper Lady. Can you switch the look you have on?"

"Why?'

"Because you it's freaking me out."

I will the change away and turn to her. "Better?"

"Thank you."

"What does he want with you?"

"The same they want with you if they have you in their possession."

"He mentions the Baba."

"He did?"

"Where's your Mama."

"Ravagers."

That mere word opens the wound I had tried to seal all these days, survival kept me from thinking about Mama, from turning back to see if she's okay. A foolish part of me hoped that maybe this was all a dream that I would wake up soon and find that Mama and Kamili were beside me, everything would be like the old days.

Mama. I miss her laughter, I miss Kamili and her I can-save-world-attitude she has going on. And how blind she is to the way Madi looks at her. Like she is his universe, his suns, moon, and stars, an undetachable part of him. Both were inseparable since their first meeting. Sometimes I just want to slap some sense into her, I mean how can you tell your sis to pay more attention to her best friend? That he's in love with her, almost everybody close to them could see it. Only she was clueless.

I suspect that something must have happened to her on pledging eve, the way he stood up for her during the trial tugged at my heartstrings. I caught a tear in my palm, Cleo whines, and I grin, she nuzzles my hand, licking my tears clean. I chuckle and she gives me an adorable yip, I burst into gales of laughter. I couldn't help it, at least I had her. I guess that I would have been more miserable if I hadn't had her along with me. She's a blessing.

CHAPTER 50

KINDRED

Calla

With Reapers on our heels, the future uncertain, I stared at the stone fortress before us. Sutukoba is the biggest place I have ever seen in my whole life. A place that gives me the shivers, I had Cleo stay out while we go in.

"I don't like this."

"I know," Chima replies, her eyes scan the streets.

I couldn't blame her; nowhere is safe anymore. The Reapers could pick her on their radar at any moment. Deafening cheers and clapping fills the air. Chima jogs towards the sound I follow hard on her heels. Two guys fight each other in a massive pit, while the crowd cheers for more blood to be spilled. A girl lay on the ground clutching her side, bodies lay strewn on the ground. The guy fighting the dark-haired guy crumples to the ground, his neck twisted at an odd angle the crowd went wild

"And now for the final specialty of the night, I give you something from your wildest nightmares." A door slid open, a growl emanates from within freezing my veins in my body, a huge beast that could put Cleo to shame steps out onto the pit. Its dark midnight coat shone scarlet with the dried blood of past kills, a malevolent intelligence shone in its eyes. The guy stood his ground, protecting the wounded girl on the ground.

Oh, god, I'm going to die.

I clash gazes with her. The beast went on its haunches in a crouch, powerful muscles bunched ready to spring. It lunges at the guy, jaws open flashing serrated teeth that would separate the flesh from bones. A boy materialized before the guy, the two collide, I wince. The guy throw the creature in the air. It hit the ground. More doors slid open, and creatures pour onto the sands. A girl with flames licking at her lashes helps the wounded girl up.

"It seems like we have volunteers, Ladies and gentlemen brace yourselves for a mind-blowing, historic night that you've never seen. Sweeten the pot, we're throwing in something new."

"What're you doing?"

" It's Kamili,"

"We won't survive this; let's get out of here."

"You go, Chima, get out." I push her towards the exit. I run for the pit, the crowd calls out for more blood. Pulsing agony rips into my head, so hard I tumble to my knees, the change takes me over in an instant, my skin reverting its previous, nightmarish look ,horrified, I conceal my hands from sight. They are here, I know it.

Don't fight the change kindred.

I am not a monster.

Being a monster resides in all of us, give in, and you could surprise even yourself kindred.

Blood on fire, I rear back. My eyes feels like they're ready to explode in their sockets. The pit shook, dust rose, billowing in the air. A creature rose from the ground and hauls itself up, and I gulp. Roped, carved muscles rippled, the huge creature approaches the small group of people. Its hideous face nightmarish it surveys the crowd, then bellows, slit-nostrils expanding, a wicked, sharp tail whiplash in the air and cuts down a man.

"Let the games begin," the man shouts fervently into the mike. I hoist my body up, hands fisted, the Dragu would be here, any moment. I need to get Kam and get out before it's too late. I stiffen when the first call boomeranged all around.

Sarek is here.

They're here.

Kindred, I hope that you are ready for the storm.

The vision of waves of snarling Dragus snaps in my head, I fight for control, trying to throw him out of my head. I yell and slam my mind shut. Cleo barrels into view, I mount her we slam into the arena's wall, burst through the sands, we land on the far side of the arena. The hideous creature is nearly upon the girl, it stops in mid-jump and swing its gaze on us. Cleo growls, I patted her with a clawed grey hand, she nuzzled my hand, slowly I slid off her, the beast changed course and heads for us, I held my hands out, stopping time, Cleo rushes at the girl. The creature growled, forcing its body forward, but his muscles didn't obey. A wave of frost slams into the creature, cementing it in place. I turn eyes on Chima, she takes hold of my hand and squeeze.

"Let's get this bastard."

I jump on Cleo, Chima sat behind me, I let go of time. Cleo hurtles at the beast.

CHAPTER 51

OF TEETH AND BLOOD

Jelika

Zen helps the wounded girl up. A red-haired girl with three others stepped out, her blue eyes glowed dangerously on her beautiful face, I look like a sea urchin compared to her queenly beauty, she reminds me of the woman who saved our lives, especially those bright, blue eyes of hers. The same nonchalant air of deadliness. Same lithe build minus the curves. I braced for the gigantic, colossal being heading for us. A snarl on the right has me eying the creatures sidling towards us, it's going to take a miracle to get us out. I close my eyes, calling forth my power, the air hummed wild with unbridled energy.

Two pale boomerangs circled my hands. I spin around to meet the creature lunging at me. It dusts the moment my boomerang comes in contact with it, the crowd went ballistic. I leapt for the huge creature dodging swipes from its lethal claws, it tosses me on the wall of the pit. I dance out of its way, a gigantic, clawed hand slam where I was seconds ago, I somersault and land on its head. I slash at it with my boomerangs, but he didn't dust as I expect, It just hissed in pain and backhands me, My body smacks so hard on the sands that stars claim my vision. I groan, a thin trail of blood slip down the corner of my mouth. Doubling over, pain joggle my body. It lifts me high in the air and hurls me on a tower, right, time to kiss the tower. Time stops, slowing my fast descent to earth. Zunaif barrels into the creature.

A brown-haired, silver-eyed girl and an older girl rode a huge wolf-like dog that came crashing into the arena, the wolf-like dog fends off the creatures twice its size, making these growls and snarls that had them back off. They were scared of it somehow, I landed shakily on my feet. Well, who would not? The thing was ferocious; right now, it's size does not matter, and it knew it. The silver-eyed girl held a hand out, and time stops. My stomach dropped or something, even my body slow, freezing me on the spot.

Seriously! Time manipulation.

Cool hands take my hands, bringing with them a warmth that I recognized." You okay." Blyte whispers, touch gentle as he checks me for injuries. He had grown up on me on our journey, growing closer than I would have liked. My gaze went to the brown-haired girl who had dismounted her mount and was crouched on the arena trying to calm her down, but it wasn't helping, she was looking a little ashy every second that went by and so was her wolf. Her knees gave way, and she crumples, her brown hair turns gray-silver, skin graying, her small hands lengthened into lethal claws; shiny, gray-silver claws that shred with just one swipe. She isn't like the Reapers or us. This's different, and it has Dr. Kaima written all over it. I will bet my life on it.

She screams, "No," clutching her head, her beast stands guard. The red-haired girl started forward panic etched on her features, inches from the creature its growls, she stops in her tracks and held out a hand for the wolf-like dog to scent.

"Cleo, it's me," she touches its nose. The beast let her pet it and let her kneel on the ground beside the girl on the ground screaming in agony, fighting a mental battle.

"We have to get out of here."

"What do you mean?"

"They are here; she is reacting to their influence."

"What influence?"

"Them" She points behind me.

I spin around to see hordes of ashy-grey creatures climbing over the wall. I stared at the huge Fly-ship soaring above our heads, figures drops down with the startling grace of a panther. If the hand holding the flaming torch isn't an indication that we should get out of here, the hordes of creatures were. Pandemonium broke out when the audience sighted the Dragus pouring over the wall, an endless wave of teeth and blood. The red-haired girl lifts the girl on the wolf-like dog, she mounts behind her. They strike.

The ground tremors, creating cracks spread on the ground like a malevolent plague, some of the creatures fell in and crawl out and spill onto the pit. Blyte stands in the center of the hole, eyes pitch-black as he tries to stop the creatures from venturing in further, more pour in. He could only stall them. In the labyrinthine, I run faster, dusting creatures that litter my way. Zen flames, not an inch of her skin in sight. A crazy, stupid grin wreathes her face. An explosion blasts behind me as she sends a massive fireball at the horde giving chase, I skid to a complete halt and regard the man blocking our path.

"Shit ravagers."

"Pleasure to make your acquaintance kids." The man takes off his dark shades, and polish it with a hankie, two creatures crouched on the ground beside him. Their eerie gaze lodges a blade of chill in my chest.

"What do you want?"

"Take it, easy flame girl, we are not the enemy. All we have to do is come to an agreement."

"Making deals with ravagers is signing your death sentence."

The one behind him chuckles, taking off his dark shades, and stared at us with eyes that had no pupil, just a complete white that reigns over his eyes, foggy and void, no hint of color or warmth in sight.

"Fine have it your own way, I tried."

He backs away ,a girl with dreadlocks, steps forward, cold eyes survey us, wedging the blade of chill deeper until it reaches my spine. A long whiplash tongue smash out of her mouth and launches at me, I sidestepped the tongue and whirl my body in the narrow corridor, Blyte and Zen fought trying to win despite its evident that the odds aren't in our favor. I pin the dread-locked girl on the wall with a wave of my hand. She looks a little startled when I did, but then a light came in her eyes, and she doubled her attacks.

Her tongue caught me on my collar bone, slams me hard on the wall she threw me away. My body thumps hard on the floor, and I groan, getting on my hands and feet. Zen's scream of pain, rose in the narrow corridor, another guy punches Blyte and sends him flying, he hacks a cough and slowly get back on his feet winded. Pain spear my neck. Hands grip my hair and pull me closer. Tongue-girl held me in place, goggle-guy pulls out a syringe, advancing, he stabs me in the neck.

" Hmm," he fills the syringe and sticks the needle in his arm, face twisting, he buckled to his knees, body jerking. "Secure them." he utters, evidently in pain

Not happening. I could feel Blyte's unease as I tapped into the part of me I had been ignoring since the ark-break, I embraced it wholly this time. Silence reigned in my head, for the first time, I see the world in a new light. For the first time, I am at peace. It started as a hum in my veins, then it was an endless blast after blast of intense light that blinds the world. Bringing only catastrophe.

CHAPTER 52

THE RESISTANCE

Kamili

I don't even know if I was doing the right thing. I don't know if I fit in with these people. We head towards what Calla had called the resistance. How come I have never heard of them? Mama never told me about them, or that Calla can change into an ashy-grey creature, nothing about any of this. I've been traveling with them for a week now since Jelika released her deadly EMP in Sutukoba. On the run being hunted by the Baba. I have the suitcase, and Calla has the parchment Mama gave her. I wipe the sweat off my brow and scan the military-like sprawling base before us.

My gaze run over the empty watchtowers, everything seems quiet, too quiet for my liking. Maybe we shouldn't stop here.

"I don't like this" flames flicker at Zen's fingertips.

Neither do I! Something's fishy going on here.

"Don't move!"

I went still as a gun is pressed to my head. Cleo growls when a girl in ripped jeans and a midriff top aims a gun at Calla, whose eyes were slowly going Reaper. Her muscles tensed, ready to spring. I glower at the one with a gun pointed at my head, a guy, he has on a rugged look going on with him, bronze-golden brown, beautiful skin, fine, dark hair, teal-gold eyes that look straight into your soul. A heartbreaking face that I knew a lot of girls would give their soul for if he so much as threw a smile their way. His arrogant smile thrown my way reminds me of Madi. My throat clogs, tears gather in my eyes for a moment. Madi. I still can't believe that he had given his life for mine.

"seach them for weapons." A heavily-built man with straining muscles commands.

Another guy step forward; I grit my teeth, enduring his too-happy hands. A shot rings in the air, and I glance back to see Zen jump out of the way of a speeding bullet. It sped past her and heads for Calla. She held a hand and stops inches from her forehead? It clatters at her feet. I shot out of my saddle in a blink, not acknowledging the bullet that's shot at my shoulder. Calla comes first. No one tries to hurt her while I still breathe. I had promised Papa, though I have failed. I intend to keep this part.

I barrel into the guy who lunges for her, we crash and tumble to the ground. I slug him in the gut hard, I rain punches on him.

A gun presses into my spine. "Stop, stop it, or she dies."

Slowly I let go of him and lift my hands in the air. The guy clips me in the stomach, I double over and glared at him. I made a mental note to pay back with interest. Mr. Hunky had Calla in a body lock a dagger at her throat. How the hell did he move that fast to where she was? Cleo takes a step forward and halts when I give her a look to stay. She stills, not knowing if she should obey me or save Calla.

"Interesting, you think that they are spies?" The huge man eyes Calla.

"I don't know serge. I think that we should just kill them. The risk is too great."

How did they sneak up on us without our knowledge? I shake my head at Jelika, pure white flicker in her eyes, this is the wrong time to act or give the game away. I want to know who we were dealing with. The guy ties my hands and bundled us into the back of the armored truck, leading us inside the small town. The large gate swings open, and we step inside. Led inside a large building, cuffed to the wall with the same cuffs that we were handcuffed in Yegun city. A jail of sorts for people like us.

"You okay?"

"I'm fine; I don't want Cleo hurt."

"They won't."

CHAPTER 53
PROGENY

Kamili

The door opens, a tall, lean guy steps in, I hid my surprise. I was expecting the heavily-built man. For days they have been interrogating us one by one, none came back? Calla was the first one taken, I itch to get some answers from them. Even if I don't get to know who they are. Calla is my first priority. He takes the seat in front of me. I meet eyes of teal-gold set in a rugged, handsome face.

"Who sent you?"

"Where's my sister?"

"You don't look like a progeny of a Malaki', not even a genimion, more human. I guess the only anomaly is the red hair. I have never seen hair that red and eyes that blue on skin such as yours."

"My sister! Where's she?" I bit out, nearly losing my control.

"You should be concerned about yourself, not your sister. She is in good hands."

"I want to see her."

"You will if you tell us who sent you here to spy on us? And I will not be forced to hurt you."

"Do your worst because I'm not telling you anything."

"Fine, you made your choice."

Sedately, he stands up. The move mesmerizing like a snake's, a snake charmer's sensuous promise flicker in his eyes. I lean back, he puts a finger on my lips, the fight rushes out of me, euphoria fills my veins.

"Sssh."

His eyes, endless pools of promise that I could drown into, the world fades, his lips warms mine, the room peel away. We sand in a sea of flowers, I wear bustier and a knee-length wrapper. Flowers braided into my hair, he in jeans, a ripped T-shirt that plays peek-a-boo, showed his sculpted body to perfection a nipple ring peek out every time he moves.

Madi

I felt different lighter, happier without any burden, am I in paradise? Did I die? Or was the experiment finally kicking into my system? The connection between us felt live bonfire, ready to engulf us. I racked my brain to remember something important, I got nothing in return, but I can't really deny the feelings coursing in my body.

"Who sent you?"

"No one!"

Was someone supposed to send me somewhere? I don't understand anything. Something's not right somewhere. What was I missing?

"What are you hiding from me Kamili?" he whispers, crowding my space, smothering me in sweet heat, I couldn't get enough air, I couldn't breathe as I stared at him, puzzled.

"What's wrong with you?"

"What do you mean?" He pulls me close for another hot kiss. His lips felt divine, and I let the sensation took me in its tide.

"Come on heart, why did you come all the way here?"

I open my mouth to answer. A drop of blood fell on the flower in my hand, marring its perfection. My hand went to my nose. I dabbed at the blood, more follow. "What is happening to me, Madi?"

"Tell me?"

Teal-gold eyes glazed impassively, when did Madi get eyes that color? A scream breaks his captivating hold on me This guy's not Madi, he was just masquerading as him, Madi can never stand to see me in pain Madi loved me, he gave his life up for me.

"Why do you want to know?"

Thick, dark blood bubbles out of my mouth. The flowers start to wilt, poisoned by the blood. Everything starts to fade, graying before my eyes, the petals starts to combust until nothing was left. I gasp and pull away. I blink, my eyes take in the interrogating room blood trails down my nose and drip on the floor. A brown-haired woman glares at my interrogator, she points at the door her face expressionless. And opened my cuffs, I massaged them scowling.

"I'm sorry, I told Muhan to not get too carried away,"

I take the hankie she offers and wipes my nose.

"I told Zeka that Olympus won't send a group of kids to end us."

"Welcome to the resistance, I'm Maira." she hold her hand for a shake.

These people were the resistance. I take her hand." Is my sister okay?"

"Calla is fine, but none of them will talk to us about where you came from. It has us frustrated, and my son got it in his head to get you to talk in the only way he knows how. I hope that you'll forgive him and put all this slight behind you, and see that we are not monsters, we are just taking precautions."

She walks towards the door, she stops in her tracks and turn to me," You coming?"

I followed her out, she led me into a building. She stops at a door." This is for you until we get you a more comfortable one."

"Thank you."

She nods and disappears from view. I step in gauging for any signs of danger. I hope what they say is true that everyone is safe, stripping I jump into the shower. I sigh in bliss as hot water sluices down my body washing the blood, grit, and grime off me. I even washed my hair, a luxury that I haven't gotten in so long, just running for my life. I strode out of the shower in a bathrobe, hair up in a towel turban style, a selection of clothes sat on the bed. I dressed in combat pants, a sleeveless blouse, and military-style boots. I pull my hair in a ponytail and rush to find out.

The mess hall is set in the middle of the camp, long tables lined the room from one side of the room to the other. Tray in hand, I head to where Calla sat. Her face wreathed into a jubilant smile when her eyes land on me, I give her one in return and trip. The floor looms closer to my face, the tray clatter to the floor as I try to catch my balance.

The soup splatters on a girl's coat , she stands up, her face, a mask of loathing, her deep, unmarred, delicate cocoa-brown skin, and beautiful features fosters jealousy, they envy her beaty, who wouldn't? I feel inadequate facing her. I open my mouth to apologize, but she held up her hand, stopping me before I could. No sound escapes my lips. She waves her hand, an invisible force lifts me off the floor and slams me hard on the ceiling of the mess hall. She pins me up there for several seconds before letting me fall on a table.

I gnashed my teeth, and slowly sit up and with as much dignity as I could muster pick up my tray and walk towards Calla. Not letting my anger get the best of me, snickers trail me. A hand taps my shoulder, and I turned around. A fist slams into my face, and I stumbled back, clutching my nose. Blood seeps from it.

Damn it, this is the second time I'm bleeding.

"Where do you think you are going?" A smirk weaves its way on her face.

"I wish that you haven't done that?"

"I thought being the child of a legend you should be powerful, you surely aren't her child, if you are this weak, I wonder what she's like. It makes me wonder if she was just a myth, a dusty fairytale to give us hope when there is none?" she hisses at the room,." I told you that we were just dreaming, and now look at this_."

What the hell was she talking about Mom being a legend?

"We can't be waiting for someone to show up to take the Baba out. The only hope we have is someone like her. A weakling who knows nothing of the legacy running in her veins. Or what's at stake."

"Enough Jankeh, stop this nonsense right now."

"She doesn't even know who she's. Is this why we waited for years? Hiding in the shadows, like rats, away from the Baba. This is what we get." She throws me at the wall, my back bangs on the wall hard, and I crumple at her feet, I suck in a breath and use a table to stand up.

I blast at her. The blue wave of current sent her flying in the huge hall to land on the far side of the hall. Power surges into me, and I welcome it. Not caring what I do anymore, let her think that I am weak, with a wave of my hand I create a blue shield-wall and give her a smile when she waves her hand, and nothing happened. Voltage crackles in my hand, I lift a hand and the shield widens, I fisted my hand and punch the air. The shield arrows towards her and blast her body straight, right out of the hall, through the wall and outside. I follow her, I grab her by the hair and jerk her body up. She thrashed, trying to get away.

I hurl us in the air, doors slam into us, my grip loosens, she falls, then rights herself in the air, we faced each other, eyes furious, ready to tear into each other.

"You are nothing. Just give up. I will lead us into the third world, back into glorious days."

"I'm not stopping you."

"Yes, you are, as long as they think you're strong. That you can replace your mother. The very one taken by the Baba."

I see red, blue chain-whips materialized out of my hands. I lashed at Jankeh, she dodge but without taking a hit on her cheek.

Tiny blades flew at me, I l dodge the lethal projectiles. Jankeh sends more blades, halfway the blades split open, morphing into lethal, flower-shaped blades.

"Stop."

The blades fall, the metal rusting in its slow descent . A force rips us out of the air. We tumble in the air, I land in a crouch, head down, trying to control my temper. A man with granite-silver hair, swathed in yellow robes stand before us, staff fashioned into a clawed hand holds a bluish arkor-stone in its clutches.

"Save your fight for the true enemy. Stop this squabble, we're the legacy of the ancients. While we fight, our mortal enemy builds an army big enough to destroys us all. It's time to see child." The arkor-stone touches my forehead, and I collapsed. "You need to understand what's at stake."

Muhan's hands wound around me.

CHAPTER 54

AGENDA, HEAVEN, MADNESS

Kamili

I vault in the air, punches landing on the dummy, not stopping just an endless stream of blows. Cleo grumbles to herself, trying to get my attention. I ignore her, after several minutes of eying me, she shuffles off to Calla.

The look in Mama's eyes; pure hopelessness.

I will get her out even though the resistance says that's too damn dangerous to do so. I will go, I will not let them use her. I've hidden the dagger in my things. Images of Mama in a place I could only guess as the third wall dance in my vision, when that stone touch my forehead I forgot what sanity is. Left to face an ancient dangerous enemy in Mama's stead without her guidance sounds daunting .

"Care to spar?" Chima's voice pulls me away from shadowed thoughts.

I whirl around and faced Chima clothed in combat pants and sleeveless blouse.

"Yeah, that would be great."

She walks to where I stand, on the balls of her feet and attacked before I could blink. I grin and deflect her second move.

"I hear that your mother is held captive by the Baba?"

"Yeah."

I shake my head going for a dagger strike, she darts to the left, her body a graceful ribbon on the wind.

"Hope city." she says.

It makes sense. That would be the place they would put her.

"How many days is it to Hope city?"

"Less than a week if you have a good smuggler to smuggle you in."

"And if you don't?"

"It could take longer, that is, if you don't get killed while looking for one in Jereja. If your smuggler doesn't kill you and rid of himself, the tiresome job of risking his neck. And even if you have one, chances of getting into the sink-ship is next to zero."

"It does not matter; I will get Mama out." The thought of Mama suffering every minute at a mad woman's hand brings cinders in my mouth.

"I'm headed there if you don't mind?"

"I don't."

"I do." a deep voice rumbles behind me.

Chima gives me a knowing look. "Uhuh," she whispers and brushes past me, a light I know too well in her eyes.

I turn to the guy who has no shame in eavesdropping. He leans on the wall, long legs crossed at the knees, jewel-like eyes sparkling on his face. He looks good as always, one of the very reasons I have been avoiding him for days now.

"What do you want?"

"I came to apologize over what I did … uh, you know."

"Know what?"

"About what I did to you, we got off on the wrong foot."

I gave him a smug smile turning my back to him, he released a great sigh and takes a step forward." Trust me, you don't want to go to Hope city?"

"Why not?"

"Because it's Olympus' base, they own that city. Why do you think we stay far away from them as possible? Even if they got someone vital to the resistance. She gives us hope to keep fighting, even though our chances of winning this war is getting slimmer every sunrise and dawn."

"Tell me more about her, about my mother, I mean."

I somersault and whip my blade with accurate strikes, back to him. I complete moves that I knew rooted from the bizarre ability I had inherited from Mama, glad that I know that I was born this way. That I belong somewhere.

"Fine as long as you agree on one condition."

"And what is that."

"Spar with me."

"Deal"

I still want my dagger at his throat, silence met my words, I whip around and gaze at the empty space. He has pull his disappearing stunt again, a fist bangs into my sternum, the pain made me nearly buckle down to the ground in pain. "What the hell."

"Don't be a wimp; you agreed, remember."

"This is not fair. I didn't sign up for this."

A voice chuckles in my ear, sending shivers down my spine. "Too bad, shouldn't you read between the lines before making a deal with the devil, isn't that what they use to say?"

I got tossed in the air, I thumped to the ground groaning in agony I think something broke on contact when I landed . Power crackles on my skin, and I scramble to my feet.

"Ooh, I'm scared, is big, bad tigress mad at me?"

"Anybody told you talk too much? I made a deal with the devil, remember, now tell me about my mama,?"

"Fine, you are no fun. I thought that I'm going to have fun wheedling a string of begging from you."

I scoff and let loose my senses. I feel the air molecules whoosh as he moves towards me, planting my feet firmly, I wait until the whooshing was just inches away from me then blast the place I guessed he would be. He hits the ground hard groaning, his body materialized out of thin air. He looks pissed.

"Are you hurt, want me to kiss your boo-boos?" I wiggle my eyebrows.

He's up in one smooth motion, I have yet to master and on me in an instant his punches assail. "She was the one who busted us all genimions out, well, my father among them. I wasn't even born then. She is our undisputed leader, who left us when it became too risky to stay with us. Olympus had a penchant for finding her, she didn't want to put her people in danger."

I flip my body backward his fist barely misses my jaw, I snatch his wrist, body soaring and use the momentum to slam my body into his, hard. He stumbles back, that was all I need for an opening. I somersault, and angled my elbow in bent in a perfect arc and plummet for him. I never reach him, the air lightens, my body levitates, the air grows light, objects float in the training room. Arms wound around my waist, spins me around. My face bumps in a wall of delicious muscle, euphoria fills my veins, giddy with it, addictive, eyes of teal-gold drink me in.

I stare back not getting enough of him. His head swoops down, his lips descend mine, I was captivated by those jewel-like eyes. In my head, a voice screams at me to push him away, to do something. Whatever it takes, this wasn't right, but every muscle's locked in place I couldn't move, a prisoner. Held captive by the euphoric feeling coursing in my veins.

It's madness, nothing I have ever felt before. Better than heaven, better than madness, better than blood lust, all merged into one sultry, divine package. I could die for it, do anything for it if it guarantees an infinity of this. His lips caress mine, and the world explodes in my head. Static charge the air, merging with his, a part of me opens, a silver haze fills my vision. I pull away, even if it's the last thing I wanted to do, I had to.

Maira stands in the doorway an odd look in her eyes, she looks like she had seen some kind of a miracle or curse I don't know which is which.

" Kamili"

What the hell was that? I shook my head to clear it, it felt like I have just woken from a dream.

"Don't!" I hold my hand out." Just step away from me." I whisper and back away, he looks bewildered and lost as I was. I brush past Maira, his footsteps follow.

"She needs space, give her some." Maira clamps a hand on her son's shoulder halting him in his tracks.

I sigh in relief and sprint to my room. Whatever the hell happened, I don't think I want to confront it. I don't even want to know what it was; it does not matter if I admit it. It has something to do with all the chemicals from the experiment zinging in my body, maybe I have reach the limit, I have only one goal, and that is Mama right now. I am not ready to feel things that will only make my life more complicated than it is right now, I don't want a repeat like Madi's, I just lost him, gaining someone is not on my agenda.

CHAPTER 55

SALAMANDER

Chima

I know they're still on my trail, following the bread crumbs of my signature. I hope going on this journey is the smartest move I have taken in a long time. Kamili rides shotgun beside me with Zen. We had left Calla behind with Cleo I have grown quite fond of her during the few days I have spent with her. Every one of us had an agenda; Kamili has her Mama to rescue. She's still close-mouthed about what happened in the training room with Muhan; we all have felt the fissure of power, something that is not to be trifled with, power like that will worry Olympus. She is bothered about it; I want to ask her about it, but I don't want her to blow a fuse. She rides her bike like a maniac. It's got to be Muhan getting to her, the guy's scorching hot and unstoppable.

Ruin and rot were the first signs showing the broken infrastructure of past centuries before the world ended, broken steel, jagged, and rutted lay in the open, a cancerous sore. I stared at the bridge, then at the rugged rocks, we are heading into. Both Reaper magnets; teeming with Reapers. Jereja; city of smugglers a smuggler to get you into hope city, people dubbed it Grail-city. Seeing that almost everyone wants to get in there. If you don't have the money to get you into Hope city, you work your way to it.

It's Mama's dream, she was sure that I would be safe if I get in there, she says that she got a contact in Jereja, a very good smuggler who can get me in. One of Mama's contacts. I just hope that he is not dead or retired. A retired smuggler is the hardest to convince to take up a job run to Hope city. I can't wait to see how the one percent elite, rich lived.

A huge, stone, arched gate stood in the pathway full of people, most of them scruffy looking. Two guys with shaved, tattooed-spike heads and bodies pound each other into the dust. I bought the passes from the small window and join the queue.

Inside I stared at the dancing strobes of light winking from the ceiling, bathing the bodies on the dancing floor in hues of light. In a corner, I spy a guy and three women making out, I head to the bar, a bulky bartender serving drinks to people.

"Welcome to Biker-lands! What can I get for ya my pretties?"

"A shot of whiskey pre EMP era if you don't mind?" Zen winks up at the guy.

"Very well missy, "

He pours a generous amount of amber-colored liquid in a shot glass, threw in several cubes of ice, and put in in front of her.

"Zen"

"Chill chime gotta loosen up a bit." She slams several bronze coins on the bar.

"On the house for first-timers' missy." He winks and push back the coins.

"Aww, thanks." She scoops the coins and give the bartender a sweet smile and weave her way in the sea of undulating bodies.

I turn to the bartender scrutinizing Kamili, who leans on the wall with a wary look. I don't blame him, there is something primal and predatory about the girl, she makes everyone around her feel like they are walking on thin ice, clueless of the kind of effect she has . Slowly, I pluck the gun from my coat, drawing his eyes. They seem scared; I shake my head trying to calm him down before he draws unwanted attention to us. Kamili straightens, staring at him with her strange, cerulean blue eyes, he gulps and stills.

"I mean you no harm, mister, just have a question. You answer it, and you get this .45mm." I let him see the jewel in my hands, he nods a new gleam in them, the fear fading from his dark orbs, replaced by an eagerness to get his hands on the weapon. I hopped on a barstool and leaned in close.

"I'm looking for a man named the Salamander, know him?"

"I don't care what brought you here, just don't try seeking him out. The man's bad news missy, a pretty one like you shouldn't seek him out. And besides rumor is that Obra is looking for kids who have stolen something of his, it's gossip fodder for all of us, Kwim's pants are in a twist in case the kids are here. Bounty hunters are crawling all over the place." he says, eyes skittish.

"Just tell me, "

He sighs and pours a healthy amount in a glass, then chuck it all at once. "Very well. Go to the last level ask for Kanje, she will take you to Salamander now give me that gun. You just might need something to save your life these days with these abominations that spring from the least places you expect them." he draws a cross in the air, and chug another glassful, slams it on the table, grinning.

I hand over the gun and surge into the crowd, Kamili shadows me.

CHAPTER 56

LELA

Kamili

I stared at the girl with the shaved head, and extraordinary, tinted- light brown eyes that nothing slips past, maybe that is why she is working for the Salamander, she wears a tight leather pantsuit, a long, wicked, hook-like blade strapped on her back. Her petite stature came with loads of attitude to make up for her slight size. Kanje smirks at me. An attitude I like, I wonder where the rest of her team were? I went in with Chima, this level is different, I could scent the blood lust in the air, huge cages hung from the ceiling, two people fought in it each trying to pummel the other to a bloody pulp. People cheer, calling out for more blood to be spilled, some rattle the cages with iron rods in their hands spurring them on. Kanje led us out of there; the scene started changing, becoming plusher as we venture deeper. The glass door slides open, a guy in his thirties stood in a room that looks like it's taken straight out of those places in the pictures before the world ended.

He turns around facing us, ash-gold, hard, flinty eyes survey us, weighing if we were worth his time. Behind us, Kanje stiffens." What are you waiting for? Come in," his voice burrows deep into my skin, digging up a long-forgotten memory. We step in, the door slid shut, sealing us inside. He gestures for us to sit, I did so reluctantly. Part of me objects at the idea of sitting down, I want to keep the man under my constant watch.

"What do you want," he asks his voice a rough whiplash.

"We want to buy passages into Hope city, and I'm told that you are the best one who can make sure that I reach hope city. And this is for you." Chima hands him the small medallion with a spider etch on; he took it and clench it in his large hands. Sorrow like no other crosses his eyes.

"Lela! Where did you get this?" he asks in an almost inaudible whisper.

"My mama gave it to me, she says that you will know what to do."

His mask slid effortlessly back into place. And once again, I am left stunned at how good he was with masking his emotions.

"Alright, be ready by dawn."

"Thank you." Chima breathes in gratitude. "Do you know anything about the Oumali tribe?"

He freeze and swing his gaze to where Chima "We need to talk." Salamander leads Chima into another room.

I stop in my tracks and let them go. They've got lots to talk about apparently, by the look of urgency in his. I made my way out of there, through the levels, and into the club. I need to get out of here, not much air for me. It's stifling, I'm ready to claw my eyes out, I much prefer the open space of Kendulusu, trees, and laughter. Outside, on top of the rock cropping overlooking the biker realm, I stared at everything, it looks kind of surreal, one of those paintings Pre EMP on a painter's canvas that was rare to find, the twin suns make their slow descent down the horizon. His scent is the first thing that hits me.

"Are you stalking me now?"

I watch him out of the corner of my eye, this is why I had avoided, him, having bringing more people will make it harder to get out. I don't want any casualty, I had my plan, and he was not included in it.

"I don't need to stalk you Kamili, I'm just doing my job? Somebody got to make sure that you don't get into trouble."

"Damn it, I am not a job or a nutcase. Why do people always think that I need saving? I don't." Electricity crackles on my fist, hitting the ground. The air tensed, charged and lethal, I glared at him.

"I don't need help, Muhan."

"Never said you did." He lights a cigarette and throws the empty pack.

I stared at the pack as it fell down to the ground its progress hastened by the wind. "Then why are you babysitting me?"

"I don't know."

"Fine just get out of my way,"

"Yes, Princess."

"Don't you dare call me that."

I stomp away and hurry to the club. Scooping the club out, I spot Brime, saliu and Muna in the crowd. Muna whispers to

Brime, who scans the room and stops when his eyes fell on me. I made my way towards them.

"Hey"

"The rescue team right."

"Kamili...."

"Hold it Muna, I don't want more of you dying like Madi, you saw what happened in the lab, this is my run, and no one else's," I whisper hugging my midriff, fighting back angry tears, I brush past her, the lights flicker immersing people in darkness cussing I sprint out of there Muna at my heels. I hate being vulnerable like this, makes me feel helpless, I don't want more carnage and deaths on my hands.

CHAPTER 57

THE BORDER ICE-LANDS

Kamili

The dogs run harder, our sleigh speed faster on the ice. Other sleighs fan out on all sides as people head to the Promised Land, a land that many die trying to get into.

Hold on, Mama, I'm coming.

I wore the same as my team, a combination of heavy, pure white, furry clothes and boots to blend in with the total, absolute whiteout, sheaths at my thighs holding my K-bar knives and guns, a long blade similar to Kanje's in a sheath on my back, my red hair up in a bun, Muhan sits beside Jelika and Zen. Muna and Brime, were in another. The driver cracks his whip, and the dogs scamper faster than ever, if I was in another sleigh and looking back at ours, we would have been a blur. Everything courtesy of Salamander.

"Hold on tight." The sleigh driver commands, his frosty breath misting in front of him. An explosion rocks the ground, and a sleigh opposite ours explodes, ice rains down on us. This place is a minefield, only fools, or kamikazes would do what we are doing right now. But thoughts of Mama spur me on, God knows what she's being subjected to right now, every minute that ticks by lances fear and worry deeper into my heart.

Another sleigh detonates, slamming into another, both veer out of control and combusts into twin balls of fire. The world tilts at the sides as an explosion rocks our sleigh, lifting it up in the air. Ice materialized into thin air, the sleigh lands on it gliding. Chima gives me a weak smile, sweat dots her brow. I hope she could keep that up, it takes a lot of power to do what she's doing. I made out people yards away from us, Kanje pulls out her blade, a smirk plays on her lips, I watch as she jumps out of the sleigh and lands perfectly on her feet, hands out to balance her.

The sleigh comes to a stop before the group of people huddling close, faces scared. I made out a girl with a baby in her hands, all bundled up. She meets my eyes and look away, she looks like she saw a nightmare. The frozen ground starts shuddering , cracks zigzag the icy ground. A contraption protrudes out of the earth, and excited murmur fills the crowd, the giant contraption emerged slowly out of the ground bit by bit. It came nearer, revealing its huge size, the sink ship's door slid open, and a guy climbed out a gun in hand. Rope ladders slid down to the ground. A gunshot slices in the air. The crowd murmus, wary. But willing to brave it out to the bitter end.

" Look, people, the drill is still the same. You have five minutes before the next patrol starts, hustle those asses up." A guy with a scraggly beard screams.

People went wild surging forward, climbing on the rope ladder, a guy pulls on a girl's leg, and she plunges down to the frozen ground, screaming the whole way down. Undeterred, she jumps back on another ladder and begin her climb. Her eyes frantic and wild with a touch of the unknown. Her breathing quickens, her limbs climb faster than before, shrieking, she jumps the guy who threw her down and buries a Reaper-blade in his eye. Blood runs down the guy's neck staining his clothes in seconds, he screams and let go of the ladder, they both tumble to the frozen ground. He didn't get up but she did, she takes a step forward and lunges at a kid in the chaotic crowd pushing and jostling trying to get into the safety of the sink-ship. steel whistle in the air,.

I vault up in the air, and it whirls by me, to hit the girl in the head. I stared at the hefty throwing star sticking out of her head, she went down clutching her head, trying to pull it out. But it's too deep to be pulled out. I stared at where the throwing star came from, and Kanje salutes me with two fingers.

Shit!

Daywalkers.

I should have known. I Pull my blade and join the sea of bodies slashing at anybody who attacks me, Chima fighs them off with the frost blades that she had materialized using her ability, Kanje's a whirlwind as she cuts down day walkers, her eyes shone with a blood hunger that matches mine. Chima collapses on the frozen ground her energy sapped. I cover Zen while she helps her up on the sink-ship, Muhan's invisible fighting the day walkers all I see where his blades.

An icy hand burst out from the ground and grips my ankle, I kick at it and got free of its grasp, a wet day walker burst out screeching revealing serrated sharp teeth. I kicked at it, but it didn't let go, more followed, the ice cracked under my weight and I was pulled into icy water. The shock has my eyes widening. I head-butted one and stab it .The girl with the baby struggles with two daywalkers underwater. I swim towards her. Her mouth opens in a scream when a daywalker plunges a blade into her chest, I throw K-bar knives, the knives hit each in the head, I help her out of the hole. She bleeds heavily, shivering from the cold. A bullet hole appears on her forehead and she crumples to the ground, I snatch the baby out of her arms, miraculously she still managed to hold the baby, I turned to the shooter. "No infected on the sink-ship!" He barks maliciously.

I gulp the biting sadness that slides across me, and look down at the little bundle in my arms, robbed of a mother in a second. I hand the baby to a woman and climb up the ladder and into the sink-ship. The hatch close soundlessly , and the sink-ship starts its slow descend into the ground. Kanje looks somber in a corner the blood-crazed killing machine she was seconds before gone, Muna has Chima's head on her lap, blood splatters on her face and body.

Olympus will pay for all this and more.

Why should they determine who lives and dies? I gazed at the ones who've managed to fight their way in, left loved ones behind, for the shining city that controls our world. A minority that think that they're superior to all of us, everyone deserves to live a life where you don't have to worry about the Reapers, and food supplies. Keeping us all hanging by dangling a nebulous thing to us, their city, and what it has to offer.

CHAPTER 58

OF TRAPS & INFINITY

Kamili

I stared at the floor, Zen takes a step forward. And I put a hand on her shoulder, stopping her. She turns to me irritation shining in her gaze.

"Wait."

Taking one of my daggers, I chuck it on the floor. Green web-like lights floats to life spanning the room. It's a death trap, and there's no way around it, we have to go through it. Zen leaps, avoiding the green light, she was nearly out of there when a single strand of her hair slipped out of her ponytail and brushes the green light, it blasted her up in the air. I move into action, catching hold of her wrist, and flip her up, she used that momentum to boost me up in the air I land on a tile, feet spread out. Gripping her hands in mine, I throw her in the air. We both cartwheel and land on the floor. Breathing hard, I switch off the death trap to let the others in. The alarm blared to life, a whooshing of air is all I got before bullets pepper the air, the defense mechanism has been activated. Good. I smile.

"I'm here Mama."

"Kamili......"

I duck out of the way of an incoming drone, it almost crashes into the wall and reversed way gunning for me. The corridors seemed endless as I run. I burst into a large room, lying on a gurney is a figure with tubes attached to his body. Machines surround his bed, eyes that I knew too well stare back into mine. The world stops, air freezes in my lungs, I wheeze and clutched my chest.

No, this can't be. The world whirls out of focus, all I could do is just stare. The tubes retract from his body, and he slowly sit up, hands that had held me once cracked a warning that I should turn back and run. But I stand my ground, I am here for Mama. I am not getting out of here without her. I take a step forward, tears prick my eyes.

"Papa..."

The man strides forward, a giant war hammer in one hand and a scythe in the other, I swallow . I stand still as the creature that I once called Papa comes forward, his soulless eyes fixed on me with an unerring intensity that had the hairs on my body stand on end. In them I seeno recognition, no humanity, no mercy, just a husk with mindless malice that shone like two beacons of lights, bright enough to burn my soul. Papa swings the hammer. I dodge, leaping back away from him; he continues his attack, never stopping.

Bricks and mortar rain behind me as he misses again, he growls showing a grayish tongue, he knew only one thing; to bey, to kill. His hand slams into me, and I smack into the wall and burst into another room, he follow through squeezing his huge body in the narrow space. Digging deep, I blast him out of the hole and squeezed out. An enraged growl had me throwing my K-bar knives at his body, he deflects them with lethal ease.

"I'm sorry Papa." I pull my blade free and meet him halfway, dodging his hammer strikes but not his sword that kisses my skin.

I attack, scarlet liquid follows my blade, he swats me on the wall, I bounce back and lunge at him, my blade sinks to the hilt in his chest. Bands of steel clamp on my neck, I gasp and claw at my throat.

"Stop it, Suleil. "

I choke harder, my legs kick at empty air, Mama leans in the doorway, looking frail, dark rings circle her eyes, streaks of grey stood out in her hair, she has aged in my absence. A faded blue hospital gown hangs on her thin frame matched her dull blue eyes, a grey band on her wrist. Her red hair hung limply down her shoulders. Guards flood the room with Dr. Kaima in tow. My companions cuffed and escorted, Muhan's nowhere in sight, at least he got away.

"Don't do this, anything but her. I will do anything you want," Mama wheezes, clutching her sides.

Tears prickle my eyes at seeing Mama, so hopeless and broken. Kaima had broken her, I wanted to do more than that to her. Somehow she had won, I could see it in her eyes. She had played the game with her and lost. Brought her to heel without doing much, her family almost destroyed. Mama is living her worst nightmare.

Dr. Kaima snaps her fingers, and I fall on the ground clutching my throat, tears cruise down my face, my blade clatters uselessly on the floor coated with thick grayish blood. They turned Papa into this creature, my gaze land on Dr. Kaima. I ball my hands and electricity crackles in the room. Dancing on every surface .

"Such power and promise." She tuts and lifts a strand of my hair.

"Let them go, you want me to remember. I promise I will be good."

"Isn't that just beautiful, on that you are correct child you are the very thing I'm looking for. Well, you and Jelika over there. And the Ra'aps if you please."

"No, please, Kaima, I have a chance you can continue the procedure with me, please, not her." Mama pleads.

"Such love, a mother's love is the best, or so they say. Eternal and bonding." her gaze lands on Zen on the floor, glaring poison at her.

" Give me the vial, "

"Don't "

"I'm sorry Mama." I hand over the vial. Mama closes her eyes, her fragile demeanor cracking in an instant, a fiery warrior taking over, electricity crackles to life when she opens them; they were all a light blue, filled with currents, tinged with red. Mama covers the distance with surprising ease, despite her fragile physical state, she crashes into papa hard, he stumbles back snarling. Glass shatters on my left, showering on us I roll out of the way of the incoming fly-ship that hurtles towards us.

"What did I miss?" Chima cracks a grin.

Kaima loads the vial onto a small snub nosed gun and fires it at me, I stared at the bullet flying towards me, I dodge out of its way, it brushes past me, and changes course heading back to me. I meet Kaima's triumphant gaze, here's no escaping this bullet when she's tagged it to my DNA. I stared at the bullet hole on my neck, it knits back just as the bullet hits my blood stream. I hurtle to the floor, a sharp pain grips my body. My breath rattled in my chest, my blood felt like it's on fire. Dr. Kaima disappears underground on descending pad, the floors clicks back into place, Zen thumps on the floor angry tears in her eyes. The hammer looms over Mama's head. It never reached her, the creature that was Papa let the hammer slide down from his hands an inch from her.

"Channeh" he rasped eyes clearing, he whirls on the guards. With a furious bellow that shook the room. My body's shook by tremors, I scream as my bones snap and mend back. The pain horrifying, green, and purple veins pop on my arms, spreading fast. Memories fought for dominance in my head, each one fading slowly, being eaten away bit by bit by the evil coursing in my veins. Forging something different, rewriting my DNA.

"I'm so sorry, petal," Mama caressed my sweaty forehead.

Muhan materializes beside Mama, I could see the uncertainty in her eyes. She wipes her eyes, grasping the gun in her hand. Tears trail out of the corner of my eyes and I struggle to speak.

" If you can't, you should let me do it." Muhan lays a hand on hers.

"No, I will. She's my daughter; it is the least I could do for her. No one deserves to be what she's turning into."

He nods, his eyes held mine. The gun blast resonates out. I suck in a breath staring at their retreating backs; the world stops and went blank. The pain dreadful, a tide carrying me to what I could only guess was infinity. Jelika's energy flared out, sharp and brutal, and the world explodes in heat, flaring out, the air went dead I felt nothing, I am just an empty vessel born into the world. I close my eyes as havoc was wreaked outside. The ground open and oblivion embraces me.

CHAPTER 59

DEATHLESS

Channeh

Seeing her haunting beautiful eyes. With one finger, I have ended my world, but I have to do it or watch the continent burn; pressing that trigger is the hardest thing I have done in my long existence, flashes of Kamili plague me, the crumbling tower. I thought that the image of watching Olympus tower would be a great pleasure, but only bitter ash covers my tongue. Mother was right; to kill the enemy, one must destroy oneself from within.

What shall I tell Calla? Would I be able to say that her sister was becoming a monster, that I had to put her down like a monster or have a much bigger war on our hands? That what she had running in her veins makes her a weapon in Olympus' hands. Would I be able to stand her tears, as her beautiful gray eyes lose the light within their precious depths? Now that we've crippled The Baba, now what? I looked at the resistance, all of that on me, I run a hand on my face, and sigh, looking out the window to see the fly-ships fly past what used to be the shield, what happened to it, I stared at what centuries of war did, everything was barren as far as the eye could see, where once used to be shining citadels, only ruin remains. At least we might be able to try rebuild what we have lost.

I could feel it in my bones, the war is far from over, it has just started, weakened is the last thing the Baba is. I am a fighter, not much of a leader, Suleil was the leader. My rock, my guru, my home. The only one of the few people that stuck by me since the destruction.

Home.

After centuries of war and rife. It doesn't look like it, home is Suleil, home is my children and my mother. Castle Gaide came into view, my eyes drink it in, not believing what they see, half of it is gone, but yet it stands, a wonder. I breathe in the air, toxic to humans now, but to my kind and kin, it was life, already I could feel my powers surging to the surface.

"Mama,"

Calla sprints towards me with Rougy in tow. She must've seen the torment in my eyes, she give me an encouraging smile. How can I tell her I murdered her sister in cold blood? I'm the one who's supposed to be the protector of all that's good and just in this world. A monster in disguise wearing the skin of a guardian. My heart nearly stutters to a stop when I think of Calla hating me, those silver-gray clouds darkening to orbs of hatred; I don't think I can survive that after losing Kamili. I forced a smile on my face and braced myself as Calla runs towards me, I clutch Calla, burying my nose in her hair, taking in her mild scent of burnt sulfur and warm sunlight. So like Suleil in so many ways. I stared at the deathtrap that's my homeland now. Death's companion, with the shield wall down, we've more than a war on our hands, back to the way it was: surviving. Fighting abominations long forgotten, imprisoned when the shield was still standing.

"Kamili?"

"No flower, I'm sorry."

The door burst open, and Calla lunges into my arms, Rougy behind her, she shrugs when I raised brows at her in question.

"I thought you were dead, promise not to do that again?"

I nod, a smile on my lips, tears in my eyes. "Please say it, Mama. I do not want to lose you, Kam's death is enough."

Pain blooms in my heart, my heart skips a beat. How could I forget her, Kam, her death a stain on my soul, "I promise flower,"

Satisfied Calla nods, and snuggle in my arms. I stroke her head, humming the familiar hymn she loves so much.

A mercury-silver tear makes its way down her smooth cheeks, and she buries her head in the crook of my neck. I stroke her head as she hiccups, I wipe her tears off and give her to Rougy. There'll be time to mourn later, right now, I have to think of how to make our people live. I hurry toward castle Gaide, a figure drops down from a turret and smoothly lands before us, hands gripping a clawed staff. Tears came unbidden to my eyes as I run into his arms and breathed in the familiar scent my lungs have been starved for a century.

"I thought you were dead, Asaile."

A dry chuckle echoes from Sheriff's frail body, a song I have craved all these times. "How did you escape."

"I am no match for The Baba; I've played this game a long, long time. Repetition makes it part of your blood. I wish Antalene could see this even though it's not much a victory, we can start taking it back starting now."

I gaze up at the orange sky, the expectant faces of my people.

"I should've known you never do things by half," I lift my head and grin at Rougy, who stood in the doorway, hands on hips, a broad smile on her beautiful face. "It's lovely to see you too, Rougyatou,"

"I know, couldn't you've come sooner? We could do with you here, we will know what to do with the exodus making their way here."

"Exodus?"

Rougy nods grimly, "Frankly, I don't know how we did it without you for a week, but if you haven't woken up, we were thinking of moving to Coparus-Ayusr with the Gaizu headed our way, they're two weeks' ride away from Gaide."

"Gaizu," I whisper, garnering Calla's attention. I thought of sending her away but dismissed the idea, it's time to stop sheltering her from our world, the real one. "How? I thought they were taken with him?"

"I thought too until the plague-horn was blown a few days ago, they're coming for us, laying waste to any in their path. The ones not sick are headed to us for protection."

Nothing seems to make sense anymore.

"What are you thinking?"

"I don't know, Rou, I don't think I can do this," I sniff. All this while being the fabled last remaining ancient, my people look up to me like I'm a goddess, if only they know how wrong that is. Leaving their lives in my hands, trusting me. Suleil was my only source of solace. He helped me through it; it was all him.

"Suleil?"

"He is ok, I made sure none harass him. Muna and the others made sure."

I released a sigh of relief, "Thank you, Rou, this soul owes you."

"Come on out, that's enough moping. Suleil can't wait to see you. It's been hard keeping him away."

I step onto the balcony, the suns-rays bathing my body in glorious light, hopes beams out from everyone down below with their faces tilted, genimion or Malaki', wanting to be told that everything will soon be right. That even though the Baba is ripping through everything ,trying to get to us, that we're a deathless republic, we can never really fade away.

" Greetings, my people, it's been so long since we stood on these soils, fleeing an enemy that wants to see our end, see our ruin. But we sacrificed and persevered through it all. It's going to be hard to emerge the winner, but we'll vanquish our enemies. Are you all with me?"

A deafening cheer rose from the crowd of people. The smile on Sheriff's face said that I have just made them see a goddess. I hate to be the one giving them hope where there's none, even if we made it into Coparus-Ayusr, what then. I can't stop their deaths. I can only delay it. I go through the speech, assuaging their fears, painting a world that even I don't believe in anymore, to stop the discord that could come if I don't. But to sow peace in the deathless republic, I must sow lies. Lies that would end everything. But with the Baba snapping at our heels, I have nothing but lies.

Printed in Great Britain
by Amazon